Frank and Red

Frank and Red

Matt Coyne

WILDFIRE

First published in 2024 by
WILDFIRE
an imprint of HEADLINE PUBLISHING GROUP

1

Cataloguing in Publication Data is available from the British Library

ISBN 978 1 4722 9742 6 (Hardback)
ISBN 978 1 0354 1687 5 (Trade paperback)

Typeset in Adobe Caslon Pro by Jouve (UK), Milton Keynes

Printed and bound in Great Britain by Clays Ltd, Elcograf S.p.A.

Headline's policy is to use papers that are natural, renewable and recyclable
products and made from wood grown in well-managed forests and other
controlled sources. The logging and manufacturing processes are expected
to conform to the environmental regulations of the country of origin.

HEADLINE PUBLISHING GROUP
an Hachette UK Company
Carmelite House
50 Victoria Embankment
London EC4Y 0DZ

www.headline.co.uk
www.hachette.co.uk

To Lyns and Charlie.

And for Lorraine.
'As is a tale, so is a life . . .'

Frank and Red

PROLOGUE

'Ah, for Christ's sake . . .'

As there was another knock at the front door.

He raked a hand down his face, forced himself out of his armchair, and, draining the last of his bottle of beer, stomped into the hallway.

Through the frosted glass he could see two figures, one taller than the other, both in black. They were about to knock a third time when Frank swung the door open.

'Hi! Good morning.' The smaller figure – a woman – singsonged, masking her disgust at his appearance with a kindly tilt of her head. The man, a pale pencil, just smiled gormlessly at Frank, as though he was staring into the face of a child.

'We're really sorry to bother you this morning. We were—'

But Frank saw the leaflet the tall man was holding, with its picture of a candle encircled by a crown of thorns, and knew what was to follow. They weren't sorry to bother him at all.

With an enthusiasm that made his left eye twitch, the woman continued:

'—wondering if we could speak to you today about happiness, your life . . .' Her eyes fly-fished to the bottle in his hand. 'And maybe what might be missing? Perhaps even how Jesus might be a part of . . .'

Frank blinked once, slowly.

And then:

'Come on in!' he said, with sudden enthusiasm, his Irish brogue dialled up to eleven. 'Please, come!'

A spark of surprise passed between the two, as he stood aside and ushered them through the door and into the cramped hallway. They wiped their feet on a tattered mat and Frank, a beaming smile on his face, held out an arm, guiding them past the stairs. 'Please, it's just this way.'

Down the hallway, they processed – past an old dresser cluttered with pictures and a long-deceased spider plant – and finally into the kitchen.

'Just . . . right through here.'

Frank then opened the back door and unceremoniously bundled the pair outside. 'Now, off you fuck,' he said, as he showed them two fingers and threw the door closed behind them, their confused faces discernible through the obscured glass.

His own face instantly returned to its resting state of weary and annoyed, and he tossed the empty beer bottle towards the nearby bin. It missed by a foot, clattered against the skirting board and disappeared under the kitchen table. Frank huffed and opened the fridge to retrieve another as his wife appeared at the bottom of the stairs.

'Well, that was a bit mean,' she said, as she leaned against the wall.

He snapped off the bottle cap using the heel of his hand against the kitchen counter, ignoring her. Taking a glug from the bottle, he returned to the living room, to his armchair, and the impression of his body that lived there on the rare occasions that he didn't. He was about to fall backwards into it when there was another knock, a light tapping, this time on the *back* door.

'. . . Jesus! What now?'

Marcie smiled. 'Well, the back gate is locked. You lost the key, like, a year ago, remember?' Shrugging, she continued: 'So, since the only way they can get out of here is by coming back through the house, I'd imagine they want to come back in.'

Frank opened the door, and, with awkward smiles, God's squad-of-two shuffled back inside. They stood in the kitchen, like tourists trying to get their bearings, and Frank impatiently pointed back down the hallway, towards the door they had arrived through just two minutes before.

Once more, they made their way past the cluttered dresser, the photographs, the long-deceased spider plant and the tattered mat. Back on the front step, they hurriedly pulled the door closed behind them with a clunk.

'You really are a dick.' His wife chuckled.

Frank took another swig from the bottle and, despite himself, smiled back.

But she wasn't there. Disappearing, the way she always did. Each time reminding him, in the hardest of ways, that she had been dead for almost two years.

PART ONE

FRANK

Skreewoing.

   Skreewoing.

   Skreewoing.

   Skreewoing.

It was the most annoying sound he had ever heard. It sounded like a squeaky toy being dry-humped by a donkey.

Apparently, the new kid next door owned a trampoline.

The only reason Frank was sitting in the back garden at all was to avoid the noise of the removal men at the front of the house. The day he'd dreaded since Mrs Palmer-Machin had moved out had finally arrived, and he had awoken to the sound of new neighbours.

Mrs Palmer-Machin had been the *perfect* neighbour. She had spoken only to say 'Good morning,' and often not even that. She rarely made any noise, and the only sound that could be heard through their shared wall was her TV, the volume of which had increased ever so slightly as her hearing began to fail.

But one evening, last December, there had been a commotion next door – the sound of something being knocked over – and Frank had looked from an upstairs window to see the old woman standing in the street in her underwear. He had gone outside, gently guided her back into her house, and found a number for her daughter tacked to the fridge. Within hours, she was spirited away to live in Clee-thorpes or Skegness, or some other disintegrating seaside dump where fun and the elderly go to die.

Since that day, the only signs of life from number 32 had come a few weeks later, when Mrs Palmer-Machin's daughter and son-in-law had arrived and begun emptying the woman's life into bin liners, and then their car. The son-in-law, as he departed, insisted to Frank that the seaside was the perfect place for the old lady to enjoy her final years.

Of course, Frank thought, the Victorians swore by the sea air – and there *was* something vaguely poetic about a person seeing out their days in a place where the land runs out. But he was annoyed by the son-in-law's cheeriness about the whole thing, and so he had replied that yeah, he was sure Mrs Palmer-Machin would be thrilled to spend her twilight years in some 'crumbling shithole where dirt meets water'.

'Shoot me first,' he'd grumbled. And his old neighbour's son-in-law had walked back to the car with a look that suggested he would quite enjoy doing exactly that.

That had been over ten months ago, and the house had stood empty since. A fact that suited Frank perfectly. Empty, that is, until today, when the sound of boxes and furniture being delivered and scraped around the house next door echoed within the walls of his own.

By 10am, Frank's teeth began to itch with every thud and thump. And so, with a sense of weary anxiety and dread, feeling he could take no more, he'd decided – with a mug of tea and newspaper in hand – to escape into the weed forest and testicles-high grass of his back garden.

Of course, it would have made more sense to escape entirely for a few hours, to head to a local pub or coffee shop, but the thought never occurred to him. That was, after all, 'beyond the gate'. The back garden would have to do.

Frank shielded his face as he stepped out of the back door, as though he was a vampire expecting to burst into flames. It felt alien to venture outside and into the glare of the sun, and as his eyes adjusted to the light, it came as a vague surprise to find the garden in quite such a state of disarray.

What had once been his neat vegetable patch was now a twisted mess of roots and garden canes. Ivy and wisteria battled against fence panels on either side of a narrow lawn that was now a meadow. And their old wooden greenhouse at the top of the garden leaned drunkenly, its glass pierced by brown tomato plants and prickly fruit trees.

'Mmh.'

Casting his eyes around, Frank spotted a plastic chair on the patio behind him. It was painted green with algae, unfolded and facing the garden, as though someone had been sitting there, the entire time, a spectator to the ruin. He put his newspaper under one arm, picked up the chair and dropped it into the middle of his once carefully tended lawn. Balancing his mug of tea on the chair's arm, he sat down with a groan.

With something approaching satisfaction, he noted how quiet it was.

Opening the newspaper to a random page, Frank's moment of satisfaction died as he found a full-page advertisement for 'Black Friday Deals!' and a picture of an impossibly perfect couple standing side by side, wearing just their pants, smiling widely, having won something called *Love Island*. He grunted again. 'Mmh.'

Everybody seemed to be in their pants these days. In magazines and newspapers and on TV. Always half-naked. Or worse. He had turned on the telly last night to find a programme in which people chose who to date by looking at bits of each other. He had turned over quickly, just as some over-excited young woman was choosing a possible mate based solely on a view of his pale legs and his weird bits, which dangled between them like a wonky turnip.

That was Channel 4 for you.

Turning a page and then another, it soon occurred to Frank that he had no real desire to read, particularly about celebrity nonsense and stuff he didn't really understand, especially with the distraction of what was unfolding next door. But he continued the pretence of reading anyway, as it felt odd to just sit there, as though he himself was simply waiting to die or be carted off to Cleethorpes.

So there Frank stewed, staring at words and pictures on a page and silently cursing the turn of events that meant that the house next door would no longer be unoccupied. He was dismayed at the piss-awful idea that the new neighbour might turn out to be 'friendly' or, God-forbid, 'chatty'.

This dismay now turned to horror at the thought of *a family* moving in, especially one with a *young kid*.

And especially one with *a bloody trampoline*.

Skreewoing.

Skreewoing.

Skreewoing.

Skreewoing.

RED

'Well, what do you think?'

Red stood on the path in front of the new house, his lip curled. This was *not* what he had imagined. In his mind's eye, he had pictured something a bit more castle-like, with big gates. Not necessarily a drawbridge and a moat, but turrets and flags, and a garden the size of a park.

Clearly, his imagination had run away with him again.

His old teacher, Mrs Rennie, used to say this all the time. 'You mustn't let your imagination run away with you, Red,' she'd say. But that just made him imagine the word **IMAGINATION** as a cartoon with arms and legs, holding his hand as the pair of them ran down the street.

Yes, this time his imagination had *definitely* run away with him. Because what he was staring at now . . . was disappointment.

This looked boringly like an ordinary house. The smallest house in the middle of a row of small houses. And staring up at the red-brick mid-terrace confirmed something Red already knew. That the decision to leave behind their house at Stanhope Gardens had been a terrible one, and if anyone had bothered to ask him, he would have told them so.

He had never wanted to move in the first place, never wanted to leave behind the house where they had lived with Dad. And just because Dad had now gone to live with 'Tits-and-Teeth', Red saw no good reason why they had to move to the other side of London – and to *this*.

But Mum had insisted. She said the new house would be 'cool'. She said it would be 'amazing'.

It was not cool. It was not amazing.

When Red didn't answer, his mum asked again: 'So, what do you think?' She rubbed his hand in hers. 'It's really nice inside. And there's three bedrooms, so we can set up a playroom with a den in one of them. It'll be great.'

Great. Amazing. Cool. Red was beginning to wonder if his mum knew what any of these words actually meant.

'Well?' she said, yet again.

It was only a tiny word, but this time Red caught something of the hope in it, the beat of sadness at his reaction, and he suddenly felt guilty.

He didn't understand everything that had happened in the last six months. In fact, he didn't understand *anything* that had happened in the last six months, but he knew his mum had cried a lot, and recently she had stopped doing that quite so much. The last thing he wanted was to make her start again. So, he closed his eyes hard, rearranged his face to look happy, turned his frown butt-side down, and tried his best to see the good.

He tilted his head and closed one eye so that he could just see the house and those on either side. 'It looks like it's in a sandwich.'

His mum tilted her head too. 'Yeah, I suppose it does.'

The metal gate whined as she pushed it open. It clattered against the wall that divided their house from next door, and the two of them hopped up the three steps to a tiny front yard of empty pots, flagstones and patches of grey gravel. For the first time, Red really took note of the neighbouring houses, and he stopped before they got to the front door to get a better look.

The house to the right was a rampage of colour: hanging baskets fireworked at each side of its front door, and flowering roses bordered its edges. It looked like a garden centre, and it made Red's nose itch.

The house to the left was its opposite, its evil twin. This house peered out from behind hedging. Its windows were dark. It was as though this house was hiding. Red liked it. It was, at least, interesting. A place where you might need a sword, or a lightsaber to—

'Red, you're blocking the way.'

He turned around to find one of the burly removal men standing behind him on the path, holding a huge box and smiling impatiently. Red quickly half-moonwalked aside. As the man grunted through the front door, he followed his mum into the hallway.

Inside, it smelled like biscuits, and was a bit more promising.

The door opened on to a checkerboard floor and steep, purpley-carpeted stairs with a wooden banister, which looked like it might be fun to slide down. The walls were white, decorated with that wallpaper with bits in it that you could pick at. And at the end of the hallway, beyond piled-high cardboard boxes, he could see daylight pouring into a small kitchen.

Another removal man entered, and Red's mum tugged him to one side again.

'So, do you want to see your room, Reddy?'

'Yeah-huh,' he said, not really listening. He was busy running his fingers up the banister to check for slidey-ness. It was about a six. The banister at Stanhope Gardens had been an eight.

'Come on then, slow-mo.'

He followed her up the stairs, taking them two at a time to keep up, and arrived at the top to find the Vimto-coloured stair carpet spilling on to a small landing.

Upstairs, it smelled less like biscuits and more like Great Grandma Irene before she 'went to a better place' (which turned out to be heaven and not – as Red had first thought – Laser Quest).

There were four doors, and his mum opened the first with a theatrical flourish. 'Bathroom,' she said, allowing them both to peer inside the first door, 'with a bath!'

They had not moved to this new house directly from the one at Stanhope Gardens, but had been staying at Auntie Steph's flat for three months while 'some money stuff' was sorted. Auntie Steph's flat only had a shower.

'A bath! Can you believe it?!'

Yes, he could believe it.

'And this one is my room.' His mum opened the door opposite. Again, they put their heads through the opening, this time to see an entirely empty double room. It had exposed floorboards, scarred with old flecks of paint, and a window that overlooked the front yard and road.

'And you, sunshine, can take your pick from the other two.'

Red looked behind him at the two closed doors and debated which one to try first. He had once read a book about a boy who was faced with the same dilemma. Behind one door had been a dragon, and behind the other had been a room full of sweets and gold, so he took his time, eeny-meenied in his head, and selected the one on the left.

No treasure. No dragon.

Just a small, dark boxroom, again with exposed floorboards, and a tiny window that was covered with yellowed newspaper. It was about the size of the food cupboard back . . .

(Home.)

The other room, though, was much bigger, with a patterned

carpet underfoot and built-in mirrored wardrobes, which made it look like two rooms. It was just as dark as the tiny room next door, but this was because of the curtains that were drawn against a large bay window.

His mum peered in over his shoulder. 'Yeah, I think this one looks best.'

'Why?'

'Well, it's a lot bigger for a start. You can't swing a cat in the other one.'

Red looked up, horrified. 'Why would you want to swing a cat?!'

'It's just an expression, Red. It just means it's not very big.'

'Well, I don't see why that's the cat's fault.'

'Wha . . .? Just – just – never mind. Look, we can paint the walls whatever colour you want. New carpet, your Captain America lamp can go in the corner. Get some posters up on the walls; it'll be amazing. There's even enough room for friends to stay over, if you want.'

Amazing. That word again.

Red was unconvinced. Not just by the house and the room, but by the idea of friends staying over. He only had one really good friend, and Noah Conway now lived on the other side of the city, two doors down from the house they had deserted.

His mum gave his shoulder a squeeze as though she'd said something wrong. 'Listen, it's a fresh start, all this. New school will mean lots of new pals. We might need to get you bunk beds.'

'Bunk beds?' A brief excitement fizzed and then died. 'Noah's got bunk beds.'

'I know.'

An uncomfortable silence.

'There is something else.' She grinned, bouncing on her toes, and clapped her hands together once. 'Open the curtains.'

Red eyed her suspiciously. 'These curtains?'

'Yeah. Look in the back garden.'

He walked over to the window. A cobweb passed across his face, and he spluttered as he pulled it away. He tugged one of the curtains back, then the other, and on tiptoes, peered down into the garden below.

And then he saw it.

'A trampoline!'

His mum laughed. 'Yep, I had it delivered here so that you'd—'

'A trampoline!' he shouted again. This time, it was a battle cry as he barged past her. 'A trampo—' Arriving back out on the landing, Red stopped suddenly. If this had been one of his cartoons, there would've been the sound of screeching brakes. He turned around, ran back to his mum, hugged her legs fiercely and then set off again, half-falling down the stairs before clambering over boxes.

From somewhere above, Red heard her shouting, 'Be careful!' as he emerged into the garden, where, with his usual coordination, he face-planted into the lawn.

'A trampoline!'

FRANK

Skreewoing.

Skreewoing.

He tried his best to ignore it. But it was less a noise and more like his skull was being punched repeatedly from the inside.

Skreewoing.

Skreewoing.

After a few minutes, Frank noticed something from the corner of his eye. Periodically, in time with this satanic noise, a mop of blond hair would appear just above the height of the fence and then, an instant later, disappear from view once more.

Skreewoing.

Skreewoing.

He looked up and accidentally caught the attention of the owner of this mop.

'Hi,' the kid said.

Frank ignored him and stared at his blank crossword.

Receiving no response, the boy continued, saying a single word each time he reached the height of his bounce and could momentarily see over the fence:

'What?'

Skreewoing.
'Are?'
Skreewoing.
'You?'
Skreewoing.
'Doing?'
Skreewoing.

Frank continued to pretend the boy did not exist. It was a tactic he had discovered worked surprisingly well when you wanted people to just sod off. With adults, at least.

'Hi,' the kid said again.

Skreewoing.

'I've got a trampoline.'

Skreewoing.

'You don't say?' Frank muttered to himself.

Skreewoing.

'Yes, I do say.'

Skreewoing.

'It's new.'

The annoyance mercifully stopped bouncing and disappeared from view.

Frank exhaled with relief, and he recommitted himself, for the tenth time, to seven across: 'Wild horse's emotion'.

This brief interlude was cut short by a clattering noise, and then the boy's face appeared once again, this time in full view, peering over the fence. It seemed he had found an upturned wheelbarrow on which to stand and continue this apparently fascinating and vital conversation.

'What's your name? . . . Mister? . . . My name's Red. Well . . . everyone calls me Red.' He sniffed. 'It's not really my name. My real name is Leonard, but I didn't like it, and so, when I was little, I pretended not to be able to hear it and my mum let me choose my own name, and I really like Red. What's your name? I bet I can guess. I bet it's something funny, like Connor or Bob or something. I used to have a hamster called Bob.' The boy frowned. 'But it died because I took it out on my bike and then dropped it, and I ran it over and it was all dead and bloody and I cried, so we went for a KFC. . . 'I like your house. It looks old. Like it might fall down. This is my house.' He pointed behind him. 'It's new and looks like a sandwich.'

A pause for breath.

'What's your name?'

Frank continued to stare pointlessly at the newspaper, hoping against hope that the kid would get bored and disappear – or, more ideally, be hit by a meteor, leaving behind only smoking shoes.

'What's your name?' the kid persisted in the same bright tone. 'Mister? Mister?'

Finally, Frank turned the paper over and placed it face down on his lap. 'Look . . . kid.'

'Red,' the boy corrected.

Frank glanced up, as much as anything to see if the boy was deliberately trying to antagonise him.

He looked about five or six, red-faced, snot glistening on his upper lip. His *bottom* lip was sticking out like that of a pipe-smoker as he unsuccessfully tried to blow his straw fringe out of his eyes. He stopped blowing and smiled broadly.

'Look, kid,' Frank repeated. 'Didn't your parents ever tell you not to speak to strangers? I'm a stranger. Okay? I' – he pointed a finger at his own chest – 'am a stranger.'

The boy drummed his fingers on the top of the fence. Frank turned the newspaper back over.

Twenty seconds passed.

'What are you reading?'

Frank closed his eyes and breathed through his nose like a bull pestered by a horsefly. He took a long sip from his cold mug of tea.

'Are you a Beedyphile?'

'Jesus Christ!' Frank spluttered tea on to his shirt.

'You said you were a stranger. Noah Conway's brother says you have to be careful of strangers, because they could be Beedyphiles,' the boy said, matter-of-factly.

Frank was patting dry his shirt. 'For God's sake. No, I'm not a bloody . . .'

A woman's voice called from behind the kid, from the direction of the house. 'Reddy, who are you talking to?'

The old man tried one final time to return to his newspaper.

'I'm just talking to the mister next door!' the kid shouted back. 'It's okay, though . . . HE'S NOT A BEEDYPHILE!'

'Unbelievable.' Frank shook his head. He was hastily gathering his things to go inside when the eyes and nose of the boy's mum appeared over the fence, next to those of her son.

'Hi,' she said.

Dear Christ. What have I done to deserve this?

Frank nodded once with paper-thin enthusiasm as he folded the patio chair and retrieved his mug from the long grass.

'Sorry if Reddy was bothering you. He's a bit . . . excitable. New house. First time he's been on a trampoline. I'm Sarah.'

With an aggressively polite, tight smile, Frank continued to make his way inside, as his two new neighbours carried on peering over the fence.

'Bye, then,' the boy's mum said sarcastically, as she ruffled her son's hair. 'Come on, Reddy, you can help me with . . .'

Something made Frank stop.

Something in her voice or her face, or maybe an alchemy of both, made him pause.

'I know you,' he said, turning to face her.

For a moment, she looked mildly confused – and then her eyes softened as she recognised him in return. She smiled gently and nodded. 'Yeah.' She thumbed vaguely behind her. 'St John's, I'm a nurse up there—'

'The hospice,' he interrupted.

'Yeah.'

'You were one of the nurses.'

'Yeah.'

'. . . with Marcie.'

'Yeah.'

Frank nodded. He attempted something like a smile. But it felt uncomfortable, and instead he found himself grimacing in a way that made his face ache and feel odd. 'Okay,' he managed. He wasn't entirely sure what he meant by 'Okay,' but he had nothing else.

And as he continued inside, he could hear the kid behind him.

'Mummy . . . who's Marcie?

'Who's Marcie, Mummy?

'Who's Marcie?

'Who is Marcie?'

RED

Red's mum continued to sort a box marked 'Kitchen' into various drawers.

'Marcie was one of my patients, that's all.'

'Did she die?'

'Yes.'

'How?'

She stopped what she was doing for a second and kissed him on the top of his head. 'She was sick, Red.'

'Oh.'

FRANK

'I see you charmed the new neighbours, then?' Marcie was looking out of the window and into the garden as he came through the back door and threw the newspaper on to the kitchen side. 'Quite exciting,' she continued. 'It's been empty next door for way too long. "There's no such thing as haunted houses, just empty ones" . . . Who said that?'

'It's an absolute disaster is what it is. Listen to that noise already.' Frank paused for a second and tilted his head, listening. After a long silence, there was a distant, barely audible scraping sound. 'It's like a herd of wildebeest charging up and down the hall.'

She rolled her eyes. 'Frank, it's just the removal men.'

'I miss Mrs Palmer-Machin. Mrs Palmer-Machin didn't make this racket'.

'*You* miss Mrs Palmer-Machin? Ha! You used to say she gave you the creeps. Remember that time her milk sat on the doorstep all day and I was worried something had happened to her? I asked you to go round, and you said to just leave it a week and we'd know by the smell.' Marcie shook her head and returned to looking out of the window, craning her neck to see if the boy and his mother were still out there. 'Can't believe our new neighbour is one of the girls from St John's. What are the chances? Do you remember her, Frank? I remember her. Really kind. And her little boy's so cute. He reminds me of Mikey – you remember him at that age? All snot and jabber.'

Frank grunted at the mention of their son and poured his unfinished mug of tea down the sink. 'Yeah, well, excuse my lack of enthusiasm. Some noisy kid *and* a constant reminder of *that* bloody place is just what I need next door. I *don't* think.'

Marcie shook her head again and gave him a withering look.

But for Frank, it was true. A kid was bad enough, but the last thing he needed was a constant reminder of St John's living next door. He did not need reminding of those weeks, those days. When he had told Marcie that he didn't want her to die. And those final moments, when Marcie had whispered back, 'Everybody dies, Frankie.'

And he had replied, 'Not you, Mar. Not today.'

And then she had.

No, he did not need reminding of that, at all.

*

Like all things catastrophic, it began in the most mundane of ways. Just an ordinary evening.

They were sitting at their corner table in The Fairfield, the pub that had become their second home since they'd planted their feet in London from Dublin, nearly forty years earlier.

The place had remained almost entirely unchanged over that time. Burgundy velvet-backed seats and cig-burned stools scattered around varnished tables. The ancient patterned carpet, worn away in a six-foot strip before an old dartboard and in a black puddle around two fruit machines. The Fairfield had resisted the age of food and big-screen TVs. And the soul of the place was perfectly captured by a framed picture that hung behind the bar: an enlarged print-out of a TripAdvisor review that read simply: 'The pub that time forgot. Total shithole. One star.' It hung laughably askew.

For Frank and Marcie, though, it was a place where New Year's Eves were counted down to zero, where birthdays were marked, and friends were furniture. A place they affectionately called The Flea.

It was a Wednesday, a quiz night. They sat around a table of half-finished drinks and torn-open crisp packets with Sal, her husband Jonny, and Frank's oldest friend, 'Fat Ken'. Collectively, they were the quiz team that regulars of The Flea knew as 'The Clueless'. The name wasn't entirely fair. But they were a team that didn't take Wednesday nights seriously; occasionally they won, more usually they didn't. But they were happy to be 'The Clueless' rather than one of the half-pint super-quizzers like 'Universally Challenged' or 'The Likely Lads' (two accountants and a bloke who worked at DFS, who would nurse half a pint for hours and agonise over the capital of Botswana as though anyone really gave a shit).

Just another Wednesday night.

Until it wasn't.

Marcie had been sitting across from Frank, facing the bar, her back to The Fairfield's huge opaque window. She was scribing the quiz answers on a sheet, laughing and drinking, and enthusiastically ribbing Fat Ken about his latest bargain: a polo shirt he'd bought in a charity shop. It was flesh-coloured, with a blue paisley design, and it was two sizes too small, so tight it looked as though the pattern was painted on his belly.

'Honestly, Ken, I thought you were naked when you first walked in.' She wiped away a tear of laughter with the palm of her hand as she caught her breath. 'I didn't know where to put my eyes, I was—'

She was interrupted by the speaker above her head:

'Question number eight! Music! In which 1964 Chuck Berry hit did a boy called Pierre marry a lovely mademoiselle?'

(There was general amusement at the landlord's French pronunciation – via Peckham. *Mademoiselle* came out *Madam Moyzel*.)

The question was repeated, and this time Frank began to sing loudly, swaying in his seat, to groans and heckles from the opposing teams as they accused him of giving away the answer. Frank didn't care. 'Ah, piss off!' he heckled back, laughing loudly before descending into a coughing fit.

He couldn't not sing the words. This was a song that he and Marcie used to dance to in the kitchen of their basement flat, their first home together in Wood Green. The memory came back with vivid clarity: the song on the radio, Marcie heavily pregnant. Frank singing as he spun her around and held her in his arms. And as she spun away, laughing at her lack of rhythm and coordination and marvelling at how little she cared. How entirely in the moment she could be.

As the clamour faded and the next question was asked, he smiled at Marcie across the table, winked and began to take a sip of his pint. And then stopped.

Rather than returning his smile, Marcie looked confused – bewildered, even. She was staring at the paper on the table in front of her, and at the words she had written there. And Frank saw that they spidered over the page. They were nonsensical, outsized and jagged, as though written by a toddler.

Her pen hovered over the paper, and she looked up at Frank. He could see that she was afraid.

'Frank?' she said.

The next eight months were like falling.

RED

It was Saturday morning, the end of their first week in the new house, and Red sat at the kitchen table, spooning Cheerios into his mouth enthusiastically. He had been awake since 6am, when he'd wandered into his mum's room, one bleary eye open, to tell her he couldn't sleep. She had allowed him into her bed, lifting back the duvet to let him in while insisting that he close his eyes for 'another hour at least'. But after lying in the darkness for two long minutes, Red broke the silence with a tiny whisper.

'Mummy.'

Silence.

'Mummy.'

'Yes, Red?' she groaned.

'Are you awake?'

'No. Go back to sleep.'

'But I need to ask you something.'

'Ask me later.' Her voice was thick.

'I need to ask you now.'

Silence.

'Mummy.

'Mummy.

'*Muuuummy.*' A little louder.

'What is it, Red?!'

'. . . What would win in a fight? A shark or a gorilla wearing some armour?'

'Aaand, I'm up,' she said, swinging her legs out from beneath the quilt, the upper half of her body joining the effort a few seconds later. She rubbed her eyes, snapped on the bedside lamp, reached for her glasses and a bobble from the side table and scraped her blond hair back into a bun.

Red began bouncing on the bed, and she looked up at him, blowing out her cheeks. 'You know you are my least favourite kid, don't you?'

He smiled down at her and continued to jump. 'You don't have any other kids.'

'I know,' she replied. 'What do you want for breakfast, you lunatic?'

An hour later, at seven o'clock, Red was finishing his last spoonful of cereal. He took the bowl in both hands and drank the sugary milk with a loud slurp.

'Yeah, buuuut, what about an octopus versus a gorilla – who would win that? Because an octopus has got tentac . . .'

Eight o'clock.

'. . . and more arms than a gorilla, so—'

'Oh, I don't know, Red,' his mum said with exasperation. 'It would depend on whether the fight was in water or on land . . . or if the gorilla had been woken up at five o'clock in the chuffing morning, and – look, why don't you check to see if the postman's been?'

Grinning, Red jumped down from his chair, almost spilling it backwards. He'd always been excited by the idea of mail: the fact that on the other side of the world, a person could put an envelope in a box, and days later it would appear on your doorstep. It seemed like strange magic. And, besides, there was always the possibility of a postcard from Seth, the syphilitic llama they had adopted on a visit to Twycross Zoo last year.

'Don't run through the hallway!' his mum shouted.

'Okay!' he called back, as he ran through the hallway.

There was no letterbox in the door of their new house. Instead, the previous owner had installed a red wall-mounted postbox on the outside, with the number *32* ornately stencilled on the front. Red fished the postbox key from the bowl on the hall table, opened the front door and shivered slightly as the early morning air turned his breath to dragon-smoke.

He was about to open the postbox when he noticed a thicker fog. It was drifting across in a plume from next door, where their new neighbour was standing on his front step, smoking a cigarette. Red was about to say something when the old man scurried back inside, his dressing gown in his wake, leaving behind only a swirl of smoke.

Red couldn't help thinking he looked a lot like a wizard.

'You're letting the cold in, Reddy!' his mum shouted.

He quickly opened the postbox with the key, retrieving some envelopes (mostly brown), a leaflet advertising conservatories, and a menu for a takeaway called Pizza Rocket. He walked back into the kitchen and set them down on the table.

'What do you want to do today, buggerlugs? Mummy's still got a few days off and you don't start school until next Monday. I've got some stuff to do this morning, but we could go to the park this afternoon, if you like?'

'Okay,' Red said. And then, cheerfully as an afterthought 'We could see if the mister next door wants to come?'

His mum looked at him as though he had suggested that they go to the park and roll around in dog muck.

'I don't think so,' she said, deadpan.

Red frowned with disappointment.

'I think the mister next door likes his own company, Red.'

'What does that mean?'

'Well. Some people just don't like to be around people so much. They like to be . . .' She paused, considering, and then continued, 'on their own.'

He didn't get it.

'Look, do you remember Mummy's old boss, when she worked at the council? Linda?'

'Yeah.'

'Well, I think he's a bit like that.'

'What? A "bitch"?'

'Wha—? No.' His mum's voice lowered. 'And we don't use that word. Mummy shouldn't have used that word.' She sighed. 'I just mean some people don't particularly like other people, and so they like their own space and company. They like to be by themselves.'

'That sounds rubbish,' Red said, doubtfully.

There was a 'clip' sound as toast popped from the toaster behind her. She dashed it with margarine, sliced it into triangles and chewed a piece while setting the rest in front of Red.

'Besides, you have fun with Mummy, don't you? We can get an ice cream and feed the ducks and stuff.'

'Okay,' Red said absently, his mind still on sharks, gorillas and octopuses – but mostly on the odd mister next door. 'I think he might be a wizard,'

'Who?'

'The mister next door. I think he might be a wizard.'

'He's not a wizard, Red.'

'He's got a beard.'

'Well, so has your uncle Martin – and he works at PC World.'

'Yeah, but this is a proper grey beard, like a wizard.'

'Red. he's not a wizard.'

'Maybe not anymore. Maybe he's lost his powers or sumthin'?'

His mum's expression changed. She stopped busying herself and looked at him closely. 'He's not a wizard, Red . . . and he's not Miles, either.'

Red looked up, confused. 'What?'

'The man next door . . . he's not Miles.'

'Eh? Well, that's a crazy thing to say. Of course he's not Miles, Miles was a pigeon.'

Miles was indeed a pigeon. A pigeon that had splatted into their patio doors when Red was four years old, and knocked itself unconscious. Red had been horrified when his dad, assuming it was dead, had suggested putting it in the bin. Instead, Red had insisted they laid it on a tea towel on the grass in the sun, where it had slowly regained consciousness.

Over the next few days, Red had nursed Miles back to health in a cardboard box. He had sung to it, given it a cuddly Chewbacca for company, and they had tearfully released the (entirely confused) bird in the park a week later.

'No . . . What I mean is, I recognise that look on your face. That "Miles" look. What I mean is, you see something that's injured, and you want to fix it. But sometimes you can't. Fix things, I mean.'

'I don't know what you're talking about. What do you mean? Injured how?'

'Look, I don't know. I don't know what I mean . . . Just eat your toast.' His mum picked up the post from the kitchen table and began to sort through it, discarding the flyers into a box beneath the counter she had set aside for recycling.

'Oh, just great,' she said with a tut, as she turned over the final envelope. It was white, textured, and the address was handwritten. A birthday card, maybe. The sloping text read:

Franklin Hayes
34 Merton Road
Finchley, London
N2 8JS

'S'matter, Mummy?'

'Nothing. I think the postman's given us a letter meant for next door, that's all.'

'I'll take it round!' Red shouted, grabbing for the envelope.

His mum whipped it out of his reach. 'It's fine,' she said, slipping the letter into the pocket of her dressing gown. 'We'll drop it in on our way past this afternoon.'

'Aww.'

'Aww,' she mimicked. 'So, the park this afternoon. But what are you going to do this morning? It's a lovely day outside. You could go on your trampoline? Or I could unpack your paints and pens and stuff? You could have a draw and a paint while I finish off sorting the kitchen.'

Red scrunched his face and thought for a second, then nodded enthusiastically. 'I could draw something for the mister next door!'

His mum's shoulders slumped. 'Great.'

FRANK

Frank stood by the living room window and cautiously pulled the curtain to one side with two fingers. Head down, he squinted through the gap.

Marcie sat on the mantelpiece behind him, her legs dangling over the side, barefoot, as though she was sat at a water's edge. She was wearing jeans, and a T-shirt with the words 'Shit Happens' in neon lettering across the front.

Frank had become accustomed to his wife appearing as she had been at different ages. It was one of the weird things about Marcie since she'd 'come back'. Some days, she would turn up in the twenty-year-old form of the woman he'd first met. On other days, she would look the way she had in the years before she died. He was all too aware that she only ever appeared in guises in which he had seen her in real life, never as a child or in clothing he didn't recognise, cementing his sorry acceptance that she was, no doubt, a figment of his imagination.

At the moment, Marcie looked as she had in the late nineties, when she'd been around forty. A time when she had become truly comfortable in her skin, and all the more beautiful for it. She looked alive and healthy. Her hair hung to her shoulders, curling in rings the way it did when they'd been on holiday and the sun and sea had untamed it. Her eyes were lively and framed by the beginning of lines at the edges. Lines that people call crow's feet, but are often just the details that come to make a person look content.

'What *are* you doing, Frank?'

He glanced over irritably, before continuing to squint through the gap in the curtain. 'I'm trying to see if that brat's still out there.'

She slipped down from the mantelpiece soundlessly and appeared at his side, looking over his shoulder. Red was sitting on the path in front of his house, cross-legged and surrounded by a mess of paper and paints and pens. His hair was sticking out in all directions, glued up with snot and paint, and his tongue – which poked out between his teeth – was pointing upwards, reaching towards his nose in concentration.

'Okay . . . Why?' she asked, vaguely amused.

'I don't know why he's out there. He's a bloody nuisance.'

'No. Not why is he out there. Why are you bothered that he's out there?'

He glanced back towards her again. 'Because. I just want to take the kitchen bin out. And he's messing about out there, and if I go out, he'll, well, he'll talk to me or hassle me or whatever. It's bad enough I can't sit in the back garden because of that damn trampoline. Now he's messing about out the front. It comes to something when a man can't even take his bin out.'

'He's just sitting on the path crayoning; he's not going to bite you, you weirdo. And why do you think he's a brat or a nuisance? He's just a friendly little boy.'

Frank looked at her and sneered. 'I tell you what he is. He's a pain in the—' He stopped short, diving suddenly away from the

34

window. '*Fuck*. He saw me.' He looked at Marcie accusingly. 'That's your fault. You moved the curtain.'

'Franklin, I'm a figment of your imagination. How the hell did *I* move it?!'

Frank crept back to the window and peered out once more. Red had abandoned his crayons and was heading towards their house. 'Shit. He's coming up the path.' Frank put his back against the wall as he waited for a knock at the door.

There wasn't one. Instead, he heard the letterbox open.

'Mister!' A tiny shout echoed down the hallway. 'Helllooooo! Mister?! It's me. Are you there?'

Frank crouched down behind the sofa.

'I've just seen you at the window. *Miiiiister!*'

Marcie returned to the mantelpiece. 'Are you not going to answer him?' she said, studying her hands.

Frank put a finger to his lips and motioned for her to shush.

'Only you can see or hear me, you bloody idiot. Why're you shushing me?'

Again, Frank signalled for her to be quiet with a hand gesture that made it look like he was patting an invisible dog.

'MISTERRR!'

There was a pause. He could hear the kid sniffling through the still-open letterbox. He waited, holding his breath.

Finally, the boy shouted again, as though he had reached some conclusion. 'So, I think you might have GONE FOR A POO OR SOMETHING?'

Frank heard the letterbox whinge closed, and then whinge open again a moment later.

'Don't rush it, though. IT CAN MAKE YOU CONSUMMATED!'

'What is it with this kid?' Frank whispered through his teeth.

In the distance, the boy's mum called his name.

'Anyway, mister! I'm GOING TO THE PARK!' The voice echoed again down the hallway. 'I'VE DRAWN YOU A PICTURE. I'll post it through and then you can get it AFTER YOUR POO.'

Frank heard something drop on to the doormat.

'ALRIGHT. SEE YA IN A BIT!' Red sang, and the letterbox slapped shut.

Frank exhaled, stood up, and braved one last look out of the window, to see Red skipping down the path.

'I told you, bloody nuisance,' Frank said, just as the kid turned around, saw his face at the window and gave him an excited wave. The old man quickly whipped the curtains closed again, but could hear the slap of the boy's sandals as he continued to skip down the path, up his own steps and, with a slam, into the house next door. Frank sighed with relief.

'Go put the bin out, you miserable old sod. By the way,' Marcie continued, 'we both know the bins don't go until Tuesday.'

'I know that, but it's, well . . . the kitchen bin's full. That's why I'm putting it out,' he said, shortly. He grabbed the half-full bag out of the pedal bin, held the handle, tied it closed and marched towards the front door.

Entering the hallway he found, lying half-curled on the floor, a large piece of lined art paper, torn at one edge. Red's gift. Frank picked it up and almost stuffed it straight into the bin liner. But curious, he dropped the bag to one side and unfurled the paper.

It was a colourful crayoned picture. It was upside down and, as Frank turned it the right way up, he could see that it was a drawing of a smiling dinosaur. It had tiny eyes and appeared to be blasting fire from its backside. It was set against a background of a sun, a volcano, a rainbow and a smattering of 'm'-shaped birds.

'What is it?' Marcie asked from behind him.

He held it up and Marcie looked at it for a moment, before she snort-laughed reading the message written in green felt-tip across the bottom:

I am sad that your wife is dead. Love Red xxxxx

PS This is a picture of a dinosaur called an allosaurus, allosauruses are dead as well.

PPS Sorry that the volcano is a bit rubbish. I can't find my yellow.

RED

I am sAd that your wife is dead. Love Red xxxxx

FRANK

There was something about the picture that reminded Frank of the leaflets they were given when they first found out that Marcie was unwell. Not that those leaflets had pictures of an allosaurus blasting fire out of its arse or anything. Only that they seemed just as ludicrous. They usually had a picture of a sunset on the front, or a kindly hand holding another hand that was wrinkled and old.

One leaflet had the cheery title 'Living with your diagnosis', and just had a picture of a plate of biscuits on the front with a cup of tea next to it. This one particularly stuck in his head. The tea, unaccountably, had too much milk in it.

Sorry you're about to pop your clogs. Here's a Hobnob, and a shit brew.

*

The morning following the quiz, Marcie insisted that what she'd experienced the night before was just 'a funny turn', probably tiredness, perhaps the beginnings of a cold or a virus. Over the day, though, it became clear that it was something more. She showed confusion in the simplest of tasks, and would occasionally begin a thought and then lose it, like a helium balloon escaping her hand.

By lunchtime, they were both sitting in a doctor's office. By the afternoon, a hospital.

At first, it was assumed to be a mild stroke, a lightning storm in the brain that had cut off Marcie's ability to concentrate and make sense of the most ordinary and everyday things. It was a 'blessing', the doctors said, that she could still speak and communicate. The fact that she would get lost in a sentence and forget would most likely improve, they said, 'slowly but surely'.

But over the next few days, as the results to each test returned like unwelcome mail delivered in a storm, this reassurance changed to 'We'll see' and 'We're not sure', and it was, in the end, concluded that a stroke was unlikely. Soon enough, it was there in black and white: an astrocytoma.

'A good name for a band,' Marcie had said to the doctor feebly.

But it was a better name for a brain tumour. Because that's what it was.

Frank didn't actually hear the doctor tell them that there was nothing they could do to stop what was to come. He had, instead, fixated on the clock on the wall above the young Asian man's head. It was ticking in a way that seemed aggressive and mocking and wholly inappropriate for a room in which people might be given bad news. A bit like going to a funeral and having one of those wind-up, cymbal-playing monkeys on the coffin. He was thinking about making a complaint about it. What a ridiculous—

He became vaguely aware that the doctor was now speaking directly to him.

'And do *you* have any questions, Frank?'

Frank turned to face Marcie. She had seen the doctor's discomfort in imparting the news, and was putting a hand on his knee to let him know that it was okay. Typically – and ridiculously – in that moment, she was thinking about how the young doctor felt.

Frank, on the other hand, was thinking about himself. And about parachutes.

He had once heard a saying that went something like: 'You don't need a parachute to skydive once.' That's what he was thinking about: that falling in love with someone, and allowing yourself to do so, was like falling without a parachute. And that's okay when it's the love of your life, because you only intend to skydive once.

But sitting in that hospital room, forty-five years to the day after they'd first met, Frank knew that in some ways, he had been falling the whole time. Falling without a parachute for decades. And Marcie *couldn't* die, because if she did, he would hit the ground hard, break every bone in his body, and his remains would be spread until he was a thing unrecognisable.

Dr Pardesi repeated his question from somewhere above the surface. '*Do* you have any questions, Frank?'

He was suddenly snapped back into the conversation by the realisation that they had just been told Marcie was dying. And he had no questions. None at all. Which didn't seem right. None of it seemed right. It was the very definition of wrongness.

They left the hospital later that day with treatment schedules, and the tea-and-biscuits pamphlets, which mapped out a future neither one of them could bear to look directly at. It was only when they were sitting in the car at the top of the hospital multi-storey that hard reality descended, and they acknowledged that the situation was as far from okay as reality ever got.

With rain pelting against the windscreen, Frank talked too much. He went over everything that every doctor had said to them over the previous week, mining each word for something positive. And, finding nothing, they cried and lied to each other about how they would deal with what was to follow.

Finally, when they were both exhausted, Frank put his hands on the steering wheel, and asked about their son.

'What about Mikey?'

Over the previous ten days, they had agreed not to tell their son that his mum wasn't well. Michael and his wife were only recently married, and had just moved into a new house. Until they knew more about what they were dealing with, Marcie had insisted that he not be bothered with her 'drama'. Frank had reluctantly agreed, but now he felt they had no choice but to tell their son everything. It was too big. Too important.

'We need to tell Mikey,' he said now.

'Frank, no.'

'Mar, he's got a right to know,' he insisted gently. 'And he'll know something's going on, anyway. They were supposed to come up on Sunday and I've already put them off until next month.'

'I mean it, Frank.' She fixed him with a stare and then closed her eyes tightly, as though she could make this part of their conversation disappear.

'Mar—'

'He's so happy at the minute.' A smile flickered in her eyes, despite everything. 'I can't be the one who spoils that. I just can't.'

There was silence for a long time.

Frank would replay this conversation over and over in his head in the coming months. Even in that moment, it felt like a mistake to keep the truth from their son. Even then, it felt as though by conceding, he was throwing a brick into a pond – and there would be ripples. But he conceded anyway.

'Okay,' he said, reluctantly. 'For now. But he'd want to know, Mar. He's—'

'I know. I know. But please. Just not yet.' She opened her eyes again, and then took his chin and turned his face towards hers. 'In fact, I don't want *anybody* to know. Not family, not friends. Just for now, okay?'

'Why?'

She grimaced. 'Come on, you know what it's like, Frankie. Everything changes the second you tell people. I saw it with my sister, my dad, with your mum. People start talking to you like you're already . . .' She trailed off. 'It's like you go from being you . . . to just being this *thing* that sucks the life out of stuff. I don't want to be that.'

Frank nodded towards the window reluctantly. 'Okay,' he said, and started the car.

RED

Red came back through the door with his pad under one arm, and found his yellow crayon lying on the floor of the hallway. He must have dropped it earlier as he carried his paints and pens outside. He quickly picked it up and put it into his shorts pocket, then sat on the bottom stair to put on his shoes.

After a few minutes, his mum called from the kitchen. 'The park will be shut by the time we get there! Have you got your shoes on yet?'

'Yup!' he replied.

She walked into the hallway and found him sitting there. He pointed at the spaghetti'd mess of his tied laces.

'What do you call that?'

'Bunny ears,' he replied proudly.

'Bunny ears? It looks like the bunny's been run over. Come here.' She squatted down and pulled his feet towards her, untangling and re-tying. Then she quickly zipped her old boots over her leggings, and pulled on her denim jacket, patting the pockets for keys and phone. 'Ready?'

'Ready.'

Finally, the two of them left the house. And as they resumed their never-ending conversation about all the things that could potentially kill a gorilla (wearing a suit of armour), they skipped straight past next door. The lost letter in Red's mum's pocket slipping both their minds.

FRANK

The thing about terminal illness is that it is a plane crash in slow motion. It begins with warning lights in the cockpit: a cough, tiredness, a lack of appetite, sometimes spidery handwriting across a quiz sheet. And then you get a diagnosis and lose control. And then everybody prays and cries, and waits to crash into a mountain.

To begin with, Frank tried to pilot. As if, by sheer force of will, he might steer them both away from the inevitable. From the day following Marcie's diagnosis, he treated her like a child. He hovered over her and pestered her with attention. He obsessed about the hospital appointments, her blood pressure, her weight, her diet. He rattled out herbal remedies and vitamins into pillboxes already overflowing with tablets that she was obliged to take. He spent hours researching obscure treatments and clinical trials.

For one whole week, for each meal, he plied Marcie with 'leafy greens', having read an article in a Sunday magazine that described them as 'superfoods'. This particular experiment ended when Marcie placed her hand on his, as he served up yet another spoon of foliage, and informed him calmly that if he put one more leaf of spinach or kale on her plate, she would use the last of her precious energy to hold him down and stuff handfuls of it up his arsehole.

For a month, he did all this obsessively, looking for a way to save her. Until one day she sat him down and said, 'Frankie, stop.'

He lost his temper. So did she.

'What do you want me to do?' he said, angrily. 'I don't know what to do.'

'Just treat me normally!' she shouted back. 'I can't stand this.'

'Can't stand what?'

'*This!*' She stood up and began pacing. 'I'm not dead yet. We don't go anywhere; we don't do anything, and you treat me like I'm so damn breakable.'

He threw his hands into the air. 'How *can* we go anywhere when you don't want anybody to know? I keep making excuses to Ken, to Jonny, to Sal – *and* Mikey. He knows something's going on; he's not stupid.'

She continued as though she hadn't heard him. 'We exist between the hospital and here, here and the bloody hospital, and nobody treats me normally – not the doctors, not you. Everybody just treats me like I'm sick—'

'You *are* sick.'

'Oh, really? I hadn't noticed.' She pointed to her hair, which had already begun to thin.

Frank looked away.

'I just want to be treated normally. Is that too much to ask? I want *you* to treat me normally.' She looked around. 'When did this place become so quiet? Put some music on, make me laugh, tell me a bloody joke!'

'I don't know any jokes,' he replied quietly.

'Jesus Christ! What do you mean, you don't know any jokes? Everybody knows *one* joke, Frank.'

Frank stared at the floor. As Marcie sat back down, he stood up suddenly. 'Fine. Let's go to the pub,' he said firmly.

'Frank,' she began to protest.

He walked into the hallway and grabbed her jacket from a hook at the side of the front door. He strode back into the room and held it out. 'It's Wednesday; let's go.'

'Frank.'

'No. I know you don't want to go. I know you don't want anybody to know. But Mar – you can't have it both ways. You want normality?' He thrust out the jacket again. 'Then let's go to The Flea.'

She stared at the jacket as though it represented a moment of inevitability. And continued to stare as Frank's arm grew tired. He was about to let it fall to his side when, finally, she conceded with a sigh. 'I'd better go change out of my pyjamas.'

*

So, for the first time since the night of Marcie's 'funny turn', they returned to The Flea and the embrace of normality.

Their arrival was barely acknowledged by the few regulars that haunted the place in the afternoon. But as the day faded into evening, the pub filled with their friends, and they were joined by Ken and then Jonny and Sal, each of them excited to find Frank and Marcie sitting there after weeks of phone-call excuses and worry.

In so many ways, as they sat at their usual table, it was as though all was normal. As though the previous month had been an odd nightmare; a hole that they had just fallen into, temporarily.

But before long, it was clear that their friends were studiously avoiding talking about the last time they had seen the pair, carefully refusing to acknowledge Marcie's appearance and pretending not to notice the moments when she would lose her train of thought and squeeze Frank's hand as though she was slipping sideways somehow.

For the next hour, the elephant in the room sat there: stubborn, huge and blocking out light.

The laughter began to go on a little too long; gaps began to appear in conversations where they never would have been before. And as Marcie started to shift uncomfortably, Frank began to feel that the outing was a mistake. Began to wish that he had, instead, stayed home, played some music, remembered a joke.

Eventually, during one of these gaps, Marcie inhaled deeply, whispered, 'Okay, sod this,' under her breath, and then told them how ill she really was.

As she finished, Sal suppressed a whimper that made it sound like she was in a box. Jonny and Ken looked at the floor. As Sal gathered herself and took Marcie's hand, they each made vague platitudes about how it would all be alright, and that they would all be there if there was anything either of them needed.

'Never mind what I need,' Marcie said, wiping a tear away and smiling. 'You lot are gonna need somebody to answer the geography questions. There's not one of you who knows Timbuktu from your arse.'

None of them laughed.

And it was in that moment, in that silence, that Frank understood exactly why Marcie hadn't wanted anybody to know. Their friends had known she was dying for less than a minute, and they were already speaking to her in voices he had never heard them use before. They spoke to her quietly and in hushed tones, as though she were suddenly fragile. Carefully, lovingly, but it broke Frank's heart nonetheless.

And then there was a long quiet, a quiet that seemed to consume even the background noise of the pub. After a few minutes, it was broken by Frank, who had been staring at his pint in silence the whole time.

When he spoke, it was barely more than a whisper.

'The pope was diagnosed with a rare terminal illness . . .' He cleared his throat and began again. 'The pope was diagnosed with a rare terminal illness. The very best doctors were called in from around the world for consultation, and after much debate and research, they determined that the only hope to save the pope's life was for him to have sexual relations with a woman.'

Their friends looked at Frank as though he had lost his mind, but Marcie smiled at him and, after a moment, mouthed, 'I love you.'

And so he smiled back and continued, louder now: 'His advisors were told, and they, in turn, spoke in confidence with the pope. The pope informed them that he needed a day to pray about it.

'The next day, the pope summoned his advisors and said: "My sons, after much prayerful consideration, I have an answer. These are troublesome times, and as such, it is not good to be without a leader of the Church, for even a short while. I have decided that you shall arrange for this most unusual treatment to preserve my life, for the good of the Church. But on three conditions."

'"What are the conditions, Your Holiness?"

'"First, the woman that you choose must be blind. For if she sees that she is with the pope, she may either get a sense of self-importance as the only woman to ever bed a pope, or she may lose her faith in the sanctity of my station. She must be blind."

'"It will be so. What about the next condition?"

'"For the same reason, she must also be deaf. While I try to be a righteous man, I am a man, and as such, I may cry out in pleasure during the act. She must not know that she is with the pope, so she must be deaf."

'"Very wise, Holy Father; it will be done. What is the third condition?"

'"Big tits."'

There was a beat of silence before Marcie exploded into laughter. A longer pause before the others joined her. And in those few minutes of hysteria, five months before Marcie died, there was a moment when Frank almost – *almost* – forgot that his world was ending.

RED

Four hours after they'd set out for the park, Red and his mum were returning home, walking down the street, hand in hand. Red was clutching an ice cream that was melting over his tiny fingers and painted around his mouth and cheeks. It looked less like he was eating it and more like it had exploded in his hand.

As they approached their house, they could see, from a distance, their next-door neighbour on his doorstep in an odd pose. The old man was awkwardly holding on to his front door frame with one hand. In the other, he held the handle of a mop or a broom, which he was waving around at arm's length. As they got closer, they could see that, in fact, he was stretching, apparently trying to use this long stick to reach over his fence and bash the door of number 36, the house neighbouring his on the other side to their own.

Number 36 was a smart and well-kept house with a pillar-box red door. It suited the occupants perfectly. They were a friendly couple in their late forties, Mark and Joe, who had welcomed Red and his mum to the neighbourhood with a bottle of wine and a, 'We won't keep you, just wanted to say hello,' before explaining they would be away, on holiday for a few weeks.

As they reached Frank's gate, Red's mum produced the envelope from her pocket. The old man hadn't noticed them; he was still busy waving the stick. They arrived at the wall in front of his front garden and stopped to watch him for a moment.

'Everything alright?' Red's mum said, finally.

Frank turned abruptly and, looking embarrassed, he let the stick drop on to the grass. He leaned against the door, trying to look nonchalant. 'Yeah, fine,' he replied.

'What ya doing?' Red asked, tilting his head to one side, although, he was largely preoccupied with his ice cream, licking frantically at its sides as he fought to keep the vanilla blob on its cone.

'Shush, Red. Don't be rude.' His mum held up the envelope. 'Sorry to interrupt . . . y'know, whatever this is. But I think we got some of your post.' As if to confirm, she looked at the name and address again. 'Franklin?' she said, with a hint of a smile.

'Yeah. Well . . . Frank,' he replied.

Red's mum held out the envelope again, but Frank showed no sign of walking the twelve feet down the path to collect it. After a while, her arm dropped.

'What *are* you doing?' she asked.

Frank had been reaching down to retrieve the wooden handle from the grass. He stood up again quickly, holding the pole at his side like a Masai warrior. 'I'm . . . I'm knocking on next door's . . . door,' he said.

'Okay, I'm going to regret asking this, but . . . Stupid question: why not just walk round and knock . . . with your hand, like, *on* the door? I think they've even got a bell.'

He looked at her as though she was an idiot. 'Oh right, yeah,' he replied sarcastically. 'Why on earth did that not occur to me? Why don't I just wander round and knock on the bloody door? Thank you so much. What *was* I thinking?' He turned away, conversation apparently over, and began to stretch once more, extending the handle over the small fence and again towards the neighbours' door.

'Okaay, then. Come on Red,' she said with an eye roll, taking Red by his non-ice-creamed hand.

Red didn't budge. 'Your stick isn't long enough,' he said, munching the edges of his cone. 'You need a longer stick.'

Frank stopped. Ignoring Red, he addressed his mum. 'Look, this is as far as I go.' He pointed at his feet, and then at the gate. He seemed to consider explaining more, and then: 'It just – It just is.'

'Look, it's none of my business. I shouldn't've asked.' She held up her hands.

He continued anyway. 'I get food delivered, but if I run out of anything, the fellas at thirty-six—'

She interrupted. 'Mark and Joe.'

'I don't know their names. The gay fellas—'

'Mark and Joe.'

'Okay, Mark and Joe, will sometimes nip to the shops for me. I normally grab them when they're going to work or whatever, but I've not seen them for a few days. *That's* why I'm trying to knock on the door.'

'They're on holiday.'

'What?'

'They're on holiday. They've gone to America or somewhere. They'll be gone for a couple of months. They asked me to keep an eye on the house.'

'Really?' A pause. And then, almost to himself. 'You've only been here two minutes. Why didn't they ask me?'

Red's mum looked pointedly at the stick in the old man's hand, and arched an eyebrow. 'Yeah,' she said. 'It's a real mystery.' She turned to Red. 'Come on, sunshine,' she said, attempting to drag him away again.

'We could go to the shops for you, couldn't we, Mummy?'

Her body slumped. She pretended not to hear him.

'Mummy, we could go to the shops for him, couldn't we?' Red repeated, tugging at her hand.

'Red.' His mum sighed as he looked up at her. 'We've got to get you cleaned up, and I've got stuff to do . . .'

Frank, though, pounced on the opportunity. 'I literally just need some bread, a few beers. Nothing big.' He began to turn to go back into the house. 'I'll get some cash.'

'Waaait a minute, Franklin,' Red's mum said. 'He's coated in ice cream.' She gestured towards Red. 'And I know it's only up the road, but have you any idea how long it takes to get a six-year-old to and from the shops? It's not like they walk in a straight line. It's just taken half an hour to get back from the park because he saw a sad-looking cat. Look, I'm sorry, but . . .'

Frank's face fell. Red tugged slightly on her hand. 'Mummy?' he said quietly.

'Red, I've got stuff to do, and—' The disappointed frown remained on Red's face. Interrupting herself abruptly, she looked back at Frank. 'Fine! I'll get your beer.'

The relief on his face was immediate.

'But you'll have to watch Red.'

Frank's smile faded in an instant.

'What? The kid? No way. Not a chance,' he blustered.

'For a start,' Red's mum said, 'his name is not "kid". His name is Red, or Leonard. Or, if he's really getting on your nerves, you could use his middle name: Gavin.'

'Mummy!' Red shouted. He hated his middle name being revealed to anyone.

With no response from Frank, she began walking the few paces to their own gate. 'Okay, suit yourself.'

Frank stood in the doorway, thinking and shaking his head. 'Alright!' he said, conceding bitterly. 'I'll watch him. But he can't come in the house. I'll watch him from the doorstep. He can sit in the front yard . . . And tell him not to touch anything.'

'Tell him yourself, Frank. He's six, not an idiot.' She opened the gate, and she and Red climbed the few steps into the old man's front garden. 'Now, what do you want?'

Frank stepped backwards into his hallway, hastily grabbed a pen and Post-it from the dresser drawer, and jotted down a list. He handed the Post-it to Red's mum. As she took it, she turned to Red. 'Behave yourself.'

'Mmmff-hmmmph,' said Red, chewing on the last mouthful of mashed wafer.

She produced a tissue, wiped his hands and his face. 'I'll be ten minutes.' And then to Frank, 'You can give me the money when I come back. And don't let him out of your sight,' she added, pointing at Red.

She stepped through the gate and began to walk back in the direction from which they had just come, but stopped abruptly after a few feet, holding up the envelope. 'Forgot to give you this.' She took the few steps back towards them. 'Your letter.' Handing it over, she kissed Red on the forehead, ruffled his hair, and set off once more.

FRANK

As she disappeared up the street, Frank turned over the envelope and recognised the handwriting.

Red squinted up at him. 'I never get any letters. 'Cept from Seth the llama.' The boy thought for a second. 'I don't think he actually writes the letters himself, though. He's only got one eye – and bum mange.' He paused. 'Frank, what's bum mange?'

Frank turned the envelope over again.

'Aren't you going to open it?' Red asked.

'Nope.'

'Why not?'

*

The days that followed Marcie's death were painfully ordinary. As though the world had ended, and the house at 34 Merton Road was the only one to notice. Outside, people continued to catch buses and walk to work and meet friends and jog, and do all the things that alive people do. The Earth continued to hurtle around the Sun. But not here.

Mikey moved in for the week leading up to the funeral, but hid himself away in his old bedroom. The room – unchanged since the day he'd left for university fifteen years earlier – still had his single bed pushed up against the wall, which was crowded with music and movie posters. Mikey had to duck slightly as he entered the room – he had been two inches taller than Frank by the time he turned eighteen – and Frank was struck, in that moment, how much Marcie would have loved to have him home, if only for a few days.

But during that week, Frank and Mikey barely spoke, passing each other in the hallway and on the landing like spectres.

Mikey was still furious with his father for not telling him how ill his mother had been. In fact, he had not found out the truth until just six weeks before she died – and even then, not from his father.

By chance, Mikey had bumped into his parents' friend Sal in a coffee shop queue at Victoria station, not long after she'd found out the news herself. She had innocently expressed her sadness for him as he smiled cluelessly, sure that she was making some mistake.

That day, Mikey did not return to work after lunch, but instead immediately drove north to his parents' house. As he entered the front door, he demanded the truth from his father, but before Frank could calm him or answer his questions, his mother had walked down the stairs and her appearance had confirmed the reality.

Frank and Mikey had been close, especially when he was a small boy. But Marcie and Mikey were twinned souls, and had been since the day he was born. And when God, fate or bad luck meant that Marcie would never fall pregnant again, she poured that love into Michael.

On seeing his mum now, Mikey crumpled.

It was only later, when Marcie was out of earshot, that it became clear how *angry* their son was. It was an anger that had spilled over even as Frank and Mikey sat at her bedside in those final days, whispering through their teeth as she slept.

'It doesn't matter that she said she didn't want me to know. It was up to *you* to tell me! I lost all that time. I could have been here . . .'

And once she was gone, that anger, fuelled by grief, meant that Mikey couldn't bring himself to speak to or even look at his father.

The funeral was organised. Frank couldn't recall making any arrangements, but at some point, sombre-looking men dressed as death had arrived in their living room. Men who spoke too quietly as they showed them both a brochure: makeshift laminates in a ring binder filled with caskets, as though it was an Argos catalogue and they were recommending a lawnmower.

Then the day came, the usual shuffling and silence: ceremony and pageantry to mark the death of a woman who hated such things. And as the funereal music faded to be replaced by the final verse of 'You Never Can Tell', Frank felt himself die too. Upon leaving the graveside later, he felt just as buried.

And still Mikey and Frank barely spoke.

It was at the wake, though, that the rift was cleaved open.

*

The Flea had been closed to the public, the main bar turned into a table for open sandwiches and tiny sausage rolls. It was a bright day, making the pub seem overexposed, as sunlight glared through the window in sharp angles of dust.

Marcie's friends and relatives huddled together in groups of three or four, chatting quietly, politely drinking tea and coffee, and waiting for the first person to break ranks and order an actual drink.

Frank stood to speak at around lunchtime. Ken tapped the side of a glass and the pub fell silent. There was the sound of a police siren outside, and he waited until it faded away before he began.

'I don't know what to say, really . . . I'm better with words on a page than . . . I know you all loved her.' He looked at his feet, and then into the middle distance. 'She loved you, too. You know that.' There were nods, and that seemed to be the end of what he had to say, but after a moment he continued. 'Y'know, the one thing I hate most about all this cancer business,' he said, gesturing at nothing, 'is when people talk about fighting it. They talk about a battle against cancer. As though it's possible to stop the unstoppable, with nothing more than courage or wishful thinking, or being positive or whatever. What a load of shite.'

'Hear, hear,' Sam, the landlord, called from behind the bar.

'There's not one person in this room that doesn't know that if that were true, if it were cancer versus Marcie, cancer wouldn't have stood a chance.' Frank raised his pint glass, and The Flea did the same. 'As is a tale, so is a life. Not in how long it is, but how good it is.'

By the afternoon, the old pub began to feel less like a makeshift church. Background music had begun to fill that weird space. Conversation had become lighter and, slowly, occasional laughter could be heard, like wind chimes. Later, as the pub reopened to the public and numbers dwindled, the funeral became one small group of eight or ten, gathered around a corner table.

It was as one of her old school friends reminisced about Marcie as a young girl, telling a story about how they'd met, that Frank had put a hand on his son's shoulder. Mikey shrugged it off, causing Frank to lose his balance and fall against the table, disturbing drinks.

It was the spark that lit the fire.

'You should have told me!' Mikey shouted, as the entire room fell silent.

Frank shook the spilled beer from his sleeve and looked up at his son. When he replied, he sounded exhausted. 'I promised her. She didn't want to—'

'That wasn't her choice to make. That wasn't *your* choice to make!'

'Mikey.'

'You took that time from me. *Months.*'

'Mikey,' Frank repeated, his hands held apart in apology.

'Don't *Mikey* me, Dad.'

Ken stepped in and put his hands on Mikey's shoulders. 'That's enough, Michael.'

'I could have done something; I could have helped.' Mikey peered around Ken's huge frame accusingly.

At this, Frank's anger sparked, and he sneered at his son bitterly. 'Really?' he said, pushing back. 'The big city boy would've done what? Got her some expensive doctor and saved the bloody day? Your money can't buy everything, Michael.'

'And what did *you* do? Eh?' Mikey looked at his father with disgust. 'Nothing. You just let her die.'

'Michael!' Mikey's wife, Ellie, ordinarily so gentle, gave voice to the shock. But the words continued to hang there in the quiet.

Frank nodded three or four times, then took a step forward and pointed at Mikey's chest. 'Fuck you, Michael. Fuck you.'

RED

Red stood on the top step of the path until he saw his mum disappear around the corner at the end of the road. Frank was sitting on his doorstep, the mop handle now placed across his lap.

Red realised it was quite a walk to the Tesco Express, and that she would be gone for at least ten minutes – maybe even longer if she saw the cat. And so he sat down, too. He began to pick at the grass at the side of the path.

'You know, your stick handle *is* too short.'

Frank didn't respond.

'You prolly need a longer one.'

Red spotted a garden cane half-buried beneath a bush. 'I've got an idea,' he said. He snatched up the cane and held it aloft. 'We could attach this bit to the end of your stick – then it'll be longer, and then you can reach their door easy!'

Frank stared into the distance.

Disappointed, Red threw the cane to one side and returned to picking at the grass.

'I know!' Red said eventually. 'Why don't we play hide 'n' seek?' He looked around the small front yard; realising how few places there were to hide, he reconsidered. Frank would easily find him. Stupid idea. 'Or I Spy, what about I Spy?'

Red settled on I Spy as though Frank had responded. 'I'll go first!' he said. 'I spy with my little eye something beginning with G.'

. . .

'G,' Red said again.

. . .

'*G.*' His eyes were now darting repeatedly towards the gate.

Still, Frank didn't answer.

'Something . . . beginning . . . with *G*,' Red repeated, twice more.

Frank was clearly struggling with his fiendishly tricky choice. Red was now staring directly at the gate, as though he was trying to laser it with his eyes, like Superman.

. . .

'Is it . . . gate?' Frank finally said, tonelessly.

'Yes! Yes, it is! Wow, you're really good at this. Your turn.'

Frank returned to staring at nothing.

'Okay,' Red said after a minute. 'I'll go again. I spy with my little eye something beginning with L.'

'Is it the last dying embers of my will to live?' Frank replied.

'Nope!' said Red, delighted that Frank was apparently now fully involved. 'Guess again.'

There was another long minute.

'It's *lamp post*! See? The lamp post over there.' Red pointed towards the street. 'Your turn.'

FRANK

Marcie sat down on the step next to Frank. She was dressed in jeans and an old jumper with 'Class of 85' printed on the front. It had been a present from Frank on the day she had graduated as a primary school teacher. A passer-by – had they been able to see Marcie – would have guessed she was around thirty, the age she had been when their son was born. She was smiling happily.

'Remember Mikey at that age? God, he never shut up.' She chuckled.

Frank looked for signs that Red could see or hear his wife sitting there, as real to him as the boy himself, but there wasn't a flicker.

'Yooour turn,' Red said, a little more insistently.

Marcie continued. 'You taught him I Spy, on that holiday to Butlin's. Remember? He just could not get it. One minute he was spying things that didn't exist, the next he was spying his nan-nan . . . Bit weird, that. She'd been dead for six months by then.'

Frank's mouth twitched a half-smile at the memory. It was the most irritated and happy he had ever been. Funny how kids could make you feel both at the same time.

'My God. You were at it for hours. But then he got that cute look on his face, the one he used to get when things fell into place.

Remember? As though a light bulb had gone off in his little head? He suddenly seemed to understand. And I remember *your* face. You were so excited, you were like, "This is it, here we go. You've got this! Go ahead, kid!" And he looked up at you, and he said, "I spy with my lipple eye, something beginning with . . . wasps." I thought your head was gonna explode.' She laughed. 'And you scooped him up and you ran and jumped into the sea. Do you remember?'

Frank's head bobbed slightly.

She nodded at the envelope in his hand. 'Are you really not going to open it?'

He grimaced as though there was a sour taste in his mouth, blew out his cheeks and ignored the question.

'The whole thing was my fault, Frank. My mistake.'

He had heard this a thousand times. If Marcie *was* a ghost, then this was the sound of her rattling chains.

'I was being selfish; you need to make it right.'

'Are you alright?' Red said, looking up at Frank and wrinkling his nose.

Frank nodded. 'I'm fine.' He looked up and down the street, rubbed his eyes, and then turned back to the little boy. 'Okay, *Gavin*. I spy with my little eye . . .'

RED

'Mummy's here!' Red shouted, spotting his mum turning the corner in the distance. He stood up and ran to the gate to welcome her. He held it open as she walked through with a carrier bag and a six-pack of cans under one arm.

'Have you been behaving, Reddy?'

'Yeah, we were going to play hide and seek, but there's nowhere to hide. So, we've been playing I Spy. Frank's dead good at it! And he made me laugh, because when I said I wanted to play again and again, he made his fingers to look like a gun and did this.' Red put two fingers together to form a pistol, then put them in his mouth and mimed shooting his own brains out.

'Nice, Frank. Really nice,' Red's mum said, as she walked up the steps and dropped the carrier bag at Frank's feet. She put down the beers, too, then stood up, out of breath. 'Right, here you go.'

'Thanks,' Frank said, awkwardly.

'It's fine.' She turned around and reached into her back pocket, producing a small packet. 'Reddy, I got you some of your Pokémon cards, too.' She held them out to Red, who shouted 'Yesss!' and took them gratefully.

'What do you say, you wretch?'

'Thank you, Mummy!'

Red tore into the packet excitedly, quickly fanning the five cards inside. He laid them on the ground and chewed his lip while he assessed his haul. There were two that he already had, two trainer cards and a Charizard. No shinies. He sniffed once. The real treasures were the shiny ones.

'No shiny ones, kiddo?' his mum asked.

'Nah, but I got a Charizard, look.' He held up the card to Frank and then to his mum.

'Cool,' she said. 'Haven't you already got that one?'

'Yes, but this one is—'

Frank stood on his doorstep and shifted uncomfortably. He seemed confused as to why they were both still in his front yard, having this conversation in front of him.

'Well, alright then,' he said, gathering the bag at his feet.

Red's mum looked at Frank, then at the shopping bag in his hand and the pack of beer still at his feet. She raised her eyebrows.

'Oh, shi—. Yeah, the money. One minute.' He left the bag on the doorstep and disappeared inside, closing the door behind him.

Red continued to explain the merits of the Charizard card. 'And it's not just a fire-type Pokémon either. Charizard's a *Flying* Fire type, so it's got lots of special moves, and that's why—'

Frank reappeared with a note and a handful of coppers and silver, which Red's mum was forced to receive in cupped hands. '. . .Wow. Great. Thanks,' She walked past Red, who was still studying his cards on the top step. 'Okay, come on, kiddo.'

'Aww, I haven't shown Frank the other ones yet.'

'Now, Reddy.'

'Okay. Okay.' He scooped his cards together, hauled himself to his feet dramatically, and then skipped down the steps.

His mum opened the gate and turned to let him through under one arm, before noticing the foil wrapper from his cards discarded on Frank's path. She pointed to it. 'Red, your wrapper. Go back, pick it up and put it in the bin, please.' She nodded towards Frank's grey wheelie bin, which stood on the pavement just outside his gate.

'Oops. Sorry.' Red returned to collect the wrapper, almost dropping the rest of his cards as he bent to pick it up. As his mum began walking up the steps to their own house, Red raised the lid of Frank's bin, peering inside before dropping in his wrapper.

A carefully crayoned allosaurus was staring back up at him. There, on top of the bags of rubbish, was the drawing he had done for Frank.

FRANK

Frank had taken the carrier bag of groceries into his kitchen and was returning to pick up the beers that still sat on his doorstep. As he stepped back outside, he looked up to see Red staring into the bin. Realising what the boy was looking at, Frank froze.

'You didn't like it?' Red said, as he looked up at him.

'Come on, Red,' Sarah called over the small fence as she unlocked their front door.

Red continued looking at Frank with a confused nose scrunch. 'Was it because the volcano was rubbish?'

Frank remained mute.

'Red!' His mum was now shouting through the open door from their hallway.

'That's alright,' the boy said to Frank. He let the lid close on the drawing and continued a little more cheerfully. 'I know it wasn't *that* good – and I've found my yellow now.' He dug into his pocket and held up a crayon. 'So, I could just do you another one, a much better one, that you'll definitely like.' That apparently decided, Red skipped towards his own front door.

'Bye, Frank! See you tomorrow!' he shouted as he went inside.

Frank looked at the sky and sighed.

'Not a word.' Frank stepped back inside the front door with Red's drawing, retrieved from the bin, rolled up in his hand.

'I didn't say anything.'

'You saw the little shit, with the eyes. He guilted me into getting it out of the bin. Besides, you heard him: if I don't accept this one, he'll just keep drawing the bloody things and posting them through the letterbox.'

'I didn't say anything, Frank.' Marcie grinned and held up her hands defensively.

He huffed into the kitchen, snapped the kettle on and threw the drawing on to the countertop. Marcie sat at the kitchen table; she was now looking at him curiously.

'What now?' he said, impatiently.

'Nothing.'

'What?'

'Nothing. It's just that that's the second time you've been to the bin this week.'

'So?'

'What do you mean, "So"?! You can't stand going to the bin! It's the furthest you have to go from the house. You hate it.'

'No, I don't.'

Marcie looked at him sceptically. 'Not only that, but you opened the gate.'

'I always open the gate.'

'Ha! No, you don't. You open the bin from the bottom step with your stupid bloody stick, and then chuck the bag in from there. This time you opened the gate. I think that's the furthest you've been from the house in over a year.'

Frank shook his head and busied himself making a cup of tea.

Was it true? He supposed it was. He probably *hadn't* been that far down the path in over a year. He certainly hadn't opened the gate.

And he *definitely* hadn't been through the gate and into the world beyond.

Even to himself, it was difficult to explain why. Just thinking about 'beyond the gate' filled him with a rising panic that made him feel hot and shivery and wrong.

But it was more than that. The truth was that Frank felt – in some instinctive and fearful way – that if he left, he might return to find Marcie gone. Really gone. As though leaving would break some spell.

That's how the home they had shared for thirty years had become his world. His horizons were the street at the front and the fence at the back: 800 square feet of universe.

And this had been true since the night he (sort of) tried to kill himself, and she came back.

*

In the months that followed the funeral, Frank fell into a familiar routine. After sleeping too little, he would wake too early and sit at the dining table, staring into darkness. As the sun came up, he would pace from one end of the living room to the other, or sit on the front step, smoking the cigarettes that Marcie so detested, unsure as to why he still felt the need to go outside to do so.

As mid-morning bore relentlessly on, he would fish clothes out of the discarded piles around their bedroom and head out to The Flea, knowing that he could rap on the door and Sam would allow him inside before opening time. He would then spend the afternoon drinking in a corner, being obnoxious to anybody who tried to make conversation.

Even as he sat there, he felt like the worst kind of cliché. But with everything that gave his life texture gone, he found that a cliché was the most comfortable thing to be.

In the evening, Fat Ken and Jonny would sometimes join him, and they would chat to one another, Frank's only contribution the occasional monosyllable. Until it began to get dark, and Sam would suggest that Ken or Jonny get Frank home, and he would leave: sometimes quietly, sometimes angrily, but usually with little memory of doing so.

On his last visit to The Flea, Frank had made his exit under his own steam by falling through the doorway and out into the street. Pulling on his coat, he'd stumbled off down the road, his oldest friend shouting after him, 'See you later, Frankie!' with sad affection as he walked in the opposite direction.

Arriving at the High Street crossroads, rather than turning left for home, Frank continued straight on and into a small supermarket, deciding that he would brave the fluorescent lights for more alcohol and a pack of cigarettes. Standing outside, he smartened himself up a little by tucking in his shirt. By forcing his eyes wide open in an attempt to see just one of everything, he successfully made it past the small, bored security guard who stood at the entrance.

The shop was busy with late commuters and students from the new university buildings that had just opened a few streets away. Frank made his way to the drinks aisle, where he swayed in front of the shelves for a full minute. He then pulled a bottle from the spirits section, and a twelve-pack of Czech beer from the shelf below, which he tucked under one arm before stumbling to the self-service tills at the front of the store.

'*Unexpected item in bagging area.*'

He hated these things even when he wasn't drunk. In fact, this is exactly why they used to avoid coming to this supermarket when Marcie was still alive: the serve-yourself robot checkouts. She hated them too. It irritated her, the way an assistant would come over to verify her age and not even look up to check that she was 'twenty-one and over' before swiping the verification card. 'I know twenty-one was a lifetime ago, but at least glance up,' she'd said, half-laughing, as she unpacked some shopping one day.

'*Unexpected item in bagging area.*'

'For fu . . .' Frank lifted up the beer, then replaced it.

'*Unexpected item in bagging area.*'

He lifted the bottle of spirits and replaced it.

'*Unexpected item in bagging area.*'

'Are you alright there?' A young, faux-cheery woman appeared from nowhere. She was tanned a burned orange and had those inflated lips that look like an allergic reaction.

'S'not working,' he slurred.

'Yeah, you've got something in your bagging area,' she said slowly, with undisguised irritation.

'Really? No shit.'

This caught the security guard's attention, and the diminutive figure strolled over, thumbs in his belt like a dwarf John Wayne. 'Problem?' he said to the girl with the lips.

Frank looked him up and down. Mainly down. 'Nope.'

'*Unexpected item in bagging area,*' the machine insisted.

'Just got an unexpected item in my bagging area,' Frank said, stumbling forwards slightly and smiling with the drunken face of a simpleton. 'Although, Christ knows what's so *unexpected* about it.' His voice was getting louder as he gestured towards the drinks. 'It's a pack of beer, not an aardvark. It's not a fucking bouncy castle, is it?' He rebalanced by stumbling backwards a little, and the queue for the tills shuffled behind him in a Mexican wave of impatience.

'Listen, mate, why don't I put this stuff back on the shelf and you get yourself off, alright?' the security guard offered.

Frank considered the proposal and dismissed it. 'Or . . . why don't *you* sod off?' he said, squinting at the man's name badge. '*Craig.*' Frank said the name as though it was a ridiculous thing to call a human being. He turned back to the machine.

'Right. You're done, mate. Out we go,' Craig said with finality, as he grabbed Frank by the elbow and began walking him to the door. Frank tried to protest, but found his limbs uncooperative, and so he flailed half-heartedly before being shoved roughly through the automatic doors.

He stumbled into the road, where a taxi's horn blared as it swerved to avoid him. When he turned back to the supermarket's exit, he found his short nemesis still standing there, arms folded. Defeated, Frank pulled his coat collar up around his neck as it began to rain.

Back home, there was a slight 'clink' as he flicked the light switch by the doorway and the bulb died.

'Of course,' he muttered, as he galumphed through to the living room, in the dark, crashing over his shoes and then the hallway table.

Throwing off his coat, his hair still dripping, he was about to fall backwards on to the sofa when instead he pulled open a cabinet beneath the living room bookshelves and withdrew a bottle of gin. It was the only alcohol left in the house, and more an artefact than a drink. The bottle was so dusty it felt like it had fur.

Frank bumbled into the kitchen, grabbed a coffee mug from the sink, and sat down at the dining table in the chair he had occupied eight hours before. He then drank and filled and drank and filled, until the room rotated.

At around 3am, he woke up with his chin resting on his chest. His neck cracked loudly, like damp wood on a fire, as he lifted his head. Slowly, he remembered where he was. After a while, he stumbled over to the living room bookshelves once more. This time it wasn't to search for drink, but to retrieve a book he had once bought for Marcie. A book that reminded him of their first year together.

They had talked a lot during those early months of their

relationship about their ambitions, what they wanted for their futures. They spoke the way that young people often do. As though the future was a map they could paint by numbers, rather than one in which life bleeds the colours.

Marcie was at college by then, already sure that she wanted to teach young children. Frank, though, had followed his father and brothers on to the railways, and was facing fifty years of a maintenance job that he hated.

It was during one of these early conversations that Frank, awkward and embarrassed, had admitted that his real ambition was to write. At school, words had been the one thing at which he had excelled, English the one subject that had made him feel the pull of possibility. But even as his talent became clear, it was strangled by real life, his lack of confidence and the expectations of his family. The one time he had shared the idea of pursuing a writing career with his family, his father had dismissed him in a sentence, describing Frank's short stories and poems as a 'fine hobby'. His meaning was clear.

To Frank, though, they were more than that. When he wrote, it felt like painting a chalk doorway on a wall and then stepping through. He had used these very words to Marcie, and he had expected her to laugh at him; he was prepared for it, and wouldn't have blamed her. Their little town was full of people with grand plans. Stories of those who had gone to seek something else and then returned humiliated were passed from generation to generation, told as cautionary tales.

And the funny thing, is Marcie *had* laughed. But not unkindly. Not in a way that made him feel small or ridiculous. She had laughed, instead, at the very idea of him dismissing his dreams. She had made him feel that harbouring these ambitions was far from ridiculous – but listening to his father and ignoring them? *That* was.

Her laugh that day had been the catalyst for his writing. For the next three decades, Marcie's encouragement had been the fuel of his career: a career that would lead to several novels, the bestselling *Aubrey Wello* series, and a poetry collection, of which he was most proud, called *Chalk*.

It was during this same early conversation, the one in which Marcie had laughed, that she had confided in him that her favourite book was not one of the highbrow, literary classics that she pretended to like when chatting with her college friends. In truth, her favourite book was one that her father had read to her as a child. A book about a mouse.

On the publication day of Frank's first book, *The Days of Aubrey Wello*, ten years later, he had presented Marcie with a small present, wrapped in brown paper. She had expected that inside she would find a copy of *Wello*, perhaps the first to leave the press. Instead, she unwrapped a first edition of the book her father had read to her. A book she had only mentioned to Frank once, in what was for her a forgotten conversation: *Johnny Town Mouse*.

Thirty-five years later, in the living room of the house they had once shared, Frank opened that children's book to the middle page, and out dropped the piece of paper he had carefully secreted there.

When Frank and Marcie had left for her to go into hospital for the final time, Marcie must have known that she wouldn't be coming back home. And so, as they were leaving the house, she had somehow left him this letter, incongruously propped against the kettle, to find upon his return.

By the point at which she had written it, her handwriting had become little more than a tangled mess of scratchy hieroglyphics, and it had taken a while for Frank to decipher the whole thing. By now, though, he knew it by heart.

Still, he read it. Again.

Frankie,

Well. Not to sound all dramatic, but by the time you read this, I will probably not be here anymore, dead, etc.

(If you are reading this and I'm still alive, then pop it back in the envelope, or this is going to be reeally weird.)

I'm writing this because you are going to be a mess. I know you, Frank. You have a poet's heart but a big dope's head. You're going to think there's no point, and you're going to drink too much and think that life beyond us is a big hole. Well, guess what? It is. Life is a big hole, unless you fill it with things, people and experiences and stuff. And that's what you need to do.

So, be sad for a bit. You should be. I was great!

But don't be mad . . . especially not at Michael. You know he is the best thing we ever made. I know he's angry right now, but he won't be forever.

And write! For God's sake, write. It's what you were made to do, and you've not done what you were made to do for so long now. Or at least read a book or listen to a tune. Christ, this place used to be full of music.

I don't know what else to put, really. Try not to think about me as this broken little bird, I was always more than that . . . especially to you.

*And . . . I guess . . . You know how at the end of those reality shows I always made you watch, they always say to the person, let's look at your highlights, let's look at your best bits? Here's the thing, Frankie . . . **You** were my best bits. You and our boy.*

I love you. I'm so sorry I can't stay.

M x

PS Stop smoking! And eat a bloody vegetable now and again. One of us being dead is depressing enough!

Frank's chest hitched as he ran his fingers over the page. He folded the paper neatly, placed it back inside the book and refilled his mug.

Around an hour later, he stumbled upstairs. As he kicked off his shoes, he knocked the bedside table, spilling its contents across the floor. The only object that survived was a bottle of Triazolam, the 'pink ones'. Marcie had been prescribed them to help her sleep.

He sat on the edge of the bed and, without conscious thought, he tapped a couple on to the table and scooped them up, swallowing them dry. And then a few more, on to the palm of his hand. And then a few more.

He closed his eyes, fell backwards and went to sleep, drifting off with only a vague and passing interest in whether he would wake up.

RED

Red had been sitting on his front doorstep for fifteen minutes, and was beginning to wonder whether the old man next door would *ever* appear.

He had decided to ask the man what his favourite colours were, so he could be sure that the next painting he did wouldn't end up in the bin. His mum, however, had said that he couldn't bother their neighbour by knocking on his door. So Red had hatched this plan: to sit on the step and wait for Frank to appear for his morning cigarette. That way he could 'bother' him, but not break his promise.

Finally, Frank emerged and stood in the doorway.

Red observed the old man from the corner of his eye as he lit his morning cigarette, pocketed his lighter and blew smoke into the air above his head. Red stayed very quiet; Frank hadn't yet noticed him sitting there.

But suddenly, Frank mumbled something. 'Yeah . . .'

Red turned to face him, sure that Frank was talking to him, but found the old man was still looking upwards.

'. . . I know that. Just take a morning off, eh?' As he finished this sentence, Frank glanced away from Red, to his right, as though the person he was speaking to was standing there. 'You gave up smoking

twenty years ago, Mar, and which one of us died? . . . I'm well aware
it's bad for me, yes. Look, it says so on the box, right here.' He
squinted at the writing on the cigarette packet. 'Here ya go: "Smoking can cause infertility and adversely impact pregnancy."' He held
out the packet, as though showing it to somebody. 'I tell you
what . . . For you, I will avoid getting pregnant. How's that sound?'

With the satisfaction of someone who has just won an argument,
Frank turned away and glanced left, finally looking in Red's
direction.

'Jesus Christ!' Frank jumped, startled, and burned his chin with
his cigarette. He frantically patted the embers that had caught
in his beard. 'What the hell are you doing? You scared the shit out
of me!'

'Nuthin'. Just sitting.'

Frank put his palm across his chest and sat down on the doorstep. 'Christ,' he said again, as he examined his cigarette, which was
now bent at a right angle. He grunted, and then tossed it into the
hedge before taking another from his packet and lighting it.

'Who were you talking to?' Red asked.

'Wha?'

'Who were you talking to? You were just talking to someone.
You were talking to someone the other day as well. When we were
playing I Spy.'

'Nobody. I wasn't talking to anyone.'

'You must've been talking to someone. I heard you.'

They were both silent for a minute.

'Are you having a baby?'

Frank replied with tired exasperation: 'No, I'm not having a
baby.'

'Well, you said something about getting preglant, and that means
having a baby.'

Silence again.

'Who were you talking to?'

More silence.

'You know, smoking *is* really bad for you. We did about it in school. They showed us this TV programme, and someone was smoking, and there were these black ghosts that came out of this mister's cigarette and they went into his insides, and they made him cough like this.' Red coughed dramatically to demonstrate. 'And he had to go to the doctor, and he had to have an operation, which means you get chopped up.'

'Uh huh.'

'Into *pieces*,' Red stressed, not sure that Frank was grasping the gravity of the situation. 'I sometimes talk to people who aren't there as well,' Red continued. 'When I was little, I had a friend called Dog, and he was a dog that was invisible. But not like a *real* dog. He could walk standing up and talk, and . . . he was an imaginary friend. My dad thought it was bad and a worry-thing, but my mum said it was normal, and I've just got a good imagination and he should stop being such a dick-stick. Actually, I used to have a pigeon called Miles, and I used to talk to him as well, even though he couldn't talk back. Because he was a pigeon. And I sometimes—'

Frank interrupted. 'I was just talking to myself, that's all.'

'My mum does that sometimes. She says it's because it's the only way you get some sense.'

He was about to continue when Frank interrupted again. 'Shouldn't you be at school or something?'

'I don't start at my new school until next week. And anyway, it's Saturday!' Red replied, as though this was the most obvious thing in the world.

'Well, where are your mates, then?'

Red shrugged.

'Well, have you got nothing better to do than sit there scaring the bejesus out of people?'

Red chewed his lip. 'Well, I *was* having something better to do but I'm not having something better to do anymore. I was supposed to be having something better to do with my daddy. But not now. He's got to work.'

*

That morning, Red had woken up to the sound of his mum on the phone to his dad.

'It's the last weekend of the holidays!'

She had taken her phone into the back garden and closed the back door behind her so that Red wouldn't be able to hear. But Red could hear just fine.

His mum's voice was getting louder and louder as his dad cancelled their weekend together, again. 'What do you mean "So?"?! You've barely seen him, Jamie! And now it's the last weekend of the holidays and you're cancelling again!'

Red was sitting on the living room sofa, but could see through the kitchen window into the garden, where his mum was pacing back and forth, gesticulating furiously.

'He's been looking forward to it all week ... And you couldn't have called earlier?'

On the sofa beside him was Red's tiny suitcase of clothes, and a Buzz Lightyear backpack overflowing with Lego and Pokémon cards. This was overseen by three stuffed animals lined up against the wall, where Red had placed them while he decided which to include for his weekend away. There was Pikachu, a cuddly Thanos and – his favourite – a kangaroo that he had won at Alton Towers when he was three. He couldn't remember why, but he had named the kangaroo 'Bonzer'. He would definitely be taking Bonzer, but had been trying to choose between Pikachu and Thanos.

Now, it didn't matter.

Red wasn't surprised that his dad was cancelling again. In truth, he hadn't really been 'looking forward to it all week'. But he *was* a bit disappointed, for two reasons. For a start, his dad had promised to take him to watch football. And even though he thought football was boring and a bit rubbish, when they had been to the football before, he had been allowed to have fizzy laces and cola. Also, they sometimes went with Noah Conway's dad, which meant there was a chance he might see Noah, and could show him his new Pokémon cards (one of which was a shiny Snorlax*)*.

More importantly, his dad had *promised*. And promises were more than just saying you would do something, they were like a definite, definite thing you said you were going to do. That you definitely, definitely had to do.

'I realise you've got a new life now, Jamie, but your old one still exists. You can't just erase us; you can't just erase Red . . .'

Red made a mental note to ask what 'erase' meant.

A minute later, his mum hung up, gripping the phone as though she intended to crush it. Through gritted teeth, she shouted 'Arsehole!' at the receiver.

This was how a lot of their conversations ended lately.

It wasn't like this before, when they all lived together. Later, after the separation, Red's dad would say that he and his mum had been unhappy for a long time, but Red just didn't remember it like that.

Back then, Red couldn't remember them arguing at all. But, in fairness, that was a lifetime ago. Back then, he had been five. Now he was six.

For Red, the first clue that there was a problem had been when his dad didn't come home from work one day, and then didn't come home the next. And then it was Saturday, and his dad didn't come home that day, either. But he did turn up in the afternoon; he'd honked his horn on the driveway and took Red to Burger King.

The only thing Red really remembered about that day was that

Burger King isn't as good as McDonald's. And that his dad had called him 'mate' a lot.

Then, a few weeks later, his dad had picked him up on a Saturday again. Only this time, they went to meet his friend Heather, in a pub with a soft-play area that was closed. And the only thing he remembered about *that* day was that he had sausages, and Heather asked him lots of questions about the things he liked. Did he like football? Not really. Did he like chips? Yes.

And then she'd got bored and looked at her phone for the next two hours.

Of course, this was all very strange, but he hadn't really known that their lives together were over until his dad had driven him home after the pub, and talked about things sometimes getting *complicated*, and saying that Red would understand when he was older, and that they didn't live together anymore, and that was that.

As it turned out, Heather was dad's new girlfriend. She wasn't just called Heather, though; she had lots of names. Dad called her *Heth* or *Babe*. And when Mum and Auntie Steph drank wine and talked about her, thinking he wasn't listening, they called her *Tits-and-Teeth*, *the Mid-life Crysix* and *the Bicycle*.

Red could tell they didn't like Heather very much, which was strange because his mum and Auntie Steph didn't really dislike anybody.

His dad, on the other hand, had insisted that Heather was 'super nice' when you got to know her. And that was supposed to be the point of the visit this weekend, to see his dad's new house and spend time with Heather – and Heather's evil twin daughters – and get to know them better.

The thing is, though, as much as he wanted to see Noah – and, more importantly, wanted his dad to keep his promises – he wasn't at all bothered about getting to know Heather better. His mum didn't like Heather, and that was good enough for Red. Besides, her teeth were too white, and when she smiled it was like her eyes didn't join in.

Red thought about this for a second and decided that he was glad that his dad had cancelled. At least he wouldn't have to spend time with *the Bicycle*.

Red's mum shouted from the back door. 'Looks like it's just you and me again, Reddy. Your daddy says he's sorry, but he's got to work.'

Red was already emptying his backpack on to the sofa and sorting his cards into piles when she walked in. 'Sorry. I know you were looking forward to going.'

'That's okay.'

'We'll hang out and watch films and eat rubbish. How's that sound?'

'Pretty good. Can we watch *Jaws*?'

'What? No.'

'What about *Harry Potter*?'

'No. That gave you nightmares last time. What about the *Paw Patrol* movie?'

'Mummy, that's totally for babies.'

'Well, that can't be you, then, because babies don't go to school.' She scooped him into her arms and tickled him as he wriggled. 'Are you looking forward to school on Monday?'

'Dunno. I'm not going to know anybody.'

'Well, strangers are just friends that you haven't met yet.'

'What?'

'I don't know. I saw it on Instagram. It sounded good.'

'Mummy, what's "erase" mean?'

'Jesus, Red. You've got ears like a bat. It . . . it doesn't mean anything. Grown-ups say stupid stuff when they're mad.'

'What does it mean, though?'

'It just means to get rid of something. Like, you know, when you use a rubber to rub pencil out: that's erasing something.'

'So, like a mistake?'

His mum's face crumpled, and she gasped, suddenly fighting tears. She hugged Red tight. '*No*. Not like a mistake. Your dad's just a bit distracted, with his new house and everything at the minute. Me and your daddy can't be together, but that doesn't mean that we were a mistake, because we made you. And, besides, when you rub something out, it's because you want to write something new and better – and that is exactly what we are going to do. Okay?'

'Okay.'

'Look,' Red said, holding up a Pokémon card. 'Shiny Snorlax.'

'Cool,' his mum said.

*

Red finished telling the story of the morning to Frank. 'See,' he said, holding up the shiny card for Frank to inspect. 'Told you.'

Frank nodded. 'Yeah, I see.' He flicked his cigarette towards the road, and stood.

Red looked up at him. 'Who *were* you talking to?'

'See you later, kid.' Frank went back inside the house and closed the door behind him.

FRANK

Wake up.

Wake. Up.

Wake.

Up.

It was the first time he'd heard her voice in a year. Longer, in fact, as for the last three weeks of her life, that voice had been little more than a fragile whisper.

She sounded distant, underwater. And even in the state between waking and sleeping, Frank knew that he was dreaming, knew that her voice was an illusion. He struggled to open his eyes. Even more than usual, his eyelids felt like luggage, weighing down his entire face. Ah, the sleeping tablets, he thought vaguely. The tablets . . . and that bottle of gin they'd got as a present in 1998 from . . . who was that from . . .?

Wake up, you idiot.

This dream was getting persistent now, annoyingly so. And his head, which had been thrumming, was now home to a repetitive thud. With one massive effort, he tried to open his eyes. Finally, they obeyed. He blinked once as he heard the voice again.

Wake up, it repeated in time with his thudding head.

Then silence. And he was suddenly more awake than he had any right to be.

He remembered the tablets again and tumbled from the bed to the floor. And, moving like continental drift, he slowly made his way to the telephone on the landing. He pressed the numbers and then fell backwards, his eyes closing again as he drifted away, dreaming that he felt Marcie's hand on his cheek.

It was two days before he woke up in the hospital. It took one day more to convince the hospital staff that he wasn't a danger to himself, and that he hadn't tried to take his own life. Which was true. The thought hadn't even occurred to him. He had just wanted to sleep, to forget, to dull himself, just for a while. He didn't *want* to die; he just wasn't overly bothered whether or not he did.

To prove that he was fine, he refused a ride home, accepted the offer of some spare clothes from the hospital charity shop, and took the bus dressed in a ski jacket, a pair of baggy stonewashed jeans and a Prince 'Purple Rain' tour T-shirt. His own clothes in a carrier bag.

Arriving home, he walked through the front door and stood in the hallway for a moment, listening. The voice he had heard, the voice that had saved him, had been so vivid and clear. But what he heard now was nothing so extraordinary, just the sound of his own breathing, the occasional creak of the old house and the hum of a car passing in the distance. The depressingly familiar sounds of nothing in particular.

Exhausted, he took off the old jacket, made a pillow of it, tucked it under his head and fell asleep on the living room sofa, where he dreamed of absolutely nothing.

And when he awoke a few hours later, sitting on the arm at the end of the sofa was his dead wife.

'Hi, Frankie,' she said, giving him finger guns.

For the first time in his life, he did an actual double take. It was cartoonish, like Wile E. Coyote seeing a box of TNT at his feet.

And the world slipped sideways, as though God had briefly turned gravity on and off again. He was still just sitting there, but it felt as though he had staggered.

She popped her eyebrows and smiled.

'Nope,' he said simply, acknowledging the impossibility. 'No. No. No.'

He closed his eyes, stood up with them still closed and stumbled into the kitchen. He leaned against the countertop and took a glass from the sink. Filling it from the tap, he emptied it in two huge gulps, then filled it again and put his fingers in it to splash some water on his face.

'No. No. No.' He breathed in and out deliberately. In through his nose, out through his mouth. After a minute, his heart rate began to slow as he calmly reminded himself of the drugs that must still be rattling through his veins. 'Okay,' he said to himself. 'Everything is normal, everything is fine, everything is—'

'Don't freak out,' she said, from behind him.

'No. No. No. No.' Frank threw open the back door and sucked in fresh air. Then he turned around. She was still there, looking as though she had just come in from a trip to the shops. The only thing amiss – aside from the fact that she had been dead for twelve months – was the fact that she was in her 'Sunday dress', a dress he hadn't seen in years. And she was a little younger. There was no sign of the ill health that had defined her appearance in those last months.

He turned back to the outside and continued to draw in gasps, glancing around occasionally to check that she was still standing there. She was. Continuing to smile, too, but now with an air of exasperation as she leaned against the dining room wall.

Frank tried to settle himself with reason. 'One: there's the drugs.' He counted off on his right hand. 'Two: trauma, that's a thing. People go crazy after trauma. I'm getting no sleep; this is perfectly normal . . . I mean, obviously I'm having a massive shit-yer-pants, mental breakdown but . . .'

He spun around with purpose and, with his head down, he carefully avoided eye-contact as he walked past her. Skirting around the dining table to avoid coming within a few feet of her, he made his way back into the living room, where he grabbed the remote control and sat on the edge of the sofa. Martin Roberts's enormous head filled the TV as an old episode of *Homes Under the Hammer* came on.

She appeared, perching on the mantelpiece across from him. '*Homes Under the Hammer*? Really?'

'Everything's fine,' Frank repeated to himself as he rocked slightly, his right leg involuntarily bouncing.

'Just talk to me, I'm not going anywhere,' she said softly, as she sat beside him.

He increased the volume on the TV until it was deafening.

'. . . and that's why we always say to view the property before the auction,' Martin Roberts shouted.

'Okay, Frankie, have it your way.' She settled back into the sofa.

And there they had remained for the next twelve hours, in silence. As the woman Frank would have given anything to have one last conversation with sat beside him, and he pretended that she wasn't there.

PART TWO

RED

Red's mum barrelled down the stairs in her dressing gown, her hair wet from the shower, to find Red was still on the living room sofa, watching cartoons. He was upside down, his feet on the wall, his head skirting the floor. He was dressed in his new school uniform. As far as his waist.

'Where's your shoes? Where's your coat? Wait, hang on – where's your *trousers*?!'

'I spilled some juice on them,' Red replied distractedly, his eyes on the TV.

'Oh, for f . . .' His mum went into the kitchen, where he had left his trousers puddled on the floor. Snatching them up, she ran back up to the bedroom. He could hear her drying them with the hair-dryer. 'TV off, Red!' she shouted down the stairs.

A few minutes later, she was back in the living room, dressed in leggings and a jumper. She threw the now-dry trousers towards him.

'Trousers. On.'

Red didn't move.

His mum grabbed the remote from the arm of the sofa. The TV went black and fell silent.

'Trousers!'

'Muuuuum,' Red moaned.

'Don't "Muuuum" me! Your *first* day, and we are going to be late. Get your trousers on. We need to go.'

Ten minutes later, they had made it as far as the hallway, where Red was again attempting to tie the laces on his shoes. Despite his protestations, his mum was insisting he had them on the wrong feet.

'I can do it!' he said, when she tried to help.

'I know you can, Red, but by the time you do, all life as we know it will be dead. Come on.' She took over 'project shoes', switched them to the opposite feet, which did seem to look less wonky, then quickly double-tied the laces. 'Better luck next time, sunshine,' she said, with a glance at her watch. 'Shit.'

She pulled on her jacket and grabbed Red's Spider-Man backpack, which was hanging over the banister. Stuffing his water bottle into the side webbing the two of them finally fell out of the front door.

It was amazing to think that Red's school was now just a short fifteen-minute walk from home. At their old house, school mornings had meant two tubes and then a harried walk to get to Wardour Street Academy on time.

Now, it was a short stroll to the gates of St Agnes Primary. Red's mum pointed out that they were probably hurrying out of habit and they slowed down a little.

'Excited?'

'Mmm,' Red replied noncommittally.

'Trust me, new broom.'

Red kicked a stone into the distance. It clanged against the base of a metal streetlight.

'What if the other kids don't like me?'

'What are you talking about, you crazy madman? How can they not like you? You're handsome, you're smart, you're funny. You know *all* the Pokémon. What does Bulbasaur evolve into?'

'Venusaur.'

'And what type of Pokémon is Charmander?'

'He's a Fire type.'

'See? You're ready.' She nudged him with her hip.

'I dunno.'

'I do.'

Red's mum continued to test him on Pokémon, and before long they joined a throng of parents and children, all headed in the same direction.

When the school gates came into view, his mum stopped abruptly. Squatting down on her heels, she smartened Red's shirt collar and fixed her eyes on his. 'Ready, Reddy?'

'I'm ready ready.'

'I'm super proud of you, baby boy.'

'I'm not—'

'Oh, I know you're not *a* baby. But you are *my* baby. Listen, I know it's not been easy just lately. I promise things are going to be better.' She looked at him with a double crease between her eyes. 'And have a great day. The other kids are going to love you, because I love you, and I think you're the best and' – she swallowed – 'I know what I'm talking about. Okay?'

'Okay.'

They entered the gates and swerved through an increasing swarm of parents and children. The occasional older kid whipped by them on a bike or a scooter. To Red, it was the gates of a foreboding castle, the scooter-kids like harpies. He imagined a crack of thunder overhead, and was about to pull his mum's hand back in the direction of home when they caught sight of Mrs Mills, the headteacher whom they had met at their induction day, weeks ago. She was standing at the bottom of the school steps and directing traffic importantly.

'Well, don't you look smart,' she said to Red, as they approached.

'Sorry, it's not quite uniform,' his mum apologised. 'We haven't had a chance to get a jumper with the badge on yet.'

'Oh, don't worry about that!' Mrs Mills shouted, and then leaned in a little, her voice dropping to a hush. 'We do have some jumpers that are passed back by parents of older children, if you'd like one of those?'

'No. No. That's not . . . We've ordered it, it's just not arrived yet, that's all. It'll be here by next week, I'm sure.' The two women smiled at one another, awkwardly.

'Well!' Mrs Mills said finally. 'Come on then, Leonard. I'll show you to your classroom. We'll get you all settled.'

'My name's Red,' he told her quietly, but it was lost as Mrs Mills admonished a much older boy for doing a scooter trick off the steps. He had landed at their feet, clutching his balls with an 'oof'.

As the boy retrieved the scooter and hobbled away, the head-teacher's attention returned to Red. 'Right then, say bye-bye to Mummy.'

Red gave a small wave as Mrs Mills began to steer him in the direction of the main doors and away.

'Love you, Reddy,' his mum called after him.

At this, he broke free of Mrs Mills, ran back and hugged her legs. And then, trotting back to the waiting headteacher, he forced a smile over his shoulder. His mum was soon lost in the chaos behind him, as he was eaten by the building.

Inside the school, it smelled like craft glue and bleach and gravy. The corridors squeaked underfoot. It was bigger than his old school, and seemed much, much bigger because the ceilings were so high. Children of varying sizes criss-crossed in front of them, each heading somewhere with purpose, but to completely different destinations. Red scurried to keep up with Mrs Mills.

'. . . And *your* classroom is just down here. It's a lovely class, and

Miss Payton is really nice.' She kept her eyes forward as she continued. 'I know it can be tricky when you join a school later in the year than the other children, but I'm sure – Joshua James!' Red was startled by the volume of the shout and the sudden change in her tone. 'What on earth is on your feet?'

In front of them, a bewildered-looking boy with spiked blond hair – presumably Joshua James – stopped. He looked at his own feet, and the bright white trainers there, as though they had spontaneously come into existence. He was about to respond when Mrs Mills cut him off.

'Never mind. Come with me, and we'll work out why your school uniform is different to everybody else's.' She leaned down to Red and pointed at a door to their left. A window at the top of it was obscured by multi-coloured handprints that spelled out 'Class Two Caterpillars'.

'This is your stop, Leonard.'

At that moment, a woman Red recognised as Miss Payton swung the door open. The only reason Red recognised this lady was because his mum had shown him her face on the school website. And her face was easily recognisable, because it was round and red, and she had brown hair with a fringe that looked like a helmet.

'Well, good morning!' she sang at them both, clapping her hands together.

'Good morning, Miss Payton!' Mrs Mills trilled back. 'Another victim for you.' And they both laughed without really enjoying it.

'This is Leonard. I found him loitering outside.'

Red made a note to ask his mum what *loitering* meant.

'He's the new boy we chatted about last week.' Mrs Mills turned towards Red. 'We've just been getting to know each other. He's really looking forward to joining you and the rest of the Caterpillars, aren't you . . . Joshua *James!*'

Red wished she'd stop doing that. The boy with the spiky blond hair stopped in his tracks; he had begun to slink off down the corridor.

'Well, good luck, Leonard!' Mrs Mills said, cheerfully. 'Have a great first day.' And then she took Joshua James by the arm and led him away, presumably to his death.

Miss Payton watched them go, and then bent down until she was the same height as Red.

'Well, welcome to Class Two, Leonard.'

'Actually, my name is Red. I didn't like my name, and now everyone calls me Red—' he began his usual explanation, but stopped short as she put out a hand for him to shake.

'Okay, well, Red it is, then. Come on. Let's show you where your peg is, and then I'll introduce you to the rest of the class.'

Red followed her through the door, chewing on his lip, concerned that his new classmates might be actual caterpillars.

FRANK

Frank was, again, sitting on his doorstep and smoking a cigarette when Sarah walked up the steps to her own front door. She was fumbling for her keys in her handbag.

Before there were all these comings and goings next door, Frank hadn't noticed how much time he spent on this step. For a long time, he had felt comfortably anonymous sitting there; now, he felt more and more like a gargoyle.

He didn't think she'd noticed him this time, but, as she continued to rummage in her bag – and without looking in his direction – she spoke. 'Hi, Frank.'

He could see that she was upset. Her eyes and face were pink, and her voice was filtered through a blocked nose.

He wasn't going to reply, but a full twenty seconds later, she still hadn't found her keys. 'Y'alright?'

'Yes, Frank. I'm fine.' She sounded annoyed.

'Okay.'

'Well, actually, no, I'm not.'

'Okay.'

'I've just dropped Red off. It's his first day at school . . . I'm just being an idiot.'

Frank continued to smoke his cigarette.

Another half minute passed.

'Bit old to be just starting school, isn't he? What's wrong with him?'

She finally turned to face him. 'Jesus Christ, Frank! Nothing's *wrong* with him. It's not his first *ever* day at school; it's his first day at *this* school. His *new* school. We've just moved here, remember.' She returned to fighting with the contents of her bag. 'Where are my damn keys?!'

'Alright, alright. Sorry I asked.'

'Y'know' – she turned to face him again – 'you don't have a monopoly on crappy days, Frank.' She dropped her bag, spilling the contents on the doorstep. Then, plunging her hands into her jacket pocket, she finally found what she was looking for. She shook her head and bent down to recover her things. Putting the bag back over her shoulder, she unlocked the front door and stepped inside.

Before she could close it behind her, Frank spoke. 'Sarah.'

She stopped. 'Yeah?'

He was trying to think of something to say. He couldn't think of anything, and so filled the silence with: 'He'll be fine.'

'Yeah.' She was about to continue inside, but hesitated. Turning around, she leaned against the door frame, slouching wearily. 'How was your boy with school?'

Frank looked up, mildly surprised that she was aware he even had a son.

'Oh, I remembered,' she explained. 'From, y'know. St John's. He used to visit.'

Frank blew out his cheeks. 'Ah, I can't remember. Michael's thirty-odd now. That was a million years ago.'

She nodded.

'I do remember his first day, though. Bawled his little eyes out. Mind ya, so did his mum.'

'What about you?'

'Nah, I knew he'd be right.'

Frank tossed his cigarette butt towards the road and turned to step back inside.

'See ya, Frank.'

'Uh huh.'

Closing the door behind him, Frank found Marcie sitting on the stairs. She looked annoyed.

'What's wrong with you?' he asked.

'You should apologise.'

'Eh? Apologise for what?'

'For being an arse, Frank. I heard you. "What's wrong with him?" What's wrong with *you*, more like?! I know you don't talk to many people these days, but I honestly can't work out whether you've forgotten how to be a normal human being altogether, or you're just an idiot.'

Frank glanced at the letter from Mikey, still unopened and lying discarded on the sideboard.

'You're still annoyed about the letter.'

'Yes, I'm still annoyed about the bloody letter! It's ridiculous. Just open it.'

Frank picked up the envelope and stuffed it into the top drawer in the hallway dresser. Marcie let out a contained scream of frustration and paced down the hall, then back up again.

'This has gone on too long, Frank. He's your son; he's *our* son. You can't just ignore him. You can't hold on to this grudge forever.'

'Grudge? Grudge?!' Frank stopped himself and spoke more calmly. 'Look, I'm not doing this again. I have nothing to say to Michael, and God knows he has said everything he has to say to me.'

'You're as stubborn as a bloody mule.' She stormed into the living room.

When Frank walked in a moment later, she had disappeared. She was angry, and would probably be gone for a couple of days.

RED

Red saw his mum before she saw him. He was standing at the top of the steps, wrestling to get his backpack on to his shoulders. This was proving tricky, as he was holding his coat, water bottle and a laser blaster he had made in the craft area using an old Rice Krispies box and an empty bottle of Toilet Duck.

He had just about succeeded when he caught sight of her in the distance. She was just inside the school gates, craning her neck to see over the chaos, trying to catch a glimpse of him in the crowd. She looked nervous and excited, shifting from one foot to the other. Her arms were folded, and she was biting her nails in the way she often told him off for.

He was about to call to her when he was roughly jostled out of the way. He dropped his model, and as he bent down to pick it up, he saw Jake Barnet half-snarling and half-smirking back at him. Red dusted off his laser blaster and started walk-running towards his mum as best he could – waddling, really, laden down with all his stuff.

'Mummy!'

She heard his voice and craned her neck a little harder, before catching sight of him and closing the gap between them at a jog.

'Hi, Red Adair!' She lifted him off his feet, almost crushing his model.

'Hey!'

'Sorry! I'm just super dead excited to see you.'

He uncrumpled the end of his blaster. 'I'm super dead excited to see you, too.'

'I missed you today, sunshine!' She took his coat and bottle and planted a kiss on his ear as he hugged her hips. '. . . And this is pretty cool,' she said, pointing to the model. 'It's a . . .?'

'Laser blaster.'

'Of course it is. I was going to say laser blaster.' She slapped her forehead with her palm.

He chuckled. He was so utterly relieved to be in her company that he felt lighter, and he held her hand tightly as they started to walk away from school.

'So, how was it?' she said enthusiastically as they escaped the traffic of the school gates.

'Okay.'

'Aw, come on, Red. How was it?'

'It was good.'

'Oh no you don't, Reddy. I want to hear everything.' She held up a shopping bag. 'I have got Nobbly Bobblies, pizza pockets, fizzy . . . And it's all for me unless you tell me *all* about your day. Not "I can't remember", not "I dunno". *Details.*'

'Nobbly Bobblies?'

'Yup. Now, what did you do all day? Tell me *everything.*'

They headed in the direction of home. As they crossed the main road, hand in hand, Red took the opportunity to think for a second.

And decided not to tell her everything.

*

Thankfully, the other kids in Class Two were *not* caterpillars, they were just kids. But they did look at Red as though he had recently landed from space. Red rather wished he had. At least if he'd had tentacles and a face like a slug, it would explain why they were all gawping at him.

As he followed Miss Payton to the back of the class, where there were pegs under the window, the curious mob parted to let him through, still observing him closely as though they were deciding whether or not he was food. Nervously, Red stumbled over his bag – it was bashing against the backs of his knees – and as he face-planted into Miss Payton's backside, there were giggles and whispers.

'Everybody, settle down,' she said, 'and take a seat.'

Red felt a wave of relief as they all dispersed. (He felt extra glad that Miss Payton had asked them all to sit down; he was quite a bit smaller than most of the other children, but only when they were standing up.)

Class Two was colourful and bright. There were pictures and paintings on every inch of the walls, of everything from rainbows to robots. One wall was dominated by a massive poster of the solar system. (Noah's brother would have made a joke about Uranus; he always made a joke about Uranus when he saw anything even a bit to do with planets, but Red didn't really get it.)

In the middle, pairs of desks were pushed together to create five squares. In his old school, desks had been in rows, all facing the same way. Here, all the children were facing each other, as though they were about to rock-paper-scissors or arm wrestle one another.

Miss Payton steered him to one of these tables and, putting one hand on his shoulder, she lowered him into a chair before introducing him to the two boys already sitting there. 'So, these are your table buddies, Red! Warren and Jake.'

Red took a seat and looked over at these 'table buddies' cautiously. One boy looked like he had just woken up, with a tuft of dark hair sticking out at a right angle above one ear. He was scratching his backside and staring blankly at the ceiling, as though a helicopter was passing overhead. But the other boy eyed Red intently. This boy had a wide face and hair that was shaved tightly at the sides, and he made Red think of soldiers.

'Well, welcome again, Red,' Miss Payton said. 'I'm going to leave you to get to know each other. We're running a bit late, so we need to make a start . . . Okay!' she called, with a clap of her hands, and walked away to begin the class.

Red was thinking about saying hello, but the boy across from him spoke first.

'Are you fast?' he said. He didn't wait for an answer. 'I'm fastest in this class.'

'Oh,' Red said.

'*Really* fast,' the boy confirmed, as though Red didn't believe him.

'Oh.'

'Okay, settle down,' Miss Payton interrupted. 'Everybody, settle down! We have got a new Caterpillar starting with us today, which is super exciting. Everybody say, "Hello Red."'

'HeLLO ReD,' they all said in unison, like a discordant piano.

But the boy across from Red did not join in.

He had mad eyes.

*

'Wow, so Miss Payton sounds nice, and you've got your own peg and everything – just like your old school. And table buddies! I like the sound of that. *Very* cool. So, what did you do then?'

*

Thankfully, it didn't take long for the class to get bored of staring at Red. Even the boy opposite – either Warren or Jake, Red was unsure which was which – stopped eyeballing him quite so keenly.

Miss Payton began the morning by asking what everybody had been doing over the Easter holidays. For the next hour, the Caterpillars chatted excitedly about theme parks and aeroplanes and swimming pools. One kid had been to somewhere called Eejit, which was hot and had pyramids. And another had been to stay at their Nan-nan's in Rotherham, which didn't have any pyramids (at least, not that the girl mentioned), but did have a big TK Maxx.

Red hadn't really done anything that exciting. He hadn't been on holiday and, apart from the park, he'd only been on two days out. One to the cinema with his dad (and Heather and 'the girls'), and one with his mum and Auntie to an open farm. It had rained all day and they'd to eat their sandwiches in a shed, where it smelled like toilets and two cows kept doing sex to each other.

He couldn't very well stand up and tell them that.

And so, he kept quiet, shrank a little and wasn't asked. Thankfully, by the time it came to his turn, everybody had become distracted by treasure: one girl, called Amelie, had brought in a souvenir from her holiday. A real-life shark tooth that she'd found on a beach in Cornwall.

The class 'oohed' and 'ahhed' as she took it from table to table to show everyone. Amelie was pretty, with hair that was the same colour as the inside of a Crunchie. When she arrived at Red's table, she smiled and revealed that one of her front teeth was missing. It made it look as though the shark tooth had fallen out of her own mouth and, although he didn't say anything, Red thought that was kind of funny.

Each of them took turns to hold the tooth, and Red carefully ran it across the back of his hand. 'Whoa, sharp,' he said, impressed, to no one in particular.

The tooth was snatched from his hand by the big boy, who turned it over in his fingers as though it was a piece of muck from his shoe.

Red thought about saying something about the snatching, but thought better of it. Amelie, however, hissed, 'Careful, Jake!'

So, the boy with the mad eyes was Jake.

Eventually, the tooth was passed back to Amelie, and Miss Payton suggested that each of them paint a picture, or make a collage, of a shark. 'We can hang them on the animal wall.' She pointed to a wall behind her that had been painted in the colours of camouflage. 'Maybe we could even add some facts that we know about sharks? What do you think?'

At this point, Red was beginning to think that *maybe* this school wasn't such a bad place, after all. Miss Payton seemed nice. Amelie seemed nice, too. He loved to paint and draw, and he really loved sharks and knew lots about them. He and Noah had been stuck inside for a whole weekend once, when the rain turned the road outside their houses into a river, and they had spent the entire time watching Shark Week on TV. They had then watched a film called *Sharknado* – but only ten minutes of it, as Noah's dad turned it off because it had a man's arm coming off and some boobs in it.

So, for the next half hour, Red happily – and carefully – painted a picture of a hammerhead shark and a normal shark swimming side by side in the sea. He did briefly consider doing a collage, but decided against it. He had tried to make one before, at his old school, but all the bits kept falling off, and instead of an image of Jesus with the words 'Happy Easter', he had ended up with a picture of what looked like a headless woman made of fuzzy felt and just the word 'YEAST' underneath it, in pasta. (Auntie Steph had laughed at it until tea came out of her nose.)

His shark painting, though, looked awesome. Both sharks had jagged smiles and were surrounded by bubbles. He was so pleased with it that, when Miss Payton asked if anybody knew a fact about sharks, his hand went up, his nerves swallowed by his enthusiasm.

'Yes, Red?'

'Erm . . . Sharks have to keep moving or they will DIE.'

'Okay—'

'AND they've got hundreds and hundreds and hundreds of teeth – like, a million.'

'Wow, it looks like we've got a shark expert in the class!' Miss Payton said, as she turned around to write Red's facts on the whiteboard behind her. 'Well done, Red.'

Red smiled, embarrassed. But continued. 'My friend Noah knows more than me; he's dead clever about sharks. But I know that there is one that's called a tiger shark because it looks like a tiger. And that's my favourite. And I've got a magnet with a tiger shark on it because I saw one once at an aquarian on holiday in Blackpool, and a boy standing next to me got in trouble off his daddy because he sneezed on the glass and then licked it off.' Red suddenly became aware that he was talking a lot, and that everyone had returned to staring at him.

And so, he was glad when Jake raised his hand, even if he did so while still looking straight at Red.

'Jake, have you got a shark fact?'

'Yes, Miss.'

'Okay.'

'Sharks are stupid. And anyway, they eat people.' He said this in a way that sounded like common sense, before folding his arms in satisfaction.

Before Miss Payton could respond, Red muttered reflexively, almost to himself, 'No they don't.'

'Red,' Miss Payton said gently. 'Remember, we put our hand up in the air if we want to say something.'

Red put his hand in the air slowly.

'Yes?'

'Well . . . they're not stupid. And they don't eat people. Not really. Most sharks are nice. The white ones bite people sometimes, but only by an accident. And they only hurt a few people, but people kill billions of sharks. So, it's no wonder they're super mad at us.'

'That is very true, Red. Some sharks are even endangered. Who can tell me what "endangered" means?'

Red could have told her, but he was preoccupied. Across the table from him, Jake had turned purple, and was now looking at Red as though he wanted to eat his head off.

'Sharks *are* stupid,' Jake said, as he tipped the paintbrush water on to Red's picture.

*

'Wow, so you did about sharks? That's so cool. You love sharks!' His mum squeezed his hand enthusiastically.

'Yeah.'

'And so, the rest of your class – what are they like?'

Red almost told her, right there and then. That he hated it, that he missed his old school. He almost told her that he didn't know what the other kids were like, because no one really talked to him all day. He almost told her that there was one boy, a boy called Jake Barnet, who was the worst person in the world ever. Jake was Darth Maul and Thanos and the Green Goblin and Team Rocket, all rolled into one.

'They're nice,' he said, instead.

'Great stuff! Y'see, I told you you'd make friends.'

'Yeah.'

They crossed another road.

'So, what did you do after that? Who did you play with at playtime?'

*

As Red dabbed his painting dry with paper towels, a bell shrieked for breaktime. A door that he hadn't noticed before appeared from behind a curtain. It opened directly on to the playground and the field beyond, and the entire class emptied in a moment of thunder-feet, leaving Red alone at his table. He was still upset, swallowing a lump in his throat that felt like a pebble.

He was taking his time on purpose. The noise of the playground had filled the room as soon as the door was flung open, and it sounded scary out there – like war.

And besides, how *could* he go out there? Who would he play with? He hardly knew anybody's name. Only Amelie, but she had been one of the first to go barrelling out the door. And Jake, of course, whom he had absolutely no intention of playing with, inside or outside, on account of him being a dangerous cycle-path.

Miss Payton was rinsing paint pots in a sink when she suddenly seemed to notice that he was still there. She dried her hands and appeared at his side. 'Oh dear, what's happened here then?' she said, seeing Red's painting and the water-smudged sharks puddled in the middle.

'Got some water on it,' he said quietly.

'Oh, that's such a shame. Accidents happen.'

He kept dabbing.

'Listen, I can sort that out. I'll put it to dry on the radiator. It'll be as good as new.'

Red looked at his picture of two sharks swimming side by side. They were now completely smudged, and looked more like a willy swimming next to a loaf of bread with one eye. He nodded doubtfully.

'Go and play. You've earned it.' She smiled. 'Amazing shark knowledge.'

'I don't mind helping.'

She sat down on the edge of the table. 'Listen, I know it's not easy . . . all this being new and making friends. But let me show you something.' She took his hand and they walked over to the open door. 'See that?' She pointed through the chaos to a bench in the far corner of the playground. It was placed against a big equipment shed and decorated with a wide painted rainbow.

'Yeah.'

'That's our friendship bench. Any time you're looking for someone to play with, you can just go and sit on there, and someone else who might be looking to play will come, and you can play together. How's that sound?'

Terrible, he thought. 'Good.'

'Okay, now go on. I'll finish tidying up your table; you go and enjoy yourself.'

Red looked out and wondered whether his old school's playground had been like this. Maybe it had. Maybe because he'd had Noah, and because he knew the other kids in the class, it hadn't seemed so loud and weird. So scary.

As he passed the threshold of the open classroom door, it felt like a spacewalk. From here, the rainbow bench seemed like a distant planet. But Red put one foot in front of the other and ventured out into the chaos.

Girls screamed past him like flocks of seagulls. One girl briefly hid behind him as she was chased, and then took off shrieking again. A much older boy shouted in his direction – 'That ball!' – as Red watched a football roll towards him and then away. The boy ran past him, a moment later to collect it, tutting loudly and shaking his head.

Red continued to skirt around the edges of the playground until, eventually, he found himself at the rainbow bench. He sat down.

Red watched the playground tribes play – the footballers, the hide-and-seekers, the chatters, the card-swappers and tiny-car-smashers – and he felt strange, as though he was both intruding and invisible. Actually, being invisible didn't sound so bad. So, he decided to daydream about being invisible, to pass the time.

Ten whole minutes passed before he turned to his side, and discovered Amelie sitting there.

'I'm very hot. I need a sit-down.'

Red said nothing. At first, he was surprised she could see him. He was, after all, invisible.

'I liked your shark picture. Before Jake spoiled it. I saw him knock the water over. He did it on purpose.'

'I like your one, too,' Red said quickly. He hadn't actually seen Amelie's picture, but it seemed like the right thing to say.

'Jake is a more-ong.'

'Yeah,' he agreed. And then, 'What's a more-ong?'

'I think it's like an idiot-brain.'

'Yeah. He *is* an idiot-brain, isn't he?'

'Yeah.'

'See ya later,' Amelie shouted suddenly, as she pushed herself away from the bench and went running into a crowd of girls, linking arms with them. Before Red could reply, the air was filled with the shrill insistence of the bell for the end of play.

*

'So, I like the sound of the friendship bench. And Amelie sounds really nice. And that's who you played with at breaktime, is it?'

Another white lie: 'Yeah.'

'Look at you with a girlfriend already!'

'Muuuum.'

'Well, what about after that? What was for dinner?'

'Er . . . I don't know. Sausages?' This was true, and it felt good to be back on truthful ground.

'And what about *after* dinner?'

'Well . . . it was raining, so we weren't allowed to go outside. And so, I played in the craft area. And that's when I made this.' He held up his blaster, which was now a bit squished where the black hole energy converter met the plasma cannon – or, more accurately, where the Toilet Duck met an empty tube of cheese and onion Pringles.

'And *that* is amazing, sunshine.'

Red looked up and saw they were almost home. He felt exhausted. He hadn't realised that not telling the truth could be so draining. Strangely, though, he didn't feel bad in the way he normally did when he told a lie. He wasn't happy about not telling his mum the truth, but he *was* happy that she seemed so pleased. And lying for that reason – to make her happy – felt like a good and grown-up thing to do.

But grown-up things were tiring, and he wasn't sure how long he could keep it up for, especially if each day at school was going to be like this.

'I'm tired.'

'Whew, I'm not surprised. What a day.' She seemed to take the hint and stopped asking questions. 'So! What did I tell you? Sounds like you had a great time. I told you it'd be alright. Didn't I tell you?'

'I guess.' A pause. 'Mummy? Do I have to go again tomorrow?'

'Yes! What do you mean do you ha—? Of course, you have to go again tomorrow, it's school. Come on, let's get home. Fizzy and pizza, and then how about a Nobbly Bobbly in the bath?'

'Okay,' he replied absently, his mind on whether he really *could* learn to make himself invisible.

FRANK

It was 7.30am, and Frank had already been up and awake for a couple of hours. He was shaving, tapping his razor against the bathroom sink, when, with the same rhythm, there was a knock at the front door: an official-sounding rap.

It was the second time someone had knocked on the door in the last month; the house was turning into a bloody drop-in centre. First it was the Jehovah's Witnesses, and now it was . . .

Frank opened the small upstairs bathroom window and peered down to find a policeman in hi-vis yellow standing on the front step. His black cap was under one arm, and he was shifting from foot to foot, his back to the door, as he surveyed Merton Road. Hearing the window open above him, the officer took a step back down the path and looked up. He waved at Frank with an oddly formal salute.

'What?!'

The officer looked behind him, as though Frank was shouting at someone else.

'What?!' Frank repeated, as a blob of shaving foam dropped from his chin and landed at the man's feet.

'Oh. Er . . .' the policeman sputtered, before clearing his throat. He ran a hand through his hair, and replaced his cap. Having seemingly regained his authority, he called up in response. 'Morning, sir. I wonder if I could just have a quick word?'

'You can have two: piss and off.' Frank began to close the window again.

The man continued as though he hadn't heard him. 'It won't take a minute.' He shouted this rapidly, in an attempt to beat the window closing completely.

Frank snorted and pushed it ajar again. He was about to offer another expletive, but the police officer took the reopening of the window as an invitation to keep talking and seized the opportunity.

'We're just in the area because there's been a number of sheds and garages broken into.'

Frank shrugged, nonplussed, so the man continued sombrely 'Quite a few just on this street, as it happens.'

Frank looked up the street at this hotbed of crime, and saw only a middle-aged woman in a long brown cardigan. She was wearing a small black bag as a glove as she waited for her golden retriever to finish having its shit.

'What do you want *me* to do about it?'

'Well . . .' The policeman was starting to lose patience. 'Look, could you just come to the door, sir? Please.'

The copper was persistent, he'd give him that.

'For fu . . . Give me a minute.' Frank snatched up a towel that had been draped over Marcie's walking frame, a relic from a couple of years ago, and wiped the remaining foam from his face. He took his time pulling on his dressing gown and slowly made his way downstairs to the door, hoping that by the time he opened it, the officer would be gone.

He was still there.

Persistent.

'Hello, sir. So . . . Sorry to bother you.'

'No, you're not.'

The man's face now offered a sour smile, which said that he had seen Frank's routine before, and he was unimpressed. 'My name's Officer Lowden. I'll keep it brief; you're obviously a busy man.' He arched an eyebrow in a way that made Frank want to bury his foot in Officer Lowden's arse. 'So, we've had a number of shed break-ins in the area.'

'You said.'

'And we're just seeing if anybody has seen anything, or needs any advice on keeping their shed safe.'

'Haven't got a shed.' Frank started to close the door.

'Well, you *have* got a shed.' The policeman placed his palm on the door. 'I've looked into all the back gardens from the alleyway; all the houses on this row have a shed.'

'Whew, nice work, Columbo.' Frank blinked slowly. 'Fine, I've got a shed. And no, I don't need any help keeping it safe.'

'OK, well, have you seen anything suspicious? Your neighbours suggested we knock here, because you don't . . . go out much?'

Frank opened the door fully again. 'Who the hell said that?' He was oddly offended.

'Well . . .'

'Look, never mind. Listen, I hope you crack the case, but is there anything else? Because—'

The policeman's face lost its last thin veneer of politeness. 'Is that your car, sir?' he interrupted. He pointed at 'Val', the blue Volvo estate parked at the kerb behind him. His tone was clear: *If you want to be awkward, I can be awkward too.*

'It's just that it looks like it hasn't moved in a while.' He took a small black notepad from his top pocket. 'Maybe it's worth checking to see if the tax is out of date? Or if it's been registered as off the road?'

Frank looked over Officer Lowden's shoulder. 'Hasn't moved in a while' was an understatement. The old car they had lovingly christened 'Val' hadn't budged an inch in forever. There was a thin layer of dust over it, which looked like sand, and weeds were growing beneath the wheel arches.

Frank almost told him that he was welcome to tow the damn thing away for all he cared, but that wouldn't have been true. They had owned that car for decades, and in its torn leather passenger seat and wonky back window, there were memories. Echoes of trips to France, of failed attempts to teach Marcie to drive, of dropping their son off at his university halls.

And besides, having the car towed away or impounded would only mean more jumped-up little shites like this one knocking on the door.

Frank sighed, defeated. He thought for a second, and realised that maybe he *had* seen something the previous week, as he passed the window for his third piss of the night. 'I might've seen a kid on a bike, early hours, wearing a hoodie.' He gestured half-heartedly towards the opposite side of the road.

'Really?'

'Uh huh. Carrying a toolbox or something across his handlebars, now I think about it.'

The officer excitedly produced a pen from his breast pocket and began making marks in his pad. He then proceeded to speak in the manner policemen tend to do when taking information, in 'by the book' copper-speak. He called Frank 'sir', and asked if he had noticed whether the 'suspect' had had any 'accomplices'.

Frank's remaining patience drained away under this questioning. And when the copper asked if the bike had approached from a 'westerly direction', he decided he'd had enough.

'*Westerly* direction? I don't bloody know. I'm not a lighthouse keeper; I'm not a fucking ship's captain. Westerly?' Frank pointed down the road. 'He came from that way!'

'Easterly,' Officer Lowden said to himself, scratching it into his notebook. 'Well, thank you, Mr . . .' Frank didn't offer to fill in the blank, and so he continued. 'That's been very helpful.'

Frank was already closing the door in his face.

'And get that tax sorted!' Officer Lowden shouted through the glass before retreating down the path.

Frank headed back up the stairs, chuntering. 'Cheeky sod . . ."Get my tax sorted." Why can't people just leave you in peace? This is what I mean, it's like Piccadilly Circus. If it's not the God botherers, it's them next door; if it's not them next door, it's the bloody police or the council or whatever. I'm gonna get a sign made, that just says, "Sod off", a picture of a middle finger, stick it on the front lawn. In fact, never mind that. I should just build a moat . . .'

Frank stopped on the landing. He realised he was waiting for Marcie to respond, to laugh at him, to call him an old fool. But she didn't.

It had been three days, and Marcie was still gone.

RED

Red was doing his best to listen to what Mrs Mills was saying, but he had become distracted by the Big Jesus.

There were pictures and statues of Jesus all over St Agnes, in the classrooms and in the hallways. In fact, one breaktime, Red – while avoiding going outside to play – had wandered around the school, counting all the Jesuses.

There were seventeen altogether: five statues and twelve pictures. He was everywhere.

It wasn't just Jesus, of course. There were also four pictures of Mary, Jesus's mum, dotted around, and a huge picture of someone called Kris Akabusi in the dining hall. A sign underneath explained that this man, who had the most enormous smile on his face, had visited to open the cafeteria a hundred years ago, in 1986.

Of all the pictures, this was actually Red's favourite, as Kris Akabusi had written his own name on it, in silver felt-tip, and also the words *Dream Big!* (This was not written on any of the pictures of Jesus or Mary, all of which were unsigned.)

The biggest Jesus, though, was the large statue attached to the wall above the stage in the main hall. And it was *this* Jesus that Red was looking at during assembly, as Mrs Mills talked about raising money for a roof, or something.

The fact that Red was distracted by the statue was hardly surprising. The rest of the Jesuses at St Agnes were smiling and happy, and looked like Red's favourite wrestler, Brett Hart. But the Big Jesus was super distracting, because he was bloody and sad, and someone had shot him in the hands.

Red looked around and found that he wasn't the only one not paying attention to Mrs Mills. To his right, he could see Jake and his best friend Callum, who were pointing at some kid in the year below who had a big belly. They were inflating their cheeks and whispering to one another.

Another kid to his left was diligently rummaging in his nose. Red watched, fascinated, and then grimaced as the kid produced something to his liking and then wiped it on the shiny wooden floor, between his crossed legs.

Meanwhile, the headteacher continued to talk about the roof in a voice that made Red sleepy. 'And so, we will be having lots of little fundraising ideas that we hope you and your parents will all join in with, and . . .'

Red looked up. He could hear the rain driving against the windows high up on the walls, and thought that a new roof was probably a good idea; this one sounded like it was about to blow off.

Good, Red thought. If the weather was really bad, the school would be destroyed – or, at the very least, playtime would be inside again. He wouldn't be forced to go out into the playground to try and make friends; he wouldn't have to sit on the rainbow bench, pretending to be invisible. He could just occupy himself in the craft area and make a robot or something.

Maybe Amelie or one of the other kids would notice how great his robot was, and ask him to teach them how to make one that was just as good, and the class would gather round as he explained how he did it . . .

Red's daydreaming was interrupted by a deeper voice from the stage, as up stood a man whom the entire room greeted with: 'Good MoRniNg Father McManus' (apart from the kid to Red's left, who had just found another winner in his nostril, studied it on the end of his thumb and then popped it into his mouth).

Red had seen this man before, walking the halls of the school. All the teachers seemed to speak to him super politely, as if he was famous or dangerous. He dressed all in black like Darth Vader, but instead of a helmet, he had a really shiny head and teeth that were yellow and all went in different directions.

For the next half an hour, Father McManus talked about God, and then told a story called 'The Good Samaritan'. It was a story from the Bible, and it was about a man who got beaten up and another man who was nice to him.

'Friendship!' the priest shouted too loudly as he finished the story. 'Is in deed as it is in words, and should be in all our hearts.' He pointed up at the statue above his head and said, 'And that's how the son of God would wish us all to behave – as, indeed, he behaved himself.'

As Father McManus sat back down, Red looked up at the Big Jesus, the holes in his hands and feet, and the spiky hat on his head. He couldn't help thinking that Jesus having friendship in his heart hadn't turned out that well.

Red sympathised. Making friends was hard.

*

There were some things Red liked about St Agnes. The crafting area was really cool, and he liked the song they sang at the end of morning assembly, 'This Little Light of Mine', because you could clap along with it. He looked forward to that.

But by the end of the second week, the other Caterpillars were still looking at him as though he was in the wrong place, if they looked at him at all, and he still hadn't made any proper friends to play with – unless you counted the caretaker's cat, Dumbledore, who occasionally appeared and weaved in between his legs while he sat on the rainbow bench.

Part of the problem was that he'd never had to make friends before. He had been in nursery with Noah since they were both two, and the other kids at Wardour Street Academy had all started school at the same time as he did, so he had been friends with *them* since before he could remember.

Another part of the problem – a very big part of the problem – was Jake Barnet. It turned out Jake was some kind of class-boss. He was the oldest, and he was bigger than everyone else. He decided who played football, he decided whose water bottles and backpacks were babyish, and he decided who was cool. And he had decided on the very first day that Red was not.

Even those who weren't friends with Jake seemed to want to avoid making him mad. And if you weren't friends with Jake, making friends with anybody at all just seemed a lot harder.

No one could say that Red hadn't tried.

Although his first day at St Agnes had been rubbish, Red had decided to go into school for his second day as though it was his first day all over again. A restart.

There had been a TV programme he used to watch when he was little. It had a song in it called 'The Friendship Song', and although he couldn't remember all the words, he could remember the main bit, which went: 'Step one, wear a smile. Step two, chat a while. Step three, don't be blue. Step four, just be you.'

And so, with these instructions in mind, Red had begun his second day with a plan.

He would smile.

A lot.

That was, after all, step one.

Arriving, he smiled at everyone he passed in the hallway. He smiled at teachers and older kids, and he smiled at each Caterpillar as they took their seats for the morning.

He even smiled when Jake's friend Callum tripped him up as he walked past to hang up his coat. ('Good one,' Red had said to Callum, as though he was in on the joke.)

It didn't take him long, though, to realise that this approach wasn't working quite as planned. Smiling at Jake and Callum just seemed to make them angrier, and it didn't seem to be working on anyone else, either.

Red was quite good at smiling, but he wasn't very good at *trying* to smile. It was why in his last school photo, he looked as though he had been photographed eating peas. So, mostly, he just seemed to be confusing people. (When he gave Miss Payton his very best smile, she had just frowned and asked if he needed the toilet.)

To make matters worse, when he sat down at his desk – with a big beaming grin on his face – he had been so busy concentrating on smiling that he hadn't noticed that Warren was in the middle of telling his classmates that his nan-nan was in hospital and might die.

So, smiling didn't work. It may have been step one, but it just seemed to make things worse. And it had the added problem of attracting attention. Over that first week, Red realised that standing out was not necessarily a good thing when you were new. It slowly dawned on him that if he wanted to be accepted, he would need to blend in, let people forget that he was the new kid. He may not be able to make himself invisible, he thought vaguely, but he could make himself small.

The first thing he did was stop raising his hand and answering questions. He had noticed that some people in the class – and not just Jake – did not like it when you answered questions all the time.

It made them think that you were someone who wore clever clogs. And so, when they did sums and adding up coins, Red stayed quiet. And when they started to learn about telling the time, he kept his hand down, even when he knew the answer before almost everyone else did.

Then, one morning, when Miss Payton divided the class into groups to talk about the things you might do at different times of the day, Red was delighted to find himself moved away from Jake's table and into the same group as Amelie, along with another girl and a boy called Liam.

Again, Red made a point of not answering questions or talking too much. Instead, he just said nice things about the other three when they came up with an idea.

'Whoa, that's really clever,' he said, nodding, when Liam suggested that twelve o'clock might be a good time to have lunch. Liam had seemed quite pleased by this comment, as he had then roared 'DINNER!' like he was a dinosaur, and they'd all laughed.

By the time break approached, Red was sure that he had made a breakthrough and this day was going better. He was convinced that he had finally made friends and playtime would be a success.

But as soon as they were excused, Amelie and the other girl disappeared to a far corner of the field to do handstands. And Liam ran off to join almost every other boy in the class to play football. One look at the boys' faces told Red that he wasn't welcome to join them.

And so, again, like he did every breaktime, Red took up his place on the rainbow bench.

But lunchtimes were the worst.

At a cafeteria table, perching on the edge of a chair, he watched the other children chat animatedly to one another through full mouths, but when he tried to join in the conversation, his ever-smaller voice was drowned in the clatter and chaos of the dining room.

The other kids couldn't hear him – or didn't want to. Eventually, Red stopped trying. Instead, he concentrated on nibbling his sandwich and thinking about what he might do after lunch, for the WHOLE HOUR he would have to survive before they were allowed to return to the classroom.

This was when wandering around the school at breaktimes had become part of Red's routine. Counting things in the corridors, finding a corner to sort his Pokémon cards, or playing with the hand dryers in the boys' toilets. Anything he could do to avoid the playground and make the minutes go faster, until he could go back to class to pass the hours until he was eventually allowed home.

And yet, as hard as all this was, as boring and lonely as all this could be, none of it was ever the worst part of his day. The worst part was always the walk home with his mum, which he would spend embellishing the truth until, by the time they reached home, Red had scored a winning goal and dazzled everyone with his crafting skills or his evolved Bulbasaur card.

In a day of bad bits, this was always the worst bit.

Because even though he was doing it for a good reason, Red hated not telling his mummy the truth. He knew that lying was wrong.

And lying when you have twelve Jesuses, eight Marys and Kris Akabusi watching you all day?

Well, that just seemed doubly bad.

FRANK

So, Marcie was *still* annoyed with him about the letter. Still annoyed about the fact that he had slid it into the hallway drawer without opening it.

Frank wasn't entirely surprised. Since Marcie had 'returned', she had disappeared like this before. Twice before, in fact. Both times angrily. Both times in protest over the state of things between Mikey and Frank; what she liked to call the 'Cold War of the Idiots'.

But, as Frank sat on the edge of their bed, trying to muster a breath of motivation to get up, it occurred to him that it had now been a whole week. Had she ever been gone for this long before? He tried to remember.

*

In the weeks and months following Marcie's death, as Frank had retreated into his own grief, Mikey had done the same, and the gulf between them grew wider and wider. Days, weeks, months passed, and as Frank brooded over his son's refusal to apologise, Mikey continued to fume over his father's stubbornness and inability to accept that he was in the wrong.

Marcie had always joked that her 'boys' were too similar and too quick to temper. And it was true, the two of them seemed to argue about everything from the moment that Mikey could say his first words. But they had rarely fallen out for long. They both had magnesium tempers that burned hot and brightly, but usually for such a short burst of time that they were like meteorites that never quite reached the ground to do any lasting damage.

This time, it was different. With Marcie dead and gone, the person who had smoothed the edges of their relationship was gone too.

By the time she *came back*, the two men hadn't seen one another or spoken in over eighteen months. And when she did return, she wasted little time demanding that Frank make contact with their son.

In those first weeks, she spent hours insisting that he apologise, even if he thought he was in the right, telling him that if he had learned anything in the past couple of years, it must be that love and time should not be things taken for granted. But his response was always the same: 'We have nothing to say to one another.'

Frank wasn't stupid; it didn't take a psychiatrist to realise that his dead wife was probably just a manifestation of his own conscience. But that didn't mean that his conscience was *right*.

Regardless, eventually, she stopped being quite so insistent.

And then, months later, Mikey reached out.

It was Fat Ken who delivered the message. Ken was the only one of their friends who had persisted in staying in contact with Frank. No matter how rude and uninterested Frank was, Ken would turn up every week with a few cans of lager and a takeaway. He would let himself in and announce his arrival, the way he had always done, before parking himself on the sofa to enjoy a three-hour one-sided conversation with his oldest friend.

It was during one of these visits that Ken mentioned he had spoken to his godson, Mikey. Had been in touch with him, in fact, the entire time that father and son had been at odds. And Ken had news that he had been asked to pass on to Frank. Good news. Happy news.

Mikey and his wife were pregnant with their first child.

Ken had paused for a moment, waiting for the news to sink in. A big, stupid grin on his face, like he was a border collie waiting for Frank to throw a ball.

'Uh huh,' Frank had eventually replied. As though he had just been told that a stranger was thinking about getting a new car.

'What do you mean, "Uh huh"? A *baby*, Frank. They're having a baby!'

'I heard you.' Although Frank wasn't entirely sure he *had* heard; he was having trouble processing this information and, for some reason, felt like he might burst into tears. After a moment, though, he felt a familiar weight fall on his shoulders, and he decided that he would do no such thing.

There was silence for a moment. Then, seeing that Frank wasn't going to say any more, Ken's face darkened. 'For God's sake, man. Has this not gone on long enough?'

'Ken.' It was a word of warning.

'So, you both said some shit – big deal. Marcie had just died! Neither of you were thinking straight.'

'Ken, I mean it.'

'Jesus. I mean, what would she say if she saw the pair of you carrying on?'

Frank leapt to his feet. 'That's it, get out!' He pointed at the door.

Ken matched Frank's fury and indignation, but not his ability to stand up quickly. He rolled sideways and then the opposite way, and then, with a groan of effort, he eventually hauled himself up to standing too. 'Fine, I will!'

'Fine!'

Frank followed him out into the hallway. Ken's huge size shaking the walls as he stormed.

'What the bloody hell do you come here for, anyway?' Frank spat as they reached the door.

'I'm beginning to wonder that myself. It's like visiting someone in a bloody coma!'

'Well, no one asks you to come. Why don't save yourself the bother next time?'

'Maybe I will!' Ken swung the door open and spun around. 'See you next week, you miserable twat.'

'Yes, I'll see you then!' Frank replied, unsure as to why they were both still shouting.

Ken nodded and slammed the door behind him.

As soon as Ken had left that day, Marcie had appeared behind Frank, shrieking with excitement. 'A baby, Frank!'

'Yeah,' Frank said.

'Our baby's having a baby!'

'Uh huh.'

'Well?'

'Well what?' He collected the empty cans from the side table next to the sofa and carried them into the kitchen. 'Couldn't even be bothered to let me know himself.'

'*What?*'

Frank couldn't quite remember the details of the exchange that followed, but it had led to Marcie storming out of the room – and temporarily out of existence, for the *first* time since she'd died.

Now Frank thought about it, on that occasion, she had only been gone for two or three days.

*

The only time Marcie had disappeared for longer was following the message left on their answering machine six or seven months later.

'Hey. Hi, Frank. Erm . . . I'm guessing you're there, but not picking
up. That's okay.'

It was Mikey's wife.

By then, Frank had long since stopped answering the phone, so
when it rang that Tuesday morning in May, he barely paid attention
as the old tape machine clicked, and Ellie's voice echoed through the
house.

That message – and the long argument that followed Frank's
refusal to return Ellie's call – was the reason Marcie had disappeared
for the *second* time. That time, she had stayed away for a whole five
days.

*

So, this was the *third* time that Marcie had disappeared – and, yes,
she had now been gone longer than she had ever been gone before.

Frank pushed himself off the bed, threw on some clothes and
walked down the stairs, where he stood for a moment taking in the
silence of the empty house. As he passed the telephone table in the
hallway, he noticed the red light on the answering machine was
blinking, indicating a new message. He pressed the play button, and
was surprised when the robotic voice said, *'You have. Zero. New
messages.'*

Vaguely confused, Frank walked into the kitchen, but the
machine continued to speak.

*'You have. One. Old message. Sent Tuesday. The fourteenth of. May.
At. Fourteen-oh-four pm.'*

A short tone followed. And the old message played.

*'Hey. Hi, Frank. Erm . . . I'm guessing you're there, but not picking
up. That's okay . . .*

*'So, just wanted to let you know that . . . yeah, you're a grandad! Baby
Mirabelle Marcie Hayes, born this morning. Frank, she's perfect. Apart*

129

from her head! Shaped like a traffic cone!' There was a slight chuckle. *'You should see her. She's got curls and big blue eyes, and . . . so, anyway. Just wanted to let you know. Hopefully see you—'*

Frank pressed stop.

RED

Red pretended to be fast asleep. It was yet another school day in a year of school days that seemed to stretch before him like a field of cowpats to be stepped in. Each time his mum shouted to him to come for breakfast, he pulled the covers over his head and decided to pretend that the world had been exploded by a nucular bomb, so he wouldn't have to get up.

Yesterday had been a particularly bad day.

Red had, by now, got used to spending breaktimes alone. Exploring the inside of St Agnes wasn't exactly fun, but it was preferable to sitting doing nothing on the rainbow bench or wandering the outer edges of the playing fields. His only problem became avoiding the attentions of Miss Payton, who insisted he should not be inside unless it was a 'rainy day', and seemed determined to make him join in with playtime, as though he had some sort of say in the matter.

'How's it going Red?' she'd said yesterday, as she caught him hiding inside the school yet again. This time, he had been squeezed into the corner of the coat room, reading a book about a man called Jonah who got swallowed by a whale and then lived in it like it was a bungalow.

'Okay.'

'You know you can't be in here.'

When he didn't reply, she looked at him with a funny look on her face, as though he was a jigsaw. She did this a lot.

'Look, Red – Leonard. I know we've spoken about this before, but you can't make friends if you insist on being on your own all the time. You know that, right?' She squeezed his shoulder. 'Do you think you might be able to try a bit harder?'

He shrugged.

She took the book from his hands and put it to one side. 'Maybe? For me?' She nodded once. 'Come *on*!'

With that, she marched down the corridor with Red trailing behind her, skipping awkwardly to keep up. Soon, they were through the main double doors and out in the brightness of the playground.

Miss Payton had moved through the chaos in a straight line, and everything and everybody parted to make way. She encouraged Red over to where the boys were playing football. When the ball rolled near her, she picked it up.

'Red would like to play. Wouldn't you, Red?' she announced. The game ground to a halt and the animated boys became confused statues.

'Not really,' he said quietly.

But Miss Payton bounced the ball back towards the boys and pushed Red forwards. 'Okay! Score a goal!' she said enthusiastically, before pulling her pants out of her bum, pouring her tea into a bush and heading back inside.

Some of the boys spoke to each other behind their hands, but none of them moved. Each of them was eyeing Red as though he was an unexpected problem, like a cow in the road.

Red stood there with his hands in his pockets, kicking at the asphalt, waiting for his fate to be decided. The whole playground seemed to fall quiet. Finally, Jake stepped forward, barged them all out of the way and picked up the ball. With a half-smile, he pretended to throw it at Red, who flinched. As the smile faded, he threw the ball for real, and it bounced hard against Red's knees. Jake looked Red up and down, and then pointed to the goal posts behind him. He was already turning away as he snarled, 'You're in net.'

Playing in goal was rubbish. At his old school, they had taken it in turns to be goalkeeper, but it was clear that they wouldn't be doing that here. To begin with, Red tried to do his best to stop the goals from going in, but soon he got bored. So, while the other boys kicked the ball to each other and tackled, Red began picking at the flaking paint on the goal post, stopping only to pick the ball out of the back of the net and roll it to whichever player's turn it was to tell him he was useless.

Red liked counting things, but even he lost interest when the twenty-third goal bounced off his backside and crossed the line. And by the end of breaktime, it had become more of a game of survival, anyway, as the aim of the other players now seemed to be not to score but to kick the ball as hard as possible at their reluctant goalie.

Red was, as usual, glad to get back to class – this time because it was warm, and people weren't shouting at him all the time. And for once, Miss Payton seemed pleased with his efforts, giving him a thumbs-up as she told him to go and wash his muddy hands.

As Red did just that, Jake and Callum appeared at the sinks on either side of him, doing the same. Red felt like a rabbit trapped between two foxes, but kept his head down, watching the dirty water swirl down the sink. Jake peered over his own shoulder to check that Miss Payton wasn't watching, and then whispered past Red to Callum, 'Watch this.'

Red could see what was coming, but it was too late to react. Jake pressed the palm of his hand into the water flowing from the tap. All Red could do was stumble backwards as the spray was directed towards him.

'Hey!' he managed, as there was a gasp from somewhere and all eyes turned in his direction. Looking down, he found that the front of his shorts was soaking wet and changing colour.

'Miss, I think Leonard's wet his pants!' Callum shouted, as he and Jake bundled away from the sinks. Jake was hiding his laughter in the crook of his elbow, while Callum pulled his jumper up and over his mouth.

'It – it – was – the tap,' Red stammered, as more kids craned their necks to see what was happening. He felt his eyes go hot, but somehow blinked the tears back. He brushed away at the damp patch on his shorts. 'It's not wee, it's from the—'

'Alright, everybody. That's enough!' Miss Payton shouted.

'It's just water, from the sink,' Red insisted.

Miss Payton continued to shush the entire class. As the clamour stopped and things settled down, she insisted to them all that this happened sometimes. Particularly with those taps, if you turned them on too quickly, or weren't careful. She looked at Red wearily and suggested that it might be a good idea if he was to change into something from lost property, just while his shorts dried on the radiator.

And it was that afternoon, sitting in a pair of Sports Direct tracksuit bottoms that were two sizes too big, unable to concentrate on learning about clouds, with his shorts steaming nearby, that Red decided that he hated Jake Barnet. Actually *hated* him.

In fact, he hated everything. He hated Miss Payton and the whole school and lying to his mummy, and everything else that had happened since they moved to the new house.

And that was why a nucular bomb was better than the thought of getting out of bed.

'Come on, sleep monster . . .' His mum threw open his bedroom curtains with a shoosh.

'I don't want to,' he mufflered into his pillow, still buried beneath the covers.

'I know how you feel.' She pulled the covers from Red with another flourish, like a magician doing that tablecloth trick where you try not to break any plates. 'But it's a school day, and it's a workday, so . . .'

Red turned over. 'I don't feel very well.'

'Really?' she said, amused.

'I'm poorly,' he insisted, attempting to sound poorly and sounding more like an old lady.

'You don't *look* poorly.' She started to lay out his uniform at the bottom of his bed. 'You didn't *seem* poorly when you had that doughnut for supper.' She bent down and tickled his feet, and he laughed and squirmed. When she stopped, he was annoyed that his cover had been blown.

'Well, maybe that's what made me poorly. The doughnut. Maybe it was poisoned.'

'I don't think so, Red'.

'You can get poisoned by lots of things, you know? You can get poisoned by licking a frog'.

'Have you licked any frogs?'

'. . . No.'

'Then you're going to school. Get your face washed and get ready. I can't be late for work today.' She disappeared from the room.

'Mummy? What day is it, anyway?' he shouted sitting up in bed.

After a moment, she poked her head back around the door. 'It's Thursday! So, only two more days, and then it's the weekend again. And don't forget, your dad's taking you out on Saturday, just the two of you. So that's something nice to look forward to, eh?'

As she disappeared again, Red brightened, jumped out of bed, and started to pull his pyjama top up over his head. He didn't know whether Saturday would be nice or not, but he *was* looking forward to it. Not just because he might see Noah, and not just because he could spend time with his dad without 'the girls'.

No, he was looking forward to it because he had a plan.

In truth, he had considered various plans over the past fortnight. It was one of the reasons why he was so tired; his plans had kept him awake.

Firstly, he had considered running away, but had soon decided against the idea. For a start, running away would make his mum sadder than she already was. (And besides, he had run away before, and it had been a disaster. He'd been three years old. He had packed up some toys, a shoe and a packet of Mini Cheddars, and had got as far as the hallway before he needed a poo and forgot why he was running away in the first place.)

His second idea involved catching a poisonous tree frog – he was slightly obsessed with tree frogs, having watched a programme about them on the Discovery Channel just a few days before – and making a poisonous dart with it, in order to kill Jake. But he decided against this idea, too. As much as he hated Jake, he didn't really want him to be dead. Besides, that would be a murder, and he would probably get sent to jail. And although jail *looked* like fun – you did get to sleep in bunk beds, after all – Noah's brother said that jails were actually full of rats and bugs and people who put mobile phones up their bums. And the TVs only had three channels. So that was definitely out.

But last night, Red had come up with a plan that was good. Really good. A plan that made sense.

It was an idea that had been cooking in his brain since his dad had called a few days earlier to say he would be picking him up on Saturday morning to go to the football. (It was a double promise this time.)

The plan was simple: Red would take the chance on Saturday to speak to his dad, man to man. He would tell him everything that had been happening at his stupid new school. He would explain that his new school was hell, and that some boys were being mean, and his daddy would know exactly what to do.

He even thought he might be able to persuade his dad to get back together with his mummy. That way, they could all move back into their old house, he could go back to his old school and back to his old friends, and they could put all this terrible mess behind them.

He just needed to get to the end of the week, and this would all be sorted.

He just had to get through Thursday and then Friday.

And so, he did.

FRANK

Marcie was still gone.

RED

As it turned out, Thursday and Friday were the longest days imaginable.

As the rest of the Caterpillars spent the mornings practising their handwriting, copying the strokes on the whiteboard carefully, Red found himself too distracted to concentrate.

They were bright, sunny days, and so Miss Payton seemed extra keen on making sure he didn't spend playtime inside. Red, wanting to avoid being conscripted into keeping goal, wandered the edges of the playing fields instead, kicking at tufts of grass, or playing with Dumbledore behind the equipment shed.

For the afternoon hours, he simply stared at the clock on the wall, using his mind powers to make it tick faster – anything to pull the weekend closer.

Eventually, late Friday arrived, and as the treacherous clock finally thought about 3pm, Red looked down and realised he had written nothing about the Great Fire Of London. Instead, he had absently doodled a picture of Jake being eaten by cannibals.

It was quite a good picture, but in that moment, Red felt a bit guilty. Not because he'd drawn Jake being eaten alive, but because he knew that Miss Payton would be disappointed when she collected the sheets and saw his work. But Red told himself that it wasn't such a big deal. After all, he would soon be leaving St Agnes behind, and since he wouldn't ever, ever be back, it didn't really matter too much.

When the bell rang for the end of school, Red's chair was the first to scrape. Grabbing his bag from his peg, he rushed out of the door without a backwards glance. He made his way through the hallways, weaving around the older children, out of the main entrance, down the steps and finally into – confusion.

Standing there, just inside the gate and waving as he walked towards him, was Red's dad.

'Hey mate! Surprised?'

Red *was* surprised. And then pleased. Really pleased. Obviously, his mummy and daddy were back together. 'Yeah! Where's Mummy?'

'Oh, I don't know, mate. Mummy's at work still, I think. She said I could pick you up today and take you for your tea.'

Okay, so they weren't back together. Well, never mind – at least he could put his plan into action sooner. He wouldn't even have to wait until tomorrow. This was a good thing.

'Okay!' he said.

Red's dad took his bag, and they started walking out of the gates. 'The thing is, Red' – his dad squeezed his shoulder – 'I said I'd take you out for tea tonight because something's come up this weekend, and we can't go to the football anymore.'

Red didn't say anything, so his dad continued.

'I know, I know. I'm sorry. I know I promised. But instead, I thought I'd come fetch you from school and we'd go to Nando's. I know how much you like a Nando's!'

Again, Red didn't say anything. He felt a bit sick. Why did grown-ups think that if they delivered bad news with a big smile, you wouldn't notice it was bad? They continued walking towards where his dad had parked his car. Red's mind raced and he chewed the inside of his mouth.

This was *not* going according to plan. Not to plan at all.

But again, he tried to see a positive. Just the two of them, having tea at Nando's: this was probably the perfect time to talk about things with no interruptions or distractions. He could put up with another cancelled weekend if it meant getting this sorted. It was fine.

'Okay!' Red said again, as positively as he could manage. And he was about to add that he had something super important to talk about anyway, when his dad interrupted.

'And there's even better news.' They arrived at the car. 'The girls are coming with us!'

Red's heart sank . . . past his stomach and through his shoes.

The twins were fighting as Red got into the car. When they weren't staring at their phones, they always seemed to be fighting about something. This time, they were fighting about Red, arguing about who was going to be forced to sit next to him in the back. Neither of them wanted to. Eventually, his dad suggested that Red sit in the middle, which was a ridiculous idea, as it meant that Red would then be sitting next to both of them, but for some reason this settled things.

Not for the first time, Red concluded that ten-year-old girls were crazy.

He shuffled over between the pair as they huffed and whined.

'Hi, hun.' This from Heather, who was sitting in the front passenger seat and sawing her fingernails. She threw the words over her shoulder without turning around.

Red hated being called 'hun' or 'hunny' even more than he hated being called Leonard. Maybe it was because she was the only person who ever called him that.

In fact, he had told his dad when he first met Heather that he didn't like being called 'hunny', but his dad said it was a nice thing to be called, because honey was sweet. When Red pointed out that he had watched a programme about bees, and honey was actually what they sicked up, his dad said not to be silly.

Red didn't think he *was* being silly.

His dad pulled out into the school traffic. 'How was school, Reddy?'

'Okay,' he replied. This was not the time or the place to discuss something so important.

'Great.'

They drove to Nando's in silence. A silence that was only disturbed by the tick-tacking of the girls' phones. Red slumped down in his seat and watched London crawl by.

As they were about to arrive at the mall, Heather dropped her own phone into her lap and yawned, touching the roof of the car. She put her hand over his dad's as he changed gear; it was a nothing gesture, but she did it in a way that reminded Red of his mum. And that made Red want to open the door and push her out. He smiled guiltily to himself as he imagined her landing in a big puddle or some dog muck.

Nando's was busy. It was Friday night, and Heather and his dad had an argument about why neither of them had booked a table. Eventually, they all squeezed into a booth at a café in the bowling alley next door. It was loud and smelled like chips and feet. Again, he was stuck in the middle, between the two girls.

They ordered burgers that tasted like chips and chips that tasted like chips. And, as the two grown-ups chatted about work and money and things, Red busied himself colouring in a clown on a sheet, with crayons that didn't colour properly and snapped if you pressed too hard.

He was waiting for the chance to speak to his dad. And he was beginning to worry that that chance would never come.

But as they each finished their food, the girls put down their phones for long enough to demand some money to play on a dancing arcade game nearby. At the same time, his dad took another note from his wallet and handed it to Heather, who disappeared to buy more drinks from the bar.

Red's dad began to pick at what Red had left behind on his plate. It was just the two of them.

This was his opportunity.

'Daddy?'

'Yes, mate?'

'Can I talk to you?'

'Course, mate.'

'It's about everything.'

'Okay, you might have to narrow that down a bit.' He turned and called over to the bar, where Heather was waiting to be served. 'Love, can you grab me some ketchup?'

She rolled her eyes in response, as though he'd asked for something really hard to get, and shouted back sarcastically, 'Anything else?'

His attention returned to Red. 'Well . . .?'

And so, Red told his daddy everything. Everything that he had not told his mum. The fact that his new school was hell, and smelled funny, and he didn't have any friends there. And how Jake was a more-ong, and how he was annoyed that Red knew loads more about sharks than he did, and how he'd ruined his picture on the very first day. How he'd made Red play in goal and made it look like he'd wet his pants, and everybody had just laughed. And how he missed Noah and his old house and his old school. And how everything was basically just a complete disaster.

Finally, he finished.

In that moment, it felt as though something heavy had been taken out of his pockets. For the past two weeks, he had felt so grown-up. He felt like he'd had a taste of what adults dealt with all the time, the complications and mess. And now that he had told his dad everything, he didn't feel quite so grown-up anymore. It came as a huge relief. Grown-up stuff is for grown-ups, he concluded. And now that he had told someone everything (and not just any grown-up, but his daddy), this would all be sorted in no time.

Red finished what he was saying and waited for his dad to speak. Just then, Heather returned, threw down three sachets of tomato ketchup, and slid a pint of beer and a glass of wine on to the edge of the table.

His dad looked up. 'Thanks, babe,' he said, with a smile.

She slid back into her seat at the booth.

For a terrible moment, Red thought his dad wasn't going to respond at all. When he did, it was through a mouthful of chips.

'Well, this situation is new for all of us. And it's a new school, I guess. It's gonna take a bit of getting used to, that's all. Y'know?' He pointed at Red's plate and the barely touched hotdog lying there. 'You gonna eat that, mate?'

Red shook his head.

And just like that, everything upon which he had been pinning his hopes disappeared.

FRANK

It was now a whole two weeks since Marcie had stormed out of the hallway and into the living room. Frank was beginning to think that this time, she really was gone for good. Waking up on Saturday morning, he stared up at the ceiling for a while and considered whether, objectively, this was a good or a bad sign. He began to wonder if no longer seeing and speaking to your dead wife meant that you were through the worst of your nervous breakdown – or if it meant you were just into another phase of that breakdown, a phase in which you imagined that your dead wife was sulking because she was mad at you, following a hallucinated argument that had never happened.

He stopped thinking about it. It made his head hurt.

The only thing Frank knew for certain was that he hated her not being there. With each day that passed, he began to feel more and more restless. As the weekend had approached again, he'd found himself feeling almost as anxious as when he thought about venturing 'beyond the gate'.

Frank's appetite disappeared, and he barely slept. He found himself unable to concentrate on reading a newspaper. He started the same book nine times over, never getting beyond the first two pages.

Time became a thing to wade through, and as he continued to stare at the ceiling, the day stretched ahead of him like an interminable chore.

How different weekends used to be. The lazy mornings in bed. The division of Sunday papers over a long breakfast, followed by a stroll along the canal to The Flea for an afternoon drink.

Eventually, Frank got out of bed and made his way downstairs. After a breakfast of coffee and a slice of toast with the black scraped away, he once again sat in his living room armchair and stared pointlessly at the second page of his book.

After an hour, he threw it aside once more. Shaking his head, he reached for the remote control, jabbed the 'on' button and spent the next twenty minutes flipping from channel to channel.

A daytime programme about a couple who had a million pounds to spend, but couldn't find a house that had 'kerb appeal' . . . merged into a cooking programme in which that angry human bollock Gordon Ramsay was screaming at a woman about the state of her shepherd's pie, as though a cat had crapped in it . . . merged into a celebrity quiz show in which all the contestants seemed to have the IQ of a spoon . . . merged into a painfully cheerful shopping channel idiot selling a revolutionary set of pans, demonstrating their non-stickability by pouring a tin of paint into a frying pan, as though that was a perfectly normal thing to do.

Frank stood up suddenly. 'This is ridiculous,' he said to the emptiness. He turned off the TV and then, as a further measure, pulled its plug from the wall. He needed to *do* something, anything, to take his mind off the quiet.

He walked into the kitchen, looked around and noticed the empty washing basket under the counter by the back door. With a firm 'Right, then,' he decided to occupy himself by tackling his laundry.

It was perfect: a task that needed doing, but didn't involve going outside. It was also a task that Marcie had been hassling him about doing *properly* for months, laughing about the fact that since she had died, he had taken to washing his smalls in the kitchen sink as though he was camping, leaving them to dry among the pots and pans of the dishrack.

Frank's clothes were scattered in tiny mounds all over their bedroom and bathroom, as though a gang of old men dressed in Marks and Spencer's trousers and shirts had been raptured where they stood. He went from heap to heap, selecting underwear and shirts. When he had a pile that was far too large, he returned to the kitchen and began to stuff it into the drum of the washing machine, closing the door with his foot.

He could feel that Marcie was back without even having to turn and face her.

'Bloody hell, are you actually going to use the washing machine?' Marcie said. 'This'll be good.'

He glanced behind him and found her sitting at the kitchen table as though she was about to watch a sporting event. Frank exhaled and felt his shoulders and neck relax. It was a sigh of relief that came from the soles of his feet. But ignoring her, he grabbed a blue bottle from beneath the sink and poured its entire contents into the detergent drawer.

'That's rinse aid for the dishwasher, Frank,' she said, as he tossed the empty bottle into the sink.

'It's fine.' He turned dials and pressed buttons, then stepped back as the machine came to life. After a few moments, it began to groan, as though food-poisoned.

'Well, you've either killed the machine or your kecks are going to come out clean enough to eat your dinner off,' she said. 'I'm proud of you.'

'Sod off,' he said, finally turning to face her.

'I'm serious! We should celebrate.'

'Celebrate what?'

'Well, the fact that you've taken the first steps towards not smelling like a tramp's balls, for one.'

That made him snort a half-laugh, and he looked back at the clattering washing machine. Due to its heavy load, it appeared to be setting off for a wander around the kitchen. Frank felt oddly pleased with himself.

Marcie came and stood beside him as he looked out of the window and into the back garden.

'I missed you,' he said in a whisper, swallowing hard.

'I know.' She nodded sadly.

*

A few hours later, Frank was in the back bedroom. It was the first time he'd been in there in a long time, and he was festooning the radiator with grey underpants that smelled like Finish Powerball.

He looked out of the window and down into the garden next door. He could see the upturned wheelbarrow pushed up against his fence from the other side. He could also see the trampoline. And there, sitting against one metal leg, was Red, his head down, raking a stick in the dirt between his legs.

He felt the strangest urge to knock on the glass – before he came to his senses and stopped himself.

'What you looking at?' Marcie said, sitting on the bed behind him.

'Nothing. Just the kid from next door, messing about,' he replied, and then continued to line up socks alongside the pants. Each of them was identically sized and faded black, apart from one sock that had a blue band across the ankle. This sock was from a novelty pair that Mikey had bought for him for Christmas years ago. As Frank placed it on the radiator, he knew without turning it over that on the sole, it read: 'If you can read this . . .' The absent sock read '. . . bring me a beer'.

Marcie stood up and peered over Frank's shoulder at the boy below, still scraping at the earth. 'Aww, he looks really fed up, eh?'

'Uh huh.'

There was a pause before Marcie continued: 'You should nip down, Frank.'

He stopped what he was doing. 'Wha?'

'See if he's alright.'

'Mar . . .' he began to protest with incredulity, as though she had suggested that he fire himself out of a cannon.

'Frank.'

'Marcie . . .' he began again, only this time it came out like a mewl.

'Frank.' She adopted a facial expression that meant that this was no longer up for discussion. It was an expression he recognised all too well, and he stopped mid-whine.

'Look,' he said, trying to negotiate. 'If I see him, *if* he's around, I'll ask him if he's alright or whatever. Okay?'

'Now,' she replied, simply.

For a second, Frank considered continuing his protests, but then he sighed and shook his head. He knew, as Marcie placed her hands on her hips and narrowed her eyes, that this was a battle he couldn't win. She had a way of planting her feet in situations like this that made her utterly immovable.

Besides, he felt instinctively that her return was a fragile thing, an impasse, and he didn't dare risk upsetting her and turning around to find her gone again.

'Fine,' he said through his teeth.

Marcie smiled broadly in a facial victory lap, which annoyed him all the more.

'Mmh,' he growled.

Frank snatched the pants and vests from the radiator. He couldn't just wander into the back garden and talk to someone, a neighbour – even a kid – over the fence, like a mad person. And so, he dropped this washing back into the laundry basket with the excuse of hanging it up on the line outside.

Then he stomped down the stairs, muttering something about the halcyon days of Mrs Palmer-Machin.

RED

Red *was* fed up. He had woken up in a bad mood. He wasn't sure he'd ever been in an actual, proper, really bad mood before, but he was *definitely* in one now.

Normally, when he felt a bit sad, he would make a list in his head of good things and bad things. When he'd tried to do that this morning, for the first time in his entire life, not only was the bad list longer than the good list, but the good list was completely and utterly empty.

For a start, it had occurred to him overnight that it had been so long since he'd seen Noah that his best friend probably wouldn't even remember who he was any more.

And the reason his dad had cancelled again was not because of work. Not this time. This time it was because Heather had booked for him and the girls to go on a surprise weekend away.

(Dad had revealed this as he'd dropped Red off, the night before, explaining that it was 'a last-minute thing', and that he could definitely come with them next time. 'And probably best not to mention it to Mummy.')

But what Red was *really* fed up about, was that his plan had completely failed.

He had told his dad *everything*. That everything was bad, that school was a disaster, that the world was just terrible, and that things couldn't be any worse if an asteroid hit and turned everything to lava.

And how had his daddy reacted? Like the whole thing was no big deal.

So, yes: Red was really fed up. Nothing had changed, and nothing would change. He wouldn't be going home, Mummy and Daddy would not be getting back together, and he would be back at school in just two days' time.

Red thought about this as he sat with his back against the trampoline, making marks in a bare patch of earth with a stick. He had never noticed how short weekends were before. It was Saturday morning, which meant just the rest of today and tomorrow, and then it would be Monday all over again. Oh and, by the way, the days *in between* weekends lasted a billion years. This felt like a very adult realisation. No wonder grown-ups were so grumpy all the time.

In fact, Red's mum was extremely grumpy today, too.

But that wasn't because weekends were too short. His mum was fed up because she had seen a photo on Heather's Instagram, of Dad and the girls getting on a big train to Brooj. Her face had turned red, she had made a noise like an angry cat, and then she had gone back to bed for an hour.

So later, when his mum had got back up out of bed, they were *both* in a bad mood. If one of them hadn't been, then maybe they wouldn't have had their big argument.

But they were.

And they did.

*

It had started over nothing.

Red had been watching cartoons from the sofa (upside down, as usual) when his mum had shouted from the kitchen.

'Red, can you turn the TV down a bit?'

He barely heard her the first time, but when she repeated herself, he ignored it. The remote was a good finger's length out of reach.

'Red!' She walked in and snatched up the remote control herself. 'I asked you to turn it down. I can't hear myself think in there.'

He grunted in her direction, and she huffed. 'It's about time you were getting dressed, anyway. We're going to go out and do something. Cinema, park – whatever. I refuse to stare at four walls today.'

He grunted again. When she tossed the remote on to the sofa beside him, he picked it up. Once she'd left the room, he turned the volume back up to twenty-four.

Barely a second passed before she stomped back in and turned the TV off at the set with a flick of her wrist. 'Get dressed – and change your attitude. I mean it!' She gave him the eyes, but for once it didn't work.

'I am *not* getting dressed. I don't want to go out. I don't want to go to the stupid cinema or the stupid park.'

She took a step back, her eyebrows high in surprise. 'You know what? Fine! Neither do I. Sit and watch cartoons all day, for all I care. It's not my fault your dad's gone off to—'

'Why don't you shut up?!'

It was as though a crack of lightning had split the sky above them. He had never spoken to anybody like this. Ever. And certainly not his mum.

'*Red!* What's wrong with you?'

Something exploded in his chest. 'Everything. *Everything!*' He kicked the wall with his heels twice, and then spun so he was upright on the sofa. Now he stood up – 'Just leave me alone!' – and stormed past her and out of the room, the way that he had seen people do in films when they were super mad. He tried to slam the living room door behind him, but found it was too stiff against the carpet and wouldn't budge. He tugged it twice more, screamed in frustration and then, conceding defeat, he continued to stomp into the hall and up the stairs.

'Get back here, Red! Right now! I've not finished speaking to you.' She was right behind him.

'I hate it here,' he shouted. 'And I hate Daddy, and I hate you, and I hate school, and I hate everything!' He reached his bedroom and was angrily pleased when this door proved to be slammable. He could hear his mum rushing to the top of the stairs with a flurry of steps before the door flew open again.

'What on earth is going on?! Since when do you speak to me like that?'

'Just leave me alone!' he said again, falling face-first on to the bed.

'I will not! What the heck's got into you?'

Red didn't say anything. He kept his face buried in his pillow.

After a while, she continued, her voice gentler and unsure. He could feel the bed soften under her weight as she sat down. 'Look, Reddy. I get that things aren't easy at the minute. But hate is a bad word, Red – a really bad word. What do you mean you *hate* it here? What do you mean you hate school? I thought you were enjoying it.' She put her hand on his back. 'You need to talk to me, Red. You know, I'm just trying to do my best. I've not exactly been dealt the best hand here, either, y'know?'

Red didn't know what that meant. He rolled over. 'I hate it here.'

'Look, we just need to give it a little bit more time. We can't afford to live where your daddy lives . . . where *we* used to live. Near your old school is really expensive. And we got so lucky with this house. With the garden and everything. Remember how we found this place?'

Red did remember. They had spent whole weekends searching for a new house, and it was as they were walking away from their last appointment – a dingy basement flat that smelled like mushrooms – that a piece of newspaper had blown past him and stuck to his leg. His mum had been about to screw up the paper and throw it into a nearby bin, but she had noticed that it was a page of property ads from the local advertiser – and there, in black and white, was 32 Merton Road. She had called it fate.

'I know it's not near where we used to live, but—'

'I don't care about it being not expensive, or the garden. I just want to go home.' He started crying then.

'Red, like it or not, we *are* home.'

She joined in with his tears, and they sat on his bed and held each other.

*

Now it was an hour later, and Red was sitting in the back garden, leaning against one of the legs of the trampoline and daydreaming about running away again.

Yes, last time it had been a disaster, but this time it would be better. After all, he was now six. Six and a half, actually. And he would definitely get further than the hallway this time. One of the last projects he had done at Wardour Street Academy had been about the London Underground. Red had lived in London his entire life, and so he was always on the tube, but as part of a school trip he'd been allowed to buy his own ticket, pass through the barrier, and then ride with the rest of his class to Charing Cross.

Back in the classroom, Red had traced the Underground map and memorised lots of the stops. He could still remember all the lines. So, yes – he would definitely get further this time.

But then he thought of all the reasons why he had decided not to run away before, and he ruled out the idea once again. Instead, he tried to take his mind off things by remembering some of the names of the stops on the Piccabilly and Central lines. He was scratching a map of those lines in the dirt when he heard Frank pretending to cough in the garden next door.

FRANK

Outside, Frank felt the familiar unease he found difficult to shake when not within the four walls of number 34, even when in the back garden. This was the other reason he had brought the washing basket outside with him. Being outside felt like being on a spacewalk, and having something in his hands somehow made him feel less untethered.

Getting hold of himself, he approached the wonky rotary line, a drunk metal tree, long abandoned in the deep grass. Unsure of his intent or plan, Frank cleared his throat loudly as he began to hang out the washing. He was certain that this would bring the boy to the fence, or that, with a single *Skreewoing*, the kid would announce himself on his trampoline. But although he waited for the blond mop to appear, there was nothing.

As Frank hung out another item (a vest that looked half the size it had been before being tossed into the washing machine), he could hear the quiet scraping of the stick. Marcie, standing on the back step, encouraged him with a 'Go on' nod of her head. And so, reluctantly, he took a step towards the fence and called over. 'Kid?'

The scratching stopped.

'Yeah.'

'It's me. It's Mr . . . well, it's Frank.'

There was silence.

'What're you doing?'

'Nothing.'

'You not playing on your trampoline today?'

'No.'

'Why not?'

'Don't feel like it today.'

'Oh, right. How's your mum?'

Silence again.

Frank was about to give up when he heard shuffling from the other side of the wooden divide: the sound of Red climbing on to the upturned wheelbarrow. His face appeared above the fence line.

'Hey, Red.'

'You called me Red.'

'Well, that's your name, isn't it?' Frank said, stepping closer to the fence.

'Yeah.' Red paused and then tilted his head inquisitively. 'Why do you smell like a big lemon?'

'Because I put the wrong washing-up thing . . . in the . . . thing . . .' Frank's explanation faded away. 'Look, er . . . How are you?' he asked, shifting uncomfortably and staring at the grass, before glancing back at Marcie. She was still standing by the back door, rolling her eyes.

'How am I what?'

'Y'know . . . just, how are you? Like, how's things?'

Red's nose scrunched. 'What things?'

'Jesus. Forget it. I was just asking if you're alright.' Frank began to turn away.

Red looked at his hands. 'Mmm, well. The things aren't very good,' he said simply. 'I had an argument with my mummy because I said I wanted to go home. And she said we *are* home, and I said no we're not. And I want to go back to my old school, because my new school is horrible, and she said that if we moved back near my old school, we would have to get a smaller house, without a garden, and I wouldn't be able to take my trampoline. And she promised we might be able to get a dog if we had a garden, and now she says we can't do that, because what would we do with a dog if we had to move to a flat? And she says that she really wants to try and make it work in this house.'

Frank nodded vaguely, trying to keep up.

'So, I said sorry. And she said sorry. But she's still a bit mad. And I'm still a bit mad. And we're both a bit sad. And I still have to go to school on Monday, which is the worst thing ever, because there's this horrible boy called Jake, and nobody likes me there, and it's not even nice.' Red stopped talking and took a breath.

Frank was unsure how to respond. He'd forgotten how little kids could spew information like this. So he just shrugged a little, and said the first thing that came to mind. 'Well, y'know. I'm sure things will pick up.'

'Okay.'

Red climbed down from the wheelbarrow on his side of the fence to return to the busyness of doing nothing. Frank turned away to hang another shirt on the sagging washing line as Marcie appeared beside him. 'Wow, you're like a walking greeting card, Franklin. "I'm sure things will pick up"?' she said, incredulously. 'What touching, heartfelt advice for a six-year-old.'

Frank continued to hang the washing.

Marcie looked towards the fence. 'Poor kid,' she said, shaking her head sadly. And then she brightened. 'I know. I've got a great joke for him. Tell him this joke, Frank. He'll like it.'

'What? No,' Frank said, speaking quietly so that Red wouldn't hear him casually chatting to himself again. 'What is it with you and bloody jokes, anyway?'

'They cheer people up, Frank, and my kids at school loved this one.' She relayed an old joke about trampolines.

When she had finished, he looked at her with disdain. 'That's not funny. I'm definitely not telling him that.'

'It's a joke for kids, Frankie. Go on, it'll cheer him up.'

'No,' he hissed.

'Frank!'

'For fu . . .' With a long sigh, he shouted back over the fence. 'Hey, Red,' he called, glancing over at Marcie, who was nodding encouragingly. 'You know . . . er . . . I once met the man who invented the trampoline.'

Red's face reappeared, curious. 'Really?'

'Yeah, he was a nice fella,' Frank continued, now with the slightest twinkle . . . 'But he was a bit jumpy.'

There was a pause.

'Oh,' Red said. 'Why?'

'What do you mean, why? It's a bloody joke. He was a bit *jumpy*. Trampoline?'

'I don't get it.'

Marcie began to giggle uncontrollably as she sat on the back step.

'Well, the guy invented the trampoline, and so he was – ah, forget it,' Frank said, getting irritated.

'Oh, wait. Now I get it. Because he was *jump*-y, like when you're on a trampoline.'

Frank held out his arms in a silent gesture meaning 'obviously'.

'I do get it. But it's not a funny joke.' Finally, Red laughed. 'You're not very good at jokes.'

Frank smiled a little in return. 'Yeah. Maybe not. Maybe not.'

'No, I mean that was *really* bad.'

'Alright, alright . . . Christ,' Frank said, offended. 'I was just trying to make you laugh, you mardy little sod.'

'Ahhh!' Red sucked in his breath and clapped his hand to his mouth. 'You said a swearing word.'

'Sod's not a swearing word, Red.'

'I think it is.'

'It's not.'

'I think it is. It's just not one of the super-bad swearing words like "eff", "shh" and the "C" one.'

'Yeah, they are the bad ones,' Frank confirmed. 'My wife hated the "C" one a lot.'

Red lowered his voice conspiratorially and cupped his hand to the side of his mouth. 'I said the C-word to my old teacher once, and I got in loads of trouble.'

Frank chuckled, amused. 'What? You're like, six? And you called your teacher a cun—'

'Crap!' Sarah shouted from the doorstep behind Red. 'The C-word is "crap", Frank. Jesus, what's wrong with you?'

'Yeah, that makes more sense,' Frank said as she approached the fence, before adding, 'Although I had a woodwork teacher when I was about his age called Mr Glover, and that fella was a real cu—'

Sarah put her hands over Red's ears. 'Red, I think Frank's finished teaching you your "word of the day".' She removed her hands and ruffled the boy's hair, then lifted his chin with her finger and thumb so their eyes met. 'You okay?'

Frank looked on awkwardly as Red nodded. 'I'm okay.'

'Good. Why don't you have a quick bounce before your dinner?' She kissed him on the forehead.

Red jumped backwards with an 'Alright!', then crawled on to the trampoline and began bouncing with a familiar *skreewoing*.

Frank turned away and continued hanging his washing. 'You need to get some oil or something for that thing . . .'

'Frank,' Sarah interrupted.

'It's like living next door to a bleeding—'

'Franklin,' she repeated, a little bit louder.

He looked up. 'What?'

'Thank you.'

'What for?

'Y'know, for trying to cheer him up.'

'Uh huh.'

'I don't know what's got into him lately. He talks more to *you* than he does to me.' She shook her head incredulously.

Frank returned to the washing, and realised there was only one thing left in the basket: a vest, now half its original size.

'Nice crop top,' Sarah said as he added it to the line.

'I think it shrank.'

'You should get your belly button pierced. It'll look lovely.'

He heard Marcie laugh loudly behind him. 'She's funny.'

'So, the boy says you're thinking about moving out?' he said.

'I don't know. I thought we'd get a fresh start here, but maybe it's too far from what he knows. We can't really afford to live back where we were. Or if we did, it would be some god-awful tiny flat, certainly wouldn't have a garden or . . . I dunno. Maybe if we moved a bit closer back to where we were, his dad wouldn't be such a useless . . .' She gestured with her hand, a bitter butterfly taking flight.

Red stopped bouncing. 'What are you talking about?'

'Nothing,' they said in unison.

Red seemed to consider this for a minute, seemed to think about querying it, but then changed his mind. He sat on the edge of the trampoline, his legs dangling. 'Did you know that a crocodile can't stick its tongue out?' he said.

They both shook their heads.

'I don't think we should move,' Red said suddenly, and with finality, as though planting a flag in the sand.

'Me neither,' Marcie called from the step.

This abrupt change of subject provoked no response from Frank or Sarah, and the three of them just stood there uncomfortably by the fence for a long few seconds.

'You know, Mummy, Frank has met the man who invented trampolines. Haven't you, Frank?'

'No,' Frank said. 'No, I bloody haven't.'

RED

That morning, it was obvious that something was different about Class Two.

As Red hung his coat on his peg and pushed his bag into its cubbyhole, all the Caterpillars were chatting to one another, one or two grasping each other excitedly. Usually, things were quieter in the morning, but not today.

Turning around, Red finally noticed what was causing all the fuss. On the large whiteboard at the front of the room was a photograph of a man with a yellow dog. He was smiling and had big dark glasses on. The man, not the dog. And above that picture, in big letters, were the words: 'Today's Visitor'.

'Take your seats, everybody! I know you're all excited.' The noise level of the class didn't change much, but Miss Payton carried on anyway. 'Let me just explain for Red, because he's probably wondering what all this is about. So, every few weeks for PSE . . .' She stopped again. 'Settle down, please! So, every few weeks at St Agnes, we arrange for a visitor to come into school and give a talk about what they do for a job, or something great they've achieved.'

Miss Payton then went on to explain that in the past year alone, they had been visited by a fireman, a woman who had run fifteen marathons, and a man from the council called Mr Massey, whose job it was to 'rod drains'.

Red thought that at least two of these visitors sounded super boring, but there was a fresh swell of excitement as Miss Payton announced what most of the children had already worked out: that today's visitors would be at least fifty per cent dog.

Despite everything, even Red was carried away by the joy of this prospect. Dogs were a billion times better than humans, and that was just a fact.

'So, I need everybody to be really well behaved and super quiet when we welcome today's guest – or should I say *guests*.'

Everybody did try their best to be quiet, and so the buzz of excitement sounded something like awe as the visitors entered the room a moment later. The man waved as he felt for his seat and sat down next to Miss Payton at the front of the class.

'Hi, everybody. My name is Amit.'

Red craned to get a better view of the yellow dog that had led the man into the room and was now lying obediently at his feet.

'And this is my best friend, Kika. Say hello, Kika.'

Kika barked once, and the entire class, even Miss Payton laughed, delighted.

'So yeah, thank you for inviting us along to chat to you today.'

Over the next hour, Amit told them all about how his eyes didn't work quite right. He explained that Kika was a golden retriever, and was not just his best friend but also his 'guide dog', which meant she made sure he didn't crash into things. He explained that Kika was super smart and had gone to school to learn how to do her job. He then showed them all a video of Kika as a puppy at guide-dog school, and another video of the two of them walking through town, stopping at traffic lights and avoiding holes that workmen had dug in the road.

The whole time, the happy dog lay at Amit's feet and panted and smiled. And Red smiled back.

Eventually, the talk came to an end, and Miss Payton asked everybody to clap. Red, thinking that the visit was over, clapped loudest of all, even though he was sad to see them go. But then, in a surprise, Amit took off Kika's harness, which meant that each Caterpillar was allowed to go up to the front of the class and stroke her, one by one.

Even Jake seemed to enjoy doing this, grinning as he tickled the dog behind one ear. For Red, though, it was a *huge* deal. He was one of the last to take his turn, too slow to join the queue, but when he finally got the chance to stroke Kika's soft fur, Amit said he could tell that Kika really liked him, because he could feel her bashing her tail against his chair leg. Red hugged the yellow dog around her neck, and Kika licked his face. Her breath smelled like a bin, but Red didn't mind. He didn't mind at all. Because it was the best day since as far back as he could remember.

And it was about to get better.

*

As their guests said goodbye, the bell rang for playtime. Rather than the usual chaotic dash for the exit, the class moved outside slowly, still chattering excitedly about that morning's visitors. Somehow, Red found himself beside Amelie, who was bouncing on her toes.

'I've got my own dog at home, you know!' she said to Red.

Red *did* know that she had her own dog at home; he had heard her telling Amit about it as she took her turn to pet Kika. But he pretended not to know. 'Really?'

'Yeah. He's a chihuahua called Mexico.'

'A wahwah?'

'Nooo! A chihuahua.' She chuckled. 'It's, like, a really small dog. But he's dead naughty. He once ate a bouncy ball.'

'NO.'

'Yeah, and my dad said that we'd have to be careful when he went to the toilet, because the ball would come out covered in poop, and it could bounce anywhere.'

Red let out a high-pitched laugh. 'That is funny. I haven't got a dog. My dad said that dogs are too much trouble, and I once squished my hamster, so I couldn't be trusted with a dog. But we've got a new house, and my mummy says we'll talk about it.'

There was a pause. Fearing they might run out of things to say to one another, Red rushed to fill the gap. 'We once had a dog come to my old school.'

'Really?'

'Yeah, but not like this. It was a dog on the loose! It wasn't supposed to be there, and it just ran around and around the playground, and we watched it out of the window. And when Miss Barnsdale went out to stop it, it dodged her, and then she slipped over on the playground and got really mad. And she took her coat off because it was covered in mud, and then she threw her coat at the dog because she *really* was mad at it. But she missed it, and then the dog came up to her coat and sniffed it and then peed on it.' Red was wide-eyed as he spoke. This was the stuff of legend at his old school.

Amelie was suitably impressed; her jaw dropped open. 'Ah. Mazing,' she said in wonder.

Red looked down and found he was standing on concrete. They had been talking so animatedly that they had, without realising it, made their way outside to the playground. Jake ran past them, kicking the ball so it hit the back of Red's legs. He had already gone back to being mean.

'Awww, is Mr Pee-pants playing with his girlfriend?' he said, chasing after the ball and not waiting for an answer.

'Shut up, Jake,' Amelie shouted back, sounding more bored than angry. She returned her attention to Red, who was now nervously flexing his Pokémon cards in his coat pocket. He scraped his heel against the ground, and was about to walk towards the friendship bench when Amelie spoke again.

'What's that?' She peered curiously.

'Oh, they're my Pokémon cards.' He produced them and fanned them out for her to see. 'See?'

'I like that one.' She pointed to the one on the top, a shiny Mewtwo.

'Oh, that's Mewtwo. He's really powerful. It's a super-rare card.'

'Cool.' Amelie wrinkled her nose. 'You wanna play?'

'Pokémon?'

'No, just, like . . . play?'

Red couldn't speak, so he just nodded once. He was worried that if he seemed too excited, she might change her mind. But at his nod, she casually turned to the two girls that had been loitering nearby and said to them, matter-of-factly, 'He's playing.'

They both shrugged, and that was that.

They played Red Light Green Light, and a game called The Floor is Lava. They chased and catched, and explored the furthest parts of the playground where the woods encroached on the metal fencing. And when they returned to the classroom, Red was beetroot-coloured and hot, and had a huge grin on his face. It was as though he had spent the last twenty minutes remembering who he was.

Even when Jake and Callum later laughed at him for 'playing with girls', he still felt happy. And he was made even more so by Amelie's response: 'Jake, why don't you stop being such a doughnut-head? Everybody knows *you* really did wet yourself that time.'

This was as they were about to leave for the day. Red had never seen anybody look quite so angry. He had once read about a bug called a termite that gets so angry it blows up. And Jake looked like that, like he might explode. He didn't. Instead, he turned on his heel and stormed off, his fists clenched at his side.

'It was in Mrs Darlow's class in Year One.' Amelie leaned in confidentially. 'He peed his pants in the book corner.'

'No!' said Red.

'Yep.'

It was Red's turn to be Ah. Mazed.

*

For once, Red wasn't dreading the walk home. Usually, his mum had to prise the events of the day from him. But not today. His enthusiasm bubbled over like a lemonade poured too quickly. Red explained about Amit and Kika, and the pooping bouncy ball of Amelie's chihuahua, and the rules of The Floor is Lava, and by the time they were sitting down to eat tea, Red had barely drawn breath. His mum tickled him under his chin and reminded him to eat.

That night, Red went to bed feeling for the first time like things would be okay. Not the same. But okay. Maybe.

The following morning, Red almost skipped to school, excited for a day like the one before. But as they got closer to the entrance, he gripped his mummy's hand a little tighter, feeling a sudden fear that something about the day before might have broken overnight. He slowed down.

'Red?'

He could tell his mum was about to ask him if he was okay. Then he saw Amelie waving goodbye to somebody from the bottom of the school steps. Spotting Red, she stopped waving and ran up to him. Without even saying good morning, she showed him a huge fresh scab on her elbow.

'Whoa.' Red was impressed.

'I did it on my roller skates last night! There was blood every-where.' She shook her head, delighted. 'Hi!' she said to Red's mum with a mini-wave, and then she turned away and ran up the school steps and inside.

'Is that Amelie?'

'Yeah.'

'She seems really nice,' his mum said, nudging him with one hip.

'Yeah. I gotta go, Mummy!'

She stopped him by the straps of his backpack 'Err, kiss, young man!' She pecked the top of his head and he followed Amelie inside, taking the steps two at a time.

Over the course of the morning, the sky outside began to darken, and it was with disappointment that Red realised that if it started to rain, there would be no outside play. Sure enough, the rain began to come down just fifteen minutes before breaktime.

'Okay, as you can see, it's raining cats and frogs,' Miss Payton confirmed. 'So we'll have inside play today. I'll open the crafting cupboards, or you can read in the book area, or I can maybe put a film on?'

There were groans, mainly from the boys. For once, Red agreed with them. Just his luck.

He decided to head into the crafting area. He had to go the long way round, because Jake and Warren were playing a game in which they slapped each other's hands as hard as they could. Some of the other boys were standing around watching, and Red didn't want to walk through the middle of them.

Successfully avoiding their attentions, he found himself in the 'busy corner', sitting alone amongst the crafting stuff. He had found some yoghurt pots and two old cereal boxes, and was figuring out what to do with them when Amelie appeared at his side.

'Being inside is soooo booooring.' She nodded behind her at Jessica and Molly, who were taking it in turns to do one another's hair. 'What you making?'

'Oh, err. Don't know yet.'

'What about a brain for Jake and Callum?!'

Red giggled, marvelling at the fact that she didn't care who heard her.

'I think I'll make a castle or something,' she continued. 'I made a castle out of cardboard boxes at home once, and made Mexico like the queen, and I made him a crown and he looked so cute – even if he did try and bite me when I tried to put it on him.'

'A castle is a great idea!' Red chewed his lip 'Can I help?'

'Yeah! I'll ask Miss Payton for some glue and glitter.'

'And I'll get more boxes!' Red said excitedly, leaping to his feet.

For the rest of breaktime, they crafted the greatest castle ever seen in Class Two – maybe even Classes Three and Four. It was a foot tall and required an entire roll of Sellotape. It was a thing of beauty and elegance, from the drawbridge made from an Anusol box, to the square shiny windows of KitKat foil drenched in PVA glue.

'I love it, it looks totally wicked!' Amelie squealed, excitedly stepping backwards to see it in all its glory.

Red grinned as he stuck down a corner on one of the turrets.

As breaktime ended, they carried it carefully over to one corner so it could be nearer the heater.

'We'll let it dry a bit,' Amelie said. 'And then finish it off after lunch.'

Red nodded. 'Wicked,' he said, trying out Amelie's word. 'See ya in a bit.' And they each skipped back to their own tables, smiling happily.

After an hour of maths and then a long half hour of PE, Red sat at his usual dinner table eating his sandwiches. The packed-lunch table was mostly kids from the years above, and as usual, Red was quiet. Amelie and the rest of his class had school lunches, but usually Red's mum made him a lunchbox, because he was 'fussy' and didn't like things like gravy and custard, and cutlery when you could taste the metal.

Red was keen to get back to the classroom to work on the castle, and so he wolfed down his sandwich of jam, ham and Nutella, and ate his Cheestring in three bites without peeling it into shreds. Usually, the kids eating packed lunch would finish before everyone else, but today two of the Year Three boys at his table had started throwing Frazzles at each other, and one of the dinner ladies had come over and told the entire table to stay behind and help clean up.

That meant Red was one of the last to make it back to the classroom.

Amelie was already there.

She was standing near where they had left the castle, but it wasn't above the heater anymore. He was about to ask why she had moved it.

'Come on, now. It's not the end of the world,' Miss Payton was saying gently as she rubbed Amelie's back.

'What's a matter?' Red asked.

Amelie stepped to one side and gestured at the floor, where the castle lay in pieces.

'Something happened to the house you were making, and Amelie's just a bit upset about it, that's all.' Miss Payton bent down to pick up the crushed drawbridge.

'It was a castle! And it's ruined!' Amelie shouted. 'It was Jake or Callum, I know it was!'

'Now, Amelie, that's a little bit unfair, I think. I've just spoken to the boys, and they didn't realise it was your house or that it was for saving. They just thought the boxes were spare. I don't think they would've done it on purpose – and obviously the boxes *are* for everyone.'

'Yeah, we didn't know, miss,' Jake said. He appeared beside Red, looking concerned and sad, as if he had never done anything wrong, ever. His face was so convincing that, for a moment, Red almost believed him.

'It was a *castle*!' Amelie repeated. 'And it *was* on purpose! You know it was on purpose, Jake!'

Jake's face changed in an instant. 'Shut up, Amelie!' The angelic expression was gone, and the real Jake was back.

Miss Payton didn't seem to notice. 'Now, you two – that's enough! Caterpillars do not speak to each other like that. I want you both to say sorry.'

Neither of them said a word.

Red spoke up quietly. 'Maybe we could try and fix it?'

Amelie looked up, her hair stuck to her face with tears. 'It was a stupid castle anyway!'

She barged past Miss Payton, Red and Jake, and flopped into her seat, her head buried in her folded arms.

FRANK

It's weird how noises can get incorporated into a dream. A fan heater becomes a helicopter; a car alarm becomes a screeching bird. Frank had slept fitfully all night, persistently returning to a dream about climbing a tree, something he hadn't done for over fifty years. The tree was one of those lightning-burned oaks, brittle, and he was climbing in a storm. Every time he tried to take a step upwards, a branch broke, and he never seemed to be able to get more than a few feet from the ground.

He awoke at 5am, feeling vaguely annoyed. In truth, he started most days vaguely annoyed, and his mood was not about to improve.

By 8am, he was standing in the back garden, a mug of tea in one hand, staring at the fence panel that was now lying at his feet. He had known something was off as soon as he had drawn back the curtains in the kitchen at first light. The garden seemed less shaded somehow. And when he craned his head, he could actually see Red's trampoline, which he definitely shouldn't be able to do – unless the fence dividing their two lawns was no longer there.

Frank continued to stare down at the fallen wooden panel and his suddenly uninterrupted view of next door's garden.

'Great.' He raised his mug slightly in a 'cheers' to the fence, as though it had betrayed him.

He was still staring at it when Red came skipping out of his back door. The kid was dressed in his school uniform and tripping over untied shoelaces.

'Morning, Frank!' he shouted enthusiastically, and way too loud. 'I heard your back door open and I—' He'd been directing his voice upwards, as though there was still a fence to shout over, but he stopped abruptly when he saw Frank and the fence lying between them.

Red's mouth fell open. 'Whoa, what did you do?'

'What do you mean, what did *I* do?! The wind obviously blew it down last night.'

Frank tapped his foot against a splintered fence post, still half-buried in the ground. 'Anyway, if anything, *you* did it, always bloody leaning on it.'

'Eh?'

'You probably weakened it.'

Red looked at Frank as though he was talking in a foreign language, and then moved on. 'I haven't really seen your garden properly before. I like it. It's like a jungle,' Red said, surveying. 'Why is your grass so long? Is there any treasure or dead bodies?'

Frank poured the last of his tea on to the lawn, while Red waved his hands in the space where the fence used to be, as though he was a mime inside a glass box.

'I like it like this. It's cool.'

'Cool? What's cool about it? What's cool about damaging someone's property?'

'Well, for a start, I won't *have* to lean on it anymore. *And* we've got one big garden now!' Red said cheerfully, as though this was something that clearly hadn't even occurred to Frank.

'Jesus Christ,' Frank said to himself as he pinched the bridge of his nose. 'Well, it'll be fixed by the time you get back from school. Don't you worry about that.'

Red's eyes lit up. 'I can help! I could tell Mummy I can't go to school because I'm helping you mend the fence.'

'I don't think so.'

'It'll be great. I'm really good at helping,' Red insisted, as he started to lift the fence panel. It was five times his size, and barely budged.

'Like I said,' Frank reiterated, 'it'll be done by the time you get back from school.'

Red's face fell, and he let the fence panel drop.

'Why are you so desperate to get out of school, anyway?' Frank added. 'What's wrong with it?'

'Everything.'

'Uh huh.' Frank turned around to walk back into the house. 'Well enjoy it, school is as good as it gets. The best days of your life.'

'It's not the best days of your life. It is the *worst* days of your life!' Red shouted.

Frank turned around again, surprised by the boy's reaction. 'Jesus wept. Is it still this bloody Jason kid?'

'Jake,' Red corrected, kicking the dirt at his feet.

'Well, what's his problem, anyway?'

'He's a stupid idiot.'

'Apart from that.'

'Well, he says that I'm a weird, and that I'm not fast. And he breaks my things.'

'Okay.'

'And sometimes he pushes me over and trips me up, and then pretends to help me up, and then shoves me down again. And he made it look like I'd wet my pants. And I have tried to be his friend, but now he makes everybody play a game where they pretend that I'm invisible, and that they can't hear me—'

'Uh huh. Have you told your mum?'

'Sort of. Not really. It'll just make her sad or something. Anyway, she'll probably get mad and go into school, and then I'll look like a baby. And I'm not a baby. I'm six.'

'Right.'

'Seven soon.'

Frank nodded. 'Well, what *are* you gonna do?'

'Huh?'

'Well, are you just going to whinge and whine, or are you going to do something about it?'

Red shrugged.

'Back in my day, if someone behaved like that with me, they'd only do it once. The kid's obviously a bully, and bullies only understand one thing.'

Red shrugged again.

'Christ, boy. My old man always used to say that in life you're either a mountain or a mouse. Which are you?'

'I don't think I'm either.'

'What I'm saying is—'

'I don't think I'm a mountain. But I don't really want to be a mouse, either. In fact, I definitely don't want to be a mouse. Y'know that mice poop a hundred times in one day?'

'What I'm saying is, sometimes you have to stand up for yourself, make sure people know you're not someone to be trifled with.'

'Trifle?'

Christ, it was like talking to a badly tuned radio.

'I mean,' Frank said, trying again, 'that if this kid's mean to you, you be mean right back. If he shoves you, *you* shove him. If he hits you, you hit him back.'

Red seemed to think for a moment. Then his face cleared. 'Ooh,' he said, suddenly on board with the idea. 'You could teach me, like on *Karate Kid* . . . This Japanese mister teaches this boy how to fight. He has to catch flies with little sticks, and then he gets dead good, and then he crane-kicks a man in the head, like this!' Red raised karate-chop hands, spun around once and kicked a leg out like a drunk penguin.

'What the hell are you on about?' Frank said, as Red repeated the move. This time, his shoe flew off, whizzing over Frank's shoulder and landing in the grass behind him. 'You don't have to learn how to be bloody Bruce Lee, or whatever. Just . . . next time he trips you up or does something mean, give him a kick up the arse. He'll soon leave you alone.'

'Really?'

'Really. Just give this kid a bunch of fives.'

'A bunch of what?'

'Look, do what you want,' Frank said, turning to look for Red's shoe.

'But he's bigger than me.'

'Of course he is, you daft sod. Bullies always are.'

'Red!' his mum shouted from the back door.

Hearing her voice, Red abandoned their conversation and scouted around for a place to hide. He back-scurried under the trampoline and looked at Frank, holding a finger to his lips. 'Shh.'

Sarah approached the gap in the fence. 'Alright, Frank?' she said, eyeing the fence panel with confusion.

'Oh yeah, I'm hunky-dory. I suppose *I'll* have to sort this mess out?'

'What happened?'

'Well, it obviously blew down in the storm last night.'

'What storm?'

Frank looked at the fence panel pointedly and shook his head. He could see where the kid got it from.

He gestured with his empty mug at where Red was hiding under the trampoline and turned to head inside.

'Thanks, Frank. Come on, kiddo,' Sarah said, as she pulled the boy out by one leg. 'Where's your shoe?'

RED

It was the day of the incident.

On the way to school that morning, his mum had asked him what he had been chatting to Frank about, and Red had told her. Not everything, of course: just that he would've preferred to stay home and help Frank fix the fence.

'Are you really not enjoying school, Reddy?' she asked as they continued up Merton Road towards St Agnes. 'I know you said you hated it the other day, but I just thought you were mad about . . . y'know, me and your dad and everything.'

'It's okay, I guess,' he said.

This made her stop. She crouched down on her heels and turned him to face her. She gave his head a single stroke. 'Come on, Reddy, I need you to speak to me.'

Finally, he told her a little more. That he really wasn't enjoying school. That there was a boy called Jake who was mean, and a few days ago Jake had broken something that belonged to Red and Amelie, and she had now fallen out with Red about it. And that was (some of the) reason why he didn't want to go to school.

Although he hadn't gone into a lot of detail, Red felt a sense of relief. It was similar to the way he'd felt when he'd told his dad everything, but his mummy didn't dismiss him like his dad had done. In fact, Red had told her just a small bit of what he had told his dad, but she responded by giving him a squeezing hug, saying that it was her job to look after him, and asking him why on earth he hadn't said anything before.

Red didn't tell her that it was his job to look after her, too. He just lifted his shoulders and said he didn't know.

'Look, we'll talk about it more when you get home, Reddy. But if there's any more of this Jake boy being mean, you need to tell a teacher straight away.'

And if that didn't work, his mum insisted, she would speak to Jake's mum, Miss Payton and Mrs Mills herself, and make it very clear that this sort of thing would not be 'toilet-rated'. Then they set off walking again, this time at a brisker pace, his mum whispering under her breath about Jake being 'a little shit'.

No more was said until they reached the school gates, when his mum left him with the parting advice that he should, for now, just try and ignore Jake.

That would be easier said than done, but Red smiled and nodded and mirrored her thumbs-up.

The truth is, though, that Red hadn't been thinking that much about Jake that morning. His priority was to make things better with Amelie. It had been days since the thing with the castle, and in that entire time, she hadn't invited him to play, nor had she spoken to him when she passed him (now back in his old spot on the rainbow bench). When they found themselves in the same group in class, she had barely looked him in the eye.

Red wasn't sure why this was. Part of him thought it was because she had realised that being friends with Red was a bad idea. It got you picked on. Jake didn't just pick on people he didn't like, he picked on people who were friends with people he didn't like.

But deep down, Red didn't think that was it. Amelie knew

exactly what Jake was like, and she certainly wasn't scared of him. Red didn't think Amelie was scared of *anything*. It was one of the reasons he liked her so much. No, Red thought the reason Amelie had stopped being friends with him had something to do with the fact that she was embarrassed to have been seen so upset and crying.

Which was silly, because Red cried all the time: when he fell off his bike, or banged his head. He'd once cried because he put his hand in some seagull poo and his mummy wouldn't let him taste it (but he had been really little then).

Whatever the reason, Red wanted to tell Amelie that he desperately wanted things to go back to the way they had been before the castle got wrecked. He wanted to explain that there was nothing to be embarrassed about, and that he really, really, wanted to be her friend again.

The problem was, he couldn't think of the right words to tell her all that. He couldn't think of how to even start. And when he tried to say anything to her, he would open his mouth and nothing would come out. Or he would just stutter and make a noise like he was trying to start an imaginary car.

Finally, it had occurred to Red that what grown-ups do when they want to make things better is buy each other something nice – like flowers or chocolates or, if you're rich, a horse. Something that said, let's be friends again. And in the absence of knowing exactly what to say, this seemed like a good idea.

Firstly, Red thought about buying some flowers, but he didn't have any money. Then he thought maybe he could get them from the corner of the road near the park where a man had crashed his motorbike, but in the end, he decided against that. His mum would ask questions and probably make a joke about Amelie being his girlfriend, and he could only imagine what Jake and the other boys would say if he turned up with such an obvious present.

Besides, he had something better.

Red thumbed the Pokémon card in his shorts pocket, being extra careful not to bend the edges. This was his gift to Amelie. A Pokémon card. And not just any card. It was the one she had noticed, the one she had admired the most. The Mewtwo card. Shiny, rare.

His best card.

*

That morning, Red didn't need to go out of his way to follow his mum's advice and ignore Jake, because it seemed to be one of those days when Jake was fine with ignoring *him*. As he passed Jake in the hallway outside Class Two, the bigger boy didn't even notice him. He was seemingly having too much fun teasing some kid in Class One for having a *Hey Duggee* badge on his bag.

But it was difficult to find a moment to speak to Amelie. During playtime, she was always playing with Jessica and Molly, or speaking with someone else. And talking to her during class would have got them both into trouble.

It was early afternoon before Red found Amelie on her own. It was in an area of the classroom called the Wildlife Area: a small corner with plants, the class fish tank, and walls adorned with crayoned pictures of animals, creeping vines and a 'circle of life' poster.

Before Red had started at St Agnes, the entire class had been involved in a project where they each had to grow a bean plant. The few that had survived from Year One and into Year Two now lived on a shelf by the window, growing towards the light.

One of those that had (sort of) survived was Amelie's. She insisted it was still growing, despite the fact that it had no leaves on it, was brown and was about the size of a toe.

Amelie stubbornly watered it every day, and occasionally talked to it. She was doing both as Red shuffled over with one hand in his pocket.

'. . . and you need to drink it all up because otherwise you'll stay tidgy, and you'll never make any beans.' She stopped when she saw Red and looked at the floor awkwardly. 'Hello,' she said quietly, chewing her bottom lip.

'It's getting pretty big,' Red said, pointing at the tiny brown stick in the pot.

'Mm. I don't know. I think it might've stopped growing altogether. Miss Payton said it's definitely dead. But I think maybe it just needs more water?'

'Mm.' Red was blinking too much; he always did this when he was nervous.

Amelie returned to drowning her twig.

'I've got something for you,' he said, eventually.

'For me?' She turned around, curious.

'Yeah.' He produced the card from his pocket, but kept it concealed, with one hand over the other. 'It's, well . . .' He revealed the card hidden in his palm. 'You can have this, if you want?'

'What?' Her eyebrows disappeared behind her fringe in surprise. 'You're giving it to me? But I thought you said it was your best one?'

'It is,' Red confirmed. He could feel his cheeks beginning to glow. 'But I'll still be able to see it. And you'll look after it super well. Like your beans plant. And after you were so sad about everything, I thought it might make you happy. And . . . I want you to have it, anyway.'

She rubbed her hands on her cardigan, making sure they were fully dry before she carefully took the card. Red had expected to feel a little regretful when it was finally time to hand over Mewtwo, but instead he felt thrilled as Amelie smiled with her entire face. She tilted the card in the sunlight, making it reflect and shine.

'And, if you look, it's got two hundred HP points, which means it can defeat, pretty much, any other—'

Neither of them heard Callum, Toby and Jake as they walked up behind Red.

'Are you having a kiss with your girlfriend?'

Red said nothing. He didn't know how, but Jake making fun of him made it feel like he couldn't breathe properly.

Callum and Toby laughed, pushing and nudging into one another. Red angled himself away from them, doing his best to follow his mum's advice and ignore them.

'Or are you making another fairy castle for all your dollies?' Jake said this in the voice of a posh lady.

Amelie huffed impatiently and moved to walk past the three boys. But Jake stepped across her path.

'What's that, anyway?'

Amelie barely had a moment to realise that he was talking about the card before he had yanked it from her hand.

'Give it back, Jake. It's not yours!'

He held it above his shoulder and kept her at bay with his other hand.

'And it's really important!' she shouted.

'I just want to look at it.'

'I mean it, Jake! Give it back!'

This got the attention of Miss Payton, who was plugging in a laptop at her desk, ready for afternoon lessons. She looked tired and bored, and barely looked up as she called over.

'Whatever it is, Jake, give it back.'

'I don't know what they're talking about, Miss Payton.'

Red joined in now. 'Give it *back*.' He lunged to grab the card, but Jake easily avoided him by taking a step backwards. Red tried again, and Jake took another couple of steps. He was now against the countertop. The small fish tank, bubbling gently behind him, rocked slightly as he backed into it.

He was laughing now, continuing to hold the card out of reach, and when Red tried to jump for it once more, Jake pushed him away easily with his free hand.

'You idiot! Jake!' Amelie screamed behind Red.

This got Miss Payton's attention again. 'For goodness' sake, what on earth is going on over there? Jake, whatever it is, just give it back.'

At this, Callum and Toby drifted away, not wanting to get into trouble. Red stopped jumping and Amelie stopped shouting. Instead, she walked forwards with her hand out, waiting for Jake to do the inevitable: concede and hand over the card.

Instead he lowered his arm, studied the card carefully, and then smiled at them both in turn. 'I tell you what.'

Everything slowed down.

Red could see what he was about to do, but could do nothing to stop it.

'Why don't you have half each?' Jake held up the card. The level 100, shiny Mewtwo Pokémon card. Red's best card. With its special attack moves of Hyper Beam and Shadow Ball, and its unbeatable 200 HP points—

And he tore it in two.

The sound was a zip of static. Red felt it as pain.

'Nooo!' Amelie shouted.

Red barely heard her.

He just stood there for a long moment, with his mouth open.

And then he was on the ground, scrabbling to pick up the pieces, as though he might somehow reverse time, as though he could some-how undo the damage.

Finding the two halves, he held them up and then against one another in disbelief. Only then did tears begin to cloud his vision.

As he stood up, Red felt anger ripple down through his body, stop at his feet and then wave back up again. He was about to turn away. The impulse to run and run–until there was as much distance between Jake, the school and himself as possible—was utterly overwhelming.

And then he saw . . . that Jake was still smiling.

Red tried to conjure the voice of his mum, the advice to 'just ignore him'. Or that of Father McManus, to 'be like Jesus', 'to be kind, always'. But another voice intruded, and it was Frank's. The old man who lived next door. And it was a voice that got louder and louder until it seemed to fill his head.

Jake saw the expression on Red's face and looked confused – and then a little uncertain.

'I AM NOT A MOUSE!' Red shouted. He stood tall now, at his full three feet, nine and a half inches. He took a step forward.

Every slight, every injustice of the past six months was condensed into a single point – and it seemed to coalesce in his right fist.

'Eh?' Jake smiled awkwardly. The bigger boy looked around for support. Finding none, the colour began to drain from his face.

Time slowed to a crawl as the rush of blood caused Red's heartbeat to thrum in his head. He took another step forward, and before Jake could react, he swung his arm back.

'I AM A BLOODY MOUNTAIN!'

He closed his eyes tightly and, with every sinew and muscle in his body, Red threw the first and only punch of his life. And it was aimed right at Jake Barnet's stupid face.

FRANK

Unbelievable. Someone *else* was at the door.

'Who the hell's that now?' Frank had been stirring a pan of tomato soup in the kitchen. As he turned off the hob and wiped his hands on a tea towel, the persistent knocking was repeated, and then turned into a constant and angry rhythm.

Whoever was at the door this time, it sounded like they were serious. It was the sort of knocking you only ever really heard on TV, when a pair of pig-knuckle-nosed bailiffs were about to kick a door in.

Frank's annoyance turned to fury as he stomped to give whoever was on his doorstep the mother of all . . .

It was Sarah and Red.

'What the hell were you thinking?!' Sarah barked as she barged past him, into the hallway and then into the living room. Red trailed in behind her, with his head down.

'Uh oh,' Marcie said simply, sitting at the bottom of the stairs in jogging bottoms and an old Christmas jumper she would sometimes wear to do the gardening.

Frank said nothing.

He was in shock. He just stared out of his own front door, as though this hadn't just happened. His facial expression was that of a cow that has just received a bolt to its forehead.

What fresh hell was this? Just moments ago, he had been on solid ground – angry. And now he didn't know what was going on. Worse than that, there were strangers in his house! *Inside* his house! Again!

On a weird autopilot, he left the door open and followed the pair into the living room, where Red stood sheepishly by the window, his arm in a sling, as Sarah paced back and forth like a caged panther.

'What the . . .?' Frank managed.

'What happened? Is that what you're trying to say, you gormless old bugger? What *happened*?!' Sarah stopped pacing. She put her hands on her hips and planted her feet. She pointed at his face, and her nostrils flared in a way that made it look as though she was considering removing his head from her shoulders – with her teeth.

'I'll *tell* you what bloody happened.'

RED

Red's trousers were still wet, and his left arm was in a sling, loosely tied at his right shoulder. He nervously fumbled with the knot as he sat on one of the five plastic chairs outside Mrs Mills's office. They were chairs that were really designed for older kids, and so his legs dangled off the edge and his toes didn't quite reach the floor.

It was his first time outside the headteacher's office. There were kids, he knew, that were called there every day for something or other: problems with lateness, uniform, being rude. There was one kid in year six who *always* seemed to be sitting on the chairs outside the office; he was tall and had a completely shaved head, apart from a tuft at the front that looked like a squirrel's tail.

Sure enough, there he was. Sitting at the other end of the row of chairs, picking at his trainers.

'What did you do to your arm?'

Red glanced behind him to check that the boy was talking to him. The boy looked up from his trainers as though Red was an idiot.

'Oh. Er. I hurt it,' Red replied, lifting the arm slightly. He winced. He had forgotten how painful it was because he was so nervous.

'Were you fighting?'

'No.' Red screwed up his face as he rethought his answer. 'Well, hmm, not really. I tried to punch a boy on the nose called Jake . . . That was the name of the boy, not the name of the boy's nose . . . And I missed.'

'You missed?'

'Yeah, and I hit the fish tank.'

'Blimey. Is that why your trousers are wet?'

'Yeah. I had my eyes closed like this.' Red squeezed his eyes shut and swung a fist (with his good arm) in demonstration. 'And I missed, and I broke the fish tank.'

The boy chuckled. 'That's amazing. You're sooo dead meat.' He thumbed towards the closed door of Mrs Mills's office.

Red shuddered. He really hoped that the punishment for breaking the school fish tank was not to be turned into dead meat. Still, he knew that this was bad. Really bad.

As if on cue, the door swung open and Mrs Mills peered into the corridor and at the two of them sitting there. Red was upright and terrified, but the older boy had returned to picking at his shoes. Looking up, the boy saw Mrs Mills and lazily began to stand, but she put up her palm and sighed in exasperation. 'Not you, Danny. You can wait. Leonard. Come on.'

Red jumped off his chair and walked towards his fate. Leaving Death Row behind, the last thing he saw was Danny, who was making a face at him by crossing his eyes and sticking his tongue in his bottom lip so he looked like a frog. Red didn't laugh. He wasn't sure he'd ever laugh again.

Inside Mrs Mills's office was a huge wooden desk, dominated by an ancient computer monitor. There was a large, padded black chair behind it that looked like the chair Noah's brother played Xbox on. Behind that was a wall filled with framed certificates. Two stumpy filing cabinets sat beneath a window that overlooked the gates and playground.

'You've got a lot of books,' Red said sheepishly, as he noticed the packed bookshelf on the opposing wall.

'Well, Leonard. Books give a soul to the universe, wings to the mind, flight to the imagination, and life to everything,' she replied.

'Oh, right,' Red replied, unsure what he was supposed to say to that.

Seemingly disappointed, she sat down and then pointed at the two chairs opposite her.

One was identical to those in the row outside, and the other was a grey spinny chair with wheels.

'Have a sit down.'

Red chose the grey chair, which was a mistake – especially with only one good arm. Like the chairs outside, it was too big, but it also swivelled as he tried to climb on. After several attempts to sit down, he found himself lying on it, bum in air, and slowly turning. He repeated three full turns before Mrs Mills suggested he sit in the other chair.

'How's the arm, Leonard?'

'Okay.'

'Mrs Moone says she thinks you've just sprained it, but it is quite swollen, so I think you should really get it checked at the hospital.'

'Okay.'

'Do you know what sprained means?'

'No.'

'It just means that it's probably not broken or anything.'

'Okay.'

'So . . . we need to phone your mum.'

'Okay.'

'Explain everything that's happened.'

'Okay.'

She tapped at a keyboard before pulling the telephone on the desk towards herself and picking up the receiver. Eyeing the computer screen, she dialled a number slowly and deliberately, and then drummed her fingers on the desk, waiting.

Red listened to the one side of the conversation he could hear.

'Hello, Mrs Evans? This is Mrs Mills? At St Agnes?' She spoke as if she was asking questions, as if she wasn't sure if she actually *was* Mrs Mills at St Agnes.

'Yes, it's . . . No, no . . . he's fine. We *have* had an incident, though.' She popped her eyebrows at Red. 'And he does have an injury to his arm.'

. . .

'No. He's really okay. The school nurse has taken a look. He's got a small cut on his hand, and she thinks he may have just sprained his wrist . . . No, he doesn't seem to be in too much pain.'

. . .

'Well, what happened is' – she raised her eyebrows at Red again – 'probably best explained in person. If you could come into the office, and—'

. . .

'Well. It was a scuffle with another boy.'

For the first time in the conversation, he heard his mum's voice, metallic and distant, as she responded: *'Red?! In a fight?!'*

'As I say, I do think that this is something better explained in person . . .?'

. . .

'Yes. All the same—'

. . .

'Okay. Any time before three is fine. I'll tell reception to expect you. Leonard will be outside my office. Okay. Thank you, Mrs Evans. That's – yes. Bye.' She hung up the receiver.

Five minutes later, Red was sitting outside Mrs Mills's office again. Danny had been summoned inside now, and Red craned his neck to listen as Mrs Mills explained how it was wrong of him to chase people around the playground with dog muck on a stick.

Red agreed.

Danny emerged a while later, scratching his backside and unimpressed by the whole ordeal. He made the same frog face at Red as he passed him on the way back to class. 'See you later, killer.'

Forty minutes passed before Red's mum came barrelling down the hallway.

'Red?! Are you okay?' She threw her handbag to one side and crouched in front of him. 'Are you okay? Let me look at you. Let me look at your hand – and your arm? What happened?'

Red shrugged and looked at his shoes.

'Red?' his mum said again.

Mrs Mills appeared. 'Hi, Mrs Evans, please come on in. Red, if you could just wait there while I have a quick chat with your mum, okay?'

His mum stroked his head. 'I'll be two minutes, okay baby boy? Two minutes.'

As with the chat between Mrs Mills and Danny, Red could hear snippets of the conversation from the other side of the office door as the events of that morning were revealed to his mum.

The headmaster explained Red had not actually hit anybody, but that was 'more by good fortune than anything else', and that 'the fish tank had come off worse, but that wasn't the point'. And that the nurse suspected his arm was merely sprained. But it would be a good idea to take him to have it checked over at the hospital, as Mrs Moone wasn't 'really a nurse, and is more accustomed to dealing with nits and that kind of thing'.

It seemed to be a one-sided conversation, his mum stunned into silence. But when the voices got louder, Red edged along the seats until he was right by the door so that he could hear better.

'Well, who is this kid??' his mum was demanding.

'He's one of Red's classmates. By all accounts, the two of them haven't been getting on too well. And Miss Payton tells me she has made every effort to bring the boys together and—'

'Is his name Jake, by any chance? Sounds like a real piece of work.'

'Mrs Evans, I can assure you—'

'Look, this isn't like Red at all. He wouldn't hurt a fly. He's the kindest, sweetest—'

'Be that as it may.' There was a silence before Mrs Mills carried on. 'Unfortunately, we have a zero-tolerance policy for incidents like this. Which means, I'm afraid, Red will have to undergo a mandatory week's absence.'

'*What?*'

'I'm afraid—'

'Hang on a minute. You're suspending him!? He's six!'

'I understand. I do, really. And it's not a suspension, it's an "involuntary break". It's for no more than a week, and it just gives everybody a chance to cool down. The opportunity to take stock and . . . think about things.'

'He's. Six. Years. Old!'

'Mrs Evans, Red broke school property.' The headteacher paused to allow the gravity of the situation to sink in, and then continued. 'A fish *died*.'

'Oh, well, why didn't you say so?! A fish died? When's the funeral?'

'I don't think there's any need to be facetious, Mrs Evans. I—'

'*Facetious?* I've got work. I've just started a new job. I can't just take a week off!'

'I understand. But policy is policy, and a school lives and dies by its . . .'

Red heard a chair scrape abruptly.

'Mrs Evans. May I ask who Frank is?'

'What?'

'Frank? Miss Payton didn't know whether he was Leonard's grandfather or . . .?'

'I don't understand.'

'Well, it's just that immediately after the incident, Red said something about someone called Frank. And how he had told him that he should toughen up, stand up for himself, that sort of thing. Be "a mountain not a mouse" – those were the words Red used . . . Obviously, we encourage children to speak to a member of staff rather than taking matters into their own hands, and, well – we just wondered who Frank was?'

The office door flew open, Red's mum took him by his good arm and began striding down the corridor towards the exit.

'I'll kill him. I'll bloody kill him.'

FRANK

'. . . And so, I've just spent the last three hours in St Mary's, having his arm put in a cast! It's broken, Frank. A hairline fracture in his wrist.' Sarah had been pacing, but now she stopped and stared straight at him again.

She seemed to be expecting some sort of response, but Frank's head was still light – and understandably so. He had entered some sort of alternate universe in which people could just walk into your house. A man's home was supposed to be his castle, and his wasn't just under siege, it had been breached by a hysterical lunatic and her one-armed kid.

'Mummy, it's not Frank's fault,' Red offered quietly.

'You stay out of this. You're in enough trouble.' She turned back to Frank. 'What the hell were you thinking?'

Frank suddenly snapped back into his body. He would not be spoken to like this in his own—

'What were you *thinking*?!' she repeated, her arms thrown in the air.

Some of the new wind left his sails, and when he replied, it wasn't as forceful as it had sounded in his head. 'I . . . I . . . I don't know what the hell you're talking about.'

'I tell you what I'm talking about. Your bloody pep talk. Is he a mouse or a chuffing mountain? "Youse need to stand up for yourself, Red,"' she said, mimicking his accent. 'Sending him off to school like he's flaming Rambo.'

'Well, it's not my fault if he—'

She guillotined across him. 'Not your fault? Not your fault?! Do you know what the biggest problem he's ever come home from school with? I mean, before today? He once sat in the toilet and ate a whole pack of crayons. He was four. In fact, that's the only time I've ever had to take him to the hospital before. He was fine, he just shit rainbows for a week. But now look.' She gestured towards the boy. '*Look* at his arm. Fighting – bloody fighting!'

Red raised his uninjured hand, as if to make a point of order. 'I wasn't really fight—'

'Red!'

There was quiet for a long time.

'Well, in my day . . .' Frank began.

'It's not *your day*, though, is it, Frank?!' She was off again. 'It's not the nineteen-bloody-fifties. It's not the good old days when men settled their problems with fisticuffs, and everybody watched black-and-white TV, and crapped in outside toilets, and you could buy a house for four quid, and everybody died of rickets at thirty-five—'

'Just how old do you think I am?'

'The point is, things have moved on. You can't just tell a kid to go and punch another kid in the face. Do you understand that?'

But Frank didn't understand that. And he had heard enough. 'Ach, Come on! This Jake kid sounds like an absolute shitehouse.'

'Unbelievable.'

'Well, the boy's being bullied. What's he supposed to do?'

'Talk to me! Talk to his teachers! Talk to anybody apart from the nutjob next door. And now! Now, it's *Red* who's been suspended from school.'

'What?'

'Yep. Suspended.'

'Suspended?! At *six*?'

'Well, they don't call it suspension. They call it an enforced absence! But's that not the—'

'For killing a pissing goldfish?'

'I know!'

Finding themselves in agreement on something seemed to come as a shock to them both, and the fire of their anger was suddenly deprived of oxygen.

There was another long silence. Sarah took a long, deep breath, and Frank shifted uncomfortably.

'And what am I going to do with him for a whole week?' She gestured at Red, but now seemed to be talking to no one in particular. 'I'm literally in the first month of my new job at work. I can kiss goodbye to that if I turn around and tell them I can't come in. And never mind the job itself, I've got patients who . . . well, you know . . .'

He did know.

'My sister's down in Devon for the next few weeks, so she can't watch him.' She paced to the window and back again. 'Honestly, I was *here* this morning' – she held a flat palm to her eyebrows, as though indicating a water level – 'and I'm *here* now.' The hand went above her head.

'What about his dad?'

'His dad? His *dad*? What a waste of . . . I called him straight away, and he's busy. Get this: his new girlfriend is having her boobs made bigger – as if she isn't basically a human bouncy castle as it is – and she's got to recuperate and . . .' She seemed to remember Red was listening, and turned to find he had sat down on Frank's sofa. 'Let's just say Red's dad is a good father in the same way that Fred West is a cracking landscaper.'

Frank had returned to silence.

Sarah sat on the arm of the sofa, then leaned over and stroked Red's head. She looked exhausted.

For the first time since her explosive entrance, she seemed to take in her surroundings, and now appeared a little bewildered to find herself inside his house. It made Frank feel all the more uncomfortable, and he noticed a flicker of surprise as she cast her eyes around. He suspected that this was due to the fact that, in contrast to the outside of the house, the inside was neat and tidy and well kept.

She sighed, long and hard. 'I dunno,' she said, shaking her head.

Frank was glancing between Sarah and Red as he tried to formulate a plan, to come up with the right facial expression or the correct formulation of words that would get these people out of his house and return the world to its correct axis.

In that moment, Sarah caught Frank's eye. She looked at him with a curious expression on her face, as though an idea was forming.

'What?' he said, uncomfortably.

She squinted slightly, her tongue clicking against her teeth. She was thinking. Finally, the idea seemed to coalesce in her brain.

'What?' he said again.

'You could watch him.'

This was in stereo, as Marcie – who was still out of sight in the hallway – said exactly the same words at precisely the same moment.

It was such a bone-crushingly terrible idea, that Frank genuinely thought he had misheard – or perhaps had a stroke. 'Wha?'

'You could watch him,' Sarah repeated simply.

'Ach ach,' Frank spluttered. Unable to form words. Yep, definitely a stroke.

'It makes sense,' she said matter-of-factly, as though it made sense. 'This whole thing's your fault, after all.' She stood up now, warming to the idea. 'For some brain-scrambling reason, he actually likes you. And, well, it's not as though you've got anything better to do; you never leave the house. You could watch him.'

'She's right, Frank,' Marcie agreed from somewhere behind him.

'Whu whu?' Okay, now he sounded like a flooded engine. Yep, definitely, definitely a stroke. Frank had a moment to hope that it was a big one, and that it would finish him off where he stood.

'Franklin, you owe me. You owe us.'

Frank finally found English. 'I can't look after your bloody kid!? Have you gone totally—'

'It's literally not even a week. Five days. I would drop him here in the morning, pick him up in the afternoon. What do you say, Red?'

'I think it's a good idea,' Red chipped in.

'See? It's a good idea,' she repeated.

'Don't touch that!'

Red was clicking a pen he had found on the TV cabinet.

'It is *not* a good idea. It's a terribly horrific idea. This is my home, not a nursery. I wouldn't know how to—'

'You owe me,' she repeated.

'We both do,' said Marcie, matter-of-factly, as she appeared in her favourite spot on the mantelpiece.

He knew that Sarah was referring to the fact that she saw this situation as his fault – that's what she meant by 'You owe me.' But that's not what Marcie meant, and he knew it.

Suddenly, in that moment, Frank vividly remembered the last time that he had seen Sarah at the hospice. It had been two years previously, long before she and Red had moved in next door. She had stayed beyond her shift and into the night to be there when Marcie finally passed. Still talking to his wife with kindness and care, as though Marcie could hear her. Still talking to her when he no longer could.

He could see Sarah placing a cup of tea on the hospital bedside trolley, next to the previously untouched one. Placing a hand on his shoulder as she left that room.

'Her job's important, Frank,' Marcie said simply.

Frank looked up and shook his head. The hope and expectation in Sarah's face had already begun to fall away when he spoke.

'Alright,' he said, quietly.

'What?'

'For God's sake. I said, okay.'

'Really?' Sarah said, with total astonishment.

This response annoyed Frank immeasurably. She clearly hadn't expected him to say yes at all, and he could've avoided this unfolding nightmare if he'd just stuck to his guns.

She rushed forward and he backpedalled like he was about to be mugged. But not before she managed to grab his shoulder and kiss him on the cheek.

'Christ,' he said, appalled.

Sarah harried and bundled Red to the door, clearly keen to leave before Frank could come to his senses, shake off his (regrettably minor) stroke, and change his mind.

'Thank you, Frank. We'll see you on Monday morning!' she shouted as the door swung shut behind them with an ominous clunk.

He looked up, expecting to find Marcie still sitting on the mantelpiece with a huge smile on her face, but she had disappeared.

Frank stood there and stared at the ceiling.

'Fuck.'

PART THREE

RED

'Red, you *cannot* take all that.'

Red looked at everything he had laid out on the sofa in preparation for his first day next door. He had been wondering himself how he was going to fit it all into his Spider-Man backpack, but somehow he would just have to.

'But I've got to take it all. I've no idea what Frank likes.'

His mum started to sift through some of the items. 'Well, I can tell you for a fact that Frank is not going to want to play with your Nerf guns.'

'You don't know that.'

'And I very much doubt he's going to be desperate to play with your Iron Man glove, either.'

'Well, he can use the Hulk Smash Hands, then.'

His mum sat on the arm of the sofa. 'Look, I don't think you understand, Reddy. I'm pretty sure you're going to have to entertain yourself. Frank's not really a "Hey, it's playtime, kids!" kind of a guy. Y'know?'

'But he's *got* a kid.'

'Yeah, who's thirty-something. That *kid* is probably older than me. Maybe just take your tablet, some Lego. What about some books?' she suggested. 'Did you know Frank is an author?'

'What's that?'

'Well, it's somebody who actually *writes* books.'

'Frank? Really?'

'Yeah.'

'Like this one?' He held up *Walter the Farting Dog.*

'Yeah – not really. More like books for grown-ups. Not my sort of thing, but he won a really important book prize once. I think he was quite famous for a bit.'

'Oh,' Red said, only half-listening. His attention had returned to the pile on the sofa. He reluctantly began separating the stuff that he simply *had* to take from the stuff that he could, if *absolutely* necessary, leave behind.

The Iron Man glove, Hulk Smash Hands and the two Nerf Ultra Blasters went straight on the 'take' pile. To the other pile, he added a small Stormtrooper keyring.

He took a step back and thought for a moment, then moved the keyring back into the main pile.

His mum was now busying herself in the kitchen. 'What do you want on your sandwiches, Red?' she shouted. 'I figure I'll send you with your packed lunch; that way you won't starve, at least.'

'Ham, cheese and jam, with Wotsits in it, please!'

'Okay.'

'All together.'

'Obviously.'

Having now completely abandoned the idea of two piles, Red added a couple of books to the mound and then wandered into the kitchen. 'But you have to do some for Frank as well.'

'Red, Frank's not going to want to eat your—' She saw his frown. 'Fiiine. I'll do some for Frank as well. The pair of you will have to share your Fruit Shoot and crisps, though,' she said, stuffing his yellow Pikachu lunchbox. 'How's the arm?'

'S'okay.'

Her voice dropped. 'Listen, Reddy. I'm really sorry about all this. Y'know, that you have to go next door and everything.'

'I don't mind.'

'Maybe it'll only be for a day or two. I'm going to speak to your daddy again tonight, see if he can sort something out. And I'm going to have a word with my new boss as well: explain things, see if I can get a couple of days off.'

'Okay.'

She made a rasping noise with her lips, like a horse. 'This genuinely seemed like a good idea yesterday.' She zipped up his lunch and handed it to him. 'Okay, so let's see what you've managed to reduce that pile of stuff down to,' she said, following him back into the living room.

Red added his lunchbox to the top of the now teetering stack.

'Red! I mean it. You are *not* taking all that!'

FRANK

'What the bloody hell is all this?' Frank stared at the bags that were now cluttering his hallway: two carrier bags, a backpack, a lunchbox and a pull-along Avengers suitcase. 'Is he moving in or what?'

'It's his stuff, Frank. And it's about half of the crap he *wanted* to bring over here. Besides, I can't imagine you've got much in the house that would entertain a six-year-old. And, seriously, if you don't occupy him, God help you.'

Frank conceded the point, swearing under his breath. It was barely audible, but she caught it anyway.

'Which brings me to a couple of ground rules,' she said, awkwardly.

'Ground rules?!'

She held up her hands apologetically. 'Look, I don't feel great about this. I know you're doing us – you're doing me – a huge favour.'

Rules in my own house, Frank thought. *Christ on a bike.*

'They're really simple. And there are only three.' She held up her index finger. 'Number one: try to minimise the swearing. I don't want him going back to school effing and jeffing. It's bad enough they think he's a hooligan without him wandering back into class telling his teachers to "Piss up a rope, yez barstards."' She said this in his accent.

'I don't sound like that.'

Ignoring him she moved on to rule number two. 'He can play on his tablet, but for no more than an hour and a half. He will say "just one more minute" until he's blue in the face, but if you say no often enough, he *will* listen – like, eventually. And . . . rule number three.' She looked hesitant about this last rule, and spoke a lot more quietly as she nodded towards the empty beer bottles on the side. 'No drinking.'

He opened his mouth to protest, but she was already talking and moving again.

'So, I've got his packed lunch – *and* yours . . . don't ask.' She held up the lunchbox and placed it on the countertop. 'I hope you like ham, cheese, jam and Wotsits.' She looked at her phone, checking the time. 'Right, behave yourself, Reddy.' With no small effort and a loud groan, she lifted the boy off the ground and squeezed him. As she set him back down on his feet, the cast on his arm clunked her on the back of the head. She didn't seem to notice.

'And have a great day.' She looked around one more time, as though she was reconsidering the whole idea.

Frank had a flash of hope that she was going to change her mind, realise how ridiculous this whole thing was, and end the madness by scooping the kid up and taking him home.

'Okay, sorry. I really *do* need to go. I'll phone you in a bit!' she called over her shoulder as Frank followed her into the hallway. The door started to close behind her, then opened again, her head appearing through the gap. 'And Frank. Thank you. Again.'

When the door *did* finally close, Marcie was standing beside it. Her arms were folded, and she had a wide smile on her face.

'Shut up,' he grumbled.

RED

Frank's house reminded Red of a church.

He hadn't been in that many churches; the last time had been for Nanna Cath's funeral, ages ago. But he *did* remember that churches were dead quiet and felt like nobody ever opened the windows. And that's what Frank's house felt like. If he tilted his head, he could hear the fridge in the kitchen making an mmm-ing noise, like it was thinking. That's how quiet it was in Frank's house.

Red sat on the living room sofa and sighed.

He had been next door for twelve minutes.

And he was bored.

He wasn't sure what he had been expecting. From the outside, Frank's house had looked interesting, with its jungle garden and general wonkiness. Inside, though, Red found it looked disappointingly like their own. He hadn't really noticed this fact the day before (he had been too distracted by everything) but the hallway and stairs were in the same place, and the living room and kitchen were, too. Even the walls and carpets were a similar colour. The only real difference between this house and his own was that Frank's house had lots of photos on the wall, and old-people furniture in it.

Red sat on the old people's sofa and looked over at Frank, who was still sitting in the old people's armchair opposite, hidden behind a newspaper. The only way Red knew that the old man was awake and not dead was that his hand would occasionally appear, pick up the mug on the side table, and then put it back a moment later.

'Do you want to play I Spy?' Red said to the back of the newspaper.

No response.

At various times during the past twelve minutes, Red had asked Frank if he wanted to play hide and seek, Pokémon, Bakugan, The Floor is Lava, Smash Hands or a game of his own invention called Ultimate Death Warrior Battle Strike (in which you clattered two plastic figures together until one of their limbs fell off). Each time, there had either been no answer or a 'no' answer from behind the newspaper.

In fact, Frank hadn't said a lot of anything since Red had arrived. Mainly, he had just muttered to himself. The only time he had said more than the word 'no' was just after Red's mum had left that morning.

He had turned, as the front door closed, seemingly surprised to find Red – his best smile on his face – standing right behind him. He had then marched past, telling him that he was nobody's baby-sitter, but, since they were stuck together, he had a couple of rules of his own. If Red followed these rules, Frank said, they would get on just fine.

Frank's rules were:

1. Don't touch anything.
2. Don't get under my feet.

Both rules were easy to remember, but they made no sense. Because, if you thought about it, you couldn't not touch *anything* unless you could somehow levitate. And there was no way Red could get *under*

Frank's feet – unless he was shrunk to the size of Ant-Man or something.

He had pointed both of these things out to Frank, who had just muttered something about Jesus Christ giving him some strength. Then he'd asked if Red wanted a drink, before putting on the kettle and making them both a cup of tea.

Red had never had a cup of tea before. It was hot and tasted like bathwater, and he left it on the kitchen table as he followed Frank into the living room. There, after sitting in his armchair and pulling a lever that made the bottom of his chair – and his legs – stick out, Frank had disappeared behind the newspaper.

'What about Lego?' Red persisted now.

'No.'

'What about *Top Trumps*? I've got Avengers and Deadly Snakes.'

'No.'

'Or we could play *Uno*, I've got *Uno*!'

A page turned; the tea disappeared and then reappeared again.

Red tried to think of a game that Frank might be persuaded to play. Then he thought about giving up and digging into his backpack to find something he could play with on his own.

In the end, though, he decided to just wait. Frank was probably like his Auntie Stephanie and not 'a morning person'. So, he'd ask him to play again, but maybe after the old man had finished reading his newspaper.

While he was waiting, Red sat back and looked around at the living room.

Taking in his surroundings, He made a bubble-popping noise with his lips, something he always did when he got really bored.

Pop.

The ceiling was white and had swirls painted in it, like icing on a cake.

Pop.

Sunlight spilled on to a desk in front of the living room window, where dust drifted lazily. In the centre of the wall opposite Red was a fireplace, above which was a mantelpiece shelf with a silver clock and photographs in wooden and golden frames.

Pop.

Frank muttered something and straightened his newspaper with a flick.

On either side of the mantelpiece were ceiling-high bookcases that reminded Red of Mrs Mills's office, but unlike the shelves in Mrs Mills's office, the books here were all higgledy-piggledy, as though someone had actually been reading them.

Pop.

Pop.

Frank looked over his paper. 'Do you have to make that noise?'

'Sorry,' Red mouthed.

Frank returned to reading, while Red went back to staring at the ceiling. For twenty seconds, he followed the swirls.

. . .

Pop.

'Jesus *wept.*' Frank turned the newspaper over on his lap. 'What's the matter with you?'

Red's shoulders went up and down. 'I'm bored.'

'How can you be bored? You've only been here five minutes.' Frank gestured to the upended backpack. 'Look at all your stuff. Just play on your computer or something.'

It took Red a second to realise that Frank was talking about his tablet. 'Mummy says I can't play on my tablet until this afternoon. And only for an hour; it's a rule. Can't you play with me?'

Frank ignored the question. 'Well, do some colouring or Lego, or read one of your books.'

Red didn't really feel like colouring; it was awkward doing it with his arm in a cast and drawing with his wrong hand was dead hard. So was trying to do Lego. Reading a book didn't sound like much fun, either. Somehow the only books he had packed were rubbish *Biff and Chip* ones, books he was supposed to read for school, so he dismissed that idea too.

'My mummy says that you used to write books.'

'Uh huh.' Frank took a swig of his tea. He was now folding the newspaper over, testing a pen in the margins of the crossword page.

'Do you not write books anymore?'

'No.'

'Why not?'

'I just don't.'

'Right. Me and Noah wrote a book once. It was for a project. It was about a sausage that fell in a hole. It was chased by this dog and it fell in a hole. It was called *The Sausage That Fell in a Hole*.'

There was a tattered paperback book on the arm of the sofa, and Red started to turn it over in his hands. 'Is this one of your books?'

Frank glanced up, looking at Red over the top of his glasses. 'No.'

Red put the book down and walked over to examine the higgledy-piggledy bookshelf, while Frank began to scribble letters in black-and-white squares. Red sat cross-legged in front of the stack of books.

'What about this one? Did you write this one?' He heaved up the biggest book he could find from the bottom shelf and held it up awkwardly, balancing it on his arm cast.

'That's a dictionary.'

'What's it about?'

'It's . . . not *about* anything.'

'Oh. Well, that sounds rubbish.'

'What about this one?' Red held up the second biggest book.

'That's the Bible.'

'Oh, right. You didn't write it, then?'

'No.'

'Well, which one *did* you write, then? Frank? Frank?' Maybe it was Frank's hearing that was the problem. 'Which one did you write, then? . . . Frank? Frank?'

Breathing through his nose, Frank leaned over to his left and grabbed a book from the middle of the shelf by his side. Without looking up, he tossed it over to Red, who almost caught it one-handed, but spilled it into his lap. He turned it over to look at the cover.

'OUR LAD YOFF TRUNPICK?'

'*Our Lady of Turnpike*,' Frank corrected, still without glancing up.

'What's it about?'

Frank rubbed his eyes under his glasses. 'It's about a boy who won't shut up for five minutes, and so his head fell off.'

Red raised his eyebrows, unimpressed. 'What's it about *really*?'

Frank sighed. 'Well, it's about a boy who pretends he's seen the Virgin Mary.'

'What's a berjinmary?'

Frank finally looked up, his lip curled in disbelief. 'I thought you went to St Agnes? The *Virgin Mary*, for God's sake. She's Jesus's mother.'

'Oh, yeah, right.' Red turned the book over. Now he looked at the cover again, he realised it did have a picture of Jesus's mum on the cover, along with a picture of a boy praying at her feet.

'Is Kris Akabusi in it?'

'. . . Wha? No.'

'Hmm,' Red said, disappointed.

FRANK

The kid may have been disappointed that Kris Akabusi did not make an appearance in *Our Lady of Turnpike*. But of all the books Frank had written, *Our Lady* had always been his favourite.

It was the story of a boy caught in a lie about having a vision of the Virgin Mary, and how that lie saves the village and brings a community together. It was, by no means, his most popular book. It sold quite well, but never made it near a bestseller list – and the critics hated it. Absolutely hated it. One literary magazine described it as 'sentimental and trite', and a review in the *Scottish Sun* was particularly scathing in its view that: 'In *Our Lady of Turnpike*, Franklin Hayes has started writing like Les Dawson plays the piano: he still uses the right words, just in the wrong order.'

And yet, still, it was Frank's favourite.

The first draft was the most fun he had ever had writing. None of the toil of his first book, nor the writer's block and difficult birth of his second. He wrote *Our Lady* as though he merely had to empty the story from his brain. It was as though the words rolled from his head, down his arms, through his fingers and into his old word processor, like marbles in a loop. The whole thing fell on to the page in just four months, over a hot summer in 1996.

And if all books have a soundtrack, this book's music was the sound of a seven-year-old Mikey, along with Marcie and their old dog, Eddie, playing with a sprinkler in the back garden. It was Steely Dan on the stereo, and a houseful of kids from the neighbourhood, all accompanied by the regular tip-tapping of the keys on Frank's old Olivetti as he wrote the novel that the *Literary Review* would later describe as 'a waste of good trees'.

Marcie loved it. That's why the paperback in Red's hands was so dog-eared and well-thumbed: it was her copy, and she had read it a thousand times. And any sting of bad reviews was salved by her love of it. She never wavered from her own opinion that the critics hated it because he had committed the mortal sin of a successful writer and veered out of his lane. He had gone from writing something 'worthy' to something shamelessly commercial.

And 'Bollocks to the *Literary Review*,' was her considered opinion.

*

Red was still staring curiously at the book in his hands. He had found the author photo on the inside cover.

'Is this a picture of *you*?' He didn't wait for an answer. 'It doesn't look like you, much. You haven't got a beard in this picture. It makes your face look weird, like a potato.' He held up the page with the photo so Frank could see. '*And* you don't look super old.'

Frank looked up. 'That picture was taken thirty-odd years ago . . . Anyway, I'm sixty-seven now. That's not *that* old.'

'*Sixty-seven*? That's really, really old. My mum's old, and she's only thirty-two.' Red shook his head, as though he was trying to fathom how Frank could possibly still be alive. 'Did you have television when you were little?'

'Yes, we had television.' Frank didn't like the turn this conversation was taking, and went back to his crossword.

Red glanced out of the window. 'What about cars? Did you have cars?'

'Yes, we had cars.'

'What about . . . what about the pyramids? Did you have pyramids?'

Frank looked up. 'Yes, Red. The pyramids existed when I was a kid. What the hell do they teach you at that school? The pyramids are, like, thousands of years old.'

'Whoa,' Red said, impressed. Then: 'What about computers?'

'What about them?'

'Did you have computers?'

'Look, just . . . just . . . there's some kid's books on the bottom shelves there. *Beano* and stuff like that. Why don't you have a look at those?'

'I want you to play something with me,' Red pleaded again. 'You can choose what. I don't mind.'

Frank tried to remember whether Mikey had been like this when he was six. Relentless. He supposed he was. In every single memory Frank had of Mikey at this age, he was talking.

He and Marcie used to wonder whether this relentlessness was because Mikey was an only child, and consequently didn't have siblings to play and chatter with. (He was not an only child by choice; they were desperate for more kids. But what was that saying? 'You want to make God laugh? Tell him your plans.')

Whatever the reason, the one thing Frank *did* remember was that when that boy set his mind to something, it was a battle unwinnable.

'Look, let me finish my crossword, and *if* you can be quiet for half an hour, then maybe – and I mean *maybe* – we'll do something . . . fun.' The word 'fun' came out as though it was the word 'corpse'.

'Okay!' Red said, excitedly. He closed his mouth with an invisible zipper, locked it and carefully put the non-existent key into the pocket of his shorts. Then he shuffled back over to the bookshelves, dragging his backside along the carpet like a Labrador with worms. He found the shelf with children's books and pulled one from the middle of the pile, a *Beano* annual from 1989. He opened it to a torn front page, read a few words, then closed it again.

'Frank?'

'What now?' Frank sighed.

'I'm hungry.'

Frank looked at his watch.

It was 9.58am.

RED

Red was worried about Frank. He hadn't touched his ham, cheese, jam and Wotsit sandwich. Not even a single bite. He had just unwrapped it, peeled back the bread and then looked at it with the face that people make when they're at the park and they've stood in something bad.

Red however, had already finished his, and was sitting across from Frank at the kitchen table, fishing in his lunchbox for his crisps.

'Eurgh. Quavers,' Red said. Monster Munch were his favourites; pickled onion flavour was the best, because the crumbs at the bottom were really onion-y and sometimes made his ears get hot.

Frank was still making that stood-in-dog-muck face.

'Don't you like it? Your sandwich?' asked Red.

'I'm not hungry.'

Fair enough, thought Red, shrugging. He squeezed his bag of Quavers until it popped. 'What are your favourite crisps?' he asked, as he continued to crunch the bag so that the insides would be crushed to dust (it made them taste better). 'Oh, wait, I'll guess . . . Monster Munch?'

'Fine, yeah.' Frank stood up and put the milk back in the fridge.

'Same as me! My dad's girlfriend says that crisps are really bad for your teeth. She's a dental high genie. She says they're worse than chocolate and sweets, because the crumbs get stuck right in between and you'll never have nice teeth if you eat them.' Red tipped the contents of the bag into his mouth. 'But her teeth aren't even that nice,' he said through a mouthful. 'They're too big and white. My Auntie Steph says she looks like a beaver. I like most crisps – not really Frazzles, though. I like Hula Hoops; they're a bit too hard, but you can put them on your fingers and pretend that you've got lots of rings on.'

It was as Frank closed the fridge door that Red noticed the birds, and then the volcano, and then the dinosaur. It was his painting, stuck to the front of the fridge. It was *definitely* his – it had no yellow in it. And his name was written on the bottom.

'That's my picture,' Red said, interrupting himself.

'What?'

'On there, that's my picture. That's the one that I did.'

'Well it's—'

'How come it's on there? Did you get it out of the bin?' Red was delighted. He *knew* that it being in the bin must've been a mistake. And Frank had literally put his hand in the bin to rescue it. Totally gross.

'Yeah, well—'

'Did you get bin juice on you?' Red marvelled.

Frank murmured uncomfortably. Before he could answer, the phone rang.

Red jumped down from his chair. He always answered the phone at home. It was usually Auntie Steph or Daddy, but the thing about phones was, it could be *anyone*. He had once picked up the phone and had a long conversation with a woman who said she was calling because she knew he had had an accident 'at work or in the home'.

Red had no idea how the woman *knew* that he'd had an accident – that the day before he'd fallen off his scooter – but she kept interrupting, asking to speak to his mummy or daddy, and by the time he was explaining how big his knee scab was, she had got mad and hung up.

'I'll get it!' Red shouted.

'You will not.'

But Frank had barely finished his three-word sentence before Red had skidded into the hallway and picked up the receiver.

It was his mum. 'Hi, Reddy!'

'Mummy!' He put his hand over the mouthpiece, like a grown-up. 'It's Mummy,' he whispered to Frank.

'I don't have long,' she said quickly. 'I'm just on a quick break and I wanted to check you're okay.' Red could hear the clatter of the hospital canteen in the background. 'How's it going? How's the arm?'

'Good.'

'Great. And how's Frank? What've you two been up to?'

'Not much. I've not been on my tablet, and Frank was telling me about the berjinmary and about his book. And my picture is on his fridge, and he probably got bin juice on him, and I've just finished my dinner.'

'Oh, okay. Well, I hope you're behaving. I'll phone you again this afternoon. I won't be too late to pick you up, and I'll grab something to eat on the way home.' There was a muffled tannoy announcement in the background. 'Listen, baby boy, just put Frank on for a second, will ya?'

FRANK

'Dinner, Frank? It's half ten.'

'Well, I figured if he had food in his gob, he might stop banging on for five minutes.'

She laughed. 'Good luck with that.'

'I'd forgotten how much they talk,' he said, almost to himself.

'Yeah. I'd like to say he's at "that age", but he's been like that since he could open his mouth. Red didn't have a first word, he had a first paragraph. I told you this morning: occupy him or kiss goodbye to your sanity. Anyway, I just had a break and wanted to check he was okay, and that you're not already driving each other nuts. And to apologise. Sorry about being a bit . . . this morning. The rules and stuff,' she said, awkwardly. 'I mean, I know I'm being daft. I know it's not the first time you've looked after a kid, for God's sake. How old's your boy now?'

Frank thought for a second. 'Thirty-eight. No . . . thirty-nine.' Was Mikey really almost forty? It made him blink.

'Not so little, then? No grandkids yet?'

Frank let the lull in the conversation do its job, and Sarah returned to talking about Red.

'. . . So, I've arranged to work through my lunch and bring some paperwork home with me, so I should be able to pick him up for three, if that's okay?'

To Frank, three o'clock still seemed like a millennium away, but he had been expecting her to say she'd be back at five or five-thirty. He tried to hide the relief in his voice as he told her that was fine.

Red was dancing beside him in the hallway, as though he needed to pee. 'Can I speak to her again? I just need to tell her something super quick.'

'Right, okay. Hang on, he says he just wants to speak to you again.' Frank handed the receiver over to Red and wandered back down the hallway.

'Mummy?' Red jabbered excitedly. 'Just *guess* how old Frank is?'

This bloody kid.

*

'Right, what do you want to play?' Frank said, with all the enthusiasm of someone walking to the gallows.

Red had finished eating a while ago, but Frank had only just finished cleaning up after him. It wasn't just the breadcrumbs and crisps; it was the raisins. Red had insisted that he was capable of opening the tiny box on his own, and they had, inevitably, gone everywhere. And apparently those miniature packets held 40,000 of the bloody things.

To make matters worse, the kid had then found a jam doughnut in the bottom of his lunchbox. Which meant everything within reach was now sticky, and Red had so much jam around his mouth and chin that he looked as though he had been feasting, not on a doughnut, but on the blood of the innocent.

Having emptied the dustpan into the bin, Frank held the edge of a tea towel under the tap and passed it to the boy to wipe his mouth.

'You've got until one o'clock,' he said, as Red scrubbed his entire face, getting rid of most of the mess but moving a good glob of jam into his hair, where it made his fringe point to the ceiling.

'Okay!' Red replied enthusiastically.

'One,' Frank repeated, pointing at the kitchen clock. 'That's what time the snooker starts.' (Frank didn't really give a shit about snooker, but it did provide the ideal wallpaper to his afternoon nap.) 'So, that's two hours. What do you want to do?'

'Mmm.' Red squinted, thinking. '*Minecraft*?'

'I don't know what that is.'

'Oh, it's super awesome.' Red bounced on his chair. 'You can build things in your biome and spawn stuff like chickens and wolves. And you can kill the Ender Dragon, but only if you go through an End Portal into the Nether. But you have to be careful, because there are Endermen and drowneds and creepers and zombies. And you can craft things if you've got, like, flint and steel and—'

Frank held up his hand. 'Wait, wait, wait. I can hear you talking, but it's just noise and words and bollocks. Is this a computer thing?'

'Well, kind of. It's on my tablet.'

'Yeah, no.'

Red looked disappointed. 'What about Pokémon?'

'What's that?'

'So, you have Pokémon that are Electric types or, like, Ground types, and my favourite is probably Mewtwo, or Rayquaza, maybe Cubone. And you have to be a trainer, and you can evolve some of them. Like, Charmander can turn into Charizard, and . . .'

Frank felt as if he had landed on a foreign planet and he was trying to make first contact. 'What happened to Meccano and stuff? Have you not just got Lego or something?'

'Yeah, but I can't do it properly because of this.' Red held up his arm.

'Well, I'm not playing bloody Pokeymoon or whatever the other one is.'

Again, Red looked disappointed. 'What about I Spy then?'

'Fuck, no.'

'Aww,' the boy gasped.

'Yeah, I said a swear – get over it. What about cards, snap or something? I'm sure I've got a pack of cards around here somewhere.'

Red wrinkled his nose.

'Or – I don't know. A jigsaw?' Frank wasn't sure if they even owned a jigsaw. But the thought loosened something in his brain.

Mikey's room had remained virtually untouched since the day he'd left for university. That night, Marcie had sat on her son's bed, sobbing. (Frank had joked that their son hadn't died, just gone to Leeds.)

Since that day, she had treated his room as though it was a memorial. Really it was nothing so morbid; she just wanted their son to know that he was always welcome to come home. Leaving things exactly the way they were was her way of saying just that. She also threw nothing away, not when it came to Mikey. Frank was pretty sure there were a couple of board games still stacked on the top of his wardrobe.

'Right, wait here,' Frank said, seriously, before leaving the boy sitting at the kitchen table, and heading upstairs.

Mikey's single bed was pushed against the wall. By standing on it, Frank could see the boxes gathering dust. *Risk*, *The Game of Life*, *Guess Who?* and other games that had provided so many rainy days with scenes of family joy – and tantrums. There were even two jigsaws, which apparently had 2,000 pieces each and would reward the person who could be arsed to spend seven hours of their life on such a thing with either a cartoonish picture of London or a depressed-looking owl. Frank pushed these to one side and began to take the board games down.

He turned to see Red standing behind him.

'Jesus! Would you stop doing that? You scared the living shite from me!' Frank put one hand to his chest to double-check that his heart hadn't exploded. 'What do you not understand about "Wait here"?'

Red shrugged. 'I thought I'd come and help.'

'Help what? Help me have a bloody coronary?' Frank exhaled noisily. 'Here, grab these.' He coughed as he blew the dust off *Connect 4* and *Guess Who?*. The boxes were barely held together with parcel tape, and pieces clattered inside them as he passed them down to Red. 'Do not drop them,' Frank said deliberately, just as Red dropped them, a hundred game pieces scattering across the bedroom floor.

'Whoopsy-daisy.'

Frank looked at the ceiling, as Red bent to pick them up. 'Just – just leave it. Just wait for me downstairs.'

Red looked up, straightened, saluted once and marched backwards out of the room.

Back at the kitchen table, Frank assembled the pieces of the board for *Guess Who?*. Astonished that they all seemed to be there, he shuffled the cards and explained the rules.

'Right, So you're *sure* you understand, yeah?'

Red nodded.

'Okay. I'll go first.' Frank studied the cartoon faces half-heartedly.

'Has your chap got a beard?'

Red looked at his card. 'No. But he's got a hat.'

'You don't have to tell me that, Red. You just need to answer the question.' Frank knocked down a few of the plastic tabs. 'Your turn.'

'Okay, so . . . erm . . . does your person have a cat?'

'What? No. None of them have cats. Or dogs. Or – just ask whether they have a moustache or blue eyes.'

Red thought for a second. 'Is yours Alfred?'

'What?! No, you don't guess yet. You have to eliminate people by asking questions.'

'You said I could guess anytime.'

'Yeah, but not on your first turn!'

'Oh, right.'

Frank looked down at his card.

Bloody Alfred.

'I mean, it *is* Alfred. But that's not how you play.'

'Cool. One nil to me!'

'Unbelievable,' Frank muttered to himself.

He started to shuffle the cards for another game, while Red disappeared into the living room. 'What are you doing in there?' Frank called.

'One sec,' Red replied. A moment later, he came back with a pad of coloured paper from his bag and Frank's crossword pen. He smoothed the pad flat on the table and then scratched down the score.

Red: 1 – FrAnK: 0

Frank shook his head. 'Lucky bugger.'

RED

It was just after three o'clock when his mum arrived to pick him up.

'Sorry I'm a bit late. I got collared in the car park by my new boss.'

'Mummy!' Red jumped up and wrapped his arms around her legs.

'Hey, baby boy! . . . Sorry, Frank, the front door was open.'

Frank hit the lever on his chair that lowered his legs.

'I did just quickly nip to the shop on my way home, hope you don't mind. Just to grab some tea.' She held up two Tesco carrier bags. 'But I got you a few bits as well . . .'

'Frank's just been telling me the rules for snooker!' Red said.

'Oh?'

'Yeah. You have to be dead quiet when it's on, and these two misters' – Red pointed at the TV; he was now sitting just a few inches away from the screen – 'have to hit the white ball into another ball with a stick, and then if *that* ball goes in one of the holes, you get some points. And if you got more in than the other man, you get millions of pounds. And this mister' – he singled out one of the men dressed in black and white – 'is a "showboat" and "an absolute tool".'

'Riiight. Okay,' his mum said, frowning in Frank's direction. She put down one of the bags at her feet, and placed the other, with bread and milk peering out of the top, on the table. There, she noticed the game laid out. 'Ooh, *Guess Who?*. I used to love *Guess Who?*. I always had a weird crush on Philip.'

Frank and Red both made a face.

'So . . .' She turned her attention back to them. 'How'd it go?'

*

Frank had been asleep in his armchair for half an hour. His snoring sounded like a cow growling. Red knew that cows didn't growl, but that's what it sounded like, anyway. The only other sound was from the TV: the dull knock of snooker ball on snooker ball, with the occasional splash of applause.

By the time they had finished playing *Guess Who?*, the score was five-two to Red. He would have happily continued playing, but they'd had an argument during the last game because Frank said that Richard didn't have hair. This, of course, wasn't true. Richard *was* bald, but he had hair on his chin.

'That's not hair. That's a beard,' Frank had said.

'What's it made out of, then?' Red had insisted.

That was when Frank seemed to suddenly remember that the snooker had started, and so that was the end of the game.

Red sat cross-legged in front of the fireplace as Frank slept. The *Guess Who?* cards were laid out on the floor in front of him. He had started out memorising the names; who had blue eyes, who had a hat. But eventually he had just begun making up stories in his head for each of the characters, imagining who might be friends with whom, which of them were married to each other, and who would win in a fight (probably Herman).

That decided, Red pulled out the *Beano* annual again and flicked through it for a while. Finding more torn and scrawled-on pages, he put it back in its place. Bored again, he stood up and traced his fingers across the bookshelves and then the photographs on the mantelpiece.

Many of the photo frames were filled with pictures of a boy. He had dark, shoulder-length hair and a wide smile. In one of the pictures, the sea was in the background, and the boy had a crab between his thumb and finger. He was holding it up to the camera.

Alongside these were a couple of class photographs and an old brown-and-white still of a man and woman getting married, a long time ago. They didn't seem to be very happy about it, and it looked like they wanted to punch whoever was taking their picture.

And then there were photos of Frank and a lady Red guessed was his wife. In one of these pictures, the boy was on Frank's shoulders, his bare feet dangling. Red wouldn't have recognised this young Frank if he hadn't seen the photo on the cover of his book earlier. He looked so happy, with his arm draped around his wife, or with a pint of beer held aloft and a face crumpled with laughter. It was an expression that Red couldn't imagine making an appearance on the face of the man now sitting a few feet away, sleeping soundly and making that growling-cow noise.

Red wandered into the kitchen. He straightened his picture on the fridge, and then decided to explore further, mapping the house in his brain the same way he did with the corridors of St Agnes.

It was ten paces from the living room to the kitchen and the back door. This was *exactly* the same as next door. (Red knew this because during Kika and Amit's school visit, Amit had explained how blind people sometimes got around by counting paces, and Red had tried to do the same, navigating his own house with his eyes closed.) It was another ten paces from the kitchen to the front door, and the bottom of the stairs.

Red hesitated here, due to the fact that Frank had said that upstairs was 'off-limits'. (This was after he had followed Frank as he'd fetched the games. 'Kitchen, garden, living room, whatever. But not upstairs.')

'What if I need a pee?'

'Well, obviously if you need the toilet, but – you know what I mean.'

Red mentally checked to see if he needed the toilet now, and decided that he didn't. But when he thought about it, he decided that this 'off-limits' thing was probably more like a guideline than a rule. And besides, Frank was fast asleep. The growling cow-noise from the living room had increased, and now sounded more like Godzilla attacking a small city.

So, slowly, he ventured up the stairs.

Red noticed a black rail running against the wall. At the top of the stairs, where the rail ended, there was a beige office-type chair. He hadn't noticed the chair earlier, as it was folded and camouflaged against the magnolia wall. But he soon worked out that the rail was actually a train track for the chair so it could go up and down. Red ran his hands over a box that dangled from it on a curly wire.

On the landing, a bulb hung from the ceiling, the lampshade for which was discarded on a windowsill to one side. The bathroom door stood open. A metal frame, with a towel slung over it, leaned beside a sink cluttered with bottles and soap.

Pushing open the door into the boxroom, Red found it largely empty but for a small bed with a bare mattress. He caught a familiar lemon smell from the clothes dryer by the window, which had oversized pants and socks hanging from it like a sad Christmas tree.

Next, he peered into what had to be Frank's bedroom. It was darker and untidier than the rest of the house. A wall of sliding grey doors to one side faced a window with half-closed curtains. There were clothes on the floor, and too much stuff on the tables that sat either side of the big unmade bed. An electronic clock with red glowing digits flickered from beneath two or three books. Its face said '14:15'. Red gently pulled the door closed without going inside.

He had been in the remaining room already, but hadn't had much time to look around before Frank had ordered him back downstairs. It was brighter in here, and was the same size as his own room next door. Instead of his Pokémon and *Toy Story* pictures on the walls, though, there were other posters. One just had a woman smoking on it, and another one above the bed said 'THE DOORS' in big letters. It didn't have any doors on it, though: just four men in black and white who looked like they were in a really bad mood.

In one corner, there was a computer desk with no computer – just a mirror standing on it, leaning against the wall. Surrounding it were tickets tucked into its edges. One was for something called 'Half Man Half Biscuit', and one was sealed in plastic and hung on a string from the corner of the mirror: 'T in the Park 2001'.

There was a rack hanging from the wall with three or four CDs in its slots, but mainly empty spaces. Red took one down and examined it, fascinated. 'CD' stood for compact discs. Auntie Steph had lots of them, and had told Red that in the olden days, you played them on a machine to get music to happen. Red looked for a machine, but couldn't see one.

Finally he looked inside the wardrobe. It was empty, just a few coat hangers swinging lazily as he closed its doors again.

Red stepped back out on to the landing and sat on the top stair.

Thinking about nothing in particular, he pulled at the spiralling wire that dangled from the chair until the control panel was in his hand. There were just two buttons on it – two arrows. He pressed one, and was surprised that the chair made a humming noise. He was even more surprised when he pressed the other button and the chair began to move down the stairs.

Cool. Like something from the future.

Red lowered the seat and armrests, then settled himself in the chair and prepared for lift-off. He whispered to himself in his best astronaut's voice: 'Five, four, three . . .'

Gritting his teeth, he reached 'one' and braced himself against the G-force as he pressed the ↓ arrow hard. And set off – in disappointingly slow motion.

By the time Red was a quarter of the way down the stairs, he was fed up of spaceflight, so he jumped off and walked the rest of the way. Back in the hallway, he realised – that was that – there was nowhere left to explore. Disappointed – and now *really* bored – he was thinking about waking Frank up. Then he passed the hallway dresser.

He stopped and took two steps back.

Wait a sec.

The dresser had two drawers, and the left-hand one was slightly skewwhiff and ajar. Just enough to get his fingertips in and pull it open further. Which he did.

The drawer was surprisingly full of stuff: Post-it notes and tiny cards, a big box of matches with a telephone number scrawled on it, a car key with a piece of card threaded through its eye, on which someone had written 'Val Spare'. There was a leaflet with a picture on the front of a candle with spikes surrounding it. And another one with a photo of a steaming pizza. Red sighed. It was full of stuff, but this drawer was turning out to be just as boring as the rest of the house.

As he pushed the drawer closed, though, it caught on something and stubbornly refused to move. He jiggled it a couple of times, but it still wouldn't budge. Red knelt down and closed one eye to peer into the gap, and saw that the drawer was caught on a ball made of rubber bands, nestled at the back.

Treasure, Red thought.

He jiggled the drawer a little more, trying to free the ball, but still it wouldn't relent. Finally, with his last jiggle, he pulled the whole thing towards himself a little too hard. With only one good arm, Red could do nothing to stop it as the drawer came off its runners and fell to the floor in front of him with a clatter.

The rubber-band ball went bouncing down the hallway and stopped at Frank's feet. He was standing in the doorway of the kitchen, bleary eyed from his afternoon nap.

'What the bloody hell are you doing?' he said lazily, scratching the back of his neck.

'Nothing,' Red replied sheepishly. 'I was just – I just wanted that.'

Frank bent down to pick up the rubber-band ball, with a groan. He tossed it to Red. 'Well, do you want to stop destroying the place?' He coughed and turned towards the kettle. Red could hear him filling it at the tap before he poked his head back into the hallway. 'And stay out of the drawers and cupboards.'

Red started to put away the stuff that had fallen out of the drawer: the leaflets, the matchbox, and the car key, which had skidded to a rest by the front door mat. It was then that he saw something familiar: the letter that had accidentally been delivered to their house next door. It was on the pile still in the drawer, and he recognised the waxy paper of the envelope and the handwriting on the front. It was torn open and had a card inside. Without thinking, Red pulled out the card and turned it over.

Michael and Ellie
invite you to the Christening
of their beautiful baby daughter

Mirabelle Marcie Hayes

on Sunday 2nd July
at St Wilfred's Church, Wimbledon at 2pm

(and afterwards at their home
148 Castlegate Road, S. Wimbledon SW19 1DE)

r.s.v.p. ellie5538@gmail.com – 07955 220981

'Just leave that drawer,' Frank called from somewhere in the kitchen. 'I'll sort it. It's awkward, and you'll never get it back in with one arm.'

'Okay!' Red shouted in return. He dropped the envelope back on top of the stuff in the drawer, then grabbed the car key and dropped that on top of the pile, too.

He picked up the ball, squeezed it in his hand and then bounced it down the hallway and into the kitchen, before hopping after it.

FRANK

'So, did Frank let you win?' Sarah asked, raising her eyebrows at him. The boy had just finished explaining that after Frank's nap, they'd had two more games of *Guess Who?*, both of which Frank had lost. He was holding up the pad for his mum to see:

Red: 7 – FrAnk: 3

'No, I won fair and square. Didn't I, Frank?'
'I don't know about fair and square,' Frank muttered.
Sarah laughed, and Red smiled at the sound.
'So, listen Frank.' She picked up the carrier bag at her feet and patted the contents. 'I'm just going to make a chilli or something. You're welcome to join us; I always make too much, anyway. I could even cook and we could eat it here, if you don't want to . . . y'know.' She tipped her head in the direction of next door.

Frank knew full well what 'y'know' meant: It meant 'if you can't walk out of your own house and into someone else's, like a normal person'.

He stood up. 'No, thank you,' he said with finality. 'I'd sooner just get my house back today, if that's alright with you.'

For a moment, he felt strangely aware of how rude he sounded; it felt like a joke falling flat. And so he heard himself adding, 'Erm, thank you, though, for the shopping, and whatever.'

'S'fine,' she replied, obviously amused. 'Thank *you* for today. I have tried again to get his dad to do his bit, but he's still "very busy" apparently.' She said this with a shake of the head. 'And I don't see me getting any time from work this week; that's what I was talking to my boss about in the car park. She wasn't overly impressed about me asking. We've got a full ward at the minute, and, well . . . So, yeah, I guess, same time tomorrow?'

Frank nodded. 'Uh huh.'

'Great!' She seemed a bit surprised by his response and nodded enthusiastically. 'Is it okay to leave his stuff here, then?'

'Well—'

'No point in us taking it back home, I suppose. Come on, Reddy.'

Red jumped up and skipped to the door behind his mum. He turned to Frank and waved. 'See ya later, baked potato.'

Frank didn't have the faintest idea how to reply to that, and so he just stood there as the door closed behind them.

'I think that went pretty well,' Marcie said.

Frank rubbed his eyes wearily. 'It'll be a long week; I know that much.'

'Kind of funny having a little one in the house again, though, eh?'

'Jesus Christ!' Frank cursed. As he'd walked back into the kitchen, he'd slipped on something. 'Funny?' He lifted his foot and began to unpeel the piece of doughnut now stuck to the bottom of his slipper. 'That's one word for it.'

RED

That night, Red felt quite grown up. He had never had to do home-work before, but it was one of the 'conditions' of his enforced absence: his daily Reflection Diary.

His mum took the first sheet from an envelope and handed it to Red, along with a pencil. Bits of the sheet were already filled in:

Name	Leonard Evans		
Class	2	Day	1

Reflection Diary

Parents note: During your child's period of absence/reflection time, it is important that they complete this diary at the end of each day. Please encourage your child to make a note of what they have done during the day, their feelings and anything that they may have learned.

What I did today:

I went to Frank's. He is very old and doesn't go out of the house, except sometimes to the bins. His wife is dead. We played a game called Guess Who and I won. I watched snooker. Frank has got a robot chair on his stairs.

FRANK

It was Frank's idea to fix the fence.

Supposedly, the longest day of the year was the 22nd of June, but Frank begged to differ. The longest day of *his* year had been yesterday. Or at least, it had felt like it. The boy just never stopped talking. And the second day of this week – a week that Frank had begun to refer to as 'the invasion' – had begun in exactly the same way.

Maybe with a project like the fence to focus on, the kid would stop jabbering for five minutes, and Frank could escape the coming days with a shred of his sanity intact. Besides, that fence was the only thing that separated his garden from next door's. And it was a vital barrier for life beyond this week, when things could mercifully go back to normal.

'Normal?' Marcie had scoffed when he had said this out loud. 'Frank, you're a sixty-seven-year-old man who does his shopping by banging on a neighbour's door with a big stick. Oh yeah, your life is super normal.'

She had a point. He didn't like it.

Actually, it wasn't just the kid's constant blather that was the problem. It was the questions. As soon as he had walked through the door this morning – endless questions. The boy could ask three questions in a row, and there would be nothing like a sane thread to connect any of them. Did Frank think dinosaurs could sneeze? Did Frank think that cheese was weird?

And then a million and one questions about the photographs.

The house was full of photos. Frank used to complain about it all the time: the walls they filled, the clutter they made on every surface. But after their second pregnancy failed, he had come downstairs one night in the week that followed and found Marcie sitting at the kitchen table, framing even more snaps from their albums. He had asked her why, and she had replied that life was full of shitty moments, so the perfect ones deserved wall space.

He'd stopped complaining.

And Marcie had added more and more as she got ill.

Now, as Frank was trying to superglue a handle on to a broken mug that had been sitting by the kitchen sink for months, Red's incessant questioning had turned to the pictures on the mantelpiece.

The boy had spent half an hour taking them down from the shelf in the living room, one by one, and holding them up so Frank could look up and see them from the kitchen table.

At that moment, Red seemed particularly fascinated by a photo he had found tucked at the back: a picture of Frank, Marcie, Fat Ken, Sal, Jonny and the old landlord, Walt, all standing outside The Flea, drinks in hand, all in fancy dress for Ken's birthday. It was clear that Red was trying hard to reconcile how the Frank sitting at the kitchen table could be the same person as the man in the picture, a Frank standing half behind the landlord, wearing a riotous shirt and caught laughing as he threw bunny-ear fingers up behind Walt's head.

'So . . . that's you?'

'Yeah.'

'That *there* is *you*?'

'Yes, it's me.'

Red put the photograph back down.

'What about this one?' he said, picking up another.

'That's my mother, that's my father, and that's me in the pram.'

Red was no less astounded to find that Frank had not entered the world as a fully formed adult. 'What?! That *there* is *you*?'

'Uh huh.'

'The *baby*?' Shaking his head, Red moved on to the next photo. 'What about this one?'

Michael.

There were a couple of school photos of Mikey on the mantelpiece, but Red was holding up the framed polaroid taken on Southend beach. Frank's son was grinning, his hair wet on its ends and dusted with sand. He was holding a crab. Frank remembered that day well. Mikey had been disappointed not to catch something in his new fishing net and bucket, and so Frank had sneaked away to a shellfish stand beneath the pier, bought a dressed crab, and then surreptitiously dropped it at Mikey's feet, as though it had just been washed in on the surf. That's what he was delightedly holding up to the camera.

'That's your little boy?'

'Yeah.'

Red examined the picture more closely. 'Why doesn't he live here?'

Frank turned his attention back to applying superglue to the mug handle. 'Because he's got his own house. He's a man now. He moved out, got married.'

'Well, why doesn't he come here to visit then? I've never seen him.'

'He just doesn't.'

'Why not?'

Frank sucked his teeth. He had almost got the handle to stick, but it had moved at the last second. 'He just doesn't.'

Red looked at a few more photographs before finally settling on a picture of Marcie. It was Frank's favourite picture of her. Unaware that her photograph was being taken, she was leaning against a tree, smoking a cigarette, and laughing with somebody just out of shot. Red held it up.

'That's Marcie.' Frank swallowed.

'Your wife?' Red tilted his head and examined the picture more closely. 'She looks like she's out of a film or something. Is this when you were getting married?'

Frank could understand why Red might think that the picture was taken on their wedding day. The dress she was wearing did look like a simple bridal dress: it had lace at the edges, and in the monochrome photograph it looked white.

But it had been pale blue. A bridesmaid's dress. And the photograph had not been taken on *their* wedding day, but on the day they met.

Well, not quite the day they met.

That had been a fortnight earlier. A moment of purest destiny for both of them. A singular moment. A moment of life-defining romance that would be forever etched on Frank's mind – not least because Ken had just been hit in the face by a large purple dildo.

*

It was 1983. A Saturday night in Neary's, a working men's club established to serve the enormous docks nearby. It was busy in a way that pubs always were back then, especially on a Saturday night. People barely had the elbow room to bring their glasses to their mouths, and a trip to the three-deep bar was an expedition of cajoling and apologies. The air on these nights was thick with clouds of rising smoke from cigarettes and the faintly sweet smell of Harmony hairspray.

Generations overlapped here. Seventy-year-olds would sit on the barstools that had been theirs for decades, raising their eyebrows and shaking their heads at the way the youngsters were dressed, as though they were creatures from outer space or wearing costumes in a play about the future.

Frank and Fat Ken were Saturday-night regulars. Not by choice. The young Frank was charged by his dad with walking his elderly grandma to and from the club for her weekly drink, and Ken was ever-present because his mum was a barmaid, and he could sneak the occasional free pint.

That night, they were sitting at a table in one corner. They were both just short of their nineteenth birthdays, and still had that peculiar awkwardness of the teenager, not helped by Ken's acne or the barely there moustache that ghosted Frank's upper lip. Each had hair that touched their shoulders at the back, spiked carefully on the top. Frank was wearing his brother's grey PVC jacket and Ken – who was, at the time, obsessed with *Miami Vice* – was dressed in a white vest under an electric-blue blazer that he'd rolled up at the sleeves, as though he was relaxing on Ocean Drive rather than sitting in a working men's club, licking out the crumbs from a packet of pork scratchings.

'Do you have to do that, Kenny?' Frank said, glancing around with concern that Ken was seriously detracting from their 'cool'.

'Do what?'

'Do that – with the bag.'

'I'm hungry.' Annoyed, Ken screwed up the packet, tossed it into the ashtray and took a swig of his pint.

And that was when a large, ten-inch purple dildo hit Frank on the shoulder, bounced off, slapped Ken in the face, and then finally landed on the table in front of them, wiping out their drinks and drenching Ken's trousers in snakebite.

'What the—?!' They both recoiled backwards.

A hush descended as all eyes turned their way: a silence that was punctured a moment later by a single voice from the other side of the bar shouting 'Wahey!', the traditional pub response to the sound of breaking glass.

Slowly, the club returned to normal as the jukebox mercifully restarted with the opening bars of 'My Sharona'. Frank and Ken looked at each other, and then confusedly at the alien object now on the table in front of them, nestling in a puddle of beer and crisps.

'Well, *I'm* not touching it,' Ken said.

'Well,' Frank replied. 'Where the hell did it come from?'

'I dunno.'

They both studied it again, for a long moment.

'Massive, innit?' Ken observed.

That's when she appeared, pushing her way through the throng. Marcie.

She arrived at their table, breathless, as if birthed by the crowd. They each just looked at her, stunned. For Frank, it was as though he was staring at an entirely new species of human.

Her eyes were framed by dark eyeliner in a way that made her seem cat-like, and her hair was black and close-shaved on one side. She wore a Boomtown Rats T-shirt, torn at the neck, and a denim jacket that hung from both shoulders. Over the top was a home-made pink ribbon sash that read 'Bridesmaid' in ornate silver lettering.

'Sorry,' she said, apologetically. She reached in and picked up the dildo by one end. 'It's not mine,' she continued, as the member flopped awkwardly from side to side in her hand.

An elderly man sitting at the bar a few metres away looked on in disgust and audibly tutted. Marcie turned in his direction and held the thing aloft like a perverted Statue of Liberty.

'It's not mine,' she repeated, gesturing with it towards the old man. She turned back to Frank and Ken. 'I really am sorry,' she said, registering the mess of their table and the beer pooled in Ken's crotch. 'It was supposed to be a joke gift for my sister. She's getting married.' The girl tugged at her 'Bridesmaid' sash, as though that explained everything.

'Marcie!' A female voice shouted from the depths of the club behind her.

'Sorry, just a sec.' Without a beat of hesitation, she turned around and threw the dildo over the heads of the crowd, back in the direction from which she – and it – had come. 'So, yeah,' she said, returning her attention to their conversation.

They were still too busy gawping at her to respond.

She looked vaguely confused by their silence but went on: 'My sister opened the box, saw it, and panicked, I think. Anyway, she threw it, and it landed on someone else. Then *they* threw it, and, well . . . eventually, it landed here.'

'. . . Erm. It's fine,' Frank said regaining his ability to speak, although his voice broke in a way it hadn't for years. 'No harm done,' he continued, in what he hoped was a more manly timbre.

She smiled at him, seeming to size him up.

'Speak for yourself, Frank,' Ken interrupted. 'You know how sticky cider is.' He pulled his trousers away from his crotch. 'My balls are already stuck to my leg.'

'I'm Frank,' Frank said. 'This is Kenny.'

'Cool . . . I like your jacket,' she said, in a gently mocking way that made Frank want to burn it and forget that it had ever existed. 'I'm Mar—'

An enormously tall blonde girl suddenly barrelled through the crowd and grabbed her by the shoulder. 'Mars, we've got to go! It's landed in the meat raffle; Terry's going absolutely bananas.'

'Right, well, sorry again. Looks like I'm off!' She turned away, but then turned back, apparently to address them both, but with her eyes on Frank. 'But we're heading into town. You should come.'

Frank's eyes widened. He almost glanced around to check that she wasn't talking to someone else.

He was about to answer before Ken interrupted. 'He can't,' he said. 'He's got to take his nan home at half ten.' Ken nodded towards an ancient woman sitting at the table next to them. Her arms were folded, and she was peering over at them with a face like a cat's arse. The old woman caught Frank's eye and casually stuck a middle finger up at him.

'Sorry. She's a bit . . .' Frank explained, twirling his finger at his temple.

'Mar!' The blonde girl tugged on her sleeve again. Marcie looked reluctant to leave, torn between her conversation and her friend's insistence.

'Okay.' She smiled. 'Well, I guess I'll see you around!'

And then she allowed herself to be dragged away by her friend and disappeared into the throng, leaving behind only a wafting disturbance in the blueish cigarette smoke. To Frank, it made her seem mystical, beautiful, a thing otherworldly.

'Twat,' his nan called over.

*

It was two weeks later when Frank and Marcie's paths crossed again.

Following their first meeting, Frank found himself thinking constantly about the girl who had crashed momentarily, and breathlessly, in and out of their lives that night. He had been vaguely aware that women like this existed. Maybe in New York, or London – but not here in Dublin, and definitely not on the Northside.

To Frank, she was so utterly out of place she may as well have ridden up to their table that night on a unicorn.

In the days that followed, Frank bored Ken to distraction as he persistently turned conversations back to the subject of *her*. She had spoken fewer than a hundred words, and Frank plumbed each one for meaning. 'What do you think she meant by "You should come"? What do you think she meant when she said, "See you around"?' he asked Ken, as though she had been speaking a foreign language.

Eventually, as they were enjoying a lunchtime pint one day, Ken decided he had heard enough. He stood up suddenly, muttering 'Sod this,' and then disappeared. He returned five minutes later with a scrawled-upon beer mat. 'Right, this is her phone number.'

'What? How the hell did you get that?'

'Long story, but that girl she was with, she used to go to our school. She was in the year above. Holly Boones?' He looked at Frank's blank expression with exasperation. 'Everyone called her Ladders?'

'Right, yeah.' Frank nodded, recognising the nickname.

'Well, we had a thing for a bit . . .'

'You and *Ladders*?'

'Yes. Never mind. Look, just – just listen,' Ken sputtered impatiently. He went on to explain that a quick phone call to Holly Boones had produced her *full* name: one Marcie Scott. 'And with a little of the Kenneth Browning charm,' he said, smoothing an eyebrow with his index finger, 'her phone number.'

He tapped his finger on the scrap of card on the table between them, before sitting back with satisfaction.

Frank looked down at the beer mat as though it had energy.

'Now, *please*, just phone her,' Ken said. 'Not because I think you're made for each other. Not because I think she's the love of your life. Not for any of those reasons. Do it for me; do it because you're boring my tits off now, and if you keep going on about her, I'm going to punch you in the dick.'

Frank never did use the number.

And not just because he didn't have a telephone at home. Three times, he'd stood in the phone box at the end of their street, his T-shirt pulled up over his nose and mouth to mask the aroma of piss and chips. But every time he'd begun to dial, he had returned the phone to its cradle again, certain that he was making a mistake.

His initial excitement at having her phone number had given way to a melancholy, a certainty that she wouldn't even remember who he was. And even if she did, in what universe would she have any interest in him, anyway? Better to avoid the humiliation of that.

And then the gods of small towns intervened.

Frank knew that the hen night Marcie had been enjoying was in honour of her sister's wedding. What had *not* occurred to him was that this might be the very same wedding he and Ken had been invited to that weekend, that of their schoolfriend, Martin 'Pilot' Winter. ('Pilot' was not Martin's occupation, but a nickname he had acquired due to the fact that – like the pilot light on a boiler – Martin never went out.)

It wasn't until the morning of the wedding itself that Frank looked at his invitation closely, saw the bride's name was 'Scott' and realised, with a feeling that made his stomach drop, that *she* would be there.

When Ken knocked on his door that afternoon, Frank answered with the invitation in his hand. 'Pilot's marrying her sister. That girl, Marcie, she's gonna be there!' he said.

'Yeah, I know,' Ken replied, leaning forward as he ate a melting chocolate ice lolly and tried not to get any on his white suit.

'What?'

'Yeah, I know. Holly told me.'

'And you didn't think to mention it to me?'

'Forgot.' Ken chased his Feast ice lolly around its stick. The last of it dropped off, a large splodge of chocolate ice cream landing on his white loafers. 'Bastard,' he said, disappointed.

A few hours later, they arrived at the wedding reception. It was being held in the 'good' room of the club, a function room set aside for weddings, funerals and birthdays: those life milestones worthy of being marked by cocktail sausage rolls, a DJ and kids doing knee skids on a varnished floor.

The room was filled with balloons and noise, and against a back wall hung a waterfall of silver tinsel with the words 'Just Married' in four-foot-high lettering.

As they entered, Frank scanned the scene, looking for her, eventually turning his attention to the long table at the head of the room. It was a classic Renaissance-style tableau of an eighties wedding. Sitting in the middle was a smiling bride with gravity-defying hair. She was wearing a shiny, polar-white dress with puffed ruffles that made it look as though her shoulders were exploding. (For one disconcerting moment, Frank thought this was *her*, so much did the bride look like her younger sister.) Next to her was the uncomfortable-looking groom, sipping a pint of Guinness. On one side of this happy couple was a mulleted best man dressed in the same brown suit and chevroned tie as Martin, and on the other side, Martin's mum and dad. Finally, a handful of bored bridesmaids stood listlessly around the table.

But no Marcie.

Disappointed, Frank followed Ken to an empty table at the back, wheeling his ever-present nan in her wheelchair in front of him. (Frank had objected to having to bring her but, 'It's Saturday, Franklin,' his dad had said with finality, and that was that.)

As Ken began to ask what they wanted to drink, Frank took a seat, and discovered that from this lower angle, he could see another bridesmaid, sitting cross-legged on the floor behind the top table. She was playing with, or telling a story to, a little girl, who was laughing animatedly.

It was *her*.

He watched her for a few moments. Her side-shaved hair was exactly as it had been the week before, but other than that she seemed every inch a copy of the other bridesmaids – until Frank noticed the black work boots that poked out from beneath the hem of her pale blue dress, rendering the whole outfit both absurd and perfect.

Seeming to sense she was being watched, she looked up and caught his eye. Before Frank could turn away, embarrassed to have been caught staring, she smiled and waved at him.

'So, what do you want to drink, Franko?' Ken said, interrupting the moment. In the seconds it took for Frank to turn towards Ken, answer him and turn back, Marcie was no longer sitting there. She was taking her place at the wedding table, as a chinking of fork against glass silenced the room and Martin stood up to deliver the first of the speeches.

For the next hour, the crowd responded to the words of each speaker in the well-worn tradition of every wedding speech since time began. They 'aahed' at the declarations of love, and laughed with enthusiasm at the jokes, whose main theme was the death of Martin's freedom and the apparent tyranny of the marriage to come.

Eventually, the best man finished his speech with a toast to bride and groom: 'They say you don't marry the person you can live with,' he said with rehearsed sincerity. 'You marry the person you can't live without. Ladies and gentlemen, to Martin and Becky!'

'To Martin and Becky,' the crowd replied.

As glasses were lowered and the audience sat back down, the best man remained standing. '. . . As a lot of you will probably know,' he said sombrely, 'Becky's dad is no longer with us. I'm sure he's looking down delighted and proud of you today.' He tilted his head and smiled towards the bride. 'But in his absence, Becky's sister Marcie would like to say a few words. Erm . . . yeah.'

He handed the microphone to Marcie, who stood up to address the increasingly restless crowd. To Frank's annoyance, people continued their conversations, chairs scraped, and old men coughed. Speaking into this indifference, Marcie began her forty-second speech.

'I didn't really know our dad.' She looked down at her sister, who was smiling through eyes already glazed with tears. 'He died when I was two and our Becks was six. And I've no idea whether he's looking down today. I'm not sure how much I believe in all that stuff.' She shuffled in place. 'But one thing I do know is that I am proud that you are my sister. You have been my best friend since the moment I drew breath.

'You are a lucky man, Pilot,' she continued, turning towards Martin. 'She is special. And you're an idiot if you don't know that.' She looked as though she was about to sit down, having finished, but had a second thought. 'And if you break her heart, I will kill you.'

The best man began to reach for the microphone awkwardly, 'Okaaay, thank you Mar . . .'

She kept going. 'I will kill you in the most painful way you could ever imagine, and then I will bury you in the woods, so you are never ever found—'

The best man finally secured the microphone, and the two sisters, both now in tears, hugged.

For a long few seconds, the room was largely hushed, apart from a squeak of microphone feedback and the noise of a laughing Ken applauding enthusiastically.

And quietly, barely audible at all, the sound of Frank's nan as she leaned over to him and said the most coherent words she had uttered in years: 'I like her.'

*

Frank tried to pick up the mug, but it wouldn't shift. He had somehow managed to superglue the whole thing to the table. After a further, more determined pull, it was finally freed – but as he lifted it up with satisfaction, the handle came away in his hand, and the body of the mug fell to the tabletop and broke into several pieces.

Red, who was carefully putting the photograph back in its place, turned at the sound of the clatter. 'I think you've made it worse.'

Frank looked at the tiny handle still in his hand. 'Yeah . . . let's go have a look at that fence.'

RED

It was bright and warm outside, and the air moved.

An unseen bird whistled, and two butterflies corkscrewed around one another, skirting the top of the long grass. As they floated by, Red followed them with his eyes, squinting as he accidentally looked towards the sun.

Behind him, Frank seemed to pause for a long time before stepping out into the garden. He had a funny look on his face, like he was trying to be brave, as though there were zombies around. There was a brush leaning against the wall, and Frank grabbed it before finally stepping out on to the back patio.

'Frank, are there zombies in your garden?'

'No.'

'What about orcs?'

'No.'

'It's just, well . . . why do you look a bit scared, then?'

Frank looked at Red as though he was talking like a crazy person. He did this a lot. 'Don't be an idiot.'

Red frowned. 'You shouldn't call people idiots, you know. It makes them feel bad.'

'Well,' Frank said, still not looking very happy to be out in the sunshine, 'I didn't *call* you an idiot, what I said was "Don't *be* an idiot".'

Red couldn't really argue with that.

Holding his broom handle like Gandalf holding a staff, Frank strode past Red and into the long brush of the lawn. Frank's garden was the same size as next door, but it didn't look like it. It seemed a lot smaller, probably because the grass was so long and the plants were growing in all different directions, gripping the sides of the fence, as though they were a sea monster trying to take down a boat.

'I need to get some tools out of the shed.' Frank pointed with his staff towards the top of the garden.

Red peered in that direction and past the drunk greenhouse. He could just make out a wooden door. The rest of the shed was overgrown by shiny green leaves, which it made it look like a hobbit house.

'So, *you*,' Frank said. 'Stop *there*. Understand?'

Red nodded, and Frank continued up the garden.

Red's legs itched as he followed Frank, wading through the grass a couple of feet behind him. Arriving at the shed, Frank stopped, and Red promptly walked into the back of him. Turning around, the old man tutted once. Then he turned back to the door and swore under his breath.

This time it was one of the *really* bad ones.

'What's a matter?' Red said nervously, still a little bit concerned about garden zombies. Maybe there was one trapped inside the shed.

'Someone's broken the lock off.'

'Eh?'

'The lock. It's hanging off.' Frank flicked the broken padlock with his thumb. He threw his broom handle to one side and put his shoulder to the door. It creaked open and Red poked his head into the gap between Frank's arm and the doorframe.

Red wasn't surprised to find that the inside of the tiny wooden building was a mess, with old, rusted tins of paint and screws strewn across the floor where they had fallen from lurching shelves. The room looked to be in the same sort of state as the greenhouse and the rest of the garden. But Frank wasn't happy.

'Bloody hell.'

'What's a matter?' Red repeated.

'Some thieving little shit's been in here.' Frank didn't sound overly angry, just tired. And he didn't seem particularly surprised, either.

Red was surprised enough for both of them. 'A robber?!'

'Yeah.'

'Whoa. We had a robber at our old house. He broke into our garage and stole my bike. My dad said he thought we'd never ever get it back, because the robber would swap it with another baddie for some crack.' He thought for a second. 'What's crack, Frank?'

'. . . I don't know.'

'Anyway, we *did* get it back, because we found it in a bush at the end of the road.'

'Well, I don't think I'll see this stuff again. Whoever's been in here has had it away with my drill, ladders . . .' He turned his head, as though imagining where these things used to be. '. . . and my saw.'

'Does this mean we can't do fixing the fence, then?' Red frowned. 'I mean, it doesn't matter too much, I suppose. At least it means we can still have one big garden.'

Frank seemed to think for a moment. Then he backed out of the shed, pulling the door closed behind him.

'I need to phone someone.'

FRANK

'Ken, it's me.'

'Who?'

'What do you mean, *who*? Don't piss about, Ken. I know my name comes up on your phone, or whatever.'

There was a barrel-chested laugh. 'Jesus H. Maloney – Franko! What are you doing on the phone? Am I on *Who Wants to be a Millionaire*? Am I a lifeline?'

Frank waited until Ken had finished entertaining himself, then said, 'I need a favour.'

'Surprise, surprise. Let me guess, the fellas next door are still on holiday, and you've run out of cigs.'

'No, I've still got those duty-free ones you bought me back from Spain.'

'Sharm El Sheikh,' Ken corrected. 'Jewel of the Orient.'

'Egypt is in Africa, Ken.'

'Well, whatever.'

'Anyway, it's not that. Some toerag has been in the shed and had it away with my saw and drill, and God knows what else.'

'Blimey. Right, right . . . and you want me to put the feelers out? See if anybody's heard anything, maybe put the squeeze on—'

'Alright, Tony Soprano. Jesus. No, I don't need you to use your "underworld connections" from The bloody Flea. I just need to borrow a saw.'

'Hey!' Ken was offended 'I *do* have connections. I *know* people. What about Trigger Pete? He's done time.'

'Yeah, for indecent exposure on a bus. Yeah, no thank you. I just need to borrow a saw and, if you've got it, a decent drill.'

'Fine.'

'Oh, and can you fetch us a bag of Postcrete and a length of two-by-four as well? I've got a fence panel that's come down and, well . . . I wouldn't ask, but I need to get it fixed sharpish.'

'No worries. I'm just in town at the minute. I'll nip to B&Q, swing by mine and then get to you. Give me an hour.'

Frank hung up and headed back into the garden.

'Who were you on the phone to?' Red asked. 'Was that the police? What did they say?'

'No, Red, it wasn't the police.'

'Why not?'

'What do you mean "why not"?'

'Why haven't you phoned the police?'

'No point.'

'But they could get *fingerprints*! They could catch the baddie and put them in jail and you can get all your things back.'

'I think the coppers have got bigger crimes to deal with than solving the mystery of my rusty saw.'

Red looked unsure about that. 'So, who *was* on the phone?'

'Fat Ken,' Frank said, sitting down on the back step and lighting a cigarette.

Red grimaced and coughed exaggeratedly as though he was in a burning building. Frank begrudgingly moved the cigarette to his other hand.

'Who's Fat Ken?'

'He's just someone who is going to lend us some tools. He'll be about an hour.'

'Okay. So, we can still fix the fence, then! What do you want to do for an hour? Hide and seek? Or . . . I know! We could look for crime clues?'

Frank didn't respond. They sat in silence for a minute.

'Frank, I'm hungry.'

'Jesus, do you not get breakfast next door or what?'

'Yeah, but that was aaaages ago.'

Frank looked at his watch. It was just before 11am. 'Fine. What've you got?'

RED

They were both sitting on the back step, waiting for Frank's friend to arrive with the tools.

Red had unzipped his lunchbox to find two sandwiches, both cut into squares and held together with tin foil. He measured them with one eye and decided that the one in his left hand was slightly bigger, and so he handed that one to Frank.

'Great. Thanks,' Frank said, in a way that meant that it wasn't really great, and he didn't really mean thanks.

Red smiled, though. He had changed the recipe. The day before, Frank hadn't touched his ham, cheese, jam and Wotsit, sandwich and so under his instruction, his mum had made them both ham, cheese, jam and Monster Munch sandwiches instead. Red found it difficult to believe that anyone could not like ham, cheese, jam and Monster Munch sandwiches. And Monster Munch were, after all, Frank's favourite crisps.

Again, though, Frank seemed to have no interest. As Red wolfed his sandwich down, Frank was tearing his bread into tiny pieces and tossing it on to the patio beside them. Red was about to ask him why, when a pigeon landed and started to peck at a piece, tossing it into the air and then nodding after it.

'Do you not like that sandwich either?'

'Mmh,' Frank non-replied, tossing another piece of bread to the scruffy-looking bird.

'I used to have a pigeon, y'know,' Red said returning to his own lunch. 'It was called Miles. What's your pigeon called?'

Frank tossed another tiny piece of bread. 'It's not *my* pigeon, it's just *a* pigeon.'

'I think it *is* your pigeon. Look.'

The bird had polished off everything on the patio and was nodding his head from side to side as he looked at Frank expectantly.

'We'll call him Miles Two,' Red decided.

Frank threw another piece of bread, and Miles Two backed away from where it landed before returning to peck at it hungrily.

'They poo a lot, pigeons.' Red continued, 'Not as much as mice, but a lot. On cars and on statues and stuff. And if you get some in your eye, it can make you dead.'

This was true. His mum had told him once when she had been wet-wiping some off his finger.

'Is that right?' Frank said.

'Yeah. My mum's a nurse and she knows lots about things like that. What can make you poorly and stuff. You know, my mummy looked after your wife.'

'Yeah.'

'The one in the picture.'

'Yeah.'

'And then she died,' Red said in his sad voice.

'Yes. Thank you, Red. I *am* aware.'

'What do you think happens when you're dead? Because Father McManus, from my school, says that when you die, you go to Heaven, and it's a place where everything is fun and super good. And you can have as many sweets as you like, and a swimming pool. *But* if you're really naughty, then you have to go to Hell, which is rubbish. And it's got the devil in it, and he's, like, in charge, and he's got horns like a cow, and he makes you on fire and he chases you around with a big fork.'

'Father McManus? He still at St Agnes, is he?'

'Yuh huh.'

'He must be in his eighties by now. He used to be at St Agnes when Marcie was there.'

'Your wife used to go to my school?'

'She used to teach there. Long time ago now. The kids loved her, though. They used to knock on the door, years later, when they got a job or got married or whatever, just to say . . .' The sentence drifted away. 'Is Mrs Mills still there?'

'Yeah, she's the boss teacher. She's the one who I got in trouble with and everything.'

'Jesus, Mills is the head now? Blimey. That place has gone down-hill. Mar was *not* a fan of Mrs Mills. Used to say she had the brains of a spoon, and was all fur coat and no knickers.'

Red wasn't sure what all that meant, but for a split second he was stunned into silence by the extreme naughtiness of someone saying something like that about a teacher. A beat later, he laughed so hard he sprayed his Capri-Sun everywhere. And Frank smiled.

They both turned at the same time then, hearing the traffic from the road as the front door opened. Red jumped up excitedly to see who it was.

Sliding into the hallway, he screeched to a halt as he was confronted by the largest human he had ever seen. The man was blocking out the daylight from the door that was closing behind him, and had sunglasses on and a grey T-shirt that stretched across his belly with writing on it that read: 'I'm no.1, so why try harder?'. In one hand, he had a large duffle bag, and in the other a drill, its cord wrapped around itself.

'Who are you?' the giant asked.

'Red.'

'Okay. Frank in?'

'He's in the back garden.'

'Huh?'

'He's feeding a pigeon.'

The giant put down the duffle bag, took off his sunglasses, tucked them into his collar and looked at Red intently. 'Frank?'

'Yep.'

'Is outside?'

'Yep.'

'And he's *feeding the pigeons*?'

'No. He's feeding *a* pigeon. There's only one. We've called it Miles Two.'

'I see.'

'Do you want a Mini Cheddar?' Red held out the bag in his hand.

'Go on, then,' the man said, as he took three. They disappeared into his mouth as he walked past Red, through the kitchen and outside.

'Frank!' the giant roared.

FRANK

'Feeeed the birds, tuppence a bag.' Ken came through the back door singing *Mary Poppins*.

'Eh?'

'Nothin'. Brought you the tools.' Ken dropped the bag at his feet and laid the drill on top. 'Who's the hobbit?'

'It's the neighbour's kid.' Frank tilted his head towards next door. 'Long story.'

'Alrighty then. I'll stick the kettle on.'

Red sat in the grass while Frank told Ken about the succession of events that had led to the boy being there. He explained everything, from the fact that Sarah had cared for Marcie at St John's Hospice, to the pair moving in next door, to the fight at school and the suspension. All culminating in this: his current living nightmare.

If Frank had been expecting sympathy it was not forthcoming.

Ken spent most of the time laughing uncontrollably – particularly at the bit about the fish tank, and even more so when Frank described being roped into babysitting for a week.

'That is amazing,' he said, wiping his eyes. 'Boo Radley bloody babysitting!' He set off laughing again. When he finally stopped, he turned to Red. 'So, Red, you've been kicked out of school, eh?'

'Yeah.' Red looked at the ground in shame. 'I have to stay at home and not go to school and do reflection time for a week. A whole week. But . . . I don't mind it too much, really, because I don't really like that school, and I'm helping mend the fence with Frank, and besides Mrs Mills is all fur coat and no knickers.'

'Is she now?' Ken nodded. 'Me and Frank were suspended from school once, weren't we Frank? Remember?'

Frank did remember.

Red's jaw swung open.

'Oh, yeah. Me and Frank grew up together in the old country, went all through school in the same class. Didn't we, Frankie boy?'

'And you got told to get out of school for a week?' Red said.

'Yeah. *Two* weeks, actually.'

'Do *not* tell that story,' Frank said simply, as Red's mouth dropped open again. He may as well have been talking to himself.

'What happened? Were you fighting or something?' Red asked.

'Yeah. Kind of.' Ken leaned towards Red. 'Thing is, I used to get bullied quite a bit myself.'

'*You*? But you're as big as a Gyarados.'

'Right, well. I don't know what that is. But yeah, I wasn't always tall. I didn't start growing upwards until I was about fifteen. I'm not exactly Kate Moss now, but back then, let's just say I was a *lot* more wide than I was high. Couple of kids at our school used to call me every name under the sun. Fatty Arbuckle, Lardy-Arse, all that sort of thing.'

'Really?'

'Yeah, and one day I'd had enough, and I just came out swinging. Got booted out of school for a fortnight.'

'So how come Frank got in trouble?'

'Well, Frankie was my best friend. And I was whaling on these two lads in the playground, and eventually this old mean bastard teacher called McGillis jumped in, broke it up and pinned me against the wall. Frank comes round the corner, sees me, and sees

262

this fella's got me by the throat. He'd no idea what was going on, and he didn't think. He threw McGillis off me and kicked him in the danglies.'

Red gasped.

'Oh yeah,' Ken continued. 'And no ordinary kick, either. He had a proper run-up. He booted this fella like he was trying to get his bollocks through the whites at Lansdowne Road.' Ken was laughing again. 'Honestly, this fella made a noise like when you let the air out of a balloon. Eeeeeeeee!'

Frank had to fight hard to keep the amusement from his face.

'Remember that, Frankie? God, your old fella gave you such a hiding for that. But I'll tell ya, Red, we had the best couple of weeks ever. We went fishing, hung out down in the glen, shoplifted booze from—'

'Alright, Ken, alright.'

'Well, anyway. Sounds like this fella at your school was being a bit of an arse himself, so don't you go feeling too bad. You know what they say . . .'

'Don't be a trifle?'

'Yeah, something like that.'

'Right, well. Thanks for the stroll down memory lane, Ken. You got all the tools and stuff?' Frank said.

'Uh huh.' Ken disappeared for a moment and came back with the long bag he'd left in the hallway. He dumped it on the patio.

'I've left the timber and the Postcrete in the car. I'll nip and get it, and then I'd better get gone. I'm meeting Little Ken and Little Little Ken for lunch.'

Little Ken was Big Ken's son. And Little Little Ken was his pride and joy: his four-year-old grandson.

Ken turned to Red. 'Come on, muscles. You can give me a hand.'

The two returned a couple of minutes later, Ken with the heavy bag of concrete in his arms as though it was no heavier than a pillow,

Red dragging the wooden post behind him and grunting with effort. Ken dropped the bag in the grass and Red let the post fall at its side. Frank, meanwhile, had been sorting through the tools in the long bag, finding that many of them already belonged to him, having been 'loaned' to Ken over the years. He was beginning to wonder if his shed had been burgled at all.

'Ken, you know half of these are mine?' he said, producing his saw from the bag.

'Well, what's mine is yours, Franklin,' Ken said pulling his trousers back up over his backside. 'Right, if you need anything else, just give me a shout. Red, it's been a pleasure.' He stuck his hand out. Red looked at it and then shook it, his hand lost in Ken's sausage glove. 'Frankie, I'll see you later. Good to see you outside.' Ken turned as he got to the back door and swivelled his car keys in one hand. 'And get your bloody lawn mowed. It looks like a nun's bush.'

Red peered up 'Frank, what's a—?'

RED

'Make yourself useful,' Frank interrupted. 'And hold this.' He produced a tape measure from the bag and handed it to Red.

Frank continued to rummage as Red examined it. He pulled the tape out a few inches before releasing it again, letting it snap back into his hand like a snake attack.

Wicked.

Frank, meanwhile, had finished emptying the bag of tools. 'Right, pass me that.' He took the tape back from Red and, kneeling down, started to measure the new length of wood.

'I'll help!'

'I don't think so.'

Frank made a mark on the post with a pencil, which he then quickly slotted back behind one ear. To Red, it was like the coin-behind-the-ear trick, and he wondered if Frank always kept a pencil there and he had just never noticed before.

Frank stood up and marched over to where the fallen fence panel was still lying in the grass.

'I promise I won't get in the way. I'm dead good at helping,' Red insisted. 'I helped my daddy once when he was making some new shelves for my bedroom. And he dropped this screw and it went under the floorboards, and I was the only one who could reach it because his hands were too big to get it. *And* they were the best shelves ever. And I put my certificate on the shelf, the one I got for "best listening" – that was at my old school, not at my new one – and my mummy thought that the shelves were a bit slopey, but my daddy said it was a good job, well done.'

Dragging the panel to one side, Frank trampled down the grass around the old broken and leaning fence post.

'Your dad's pretty busy at the moment, eh?' he said, as he held the old post against the new one and made another mark with the pencil.

'Yeah,' Red replied quietly. 'He's got lots of things to sort out. And he's got a *really* important job,' he added seriously.

'Right.'

In truth, Red didn't really know what his dad did for a job. He had once asked, and his dad had told him that he was a 'senior project manager' or something, and Red had never bothered to ask again, because that sounded very boring. But as far as he could work out, being a 'project manager' meant having lots of meetings on the computer and getting mad because Jeff had dropped the ball again. Whatever a project manager did, Red had decided a long time ago that he didn't want to do *that* when he grew up. Instead, he wanted to be a shopkeeper, a vet, or a dragon-rider.

Red brightened. 'But he's going to take me camping this summer, just us. And not in the garden.' Red shook his head, in case Frank thought he might be kidding. 'Like, properly camping.'

'Uh huh.'

'Just us.'

'Right.'

'And not in the garden.'

Frank stood up. 'Look, if you listen properly, you can help me measure. Just don't get in the way.'

'Okay!' Red said, spinning around once in a celebratory dance that ended with him on his tiptoes.

Red considered it a tiny fib to not mention that the shelves he had put up with his dad had fallen down during the night with an almighty crash. The last thing he wanted was for Frank to know that he wasn't actually very good at this sort of stuff.

*

There was no argument this time about who would answer the phone. Frank probably hadn't even heard it ring. He was still in the garden sawing, and Red had come inside to get them both a drink.

It was hot outside, and Red's hair was stuck to his forehead. Frank had loaned him a baseball cap that was three sizes too big, and he'd turned it back to front as he pulled a chair up to the sink. He was filling two mugs from the draining board with water when the telephone rang.

It was Red's mum again. Apparently, she had been telling the truth when she said that she was going to be calling every few hours to check on him.

'Hey, Mummy!'

'Hey, Reddy. How's it going? How's—'

'Good. I can't talk for very long. Frank needs me.'

'Oh, okay. What are you doing?'

'We're fixing the fence and I'm helping.'

'Okay.'

'Okay, bye.'

'Wait!'

Red put the phone back to his ear.

'I just wanted to check that you're okay. Are you being careful in the sun, if you're outside?'

'Yeah, I'm mainly in the shade and I've got a hat on that Frank gave me.' He took it off and looked at it properly for the first time. 'It's got a picture of a dog on it, and it says Churchill Insyoorance.'

'Nice. Listen, sunshine. I've spoken to your dad, and he still can't get any time off, so it looks like you're stuck at Frank's all week. I'm really sorry, kiddo. But he says he's definitely, definitely coming to pick you up on Sunday. Definitely.'

Three definitelys.

'Okay. I'll see you later!'

'Oh . . . alright. Okay, bye. See you—'

Red hung up and ran back to the sink. He carefully carried the two very full mugs over the threshold of the back door, now propped open with the discarded broom, and back to where Frank was still sawing.

'Here ya go, Frank,' he said, dribbling most of the water down his arms.

Frank stopped and drained his mug in an instant, with a gasp.

Three *definitelys*. That's what Red's mum had said. Three *definitelys* that his dad was going to pick him up on Sunday. And that was fine by Red. He had been dreading the possibility that his dad *would* find some time, and he would have had to go there all week instead of coming to Frank's. True, his dad would've let him have pizza and play on his tablet as much as he liked, but that wasn't important work.

Red drained his own mug in one go, too.

Not like this.

FRANK

Frank's shirt was clinging to his back, and sweat was making his beard itch. His back and the palms of his hands felt heavy and ached, but it felt good to be exerting himself, his body remembering muscles that it had all but forgotten.

The kid hadn't listened, of course, and had insisted on not just assisting with measuring, but also 'helping' to dig out the old fence-post. That's what he was doing now, working one-handed and with a small potting trowel he had found in the bottom of the tool bag. For the half an hour that Frank had been using a spade to break up the earth that surrounded the stubborn post, Red had been scraping at the other side of it, removing precisely no soil, but doing so care-fully, with his tongue between his teeth, as though he was an Egyptologist excavating a pot.

Curiously, each time Frank blew out his cheeks with exertion and stood up to stretch his back, Red would do the same. The first time he did it, Frank thought Red was taking the piss, but the boy seemed entirely sincere, as he then squatted back on his heels and continued scraping at the earth diligently.

'If we keep digging like this, we'll get all the way to America or Australia!' Red announced.

Marcie was lying on a low wall behind them, sunbathing in Audrey Hepburn shades. 'Actually,' she said, lazily, 'if you were to dig straight down, you'd eventually come out just off the coast of New Zealand, in the middle of the Pacific.'

Out of habit, Frank did a quick mental check to see if he knew this fact already.

He had figured out a while ago that if Marcie was just a manifestation of his own subconscious, then anything she said would, by necessity, already be tucked away in his brain somewhere.

Check over. He *did* know this already. He had read it in a *Nat Geo* article somewhere years ago.

He felt none of the disappointment that he used to feel in this scenario. He had got used to these confirmations that his deceased wife was just a product of his own brain.

In the early days, when she first came back, he hadn't been quite so sure.

*

In that first week, Frank had simply refused to acknowledge her existence.

'Why don't you just speak to me, you big idiot?' she said, as he lay in the bath, exhausted from lack of sleep, just his face above the water as he tried to shut out the sound of her voice.

It had been five days before he finally replied. 'Because you're not there. Because you're not real. Because my wife is in the ground.' The tears came in sobs like punches, but he continued. 'Because I know I'm going mad, and the only thing about that fact that scares me is . . . I don't care. Because if that means that I get to talk to her again, I'm fine with that.' He stopped suddenly, wiping his eyes hard, disgusted with himself.

'Look at me,' she said. 'Look at me, Frankie.'

He looked. Looked straight at her for the first time since she had appeared on the sofa, five days before. And he felt himself collapse, his entire body crumpling under this new gravity. And then he really wept, in a way he hadn't since he was a kid. Cried until he couldn't.

The following day, he began to ask his questions, but they always went around in circles.

'But how do I know that you're real? Prove it.'

'And how am I supposed to do that?'

'Well, tell me something that I couldn't possibly know.'

'Jesus, Frank. I don't know. Those cargo shorts you bought from Millets make you look like an arse?' Her voice became softer. 'That's not how this works, okay?'

'Then how does it work?'

'I don't know.' She sighed. 'Maybe I am just a figment of that imagination of yours. Or maybe I'm a ghost, or whatever. The truth is, you're drowning, Frankie. Maybe I'm just armbands.'

*

'Actually, if you *were* to dig straight down, you'd eventually come out in the middle of the Pacific Ocean,' Frank said, repeating Marcie's fact.

'Right.' Red looked impressed, but then concerned. 'We'd better be careful, then.'

'Whew.' Frank stood up. 'I think we deserve another drink,' he said, wiping the sweat from his forehead

'I'll get it!' Red disappeared through the back door and into the kitchen.

Frank unbuttoned the top button of his shirt and untucked his vest, then began rocking the old rotten fence post out of the hole they had dug around it.

'Switswoo!' Marcie fake wolf-whistled. 'It's like watching that Diet Coke advert.'

'That's funny.'

'Like I said, "switswoo".'

'You never could whistle properly.'

'Who can't whistle properly?' Red said, as he emerged from the back door. He was walking towards Frank, his eyes darting between the mug in each hand. Water sloshed over the sides, though, with each step. He was like a drunk with tremors heading back from the bar with too-full glasses. 'Who can't whistle properly?' he asked again.

'No one.'

'I can whistle. Listen to this.' Red pursed his lips and blew. There was no whistle, just a noise that sounded like an asthmatic blowing out candles on a cake. He stopped, red-faced, as he handed a mug to Frank.

'Right, we'll chuck some concrete in this hole, drop the post in, and then call it a day until tomorrow. I need you to go and sit out of the way,' Frank said.

'But I'm helping.' Red looked disappointed.

'If you can call it that.'

Red frowned, and Frank felt that unwelcome twinge of guilt again. 'Look, you *are* helping. I'm just . . . joking with you. But concrete dust can be bad for you, if it gets in your eyes or you breathe it in . . . so I need you to listen and just stay out of the way, okay?'

Red clearly thought this was just an excuse to stop him being involved, but he agreed begrudgingly. He climbed on to his trampoline and sat, his legs dangling over the edge, to watch.

When Frank had finished emptying the bag of grey powder around the post, he went over to the tap attached to the back of the house. Unclipping the hose, he filled a dented metal watering can with water and carried it back to the hole. By this time, Red was lying on his back on the trampoline, staring up at the clouds and twisting a dandelion in one hand.

'Red?'

'Yeah?'

'You want to pour the water in?'

'You want me to pour it?'

'Well, I can't stir and pour at the same time, can I? I'm not an octopus. You want to make yourself useful or not?'

'Yeah!' The kid jumped up.

'Okay . . . gently.'

Red dribbled water from the heavy watering can into the hole as Frank mixed the grey powder in with the trowel.

'Okay, that's enough,' Frank said after a minute. Red backed away and Frank continued to mix. 'Right, grab me that.' Frank pointed to the spirit level, which was lying on the fallen fence panel.

'The long yellow stick thing?'

'Yeah. I'm gonna hold it up against this post,' Frank said as Red handed over the level. 'I need you to look and tell me when it's straight.'

'Huh?'

'Just tell me when that bubble is in the middle.'

Moments, later the pair stepped back, and Frank dusted his hands as he looked at the post with a tilted head. Red did the same.

'That looks spot-on to me,' Frank said, with something approaching satisfaction.

'Me too.'

'Right, well. We just need to let that set, and then we can put the fence panel back in.' Frank turned to find Red standing there with his hand raised.

'What?'

'High five?'

'No.'

RED

By the time Red's mum came to pick him up on the second day, they were both fast asleep. Frank was snoring in his armchair and Red was dozing on the sofa.

After working in the garden, Red hadn't been in the mood for a game or anything. He was tired. It was hard work fixing things, especially in the sun, and so when Frank relaxed into his armchair for his afternoon 'eye rest', Red had happily settled on to the sofa across from him.

Turning on the TV, Frank was asleep before an advert for bingo had even finished. Red pulled his tablet out of his backpack and played *Roblox* for a while. Half an hour later, the tablet chirruped to say the battery was about to die, and before long the screen went to a pinpoint and then dark.

Red tossed it aside, looked at the ceiling for a bit and then stared at the TV lazily. The news was on, and two men were pointing at a wall with lines on it and talking about money.

'And so with global interest rates and the compounding of the fumdi-fump of the bloombiblart in the dangle dongle . . .'

'Frank.' He said in a whisper, and then again, a little louder. 'Frank?'

There was no answer, so Red crept over to where the remote control was resting on the arm of Frank's chair. He picked it up between thumb and forefinger and then retreated to the sofa, tiptoeing backwards like a cartoon villain.

'Frank, can I watch something else?'

The old man grunted slightly, and Red thought this probably meant 'yes'.

Frank didn't have Netflix or YouTube or anything like that on his TV. There were *some* channels Red recognised, like BBC One and Channel 4. But as he kept clicking upwards, there were many that he had never heard of before, like UK Gold and Lifetime, and a channel that said 'GodTV' in one corner and had a man shouting and selling plates with a picture of Jesus hugging a sheep on them.

Clicking back down the channels, there was just a lot of people gardening or talking about old things they'd found in their lofts. For five minutes, Red *did* get a bit interested in one woman who was showing off a big bowl with flowers on it.

The man in charge had told her that it was something that people used as a toilet ages ago, and the woman got sad when he told her that it wasn't worth much money. Which made Red think that the woman was a bit stupid, because why would anybody buy a bowl that people had used to poo in? No matter how well you cleaned it, you still definitely wouldn't want to put your Coco Pops in it.

Disappointed, Red flicked the TV back to the news. 'Frank? There's nothing on.'

The old man mumbled something.

'Frank?'

He didn't open his eyes, but stopped snoring abruptly. '. . . What?'

'My tablet's got no battery left, and there's nothing on.'

'There's about a thousand channels, Red.'

'Yeah, but they're all weird or about boring things. There's no cartoons or anything.'

Frank opened one eye. 'Well just watch a DVD or something. There are loads under the telly there; just grab one and put it in the thing.'

'What thing? What's a DVD?'

'What?' Frank rubbed his eyes before finally opening both. 'I thought all you kids were supposed to be up with the latest gadgets and stuff. A DVD. It's like a video tape.'

'What's a video tape?'

'Jesus. Look, just open the cupboard underneath the telly.'

Red did as he was told. Inside, there was a slim silver machine, and beneath that, two shelves full of boxes that looked like Xbox games.

'Just choose one, take the disc out and stick it in the DVD player.'

That seemed like a lot of trouble to go to just to watch a film. 'Why don't you just download it?' Red asked.

'Oh, I don't know, because we're not all Elon bloody Must?' Frank replied, adjusting the cushion behind his head and closing his eyes again.

Red traced his fingers down the spines, reading the titles. 'I don't know any of these films. Have you got *Minions* or the new *Lego Movie*?'

'No.'

'What about the *old* one? Or *Avengers* or *Iron Man* or *Thor: Ragnarok*?'

Frank opened his eyes again. 'Never mind *Iron Man* and all that superhero bollocks. Those there are classics: *Blythe Spirit*, *The Cat and the Canary* . . . some of the best films ever made.'

Red took another one from the middle. He frowned. '*The Flying Deuces*, Laurel and Hardy.' He put it to one side and slid out another and then another.

'*The Godfather* . . . and *Miracle on 34th Street*,' Frank offered. 'Marcie's all-time favourite film. We must've watched that a thousand times.'

'Alright, so shall we watch this one then?'

'Well, it's a Christmas film, but . . . whatever.' Frank shifted to make himself comfortable again, plumping the cushion behind his head once more. 'There's a couple of Michael's old favourites on the bottom shelf there; have a look at those.'

Red pulled out one that had a black sports car jumping over a police car on the front. In one corner, it had a picture of a fat man dressed as a superhero. It was the closest thing to *Avengers* he could find. 'I'm choosing this one. *The Cannonball Run*.'

Frank closed his eyes again. 'Fine. Just keep the volume down.'

*

It was halfway through the second film Red put on, *The Flying Deuces*, that Red's mum arrived to find them both sleeping.

Red didn't stay fully asleep when she scooped him up, but he pretended to be, because it was his favourite feeling in the world: to be lifted by her, weightless in her arms. It reminded him of something, but he could never quite remember what.

'Come on, baby boy,' she whispered in his ear.

Frank stirred. 'Shit. What time is it?' he said, yawning blearily.

'It's nearly four. You've obviously had a busy day; he's absolutely knackered.'

'Yeah.'

'Well . . . we'll see you tomorrow.'

*

Reflection Diary

Name	Leonard Evans		
Class	2	Day	2

What I did today:

Today was the busiest day in the world ever in a million years. Frank's shed was burgled by a thief! Fat Ken had to come round and borrow us some tools to mend the fence. Fat Ken is Frank's friend and he is a giant.

I helped mending the fence, but it's not finished yet. We watched CannonBall Run and it was really funny. To begin with Frank pretended to be asleep but he wasn't really, I could tell because he kept opening his eyes at the best bits.
I especially liked the bit at the end when they showed all the stuff that had gone wrong when they made the film because Frank laughed really properly and got some tea on his vest and said bugger.

Cannonball Run is Mikey's favourite film. Mikey is called Michael and is Frank's son. But I don't think they are friends with each other anymore.

We both fell asleep and then mummy picked me up to take me home and we had lasagne. It had bits of carrots in it.

FRANK

Frank had just sat down for his mid-morning cigarette.

He ordinarily perched on the front step to do this, and had done for the last year or so. He was more comfortable there; the front yard was permanently in the shade of the house, which made it feel like an extension of it. But from the back step, he could keep half an eye on Red as he sat at the kitchen table and sorted jigsaw pieces.

There was less room on that step this morning, though. Marcie was already sitting there, her face turned towards the sun.

'I could listen to you two bicker all day.' She was smiling. 'You're like a pair of old washerwomen.'

It was annoyingly true.

It was the fourth day, and Frank had been surprised by how quickly they had fallen into a morning routine. Red would arrive noisily and in a burst of colour. As his mum left, the boy would kick off his shoes and throw his newest bag of stuff at the bottom of the stairs. He would then help himself to a glass of milk or orange juice from the fridge (always adjusting his picture to make sure that it was straight), and then join Frank at the kitchen table.

'So, what do you want to do today?' would be his first question.

'I don't know,' was the answer. Usually followed by, 'Let me drink my coffee.'

Red would then talk about *Minecraft* and Pokémon cards and everything and nothing, until eventually Frank would have no choice but to lay down the day's news and respond. And then they'd bicker about something.

This morning, Red had asked Frank why he didn't own a mobile phone. Before he could even think about answering, the boy was busily explaining that he wasn't allowed to have one until he was ten, but that he *needed* one now.

'Why do *you* need a phone?'

'So, I can play games and phone people and stuff.'

'Who the bloody hell are you gonna phone?'

'I don't know.' He shrugged. 'Mummy, Auntie Steph? You?'

'Well, there's another good reason not to have one, right there.' Frank had then made the case for the fact that mobile phones were the worst thing that had happened to humanity since it had crawled out of the mud, and told Red he would rather set fire to himself than own one of those godforsaken things.

'You know there's more computer stuff in them than NASA took to land on the moon. And what do we use them for? You see 'em out front there, walking down the street, the gormless buggers, their heads buried in the things. There could be a hole in the road the size of the Grand Canyon and they'd walk straight into it and still be tippy-tapping away on YouTubes and Instantgran and Arsebook. And not even bloody words: smiley faces and L.O.L. and D.F.S. and God knows what else. People don't talk to each other anymore; it's all texting. And you see them at these concerts, filming it instead of watching the thing, and—' Frank stopped abruptly.

Red was grinning. He seemed to enjoy nothing more than listening to Frank rant about something, and it short-circuited his irritation to see the kid smiling up at him as he got worked up.

'Drink your milk.'

'You know you've hardly smoked in the past couple of days?' Marcie said, as he took another drag.

'Yeah, well, every time I light one, the kid is in my ear. He's worse than you. He drew a "before and after" picture of me yesterday. In one, I was smoking a cigarette, and in the other I was dead. Literally, "x"s for eyes and in a coffin.'

She chuckled.

'And he wanted me to put it on the fridge with that other monstrosity. Just the thing to brighten up a man's day, that: a crayoned picture of your own corpse on the fridge door.'

They fell into comfortable silence.

'Fence looks good,' she said.

It didn't. It was wonky, and you could drive a bus through the gap between the panel and the ground underneath. But Frank felt oddly pleased, looking at it.

'Kid reckons it needs painting. Probably right. Might have to paint the rest of the fence, as well. It'll stand out like a sore thumb otherwise.'

'So, that what you're gonna do today?' Marcie asked.

'I don't know. Anything but bloody *Guess Who?*.'

The day before, they had finished mending the fence in the morning, slotting the old fence panel back into place around lunchtime. They had then watched a double-bill feature of *Smokey and the Bandit* and *Cannonball Run II*, before playing a marathon session of twelve games of *Guess Who?*.

'If I never see that game again, it'll be too soon. Thankfully, he's started in on that London jigsaw. Two thousand pieces, should keep him busy for a bit.'

Frank turned. She was gone.

RED

Red was painting the fence. But not really concentrating. Partly because of the noise of Frank mowing the lawn, and partly because he was thinking. He was trying to work out how to ask Frank the question that he wanted to ask him.

He wanted to ask him about Michael.

Red's mum had told him that Frank had a son, but he had only really become curious about it after seeing all the photographs of the boy – that became a man – dotted around the house. This curiosity had grown when Frank had told him that the two of them didn't really see or speak to each other anymore.

But what had *really* caught Red's interest was overhearing the conversation between Ken and Frank, and finding out that the invitation that had arrived next door – and was now hidden away in Frank's drawer – was from Mikey.

*

It had been lunchtime (10.30am), and Frank was eating his ham, cheese, jam and Space Raiders sandwich. This time, the pigeon didn't even get the crust, and it bobbed back and forth on the patio looking annoyed, as Frank stared into space and ate the entire four squares in his tin foil.

He was still chewing the last bite when he saw Red looking at him. 'Wha?'

'You've eaten your sandwich.'

Frank actually seemed a bit surprised to hear that any of the sandwich had been in his mouth, and looked even more surprised that the tin foil in his lap was now empty. 'It's actually not that bad,' he said, snorting a laugh, before continuing to chew.

Red grinned. Then, seeing Miles Two looking on in disappointment, he tossed the whole of his final square of bread to the bird. The pigeon pecked away as Frank stood up with a groan, a rub of his knees, and a 'Right, then.'

'Are we painting the fence?' asked Red.

'I guess so.'

'Yes!'

Red stood outside the shed, listening to the commotion within as Frank banged and bashed, looking for something, until eventually, through the open door, there flew a couple of paintbrushes, which landed in the grass at Red's feet. These were followed by a tin that looked a million years old. It was rusted on the top, and dried paint had dripped down the sides.

Red waited for Frank to come out again and close the door behind him, but instead there was a louder and more substantial racket, punctuated by cursing. Finally, Frank exited the shed, wrestling an orange lawnmower behind him.

'Might as well mow this lawn while we're at it.' He looked at the long grass and the lawnmower, as though he was already changing his mind. 'It's only a matter of time before one of the neighbours starts moaning about it, and the council starts coming round.'

Red looked at the neighbouring houses and couldn't think why anybody would complain; you couldn't even see into the back garden unless you deliberately looked over the fence. But he chose not to say anything.

Frank uncoiled an extension cable from the kitchen, then plugged in the lawnmower. He gave it a quick rev with his right hand; the lawnmower crunched and clattered and sounded generally poorly. Apparently satisfied, though, Frank then went back into the shed and returned with a long sheet. As he shook it, a cloud of dust leapt into the air, along with cobwebs and a dead fly that nearly landed in Red's hair. Frank laid the sheet in front of the fence panel, pried open the tin of paint with the garden trowel and dropped one of the paintbrushes into the gloop.

'Right, you paint. I mow.'

Red had been happily painting when Ken arrived.

'Alright, lads!' Ken shouted over the sound of the lawnmower, which whined to a stop. 'Just passing. I thought I'd come and pick up my tools. I'm building a treehouse thing for Little Little Ken this weekend, and I need the saw.' He grinned at Frank as he nodded at the fence panel. 'Bloody hell, top job there, fellas. How many beers did you have before you knocked that up?'

'I'm painting it,' Red offered.

'I see that. And a top job you're doing, too, sir.' He turned to Frank. 'I see you took my advice about the lawn, Franko. Let us know if you find Stanley.'

'Who's Stanley?' Red asked, squinting as the sun reappeared from behind a cloud.

'He's a bloke who went missing in the jungle years ago,' Frank said, leaning on the lawnmower. 'You'll have to excuse Kenny. He thinks he's funny.'

'Oh,' Red said, as he got the joke. 'That *is* funny. It's 'cos your garden is like a jungle.'

Frank rolled his eyes as Red got a high five from Ken without even asking.

'Right, I can't stop,' Ken said.

Frank nodded. 'The tool bag's just by the back door there. Drill's on the kitchen side.'

'Righto.' Ken picked up the holdall of tools and the long saw that was laid on top. He was about to leave, but then he turned to look at Frank. It was a few seconds before he spoke. 'I take it you're not going? To the . . ."do"?'

Frank didn't reply.

Ken continued, sounding serious and sad. 'Ellie told me they were sending you an invite. You should at least reply.'

The lawnmower started up again. The conversation was over.

Ken looked at Frank, and then at the ground, as though he was thinking about saying something else, but he didn't. Finally, he turned, but a slight breeze closed the back door as he was about to walk through it. 'Red, you want to give a man a hand with the door?'

'Okay.' Red skipped in front of him and held it open. He followed Ken into the hallway so that he could open the front door for him, too. 'Ken, what's the "do"?'

'Don't ask, bud,' he said stepping outside.

'Is it the thing at the church, in July?'

'Yeah.' Ken turned. 'The christening. How do you know about that?'

'Because Frank *did* get an invitation; it was in an envelope delivered to our house by mistake. We gave it to him, though. I've seen it.'

'Okay.'

'It's in that drawer.' Red pointed at the dresser behind him.

'Is it, now?' Ken laid his tools down on the front path and stepped back into the hallway.

'Be careful, because that drawer is hard, and stuff falls out everywhere,' Red said as Ken pulled out the drawer easily.

He quickly found the beige envelope on the top of the pile, and then rummaged further. Finding a pen, he freed the invitation and, resting it flat on the dresser, he wrote a sentence above the ornate text. Satisfied, he then took it into the kitchen.

A moment later he came back, ruffling Red's hair as he walked past. 'See you later, kid.'

Red closed the door behind him and walked into the kitchen himself, the sound of the lawnmower filling the space. Stuck to the fridge over his drawing was the invitation. And in blue biro were the words Ken had added:

'Frank, don't be a bloody idiot'.

FRANK

As far as Frank was concerned, he *wasn't* being a bloody idiot.

There was no point in lying to himself. Part of the reason why he couldn't go to the christening, even if he wanted to, was that it meant leaving the house and going 'beyond the gate'. And not just beyond the gate; Mikey lived south of the river, on the other side of London. He might as well live on the moon.

Besides, Ken had just confirmed that it was Ellie who had sent the invitation, not Mikey. So he was still sure that his son wouldn't want him there, even if he could make it those 384,400 kilometres.

Frank continued to wrestle the lawnmower through the long grass, trying to put the whole thing to the back of his mind.

But there was another reason why he couldn't go, wasn't there? It was a reason that sat somewhere in his chest, and it was only recently that he had come to accept the truth of it.

His son had moved on in a way that Frank couldn't. He didn't resent Mikey for that – far from it. People were *supposed* to move on. And in his more lucid moments, he couldn't have been more pleased. He caught himself smiling sometimes, as he imagined Mikey – his gentle, imaginative and funny boy – as a father. But this was why Frank had finally given up on reconciliation altogether: because his son was happy. And like his wife when she was dying, Frank couldn't bear to be a cloud on that happiness, to be the Reaper at a birthday party. He had made so many mistakes with Mikey over the past two years, but he wouldn't make that one.

Red came back outside and sat cross-legged in front of the fence, picking up his paintbrush once more. Frank continued to force the lawnmower through the meadow, wincing occasionally at the sound the machine made as it passed over a particularly crunchy piece of grass, and whatever objects it had stumbled upon went rattling around its blades. Still, he persevered – until there was a particularly apocalyptic clattering, and the lawnmower whined to a halt.

'Bollocks.'

'What was that?!' Red turned around with his mouth open, dripping paint on to his trousers.

Frank turned the lawnmower over and examined the underside.

'Well, I found your shoe,' he said, as he pulled a shredded black trainer out of the blades and held it up like roadkill.

'Woah, that's cool.'

'Mmm. I don't think your mother'll see it that way, especially when she sees the state of your T-shirt as well. Have you got *any* paint on the fence yet?'

Red looked down and tried to brush the paint off with the palm of his hand, succeeding only in smearing it around until more of the T-shirt was brown than was its original white.

'Well, I didn't like those shoes anyway. Jake and Callum said that they were slow shoes and weren't fashion.'

There was still a shredded shoelace wrapped around the blade, and Frank started to disentangle it. 'Fashion,' he muttered with disgust.

'Frank?'

'Yeah.'

'What month is it?'

Frank wiped the sweat from his eyebrows with the upper arm of his shirt sleeve. 'April? No, May.'

'Oh.'

'Why?'

'No reason.' Red dipped his paintbrush and stroked paint up and down a couple of times. 'When's July?'

'In two months' time. It goes May, June, July.'

'Oh, right.'

Another couple of strokes of paint.

'What's a christening?'

Bloody kid really did have ears like a bat. Even when he didn't seem to be listening, he was taking in every word.

'. . . It's like a party for a new baby. They pour water on its head and give them their name, and then you all go the pub. It's a church thing.'

'Why would they pour water on a little baby's head? Did that happen to me? I don't remember.'

'Well, I don't know. You'd have to ask your mum. Not everybody does it, depends on if you're religious or whatever.'

He tried to start the lawnmower again, but it just spluttered and died. Damn thing.

'Did you be christened?'

'I did,' Frank said, giving the lawnmower a kick.

'What about Mikey?'

'Yeah.'

Frank hadn't really cared whether Mikey was baptised or not. Neither Marcie nor Frank were particularly religious; they came from a community that thought of God as a part of daily life, like wearing shoes. But by the time Frank was ten, he had already begun to see Catholicism as mean-spirited and scary. Marcie, meanwhile, had always just thought of the whole thing as a bit daft.

In their adulthood, they had settled on the idea that the Church was kind of irrelevant. But Marcie wanted to have Mikey baptised; it was, she said, like their boy planting a flag in the sand and saying, 'I'm here.' And it was a good excuse for their family and friends to celebrate together. So Frank had agreed.

It had been cold in the church: mid-February, with snow on the ground. They had joked about being able to see their breath in clouds, even inside. And Frank remembered looking out at their family and friends, and finding that Marcie had been right. There were few times he could remember being happier than in that moment. Watching the people he loved most in the world smile and laugh as the priest poured water over Michael's head, the baby protesting with a screech that sounded like he was being lowered into an active volcano.

'Did he cry?' Red asked.

'Screamed the bloody place down.' Frank tried the lawnmower again. Nothing.

'Frank?'

'Yes, Red?' he said, with diminishing patience, partly due to the lawnmower, and partly because, unlike the lawnmower, Red's question machine had started up again.

'Why aren't you and Michael friends anymore?'

Frank stopped what he was doing and looked directly at Red. Reflexively, he tried to react angrily, but when he replied, he found that he just sounded tired. 'It's complicated.'

'Why?'

'It just is. We fell out a long time ago.'

'Well, that doesn't sound very complicated,' Red said matter-of-factly. 'You could just say sorry, and then he could say sorry, and then it's all fine again.'

'It doesn't work like that for grown-ups.'

'Why not?'

'Because.'

'Because what? Are you scared? Like you are of outside?'

'I'm not scared of outside, Red.'

'Well, maybe you should go to the christening then. Are you a mountain—'

'Red. Do not even think about—'

'—or a mouse?' he finished simply.

'Christ,' Frank whispered to himself. He was still having no joy with the lawnmower, and he started to check the cable, getting more and more annoyed.

'I mean, maybe you don't have to go to the christening to begin with. Maybe you could just phone him or something. Or send him a present, even.'

'Red, enough.' Frank was following the cable back to where it was plugged into the extension reel in the kitchen. It had probably tripped and needed resetting.

Red was warming to his idea, though, and followed him inside, chattering away. 'Maybe you could get him some flowers – or, if you've got lots of money, a horse or something. When I fell out with Amelie, I gave her my Mewtwo, or I tried to, anyway. And when me and Mummy fell out I made her a heart card with a thousand kisses on it and a picture of a toilet. I didn't mean to draw a toilet; I messed up one of the hearts, so I had to *turn* it into a toilet.'

'Red.' Frank raised his voice a little. 'This is grown-up stuff. And you need to . . . maybe just mind your own business.'

'But if you could phone him and then ask him what he likes, or even—'

'*Red*! Enough!' Frank shouted.

Red's mouth slammed shut and he looked at Frank, his eyes wide.

'You're as bad as bloody Ken.' Frank pulled the plug out of the extension reel socket and looked at it accusingly. He continued chuntering to himself, not looking in Red's direction. 'I knew this whole thing was a mistake. You try and do somebody a favour. It's always the same: you give an inch, and people take a mile. Always being nosy, always in your business. Basic bloody respect, that's all it is.' Finally, he stood back up and, for the first time, he noticed the invitation stuck to the fridge.

He stopped talking, confused for a moment as to why the card should be there. He approached it and squinted slightly as he read Ken's block letters written over the text.

'For God's sake!'

Frank took the card from the fridge and, tearing it into pieces, he marched into the living room, and tossed the scraps into the waste-paper basket beneath his writing desk.

'There, that's the end of it.'

Outside, the lawnmower fired into life.

'Oh, *now* it bloody works!' he said, his hands thrown in the air.

RED

Red had never really seen Frank mad before. He'd seen him fed up, grumpy, annoyed and definitely sad (sometimes when Frank was staring off into space, he had a face like the rabbits at Pets at Home), but never properly angry. So, as Frank marched outside, Red stood there in shock. He trembled and felt like he was going to cry, and didn't know how to stop himself.

But, as his bottom lip started to quiver, Red closed his eyes. His breath began to quicken. His hands flexed and then balled at his sides, and his back teeth began to grind together.

Red was angry, too.

Angrier, in fact, than he had ever felt before.

Just because you weren't a grown-up, it didn't mean that bad things didn't happen to you. Things were complicated for Red, too. Really, really complicated. They had been since the day his dad had taken him to Burger King and started calling him 'mate' all the time, and explained that everything that had been good was now rubbish.

Rubbish new house and rubbish new school with rubbish mean people and stupid teachers, miles away from his friends and his old life, and with a stupid new step-mum (whatever that was) who had stupid big lips and called him 'hunny' all the time, and two new pretend demon 'sisters' who hated him. And no dog, and no Noah, and no Mewtwo card (with its special attack moves of Hyper Beam and Shadow Ball and its 200 HP points). And he had a bad arm, and he felt terrible because he'd killed a fish, and EVERYTHING WAS RUBBISH.

Including the rubbish old man who lived next door, who had just shouted at him for no reason at all, when Red was just trying to be nice and help.

He stormed out of the back door and outside. 'You're mean!'

'Eh?' Frank shouted over the sound of the lawnmower.

'You're the meanest person in the world, ever.'

The lawnmower fell silent.

'Really?'

'I wasn't being nosy, you – you . . .' Red couldn't find an insult bad enough, so carried on, even more frustrated. 'I was just looking, and the drawer was just open. And it was Ken who wrote that on the card. And you shouldn't say such mean things to people. . . . No wonder Mikey doesn't want to be your friend anymore!'

Even in his anger, Red felt that with this last comment, he had maybe gone too far. All the same, he replanted his feet, stuck out his chin and folded his arms across his chest defiantly.

The shock on Frank's face soon fell away. 'Oh, really?' Frank said. 'Well, maybe the way you pry into other people's business is why you get bullied at school so much. Have you thought about that?'

Amazingly, Red's fury clicked up one more notch. He could hear his heartbeat in his ears now, and he had to fight the almost-forgotten urge to fall to the ground, rolling and kicking like a toddler.

'You're a mean old – old – *shitterhead*!'

Yes, 'shitterhead' was the only insult bad enough for this situation, and Red saw with some satisfaction that Frank's eyebrows lifted as it hit him.

'And you're a big bully as well. As bad as Jake. And I hate school, *but* I cannot wait to go back to school, just so I can get away from you.'

'Yeah?'

'Yeah.'

'Well . . . you're a spoiled little arse.'

Red's mouth fell open. Closed. Fell open once more, and then closed again. The only noise that came out was 'Nggnnhh.' He turned away, furious, and Frank fired up the lawnmower once more.

FRANK

Marcie was walking beside him. She was talking animatedly, gesticulating with her arms. But Frank found that if he really concentrated on the sound of the mower, he couldn't hear her.

RED

For the rest of the day, Red and Frank ignored one another.

While Frank finished mowing the lawn and piling up the grass cuttings into a big mountain in one corner, Red continued to paint the fence, but without really trying to make it neat. He threw the paint on sulkily and in big splotches, and let it drip down on to the grass.

He was still amazed that he had called someone a 'shitterhead', and even more astonished that he had called a *grown-up* something like that. It was the baddest thing he had ever done in his entire life, worse even than trying to hit Jake, or that time he and Noah had been in class and drawn on a *Topsy and Tim* book. (In fairness, Red had only done the moustache; it was Noah who had drawn the willy and balls on Topsy.)

But what Red was really surprised about was the fact that he didn't care. After all, Frank had called him a name, too. And somehow, that was worse.

In the immediate aftermath of their row, the only time the two spoke to one another was when Frank, who had finished in the garden, asked Red if he wanted a drink, and Red had replied 'No,' with all the moodiness he could muster.

'Suit yourself,' Frank had said, before heading inside to nap.

Red didn't follow him for a long while, and when he did, he could hear Frank's usually comforting snore echoing through the down-stairs. Today, Red found it annoying. By now, though, he was feeling less mad about everything. And as he sat at the kitchen table and half-heartedly added a piece of sky to the London jigsaw, he felt sad.

He realised he had made a mess of everything. Again. Frank was no longer his friend. And, at the moment, Red thought, he didn't have so many friends that he could afford to start losing the ones he had.

He added a piece of black to a palace guard's bearskin hat.

He *had* been trying to help, but there was no point in denying it: he had made everything worse. Not for the first time, Red was disappointed not to have a time machine so that he could go back and do things differently. He stopped messing with the jigsaw and sighed. His head felt heavy, and he put his elbows on the table and rested his face in his hands.

Red wasn't quite sure what made him decide to retrieve the torn pieces of the invitation from the wastepaper bin. He glanced into the living room, and his eyes fell on the desk and then the wire basket beneath it, and it just felt wrong that the card was in there, destroyed.

And it was *his* fault that it was.

Red got thinking. The next best thing to a time machine, he decided, would be to stick the invitation back together and put it back in the hallway drawer. If he couldn't make things better, he could at least put things back to the way they were before Frank got angry. It wasn't time travel, but it was the next best thing.

A moment later, Red was tiptoeing past a snoring Frank, cau-tiously watching for any sign that the old man was stirring. He quietly slid the wire basket out from underneath the desk, and was about to start fishing for the torn pieces when he realised that this might make too much noise. So, instead, he picked up the small bin, and carried it back into the kitchen.

Most of the bits of the invitation were near the top of the bin, but as Red knelt on the kitchen floor and pieced them together, he found that one corner was missing. Looking through the sides of the basket, he could see that it had jiggled its way down the side, where it nestled among several balls of screwed-up paper at the very bottom.

Continuing to keep an ear out for any change in the rhythm of Frank's snores, Red picked up the basket and turned out the contents on to the floor.

Finding and retrieving the corner piece of card, he then scooped up all the other rubbish and dropped it back into the bin. All apart from one scrunch of paper, which had rolled slightly out of reach. Ignoring it, Red set about sticking the invitation back together with a roll of Sellotape he'd found in a kitchen drawer.

It wasn't perfect. Sellotape is tricky, and finding the end of the roll almost impossible. He had seen people bite Sellotape to break it at the right length, but when Red tried to do that, it just stuck to his lip, then his nose, and then one finger, before twisting around itself. Eventually, Red had succeeded in taping two fingers together, but also putting the invitation back to 'as good as new'.

Satisfied, Red peeled the tape from his fingers and held up the card, pleased. He carried it carefully in both hands so that it wouldn't fall apart again, and placed it back in the hallway dresser. Right where it had been when he'd showed it to Ken that morning.

After pushing the drawer quietly closed, he returned to the kitchen, where he gathered up the remaining slivers of tape and mess that he had left behind. He dropped these bits into the wire basket too, put the tape back where he had found it, and then, with ninja-like stealth, he cautiously put the basket back in its place, rearranging the rubbish a little so that there was no evidence of his rummaging.

Back in the kitchen, Red made one last check to see that no mess remained, and that's when he noticed the ball of scrunched-up paper against the skirting board. Unsure how he had missed it, he snatched it up and was about to take it to the bin when curiosity stopped him. It was identical to the other scrunched-up balls that lined the bottom of the wastepaper bin, and Red found himself wondering whether it was bits of a new book that Frank was writing, or something.

Quietly, side-stepping to keep one eye on the sleeping Frank, Red began to unfurl one corner, then another. He was about to unfold the entire page when there was a snuffle and a momentary pause in Frank's familiar snore. In a panic, Red quickly stuffed the paper into his hoodie pocket.

But not before he had read two words, written in blue pen:

Dear Michael.

FRANK

Frank couldn't sleep. He had gone to bed early that night, with Marcie's words stumbling around in his head, bashing into the furniture like an uninvited drunk.

They had argued about Red since the moment the boy and his mum had left for the day. Frank had pretended not to understand what the big deal was. They'd had cross words, and both had called each other names. So what? By the time the boy had gone home, things were fine.

'It's fine. He's fine.'

An hour before he'd left, Frank had offered the kid another drink and a Penguin bar, and Red had accepted both gratefully. They had even had a quiet game of *Connect 4* while he ate his snack.

But, in truth, Frank knew that that afternoon, as they'd added more and more pieces to the London jigsaw, Red hadn't been anything like his usual self. There was no endless flow of chat and questions. And even though when his had mum arrived, the boy had said goodbye cheerfully enough, the truth is that they had spent the latter part of the day awkwardly, as if the ground was littered with eggshells.

And despite the fact Frank knew this was entirely his fault, he argued anyway.

'He's not fine, Frank! You need to say sorry!' Marcie demanded.

'For what? . . . I wouldn't mind, but this whole thing is *your* fault, if you think about it.'

'What?!'

It was a fact. He had told Marcie the whole thing was a bad idea, and he had been right. Against all his better instincts, he had let these people into his home, and it was turning out just as he'd known it would.

'You know what your problem is, Frankie? Why you're such a dick to everyone? Why you can't even be decent to a sweet kid who, for some unknown, miraculous and baffling reason, actually likes you?' She was gesticulating wildly.

'No, but I'd imagine you're about to tell me,' he said, as he busied himself with the washing-up.

'You're comfortable being miserable. You wear it like a pair of slippers. That boy . . . it's like . . . it's like he's opened the curtains.' She held up her finger and thumb, spacing them a centimetre apart. 'Just the slightest little bit. And you don't like it. And so, you'll do whatever you can to close them again, just so you can go back to sitting down, doing nothing, and being mad at the world in your shitty, ugly chair and your misery slippers.'

'That chair is not ugly.'

'What if you just stopped fighting the possibility of something good happening? What if you just stopped fighting full-stop? Just for five minutes. What's the worst that could happen?'

He dried another mug. 'Well, that's easy for you to say, Marcie. You're dead.'

'Yeah,' she replied simply. '. . . Well, so are you.'

And these were the words that continued to wander around Frank's head as he stared at the bedroom ceiling.

Realising he wasn't going to go back to sleep, Frank pulled on his dressing gown and went downstairs.

'Can't sleep?' Marcie was in her pyjamas. This had long since stopped being absurd.

He sat across from her at the kitchen table, the nearly completed jigsaw between them.

One of the remaining pieces was upside down. He picked it up and turned it over: a random piece of St Paul's. Frank leaned forward to slot it into place, pressing it down with the heel of his palm.

'Nearly finished.' She nodded at the hundred or so pieces still scattered to one side.

'Mmh,' Frank acknowledged. 'Kid did most of it.' He held up the box lid. 'Supposed to be for over ten-year-olds as well. He's smart, I'll give him that.' Frank heard something that sounded like pride in his voice, and he self-consciously coughed it away.

He deliberately avoided eye contact with his wife. 'Look, about today. Maybe I *was* a bit . . .'

'Of an arse?'

'I was going to say "a bit harsh on the kid". But . . . yeah.' He looked up.

'You *should* apologise.'

He scoffed. 'Let's not get carried away.'

He added a few more random pieces to the jigsaw.

Marcie watched him, her facial expression unchanged. It was almost as though she was paused.

'Look, I'm not going to apologise to the kid; I've nothing to apologise for,' Frank said. But he wasn't sure that that was true anymore. In fact, he *knew* it wasn't true anymore. 'But I *will* have a word with him. Y'know, in the morning. Maybe I should've been a bit more . . . I dunno.' Frank abandoned that sentence, then continued more solidly. 'Besides, I could do without him moping around here all day tomorrow. Face like a smacked arse. And now I think about it, we need to finish painting that fence. It's half the problem with kids today: never seeing anything through. I mean, it was Mikey's idea to paint the bloody thing in the first place, and he shouldn't get away with a job half done. It's not right. Mind you, the way he daydreams and slops it on, it'll be Christmas by the time he's finished.' Frank sighed. 'And so, yeah, I'm not apologising, but I guess I will speak to him and, y'know, draw a line.'

'Red.'

'What?'

'Red. You said "Mikey". You said, "It was Mikey's idea to paint the thing."'

RED

Red had come home tired and still a bit upset. His mum had asked him why he seemed down in the dumps, and eventually he had told her that him and Frank had had a bit of a falling-out.

'What about?'

'He said I was being nosy and snooping in his stuff.'

'Well, Red, Frank's a very private man. Did he ask you not to look at his stuff?'

'Well, yeah, but . . .'

'So, maybe he's got a point then.'

'Maybe, but . . . did you know that he was a grandad? And do you remember that letter? The one that came to our house? Well, it wasn't a letter at all. It was an invitation to his—'

'Red, you definitely shouldn't be reading other people's mail. That really is being nosy. No wonder he wasn't happy.'

Red huffed. She didn't understand. She did that thing adults do when they don't really listen to the important bit, and get stuck on the bit about you doing something wrong.

That night, Red couldn't really be bothered to do his reflection diary. He sat at his tiny desk in his bedroom, listening to the sound of his bath being run on the other side of the bedroom wall, and staring at the sheet of paper. After ten minutes, all he had added to the form was a small doodle.

His mum entered the room with an arm full of balled-up socks. She dropped them into the bottom drawer of his wardrobe, and then peered over his shoulder. 'Maybe leave it tonight, buster. It's getting late and you can catch up with it tomorrow or over the weekend.' She left the room again.

Red put his pencil down, but then quickly picked it back up.

Reflection Diary

Name	Leonard Evans		
Class	2	Day	4

What I did today:

I painted the fence today but i fell out with Frank. and i swore at him and he swore at me and we didn't watch any movies or anything and today was the worst day ever.

What I have learned:

Nothing.

*

It wasn't until later that Red remembered the scrunched-up ball of paper in his pocket. He'd only stuffed it in there because he thought Frank was about to catch him 'snooping' again. After that, any curiosity he'd had about it had been forgotten and faded like dreams do when you wake up.

It was after his bath, after his bedtime story, after his kiss goodnight from his mummy. He was lying in bed, waiting to feel tired, when he looked at his clothes, puddled in the corner of the room where he had removed them an hour or two before: his jeans, his vest, his socks – and his hoodie, lying on top.

Red snapped on his bedside light.

Rummaging in his hoodie pockets, he retrieved the paper ball quietly and returned to his bed. Lying on his belly, he uncrumpled the paper on his pillow until it was flat and illuminated by the yellow glare from his Captain America lamp.

Red was a good reader (he was already on Band 12), but this was an entire page with small and slopey handwriting. He took his time.

Dear Michael,

I've started this letter a hundred times in my head. I don't know whether I'll ever send it, and if I did whether you'd read it.

I know I should just pick up the phone. But God knows, I was never as good at talking on that thing as your mother. And me and you were never that good at letting each other get a word in edgeways.

I just wanted to let you know that I got the messages about baby Mirabelle.

I don't know a lot, but I know that your mum would have been SO happy. God, it seems like something out of kilter with the universe that the two of them missed each other.

But you need to know how proud she would've been of you. How much that baby would have been loved by her.

~~I know it's daft, but I still talk to your mum sometimes. I don't know why I'm telling you tha~~

~~I was going to write something about how I don't know how things got so complicated between us, but that isn't true. I know how things got so bad.~~

I'm sorry for not telling you when your mum got sick. We didn't tell you because neither of us could ever bear you being sad. Simple, stupid, but the truth.

When you have a kid, you do anything to protect them, to hold their misery for them. You're about to spend the rest of your life finding that out. ~~We did th~~ I did the wrong thing, but it was for the right reasons. Maybe it was selfish, but I'm not sure that I regret it. Not sure I ever will.

I do regret . . . after. I behaved like an idiot. Said some stupid things – nothing new there. But I didn't say them to hurt you. I don't say that to excuse myself, because the truth is much worse: I wasn't thinking about you at all.

You know that I didn't deserve your mum; she was everything to me. But I was so hollowed out when she died that I lost sight of the fact that she was everything to you, too.

And I will be sorry for that until I'm in the ground myself.

Give my love to Ellie and baby Mirabelle. I hope you'll be a better father than I've been.

I know you will be.

Dad.

FRANK

'What?'

'Nothing.'

Red was standing in the kitchen and looking at Frank with an odd expression on his face. He had been acting weird since he arrived.

But then again, Frank was acting weird too.

The eggshells of the previous day were apparently still littering the floor.

It was ridiculous, but standing there, Frank realised he was feeling nervous as he worked himself up to *not* apologising.

Might as well get it over with. His left eye twitched slightly, and he cleared his throat. 'So,' he said putting his hands on his hips and looking everywhere but directly at Red. 'So, yeah.' He began again, blowing out his cheeks. His eyes finally alighted on the kitchen table. 'The . . . jigsaw's nearly finished.'

'Yeah.'

This *really* was ridiculous.

'Look, Red.'

'Uh huh?'

'I'm y'know. I'm *sorry*.' He almost did the finger air-quotes thing, like some absolute twat. What the hell was wrong with him? 'Sorry for what I said about you being bullied at school. That was just a stupid thing to say. People – er, and by people, I mean me, y'know, specific-ally . . .' Well, this was going brilliantly. 'People sometimes say stupid things when they get mad. And yeah, I didn't mean that.'

Red seemed to think for a long time about what Frank had said, and then looked almost as awkward as he replied. 'Well, I'm sorry that I said that about Mikey.'

There was another long silence.

Red looked at the floor, but when he looked back up at Frank, he was smiling. 'You called me an arse.'

'Yeah, well,' Frank replied, sheepishly. 'You did call me a shitterhead.'

'I know,' Red said, still apparently amazed that he had done exactly that.

'I'm not even sure that's a thing. I think you might have invented a new swearword there.'

'I really am sorry that I said that about Mikey. That he didn't want to see you. I'm sure he does want to see you, really, otherwise he wouldn't have invited you, y'know, to the baby party. I mean, I know sometimes you have to invite people you don't like, because for my fifth birthday party, I had to invite Jareth Pinnock, because my mum said that it was the right thing to do, even though he said my ears were big and my bag smelled like fish. But he came, and we were really good friends after that. It's really hard to be mad at some-one for a long time.'

'I don't know about that.'

Red nodded thoughtfully. Then: 'Friends?' he said, with his hand held out to shake.

'Okay.'

'You have to say it.'

'What?'

'Friends, Frank. You have to say it.'

'Red, I—'

'You have to say it.'

'Jesus wept. Fine. *Friends.*'

'And shake on it.'

Frank looked at the ceiling, then reluctantly stepped forward to shake him by the hand. Red shook once, then slapped the back of his hand, did some sort of daft potato move on top and finished by bashing fists.

'What the bloody hell was that?'

'It's a handshake me and Noah made up,' Red said proudly, wiping his nose with the palm of his hand.

'Right. Well,' Frank said, unconsciously wiping his own hand on his trousers. 'I think I'll make a brew.' He turned and shook the kettle, found it empty and carried it over to the sink.

'Frank?'

'What?'

'Can I ask you *one* question about Mikey?'

'Red,' he said, with a long sigh. The kettle suddenly felt heavy. He carried it back to its base and snapped it on.

'OK, well . . . can I show you something, then?'

Frank leaned back against the counter. 'What?'

'Promise you won't get mad.'

'Red, I . . . Okay, fine, whatever. I promise I won't get mad.'

Red produced a piece of paper from his pocket. It was folded into squares, but as he unfolded it, Frank recognised his own handwriting.

'Where did you get that?'

'It was in there.' The boy nodded towards the writing desk and the wastepaper basket beneath it. 'I honestly wasn't spying,' he said, quickly. 'I wanted to fix the invitation with Sellotape, and I did, and I put it back in the hallway drawer, good as new. And I didn't mean to take this. I only put it in my pocket because I thought, well, I don't know what I thought. I thought you were going to wake up and that you'd get mad again, and I didn't mean to read it or steal it—'

'Red, it's fine.'

'—although actually it's not really stealing, because it was already in the bin, and you can't really steal something that's already in the bin.'

'*Red*. Really. It's fine.'

Frank took the paper from his hand gently, turned it over and glanced at it. He had written many versions of this letter, mostly in his head, a few on paper. This had been the last.

'Did you read this?'

'Not all of it. There's lots of long words . . . but I do know it's to say sorry.'

Frank scanned the letter again.

'Why didn't you send it?' Red asked. 'Is it because you don't like to go outside? Because I could put it in the postbox for you next time I go to the park. Easy. I could get it to Mikey, no problem. It would be like a cool mission,' Red said, enthusiastically.

'Red, I've told you. It's more . . . complicated than that.'

'Why?'

'Well, for a start, I don't know that Mikey *wants* to read a letter from me.'

'Well, how do you know unless you send it?'

'Look, Mikey's getting on with his life. We said things – a long time ago – that are difficult to unsay.' Frank stopped. 'Why am I telling this to a six-year-old?!'

'I'm nearly nine.'

'Eh? I thought you were six.'

'I am. But I've been thinking: soon, I'll be seven, and then I'll be eight. So, I'm nearly nine,' Red said, as though this was basic common sense.

'Red, I know you're just trying to help. But adult stuff is hard. And when things have been left for a long time, it can make things worse, not better. All this stuff about, "Ah, it's water under the bridge." Fact is, sometimes so much water can flow under a bridge that the whole thing gets washed away and destroyed.'

It was Red's turn to look at Frank as if he had strayed into a foreign language. 'Well, I think you should send him the letter,' the boy said eventually. 'Because if you don't send it, then you'll never know.'

'Red.'

Red pushed his luck. 'And that would be stupid. You never really know what people are really thinking unless you ask them . . . And, if you think about it, *we're* still friends, even though you called me an arse.'

'You're not gonna let that go, are you?'

'Nope.'

Frank nodded. 'Listen, I know you're like a dog with a bone, so I'm just going to say this once, and then you're going to stop asking questions about it, okay? I appreciate that you're just trying to help. I really do. But I don't need help with this. There are certain things about grown-ups when they fall out that you just won't understand until you're all grown up yourself. And where you got this from' – Frank folded the paper in half – 'is probably exactly where it belongs.' He took the few steps into the living room, pulled the wastepaper basket out from under the desk, and dropped the letter back where Red had found it. 'Okay?'

'Okay.' Red nodded reluctantly.

But it wasn't okay.

RED

It was the most stupidest thing Red had ever heard.

So, Frank and his son Mikey had had a big argument, Red didn't fully understand what about. But, whatever. Frank had written a letter saying he was sorry, and he was now too scared to send it . . . just in case Mikey didn't want to read it.

What?

It didn't make *any* sense.

If Frank never sent the letter, how the living heck on earth would he know whether or not Mikey wanted to read it?

Stupid. With a capital *Stu*.

Red stirred the fence paint.

It had only recently become apparent to him that adults could *be* stupid. For a long time, Red had been certain that adults knew everything. When he was little, it didn't seem to matter what problem popped up, or what questions he asked; his mummy and daddy would have an answer, just right there in their brains.

But in the past year, Red had had a thousand questions – about why his mum and dad were arguing so much, about why they had to move house, about why his dad had a new girlfriend, about what on earth was going on – and suddenly those answers had been full of 'I don't know's, 'I'm not sure's and 'We'll have to see's.

And if it had come as a surprise to find out that adults did not know everything, it was even more of a shock to find out that, in fact, it was worse: adults were *idiots*.

Yeah.

They *pretended* to be super clever, walking about wearing suits and drinking coffee and eating salad, and driving and tying their own shoelaces, but when it came down to it, they were nowhere near as clever as they pretended to be.

And Frank's decision not to send the letter was just more proof of that.

Red stirred the paint more roughly, and it sloshed over the sides of the can.

He had a good mind to send the letter himself.

. . .

. . .

He stopped stirring.

. . .

Hold on a minute.

It felt like an idea that had been waiting.

An idea that was now pushing every other thought aside as it made its way to the front of his brain.

Red looked up at Frank, who was busy painting the jagged bits at the top of the fence that Red couldn't reach.

Red could get the letter to Mikey himself.

His first instinct was to dismiss the idea.

For a start, he had promised Frank, only half an hour ago, that he would mind his own business. And this would be doing the opposite of that. Frank would almost certainly be mad. *Really* mad. Maybe he would even stop being friends with Red altogether.

No, it was a bad idea.

. . .

. . .

But only if Frank found out.

Red couldn't stop his `IMAGINATION` from running.

What if Mikey read the letter and stopped being his dad's enemy? Frank *couldn't* be angry then. In fact, in a way, that would make Red a sort of hero. And no one was ever mad at a hero.

Also, now Red thought about it, if Frank had not wanted Mikey to read the letter, he wouldn't have written it in the first place. That was just common sense.

And, actually, if he *really really really* didn't want Mikey to read it, he would have ripped the paper into pieces and put it in the outside bin, not just crumpled it into a little ball and put it in that tiny bin under the desk where literally *anyone* could find it.

In fact, in a funny sort of way, if you really thought about it, it was almost as though Frank *wanted* him to find it.

Wanted him to send it.

In the space of a few minutes, Red had not just managed to convince himself that getting the letter to Mikey was the right thing to do, he had also somehow managed to convince himself that the whole thing was kind of, in a way, Frank's idea.

Okay, if he thought about this too much, it didn't make a lot of sense, but Red managed to get around this particular problem by *not* thinking about it too much. Instead, he began to concentrate on *how* to put his plan into action.

'What are you up to?' Frank was looking at him suspiciously, and Red realised he had been frowning while staring at nothing in particular.

'What do you mean?'

'You've got a look on your face. Like you're up to something.'

'I'm not up to anything. Maybe *you're* up to something?'

Frank shook his head and continued to paint.

That was a close one. Red would have to be more careful. His mission depended on it.

*

For the rest of the day, Red found it difficult to concentrate on anything else.

After the pair had finished painting the fence, he helped Frank to wash the brushes in a bucket on the patio. Frank then sat in a deck chair and did that morning's neglected crossword, while Red lay on the now patchy and brown grass and flicked through a *Bunny Vs Monkey* book that he had tossed in his bag that morning. He wasn't reading it, though. He was just pretending to. Really, he was thinking.

The first part of his plan was simple: retrieve the letter from the wastepaper basket and hide it in his bag. He would just have to wait until Frank was busy doing something or having his afternoon nap.

What was proving harder to work out was what to do next.

'You hungry?' Frank asked, without looking up from his lap.

'Not really.'

Frank looked at his watch and raised his eyebrows. 'It's nearly twelve.'

'Mmh,' Red non-replied.

The simplest thing to do with the letter was to just put it into a postbox. You couldn't just put a piece of paper in a postbox, of course. Red knew that. It had to be in an envelope and have a person's name and address on it, so the postman knew where to take it. But that was fine. Red had some envelopes. They had the Gruffalo on the front, but that didn't matter too much.

He could also get Mikey's address; it was printed on the

invitation that he had Sellotaped back together. He could get that at the same time as he got the letter, while Frank was sleeping. Easy.

He *would* need a stamp. The postman didn't take letters unless they had a stamp on them. But, after some hard thinking, Red knew what to do about this, too. He could just tell his mum that he wanted to send a letter to Seth the Llama, and she would give him a stamp.

Then all he would have to do, next time they were going to the park or the shops, would be to pop the letter into the postbox at the end of the street.

Mission accomplished.

It seemed like the perfect plan, but as Red and Frank settled down in front of the TV to eat their lunch (ham, cheese, jam and Space Raider sandwiches again), Red began to see the holes. It wasn't the perfect plan at all.

For a start, he hadn't written to Seth in ages; his mum would definitely be suspicious. And what if she saw the address on the front of the envelope? She would ask questions – and not ones he could answer without jeopardising the whole thing.

And there was another problem, too: a much bigger problem. There was no guarantee that the letter would even get there. After all, the invitation had been delivered to *their* *h*ouse instead of Frank's in the first place! Postmen made mistakes all the time.

Disappointed, Red ruled out the idea of sending the letter like this; it was too important, and posting it was just too risky.

An hour later, Frank and Red were at the kitchen table, working on the jigsaw.

Perhaps, Red thought, with a sudden flash of inspiration, he could just give the letter to Ken? That way, he wouldn't be risking a postman losing it. And Ken would pass it on to Mikey, no problem.

Red looked up from the jigsaw and asked in a voice that he hoped sounded normal, 'Is Ken coming today?'

Frank searched through the puzzle pieces as he answered. 'Don't think so. Why?'

'Oh, nothing. Just wondered.'

Damn.

Again, Frank looked at him as though he was up to something, but soon returned his attention back to the puzzle.

Actually, Red thought, maybe it was a good thing that he *couldn't* send the letter through Ken. What if Ken told Frank what he was up to? After all, those two had been friends forever, and friends forever told each other everything.

Another idea for the dustbin.

This was hopeless.

He continued to try and think of a plan that might work, but it was no good. Maybe grown-up stuff *was* just too hard. If he had learned anything in the past few months, it was that some things just could not be made right, no matter how much you tried. Maybe this was one of those things. Maybe this really *was* just too complicated.

Red was about to give up on the whole idea.

'You want to do it?'

'What?'

Frank was holding up a piece of the jigsaw.

Red had been so busy thinking about the mission that he had almost entirely daydreamed his way through an hour of adding pieces to the scene of London. And now, when he looked down, he discovered that there was only one squiggly space left. The final piece.

'Whoa,' Red said. It was like coming out of a trance.

Frank held up the box. 'Two thousand pieces, and only one left.'

'Blimey.'

Red took the piece. It had a letter 'E' on the front, and when he slotted it into place, it completed the word 'Covent' in Covent Garden. It was on a destination sign on the front of a cartoon tube train, which was racing over London Bridge.

That was daft. Tube trains didn't go *over* London Bridge. They went underground; that's why it was called the underground. And even if they *did* go over London Bridge, this particular train was going in the wrong direction. *And* it was the wrong colour; it had Central line written on the side, and Covent Garden was on the dark blue line, not the red one. Everyone knew that.

'Six hours of our lives we'll never get back. Doesn't even really look like the box.'

Frank had a point. On the box lid there was a black cab in the middle of the picture, swerving through traffic.

But Red wasn't really listening. He was looking at the completed jigsaw: the tiny overhead map of London in one corner, the tube stations listed in a box in the other. The big river snaking through the centre of the whole thing.

He was thinking about how wrong it was.

It wasn't just the ridiculous tube train on London Bridge. The big wheel, the Millennium Eye, was missing from the final picture, and so was the super-pointy building in the middle. And although the lines for the underground were on there – zigging and zagging around the landmarks in red and black and yellow and blue lines, they weren't quite right. Because when they got to the edges of the puzzle, they disappeared.

But Red knew that those lines went further: to Chorleywood and Hatch End and Tooting. And he knew all this not just because he had done a project on the London Underground at school, and not just because he had memorised so many of its stations and stops. He knew this because he had lived in this city his entire life, and he knew that the underground could take you wherever you wanted to go.

He felt a buzz of excitement in his feet as the mission began to come together.

He would deliver the letter himself.

Simple.

FRANK

Frank wasn't entirely sure what he was feeling. There is a scene in the film *Life of Brian* in which the main character is suddenly scooped up by a UFO, taken on a whistle-stop tour of the galaxy by aliens, and then dropped back in the desert of Judea. The film then just continues without anyone really mentioning it.

And that was close to how Frank felt: like his life had been briefly turned inside out. And now things were about to go back to normal in a way that made the previous week seem unreal.

'Just admit it. You're gonna miss him . . . maybe, just a little bit?'

Frank raised an eyebrow in Marcie's direction. 'Mmh.'

'Mmh,' she mocked.

'Mummy's here!' Red shouted from the living room, as he spotted Sarah coming up the path from the window. He raced to greet her at the door, and when he opened it, she hugged him without dropping the bags in her arms.

'Hey, Frank,' she shouted over Red's head. He waved once and nodded, and Marcie disappeared as she walked through the kitchen wall.

'I've brought fish and chips,' Sarah said, as she held up the bags in her arms. 'No arguments.'

She seemed mildly surprised when he didn't protest. She hugged Red once more. 'You don't have to lift a finger, Frank. I'll get the plates – and I'll *even* do the washing-up.

'I know it's not much,' she added, unpacking the bags on the countertop and opening the steaming parcels of paper. 'I just really wanted to say thank you for this week.' She stopped being busy for a second. 'I don't know what we'd have done if . . .'

Oh God, Frank thought. *She's going to turn around and be crying.*

'Anyway, plates?' Sarah said, gathering herself and turning to face them.

'Door above the toaster. Knives and forks in the drawer under-neath.' Frank was already sliding the jigsaw carefully to one side so that they could all fit around the kitchen table.

'Sit. Eat. And then I promise you can have your life back,' Sarah said, as she presented Frank with a plate of fish and chips. Returning to the bag, she produced a bottle of beer. Opening the cutlery drawer again, she found a bottle opener and, popping the cap, she put the beer next to Frank's plate. 'Happy Friday, Franklin.'

Frank and Red ate. As Sarah talked. A lot.

'. . . Mark and Joe'll be back in a couple of weeks as well, so that'll be a relief, I guess? Not that you can't ask us to nip to the shops and stuff,' she added quickly, as though she had said something wrong. 'Honestly, any time at all. It's no problem.'

She was one of those people who filled silences as though they were dangerous. Marcie could be the same, especially when she was nervous; it was one of her most endearing qualities. Frank had always hated small talk, but for some reason he enjoyed the sound of it.

'You're quiet, Reddy,' Sarah said.

'Mmm. Just thinking.'

'Worried about school on Monday?'

'A bit.'

Of course, Frank thought. That explained why Red had been so quiet and acting weird all day.

'We've got a return-to-school meeting before you go back to class. I think it's gonna be fine.' She tickled him under the chin. 'I think you're gonna miss Frank a bit as well, aren't you? We're not going anywhere, Red. Neither is Frank; we'll still just be next door.'

Red smiled without teeth. Frank said nothing. And Sarah awkwardly moved on to her day at work, the fact that Red's dad was picking him up on Sunday to *finally* take him to the football and the news that Red's auntie was coming to visit soon.

Suddenly, she stopped talking and licked the grease from her fingers. 'And oh! I nearly forgot. Look what I bought.' She jumped up and rummaged in one of the remaining carrier bags, producing, with a flourish, a bottle of WD40. 'The man in the shop said it'll stop the trampoline from squeaking.' She sat back down.

Frank turned the can over in his hand. In that moment, he found himself thinking about the day that the boy's blond mop had first appeared over the fence. And then the crayoned picture of a dinosaur, which had somehow found its home on his fridge door. He half-smiled at the memory of himself trying to tell the kid a joke about trampolines, and the spinning karate kick that had sent Red's shoe flying past his ear—

'Well, thank God for that,' he said, putting the can to one side. He looked over at Red, who was folding some chips into a slice of bread. The boy took a single bite, and then put it down on the plate.

'I'm full,' Red said, with a groan.

'Right, well—'

But she was interrupted by Red unleashing a mighty burp, deep and impressively long.

'Jesus,' Frank said, as it continued.

'Red!' Sarah laughed in astonishment.

''Scuse me,' the boy said, wiping his eyes.

'Sounded like you were bloody possessed,' Frank said. Sarah chuckled again.

Red's mum tidied the chip papers away, while Red collected his things, stuffing them into his bags and pull-along case. There were bits scattered all over the house: books, figures, toys and cards. After a final scout around the living room and garden for anything left behind, the three finally gathered awkwardly in the hallway.

'So, what do you say to Frank?'

'Thanks, Frank.'

Frank nodded. 'Have you got all your stuff?'

'Think so.' Red was stood clutching his backpack tight to his chest, as though it contained treasure. He tapped it a couple of times, as though he was reassuring Frank about the contents, and then gave an exaggerated wink.

Weird. Kid.

'Okay,' said Sarah. 'We'll leave you to it. We really do appreciate everything – and, like I said, anything you need, anything at all, we're right next door.'

'I'm fine.'

'Right.'

'And, er . . .' Frank coughed. 'Good luck at school, Red.'

They were still shuffling towards the door, and somehow Frank's comment about school didn't seem to be enough. It felt like the moment called for something more profound, something poignant, perhaps even touching.

And so he continued. 'And if that Jake kid gives you any more crap, come and tell me. I'll go down there and volley the little shit over the school.'

'Jesus, Frank! This is how we got in this trouble in the first place!' Sarah said, throwing her hands up in exasperation.

But Red was beaming from ear to ear.

Eventually, his mum smiled too. 'We'll see ya, Frank.'

'Yeah.'

The door closed behind them.

Frank went back into the living room and sat down on the sofa. His hand settled on a card that was stuck between the cushions. One of Red's Pokémon cards. Mega Blastoise.

A Water type, Frank thought, distractedly.

RED

Red read the message again, then crossed out the words 'See you later, baked potato,' as that seemed a bit babyish for such an important note.

Then he looked at the number of kisses. His hand was aching from the number of 'x's he had drawn; there were so many. But he shook his hand to get rid of the cramp and drew seven more.

He then underlined the word 'importint'.

> Mummy, don't worry I have not run away again.
> I am just gone on a importint mission. It is importint.
> ~~See you later baked potato.~~ Red x
> xxxx ₓxxx x xxxˣₓxx ₓxx xxxx xₓxxxx x xˣxxˣ xxx xₓx xˣxxx ₓx ˣ

Hiding the note under his pillow ready for the morning, he then went through his backpack, double-double-checking its contents.

Dairylea Lunchable. Check.

Fruit Shoot. Check.

Quavers. Check.

Pokémon cards. Check.

Book about Marvel Monsters (just in case he got bored on the journey). Check.

Bonzer. Check.

And lastly, in the waterproof pocket at the front of the rucksack, the pieced-together invitation and the crumpled letter from Frank to Mikey. Check.

Red had spent most of Saturday secretly preparing for his quest. Squirrelling away the things he would need over the day, whenever his mum was distracted, and thought he was playing in his room or watching TV.

And now he was ready. Red slid the rucksack under his bed and went over the plan one more time.

Tomorrow was Sunday morning. Red would leave well before his mum woke up. She always got up late on a Sunday – and even if she heard him, she wouldn't think it weird that he was up and awake before her. He was usually downstairs and watching cartoons for ages before she appeared, anyway.

Red would then quietly get dressed, grab his things, sneak out the front door and walk all the way to the Tesco shop, past the park and then to the underground station at the top of Edgerton Road.

He had caught the tube from there lots of times with his mum since they'd moved here, and he knew exactly where to get on to go in the direction of London. There were only two platforms; he needed the one with a Greggs.

Red unfolded the tiny tube map and smoothed it out on his bed. Tracing his finger, he followed the line as it left Finchley Central Station. It was on the black line (that was also called the North line), and it went through Highgate and Archway, and then eventually into the middle of the city. But if Red *stayed* on the train, it would go all the way through London and out the other side, and eventually stop at South Wimbledon. And that was where Mikey lived:

148 Castlegate Rd
South Wimbledon
SW19 1DE

to be exact.

Red's finger stopped at South Wimbledon station. He wouldn't even have to change trains or get off and back on again, which was good. Some stations had a million platforms, and once you got closer to the city, all the lines got tangled up and confusing. The risk of getting lost was big.

He had read a story once about a boy who got lost in London and had to join a gang of other boys who stole things from other people's pockets. Which actually sounded quite fun. He quite liked the idea of . . . Red was starting to daydream, and he scolded himself for getting distracted.

Once he was in Wimbledon, things would get a bit trickier. Red had no idea how far from that station the house would be, but he had thought about it, and he was pretty sure that it wouldn't be a huge problem. After all, part of the address said 'Castlegate', so it made sense that the house he was looking for would be near a big castle. And that should be easy to spot, because castles were massive.

So. This was it. The plan. Get to the end of the road. Take the tube train to Wimbledon. Get off and look for Frank's son's house (near a big castle). Give the letter to Mikey.

Mikey would then read the letter, and Mikey and Frank would make friends. And then Frank wouldn't be so super sad that his wife was dead.

And Red would basically be a hero.

'Red!' his mum shouted from downstairs. 'Look at the time. Supper and bedtime!'

'Okay!' he shouted back. Red folded the tube map roughly and stuffed it into his backpack, which he then slid under his bed. He changed into his pyjamas and skipped downstairs for a glass of milk and a biscuit, and after a bedtime story (which he was too distracted to really listen to), he kissed his mummy goodnight.

It was as he lay awake, waiting to doze off, that Red remembered he had forgotten to do something the night before. He found the sheet of paper he was looking for on his bedside table, and also a pencil.

After writing his final Reflection Diary, he went to sleep, dreaming about adventure.

Reflection Diary

Name	Leonard Evans		
Class	2	Day	5

What I did today:

Yesterday was my last day at Frank's house. I am sad about that because he doesn't have a lot of friends and will probably miss me not being there all the time. But tomorrow I am going on a mission that I think will make him less sad. I am a bit scared because it will be scary and hard and I will have to go on a really long journey on my own, like a million miles.

But he is my friend.

And it is what Jesus and Kris Akabusi would do.

PART FOUR

RED

Bradley Darwent
smells like scotch eggs!

Red wasn't sure who Bradley Darwent was, or whether he did, in fact, smell like scotch eggs. But people on the busy tube train kept looking at him, and so he was distracting himself by reading the graffiti on the wall opposite.

Red wasn't all that surprised that people kept looking at him. He knew that it was weird for someone as small as he was to be outside on his own. When you were six, you were supposed to be with an adult wherever you went. This was because there was always a chance that you might be run over or kidnapped.

It was quite a sensible rule, Red thought, but that was only *most* of the time – and this was *not* most of the time.

Rules changed when you were on an important mission.

A mission that, so far, had gone pretty well.

But not perfectly.

*

Getting out of the house had been easy enough.

It was cold and still a little bit dark when Red quietly pulled on his clothes and checked the contents of his bag one final time. He didn't like the dark too much, and he had to fight the urge to climb back into bed, pull his Iron Man covers over his head and forget about the whole thing. But by the time he was tiptoeing downstairs, fishing the front door keys from the bowl, unlocking the door and carefully slipping outside, Red was greeted by bright and glaring sunshine. So bright, in fact, that he left his bag on the doorstep and sneaked back inside to grab his *Paw Patrol* sunglasses from the shelf in the hallway.

Back outside, the only sound was wittering birdsong and a distant car alarm. As Red eased the door shut behind him, it closed with a rattle that sounded deafening after the silence of the sleepy house. He paused for a moment, his head tilted to one side as he listened to see if the sound had disturbed his mum.

Satisfied that it hadn't, he turned to face Merton Road. He breathed deeply, summoning his courage for what lay ahead.

Red looked up and down the empty street, and for one worrying moment, he couldn't remember which direction Finchley Central was in. Every time he had gone to the tube station before, his hand had been in his mummy's. Without her hand, it felt as though down was kind of up and up was kind of down.

But, shifting his backpack on his back, Red looked up the road again, saw the flash of traffic lights in the distance and scolded himself for being so silly. Of course he knew which way to go. If he turned right past Frank's, it took him to the park, the mini Tesco and then the tube station. The other way would take him past the little dog that always barked at the fence, the Chinese takeaway called the Jade Plum, and St Agnes.

Feeling reassured, and with this tiny map in his head, Red put on his sunglasses and hopped off the doorstep, then walked down the path and through the open gate.

Walking to the station was pretty straightforward, too.

The streets were quiet; most people were still in bed. And if anyone thought it was strange that a little boy was hurrying past on his own, they didn't say anything. Everybody he passed was either in too much of a rush of their own, or were one of those 'gormless buggers' that Frank talked about, who were so hypnotised by the tiny screens on their phones that they wouldn't notice if an elephant strolled past.

CHELSEA FC

D.J. Ripcord

So, Red thought – as he read a little more of the graffiti – up to that point everything had gone according to plan. It was only when he got to Finchley Central that things got a bit tricky.

It wasn't a big station. Not like the massive ones in the middle of London that had billions of people in them. But there were still plenty of travellers jostling one another as they headed to the exit, joined a queue for coffee, or darted in and out of the shop that sold magazines.

Thankfully, all of them were, once again, too busy (or too tall) to notice the boy half their size standing on the concourse, trying to get his bearings.

Red had been certain that he would know which way to go once he was inside. But now he wasn't quite so sure.

A woman's voice announced that there were 'engineering works on the Circle and Pickabilly Lines' and that the next train at platform two would be 'bound for Highbar Nit', and to 'Mind the gap between the train and the platform.'

He didn't remember the station being quite this loud and confusing. The constant dodging to get out of people's way wasn't helping either. At one point, he found himself completely turned around. And despite thinking he'd been heading in the right direction, he somehow ended up on the pavement outside the station again, staring at the road.

'Dammit,' he said to himself, before heading back inside.

Refusing to be defeated so early in his quest, Red took off his sunglasses and slid them into the webbing on the side of his bag. That was better.

He looked around properly, and noticed a group of people standing motionless. They were staring up at a set of TVs above their heads. Red looked at the orange glow of the changing screens himself, and found nothing useful there. But to the side of it, he found something *very* useful indeed: 'This Way to Trains' was written on a big sign, along with a pointy finger. Just below that were the barriers.

Brilliant.

Newly pleased with himself, Red took a purposeful couple of strides in that direction, before stopping again.

Oh.

The barriers.

This bit of the mission was really not going well at all. Red had forgotten about the barriers: the little gates that flew open like batwings to let you on to the platforms. You needed a ticket, or to tap a special card to make them work. And he had neither.

And as if that wasn't bad enough, there was a man in uniform standing right next to the barriers, making sure nobody sneaked through. He looked half asleep and was picking at a crusty stain on his tie, but Red wasn't stupid. That was probably a trick. If you tried to get past him without a ticket, he would no doubt spring into action, like a killer ninja, and take you down.

Red turned away. The last thing he needed right now was to have to fight an expert in Kung Fu.

He leaned against a pillar and pretended to study the big map on the wall behind him while he had a think.

He was beginning to wonder if this was such a good idea. His plan had seemed foolproof the night before, but it was looking more and more likely that it would fail before he even made it as far as the train.

He was still standing there a few minutes later, half thinking about heading home, when, out of the corner of his eye, Red saw an opportunity.

A gaggle of older children entered the station. There seemed to be a hundred of them, all chattering in a language that Red didn't understand, each wearing identical purple backpacks. There was a woman with them, holding a closed umbrella above her head, and they followed her like ducklings. The woman said something to the ninja, and without even looking up from his tie, he opened one of the gates for them.

Trying to look casual, but holding his breath, Red fell in step with the crowd of teenagers as they started to flood through the gate. Lost among them, he found himself on the other side in no time at all.

Glancing back, Red saw that the ninja warrior hadn't spotted him – he was too preoccupied by the fact that he had apparently scraped enough of the stain from his tie, and was now sniffing the tip of his finger with a grimace.

Some of the boys and girls did notice the newest member of their group with some confusion, but Red continued to be carried along with the gaggle, across the station floor and down an escalator, until he was standing among them on the platform. And it was the right platform. The one with a Greggs.

The mission was back on.

Red looked up at the electronic board above their heads as it changed: *Morden (via Bank) 1 min.*

He felt good. But then he saw that the woman with the umbrella, the one in charge of the group of teenagers, was looking his way with a frown and a curious look on her face.

Uh oh.

Making himself small, Red pretended not to notice as she leaned over the children to say something to him. But as the woman opened her mouth to speak, there was the familiar metal-on-metal screech of a train as it turned the corner and arrived at the platform in front of them. Before she could say anything, she was carried away by the group as it surged onboard.

Red could just make out the lady, now on the tube train, peering over the sea of heads to see where he had gone. And so he slipped away from the group and entered the carriage to the left. The doors began to beep before closing as he hopped inside.

There, amongst the busyness of the other passengers, he took his backpack from his shoulders and, holding it to his chest, he found an empty seat. It was next to a man with big boots and paint on his trousers, and Red was pleased to notice that, unlike some of the people sitting opposite, the man didn't pay him any attention. Didn't even look up from *Candy Crush* as Red squeezed into the seat beside him.

As the train pulled away from Finchley, the driver's voice came over the tannoy: *'Passengers are advised that due to overcrowding related to the London Marathon, this will now be a partially disrupted service and will terminate at Euston. All passengers travelling for stations further south, including Morden, Balham and South Wimbledon, are advised to change at Euston for southbound services.'*

Red wasn't really listening. He was already too busy reading the words that people had scrawled on the wall opposite.

TORIES OUT!

THE WILDHEARTS

Yer Da' sells Avon

. . . It was probably nothing anyway.

FRANK

It was quiet.

Probably no more so than any other morning at 34 Merton Road. But after a week of Red, it *felt* quiet.

The whole of Saturday had felt like the air was more still, and as though the volume of the ticking clock on the mantelpiece had been turned back up.

Frank had long taken comfort in that stillness, that contrast to the outside world, with all its busyness and nonsense and sharp edges. But this morning, it felt funereal. It was, like Gary Cooper used to say in those Sunday afternoon Westerns, *too* quiet.

Until he heard the commotion next door.

It began slowly, with a vague noise of frantic movement in the neighbouring hallway, or maybe someone running up and down the stairs. It was difficult to tell. A moment later, it sounded like someone was running from one side of the house to the other.

This was followed by a minute or two of silence. And then, just as Frank was beginning to return to his newspaper, there were more rapid footfalls, and then a too-loud, one-sided conversation that could only be someone shouting into a phone.

'What the hell?' Frank muttered to himself, putting the pages to one side, taking off his glasses and stuffing them into his shirt pocket. It was the most noise he had heard from next door since the day Red and his mother had moved in.

Curious, but telling himself that he was just checking to see if the morning post had arrived, Frank opened the front door and was surprised to see Sarah already halfway up his path, phone pressed to her ear.

'Is he here?' she shouted frantically in Frank's direction.

'Eh?'

'Red, Frank! Is he here?'

'What? No. Why would he be?'

But she had already spun on her heel, and was hurrying back down the path, resuming her frantic phone conversation as she disappeared back inside her own house. In her haste, she didn't close the door behind her, and Frank could hear snatches of the conversation as it continued.

'I don't know! . . . No! You're not listening! No . . . Jamie! I've checked. What friends from school? He hasn't *got* any friends at this bloody school? You'd know that if you spent five minutes . . . He's *missing*! No . . . I've checked. Red is missing!'

It took a moment for the words to take on meaning. When they did, Frank felt a descending in his stomach that he hadn't felt in a long time. He was immediately spun back to the sounds and smells of a moment thirty years earlier, while on a summer's weekend in Morecambe Bay, in an arcade on the pier. Turning around for a moment to use a change machine, and turning back a second later to discover that Mikey had disappeared. Vanished amidst the flashing lights and noise.

It had taken a whole seven minutes to find him. The longest seven minutes of Frank's life. Seven minutes when every possible calamitous and fateful end for their son had run through his mind.

And then they had found him. An everyday miracle. Standing in front of a stall, happily and cluelessly watching as people threw darts at balloons.

At first, the memory had been disconcerting, but as Frank stood there on the doorstep, and the adrenaline of the flashback dissipated, he found it strangely comforting.

So, *apparently* Red was missing.

But kids at this age went 'missing' all the time, causing a load of fuss over nothing usually, he told himself sensibly.

It wouldn't surprise Frank if the boy's dad had let him down again, and Red was fed up and hiding away under his bed or in a wardrobe – or, more than likely, under his trampoline.

Yeah, that's exactly the way that this sort of thing turned out.

Still, Frank walked down the path to the gate and looked up and down the street for any sign of the boy. Then he walked back inside, through the house and into the back garden. He peered over the fence at the trampoline, angling his head to see underneath.

Nothing. No sign of Red, apart from the bare earth beside one leg and the scratchings left behind by the boy's doodling with a stick.

Heading back through the house, Frank found himself once more on his front doorstep. Sarah was outside, frantically looking up and down the street herself, the phone still pressed to her ear.

'Well, he's not under the trampoline,' Frank called over to her.

'I know,' she said, rubbing her forehead frantically. 'It was one of the first places I checked. Have you checked *your* garden? He could've slipped under that big gap under the fence.'

Even in these circumstances, Frank found himself slightly affronted by the criticism of the fence repair. 'The gap's not that big.'

'Frank!'

'What? He's not in my garden.'

'Are you sure? Have you checked your shed?'

'. . . I think that's if you're missing a cat?'

'Jesus, Frank. He could be hiding. Just bloody check.'

'Alright, alright.'

He disappeared back through the house, into the garden and pulled open the door to the shed.

Nothing.

Back at the front of the house, Sarah was still looking up and down the street as though she wanted to run in one direction or the other, but didn't trust her feet to take her the right way.

'Anything?'

'No, nothing. Have you tried under his bed? I remember Mikey once—'

'Frank, he's not under his bed. The front door was unlocked. He's taken his bag, some food – he's taken Bonzer, for God's sake. He wasn't here when I got up. God only knows how long he's been gone!'

'What? You think he's run off? Y'know, because of school and everything.'

'Maybe. I don't know. I don't think so. He left a note. But it just makes no sense.'

She started talking into the phone again. 'I *have* been holding – for *five* minutes! Yes, I know that you're short-staffed. Don't put me on hold. *Do not* put me on hold.' She silently screamed at the phone. 'They put me on hold.'

Frank took the opportunity to speak. 'What about that friend of his, Noah?'

'I've just spoken to his mum. He doesn't know anything. Him and Red haven't seen each other in weeks.'

'What about his dad? Could he be trying to see his dad?'

'I've just got off the phone with him as well. He doesn't have a clue where he could be; he's on his way over.' That seemed to reinforce the seriousness of the situation, and she became frantic again. 'I'm on the phone to the police now, they're sending someone. But they said it could take longer than usual because of the marathon. They've just said to "sit tight". What the hell does that even mean?! He's six, Frank! Sit *tight*?! Did he say anything to you? Yesterday? Anything at all?'

Frank thought for a second. 'No. He was behaving a bit weirdly, but . . . well, it's Red we're talking about. Look, I'm sure he's just—'

He stopped talking as someone approached along the road.

If Sarah had been hoping for sirens, and the flashing blue lights of the modern cavalry, she was going to be sorely disappointed. Officer Lowden cycled to a stop outside their front gates.

Great. They've sent bloody Poirot, Frank thought . . . *And from a westerly direction.*

RED

Thankfully, the other passengers had stopped paying much attention to Red. With each stop, some people had got on and some people had got off, and the faces around him had changed with each station.

And because it was now really busy, anybody who did notice him wouldn't guess that he was on his own. They would probably think he was with one of the grown-ups who were now packed together, holding a nearby bar or a strap above their heads.

Red relaxed a little.

His backpack was still on his lap. He was hungry, so he delved inside and pulled out his Dairylea Lunchable. Tearing off the foil lid, he turned his bag over so that it was flat, and resting the pot on it, he started to assemble the tiny crackers. Eating them crunchily, as his legs dangled from his seat, he started to look around the carriage.

Most of the people were staring at their phones; others swayed with the rhythm of the train as they stared off into space. Through the standing crowd, Red could see a man sitting opposite. He was wearing a suit and tie and reading a book with a pair of scissors on the front, and pretending not to be annoyed by the woman beside him, who was making mischievous faces at her baby in a pram.

As they got closer and closer to London, the carriage continued to fill, only now it was with couples and groups, almost all dressed in their PE kits, some with numbers on their chests. One man had a big orange wig on, and another man was dressed in a furry costume. He had a bear's head, which he held in his arms, as though he'd just chopped it off.

Red continued to swing his feet as he added a circle of cheese to his last cracker. Finally, the driver's voice sounded over the speakers as the train lights flickered and, with a squeal, the train slowed once more: *'Due to overcrowding related to the London Marathon, this service will terminate here. All change, please. Passengers for the Northern Line to Morden should take the Victoria Line and change at Stockwell.'*

Red didn't understand any of that. But it couldn't have been all that important, because the driver sounded super bored.

He cheerfully scrunched up his Lunchables rubbish and dropped it into his bag. Taking out his crisps, he clipped the top of his backpack closed. then licked his fingers and brushed the cracker crumbs from his trousers. As the train came to a stop, he looked around. There was a surge towards the exits, and Red seemed to be the only one in the carriage not moving. The man in the boots, who had been sitting there next to him for the entire journey, continued to smash fruit into diamonds as he stood up and joined the shuffle towards the doors.

At the same time, nobody was pushing to get on, and within a minute, the carriage was completely empty.

Very strange, Red thought, as the lights faded slightly. This was followed by a judder as the train's engine went quiet.

They were probably just giving the engine a rest, he thought, as he opened his Quavers.

*

It was ten minutes before Red started to get nervous. He had never been on a tube that had stopped for this long before, and had certainly never been on one so completely empty. He was taking his map out of his bag to double-check his route when he spotted a man walking through the next carriage along, coming his way. The man had a shaved head and tattoos on both arms, and he was wearing one of those really brightly coloured vests. He also had a bin liner in one hand, which he was filling with any rubbish that he came across. The door to the adjoining carriage swung open. As the man entered, Red could hear that he was singing in a high-pitched voice to himself, about players playin' and haters hatin'.

To begin with, the man didn't notice Red sitting there, and Red was beginning to consider the possibility that he had finally achieved invisibility. After all, nobody had paid him much attention on the busy train, and this man seemed not to be able to see him either. Suddenly, though, the man stood up straight, took an earbud out of one ear and looked him up and down.

'What you doing on here?'

Red wasn't sure what to say. 'I'm just . . .'

'You can't be on here, it's . . . Hang on, where's your mum and dad?'

'I'm just. They're just . . .' For the first time, Red was getting a little scared. 'I'm sorry, I . . .'

'Well, are you lost, or what?' the man started to say, taking the other earbud out of his ear.

But Red was already standing up and pulling on his backpack. 'Sorry,' he stammered as he hurriedly walked to the open door.

'Hold up kid, wait a minute!'

But Red was already on the platform.

To begin with, he just walked away super fast as the man stepped off the train behind him. But as he shouted again to wait, the noise echoed down the tunnel, and Red started to jog – and then run.

The station seemed to be entirely deserted, the slap of his feet the loudest thing. But as he reached the end of the platform, without looking back, he turned a corner – into noise. Into chaos. A seemingly infinite number of passengers, heading in all directions.

Red could no longer hear the man shouting as he dove into the crowd. He had lost him.

But there was a bigger problem.

Because Red was now lost himself.

Among the legs of nine million people.

FRANK

'Mrs Evans? I'm Officer Lowden. I understand your little boy has disappeared.'

Sarah clicked the phone off and was clearly about to respond incredulously, angrily, when Frank spoke for her.

'What?! Where's the rest of you? Where's the real police!?'

'Mr Hayes,' Lowden said, way too calmly for either of them. 'Please. Mrs Evans, the other officers will be here soon. This is my beat, and I was just around the corner when I heard it on dispatch.' He tapped the radio on his shoulder, then leaned his bike against the wall and removed his cycle helmet. 'In the meantime, why don't you tell me what you know: how long he's been gone, whatever you can.'

'I've been through this on the phone ten times already!' But Sarah filled Lowden in on the details. '. . . and so, I woke up, the door was unlocked from the inside. His bag's gone, his favourite teddy's gone, even some food.'

'Food?'

'Yeah. A Dairylea Lunchable.' Sarah was shaking her head again.

Lowden stood with his legs too far apart, taking notes in his black book. He was trying to look authoritative, but was clearly struggling with the spelling of the word 'Lunchable'. Finally, he finished writing with a dot of his pen on the page. 'So, he's obviously left of his own accord.'

'Well, yeah. Obviously.'

'And you say he's run away before?'

'No, he's *threatened* to run away before,' she said, through gritted teeth. 'Like, when he was three, or whatever? Not like this!'

He nodded. 'And is there anything that might have upset him: an argument, or any trouble that might have made him want to run away?'

Sarah shook her head vigorously, but then stopped. 'There's been some bother at school with another kid. There was a – I don't know . . . not a *fight*, an incident. We were told he had to stay home for the week. He's due back on Monday.'

'I see.'

'No, you don't see,' Frank interrupted. 'Instead of asking daft questions, why don't you get on that stupid bloody posh bike of yours and start looking.'

'Like I said,' Lowden said, patiently, turning his attention to Frank, 'the patrol cars and other officers are on their way. The more information I've got for when they arrive, the better, okay?'

Frank turned away, rolling his eyes.

'Now, Mrs Evans, you say he left a note?'

Frank had forgotten about that.

'Shit. Yeah, I've put it down somewhere. I'll get it.' She raced back into the house.

Sarah was taking longer to retrieve the note than either of them were expecting, and the two men found themselves standing there awkwardly. Lowden began self-consciously re-reading his notes, and Frank looked up and down the street as though there was a possibility that Red might, at any moment, jump out from behind a tree.

Marcie leaned in the doorway behind Frank. 'Little Jimmy Lowden,' she said. 'I used to teach him at St Agnes. Long time ago.

Class of ninety-eight. Good kid, very sweet, but he was a hell of a handful back then.' Frank could hear the smile in her voice without turning around. 'Look at him now.'

'Listen, how long are these mates of yours gonna be? You're about as much use as a chocolate teapot stood there.'

Jimmy Lowden leaned on the wall and sighed. 'Jesus, Frank,' he said, more in exasperation than anything. He was putting his black book away in his top pocket. 'Can you *please* give me a break? I'm genuinely just trying to do my best here.'

Frank was surprised at the reaction: maybe because the copper had used his first name, maybe because he suddenly looked so uncertain and young. Or maybe because he realised that he was starting to feel anxious about Red, and had been choosing to take it out on the man in uniform.

Frank sighed and nodded.

It was Lowden who broke the silence, suddenly human. 'You know we've met before?'

'Yeah, I know. I'm not senile. The great shed heist.'

'No, I mean before that.'

Frank frowned. 'Yeah?'

'Mrs Hayes's funeral.'

'You were at Marcie's funeral?'

'Yeah, your missus was my teacher. At St Agnes. I was really sorry to hear she'd . . . passed.' It was as though the uniform was a fancy dress. The bravado fell away, and he looked like a different person. 'She got me through a bad time, parents and school and all that. Got in quite a bit of trouble, if you can believe it, and she was always y'know . . . *there*. In fact,' he pulled at his jacket, 'I wouldn't have even got into police training without her; she wrote me a reference and everything.'

'I didn't know that.'

'Well.' He looked at Frank with a shrug. 'Why would you?'

'This is it.' Sarah rushed out, handing the note over to Lowden.

The officer unfolded the paper and read it carefully with a frown, deciphering the childish scrawl. 'I don't get it. What's he talking about?'

'I have no idea,' Sarah replied. 'Your guess is as good as mine.'

Lowden read it again. 'What's this "mission" thing he's on about?'

He handed the note back to Sarah, but Frank intercepted it, with a vague sinking feeling.

Sarah and Lowden continued to talk as he read it carefully.

It began as just a nag in Frank's recent memory. He tried to recall the conversation in which Red had used that exact word. It was something about—

Suddenly, it came back with vivid clarity.

It had been over the letter Frank wrote to his son.

I could get it to Mikey, no problem . . . It would be like a cool mission.'

Shit.

RED

'Excuse me . . . Sorry . . . Excuse me.'

Red was slowly making his way through the crowd of people. He was just trying to find a little space where he might be able to check his map, work out where he was, and think about what to do next. But it was like trying to cross a really fast-flowing river, and it seemed like now people *really* couldn't see or hear him.

He had never felt smaller, and his tiny voice was being squashed by the sounds of so many. Drowned out, too, by the persistent noise of departing and arriving trains on unseen platforms. And a man standing at the bottom of a nearby escalator, who had mucky hair and was playing bongos.

Red really wished he'd shut up for a minute.

He had been hoping that the announcer on the train had made a mistake about where they had stopped, and that he had already arrived at Wimbledon, but a new voice in this enormous station killed any hopes he had of that: *'Welcome to Euston. If you see anything suspicious, please report it to a member of station staff or British Transport Police. See it, say it, sorted.'*

Red thought that the man with the mucky hair looked a bit suspicious. But right then, Red had his own problems to see, say and sort. He was now fully regretting not giving up when he'd got stuck at the barriers at Finchley station. Regretting, in fact, not turning over and going back to sleep that morning and forgetting about this whole thing.

But that seemed like a lifetime ago, and now it was too late.

Slowly, Red succeeded in pushing his way through the crowd and eventually found a small, unbusy space against a wall. It was close to bongo man, and it was a space that existed because people were steering around the man on purpose. Red didn't blame them. The man smelled like plants. Definitely suspicious.

Red fished in his bag for his map and found it gone. He must've dropped it. Now he thought about it, he had a vague memory of it flapping away as he went running from the train.

Things were going from bad to worse.

Trying not to panic, he sat on his bag, his back against the wall, and tried to think about things. After a minute, he decided to do what he always did when he got scared: make a list in his head. Of the good things and the bad things.

Okay, so he wasn't in Wimbledon. He didn't really know *where* he was. And he didn't have any food left. And he didn't have a map any-more. And the man playing bongos next to him smelled like compost.

These were all things for the bad list.

Now, for the good list . . . He thought hard for something for the good list. But the only thing he could think of was this: he had got this far.

What would his mum do in this situation? He thought. Hmm. Probably shout at him for doing something dangerous. What would Frank do? Well, that was just as useless to think about: Frank would just tell bongo man to shut the flip up. Besides, *he* wouldn't have left home in the first place.

Red sighed. He really was on his own.

He looked up at the flashing lights of the electronic billboard above the escalators as it changed.

'*Just Do It*,' it said, helpfully.

Okay, then.

The way Red saw it, he had three choices. He could head up the escalator and out of the station, and try to find Castlegate Road that way. Or he could join the river of people flowing left, or the river of people flowing right.

He immediately ruled out leaving the station. That would be a mistake. He wouldn't know which way to go once he was outside, and there would be no barking dog or Jade Plum to guide him.

So he looked again at the competing flows of people. Each river was heading to a different platform, a different line, a different train. He had no reason to think that one was better than the other, and so he did the only sensible thing he could do in the circumstances. He eeny-meenied in his head. Having chosen one of the rivers, Red stood up, put his backpack over his shoulders and stepped into its flow. He was carried along like a twig.

Red could no longer see where he was going; he was simply following the striding legs in front of him and the harrying legs behind. He was still a bit scared, but it felt good to have made a decision and to be back on the move. And with so many people going the same way, it somehow felt like the *right* decision.

If you thought about it, Red reasoned, it made sense that people would be heading to the same place he was. After all, he was going to a castle. And **everybody** thought castles were cool.

Before long, the river of people had spilled on to a new platform and Red continued to be swept along, through the open doors of a carriage and on to a new train. Again, it was super busy, which was good. But it looked like there were no available seats, and Red was starting to feel quite tired. As the train pulled out of the station, he was thinking about sitting on the floor – but then he noticed a very big man sitting a little further down the carriage. He was so big that he was taking up nearly two seats, and the space that remained was not big enough for a grown-up. But Red thought that it was probably big enough for a six- (nearly seven) year-old to squeeze into, and so he weaved between the legs of the other passengers to where the big man was sitting.

Again, nobody paid much attention, as he climbed into the seat. The big man acknowledged him with a smile, but then returned to staring off into the distance.

Red began to relax again, feeling certain that he was back on track and heading in the right direction once more. Of course, he had been scared. But that was understandable. Even the bravest people got scared on missions – even *astronauts*. Noah's brother said that when astronauts went to Mars or the Moon or whatever, they had to have their toilets fitted into their spacesuits.

'Why do you think they do that?' he had said to Red and Noah.

The pair had been sitting on the top bunk, and both answered this question with a shrug.

Noah's brother had just shaken his head. 'Durr. It's because they shit themselves all the time,' he said. 'Obviously.'

Red wasn't sure if this 'fact' was true, but remembering it made him feel better. He started to yawn. He really was tired, and the rhythm of the train was making him feel extra sleepy. He had woken up really early that morning, and hadn't slept very well the night before, too full of excitement.

Before long, he was struggling to keep his eyes open.

And so he closed them. With his head resting against the back of his seat, he dozed off and dreamed of nothing in par . . .

. . .ti

. . .cu

l

a

r.

FRANK

'What do you mean, you think you know where he might have gone?'

Frank was already hurrying into his hallway. Sarah and Lowden were right behind him, and they almost bundled into his back as he stopped at the hallway dresser.

'Frank!'

'Just a second.' he said as he rifled through the drawer. Dammit. The invitation wasn't there.

Still refusing to accept that he might be right, he headed into the kitchen and checked to see that the card hadn't magically appeared back on the fridge where Ken had stuck it. He ran his hand over Red's drawing. Not there. Obviously.

'Frank! Tell me what the hell is going on?'

He hurried into the living room, and again Sarah and Lowden followed. He reached under the writing desk and dragged out the wire basket, emptying the contents on to the floor. A piece of rogue Sellotape stuck to his thumb.

'Frank!'

He quickly sifted through the discarded paper and unballed the scrunches in the bottom of the basket one by one. Having looked at each, he stopped abruptly.

'It's gone,' he said, simply, looking up at the others.

'What's gone? What the hell is going on?!'

Frank explained.

He told them he and Red had had an argument about Frank's son, and the fact that he and Mikey no longer spoke to each other.

'*That's* what you two fell out about?'

'Well, yeah. He found an invitation. It was to a christening. He wouldn't shut up about it. And then he found this letter that I'd written to Mikey. And – I don't know – he got carried away with this idea of getting it to him.'

'Wait, I can't keep up. What does this have to do with anything?' Lowden asked unhelpfully. But Sarah was already beginning to understand what Frank was saying.

'He got it in his head that if Mikey read this letter, then everything would be hunky-bloody-dory,' Frank said. 'He actually talked about getting it to him. He said it would be like . . . a *mission*.'

'Jesus,' Sarah said to the ceiling.

Lowden was slowly catching up. 'And you think . . . what? That Red has gone to put this letter in a postbox or something?'

'No. He doesn't trust the post anymore. Not since they buggered up by delivering the invite to the wrong address in the first place. And besides,' Frank said, nodding at Red's note, which was now back in Sarah's hand, 'he says a "long journey". The local postbox is not a long journey. Not for Red.'

'He's gone to deliver it himself,' Lowden finally concluded out loud. 'And where does your son live?'

'I dunno. Wimbledon.'

'*Wimbledon*? That's the other side of London!' Sarah spun around, clutching a handful of her own hair. 'And how—' Sarah started again. 'How would he even know where to go?'

'Well, the address was on the invitation. The letter's gone, but the invitation's gone as well.'

'Okay, so would he try and walk there or what?' Lowden asked.

'What? No,' Sarah replied. 'He's not an idiot. He knows how to get on a tube or a bus or whatever.'

'Right,' Lowden said to Frank with a new practicality in his voice. 'What's your son's address? I can get officers checking the route, and we'll send someone over there.'

Frank realised he had no idea what his son's address was. 'I don't know.'

'What the hell do you mean, you don't know?' Sarah was incredulous.

Frank knew how it sounded. 'I don't know! They moved in just before Marcie got sick. I've only been a couple of times. And whenever we went, I just drove. Marcie directed me. It's South Wimbledon somewhere – or North Wimbledon. I know it's Wimbledon.'

'Wimbledon's a pretty big place, Frank,' Lowden offered uselessly.

'Yeah, no shit. Thank you for that, Officer Fucking Obvious!' Frank thought harder. 'Palace Gardens . . . or Castle Street, or something. I don't know. I can't remember.' He looked up at the pair of them. 'Don't look at me like that, like I'm some kind of doddery old bugger. I know *where* it is. I can see the route in my head, but I don't memorise people's addresses. I'm not bloody Rain Man.'

'Well, have you got a phone number for him, then?'

'No.'

'Do you know anybody who might?'

RED

Red blearily opened an eye and then closed it again. The noises and light were odd, and it took him a moment to remember where he was.

Noisy. A moving train. He was still on the tube.

When he opened both eyes fully, he found himself still sitting where he had dozed off twenty minutes before, in a seat next to the doors. It was the swoosh of those doors that had woken him up, and he looked around as he slowly started to shake off the fog of his nap. The big man to his left was gone. In fact, the carriage was now almost completely empty, apart from a couple at one end who were sitting side by side, chatting, and a man with a moustache standing at the other end of the carriage, who was looking at his own reflection in the windows as he smoothed his hair.

He didn't notice the woman with dark skin and thick glasses sitting opposite until she spoke. 'Hello,' she said, trying to catch his eye.

Uh oh, Red thought. *Don't panic.* Perhaps she wasn't talking to him. He quickly looked away, left it a few seconds and then looked back. The woman was still staring straight at him, with a look of mild confusion on her face.

It was a face that was framed by short, curly black hair, with flashes of silver, like fish. Her magnified eyes seemed amused as he hastily looked away again.

'Hello,' she repeated.

Red realised that he couldn't continue to ignore this woman. It was no good pretending that she wasn't talking to him. There was no one else she *could* be talking to.

'Hi,' he said quickly, pretending to look at something above her head. He started to whistle to himself; he was good at whistling, and that's what people did when they were fine and not being suspicious.

The woman seemed to think for a long time as Red, continuing to whistle, pretended that she wasn't there.

'I like your bag,' she said, eventually. 'My grandson has a bag like that. He loves superheroes, Batman and Superman and all those.'

'Well, that's DC, really,' said Red. 'This is Spider-Man; he's Marvel.'

'Spider-Man. Right.' She nodded.

Red stopped whistling and traced his fingers over Spider-Man's face. He had accidentally found himself in a conversation.

The woman picked up the huge handbag on her lap, crossed the carriage and sat next to him. Red shuffled a few inches away, but the woman pretended not to notice. Producing a bulging purse, she took out a small photograph of herself and a boy, who looked a little bit older than Red, with his arms draped around her neck. They were both laughing.

'This is my grandson. Leo. Total rascal.'

Red looked at the photograph. It was one of those photos that made you smile, but he didn't say anything.

'So,' she said, putting her purse away. 'Where's your mummy and daddy, little man?' She said this gently, as though the question might scare him.

Red looked up, ready to point at a random group of people and say that he was with them. But when he looked around, he realised that the carriage was now entirely empty. Red swallowed his panic and thought quickly. 'Oh, my mummy's meeting me.'

'Oh, is that right?' the woman said, doubtfully.

'When I get off. At Wimbledons.'

'I see. And how old are you?'

He tried to think what a reasonable age would be to be on the tube on your own.

'I'm twenty-four.'

She chuckled. 'Twenty-four, eh?'

Stupid. Stupid. Of course he wasn't twenty-four. Auntie Stephanie was twenty-four, and that was like a full-grown grown-up.

'No, I'm eleven.' The same age as Noah's brother.

'Eleven?'

'Yup.'

'You look a little bit small to be twenty-four – or eleven.'

'Well. The smallest person in the world is only, like, this big.' He put his hand and held it a couple of feet above the floor. 'And she is, like, forty or something.'

'Is that right?'

'Yeah, she's called Jyoti.'

'Wow, I did not know that. Y'know, you're pretty smart.' She smiled. 'How old are you really, wee man?'

Red thought for a moment. The woman had one of the kindest faces he'd ever seen. He could tell that she wasn't believing him, and he felt squirmy about lying to her. 'Okay,' he said. 'I'm six. But I'll be seven next year, and then I'll be eight, and then nine. So, I am *nearly* eleven.'

'Still. Kind of young to be out here alone. And you're headed to Wimbledon, eh?'

'Yeah.' This, at least, was true.

'And you said your mum was meeting you there?'

Red thought about how much he should confide in her. And

then made a decision. 'Hmm. Not really,' he confessed. 'I'm kind of on a mission.'

'Oh.' She smiled. 'A mission?'

'Uh huh. For my friend.'

Her face turned serious. 'Well. You know it really isn't safe to be on your own?'

Red said nothing.

'And here's the thing. Don't panic, but to get to Wimbledon, this is the wrong train.'

'What?'

'Uh huh.' she nodded. 'Wrong line too . . . and headed in the wrong direction.'

Red's heart stopped. This was a problem.

He wasn't sure how long he had been asleep, but he was pretty sure that by now he had been gone for *days*, and his mummy would be starting to get worried. Worse than that, the mission had now gone totally and completely wrong. No – this was worse than a problem. This was a disaster. Red could feel the first signs of panic in his tummy.

'You want to hear something funny, though?'

Red did. Right then, he desperately wanted to hear something funny.

'The funny thing is, *I'm* going the wrong way too.'

Red scrunched his nose and looked up to check that she wasn't pulling his leg. 'Really?' he asked, confused.

'Yup. I've been getting the same tube to work every day for twelve years. Today, I got distracted and took a left instead of a right, and here I am, going the wrong way, with you. How about that?' She smiled. 'But don't you worry.' She took a paperback book out of her deep bag. 'I think I'm just going to hang out with you until the next stop, and we'll see what we can do about getting us both sorted there, okay? Sound good?'

Red nodded. It *did* sound good. So much had gone wrong lately. This whole bit had been harder than he thought it would be. But if this woman could help him get back on track, get to the next station and then put him on the *right* train, in the *right* direction then that was just fine. All was not entirely lost.

'You hungry?'

'Little bit.'

'You wanna share?' She produced some Fruit Pastilles from her bottomless handbag and offered one to Red. 'Well, I can't keep calling you little man. What's your name?'

'It's Red,' he said, chewing on a yellow one.

'Okay, my name's Carmel.' They shook hands. 'It's nice to meet you.'

She popped a Fruit Pastille into her own mouth. Green.

'What's that around your neck?' he asked.

'This?' She held up the laminated card at the end of the ribbon she was wearing. 'That's my ID, for work. See? That's me – Carmel N'Sungu. It's a terrible picture. It makes me look ancient.'

He read the title under her name. 'Staff. Nurse. My mum's a nurse as well. She looks after old people and people who are poorly to death. She says it's the best job ever ever, but what money you get paid is an F-word joke.'

'Well, I don't think she's too far wrong about that.' Carmel laughed. 'But I don't look after old people, I look after children. Some even younger than you.'

Red nodded, and she offered him another Fruit Pastille. Carmel then opened her book and began to read, and the two of them chewed in companionable silence.

After a while, a woman's voice sounded through the train's speakers. *This service will shortly be arriving at* . . .

'Okay, Mr Red.' Carmel said, filing her book away. 'This is us. You okay?'

Red nodded, pulled his rucksack on to his back, and jumped down from his seat. The train lurched to a stop and the door shooshed open. Carmel held his hand as they stepped off the train.

The doors behind them beeped and closed again, and as the train pulled off into the tunnel, Carmel looked up and down the platform, apparently unsure which way to go. A little further down, she found what she was looking for: a white box attached to the wall which had a big button on it and the words 'Help Point'. She told Red to sit on the bench next to it.

The white box made a noise like a telephone connecting, and then a woman's voice came through the speaker: *'Hello, British Transport Police, can I help you?'* It sounded like she was far away, talking through one of Red's Buzz Lightyear walkie-talkies.

'Hi. Yeah, I've just been on the Victoria line. And there was a little boy on there.' Carmel leaned in and turned away from Red slightly. 'I think he's lost, but he's way too young to be out and about on his own.'

'Okay,' the woman responded, sounding like she was mid-yawn. *'Just stay where you are; I'll send someone down.'*

There was a fumbling noise, and then the sound of the woman talking to someone else. *'Code twelve for Victoria southbound, we've got a lady at the—'* She was cut short as the help point fell silent.

'Okay . . . I guess we wait,' Carmel said, as she sat down next to Red, and he accepted another Fruit Pastille.

Orange.

FRANK

'You have reached the voicemail of Ken Browning. I'm probably avoiding someone who gets on my tits. Leave me a message and if I don't call back, it's you.'

Frank returned to the living room. 'He's not answering.'

'Right.' Lowden was referring to his little black pad again. 'I've just spoken to dispatch. There are seven M. Hayes in Wimbledon, so they'll call those they've got a number for. And they're gonna get local to check in on the others. In the meantime, they've got an alert out with BTP. The best thing *we* can do is wait for the responders.'

'And how long's all that gonna take?' Sarah was pacing. 'My little boy is on his own, God knows where, in one of the busiest cities on earth.'

Jimmy Lowden frowned, and then something seemed to occur to him. 'Well, when the squad car gets here, maybe . . . I don't know? Maybe they could take Frank, and he could direct them to the address, if he remembers the way. Might be quicker? At least it'd be the right one.'

'I can't do that,' Frank said. It was barely audible.

Sarah certainly didn't hear him. 'We can't wait for the squad car;

they could be Christ knows how long. They've said on the phone that they're tied up all over the place because of the marathon.'

'Look, Mrs Evans, try to keep calm.'

'Don't tell me to calm down. And do not tell me to sit tight. Jesus, if one more person tells me to sit tight, I will lose my shit.' She perched on the arm of Frank's sofa and started chewing at her fingernails. Frank could think of nothing to say, and when Lowden tried to speak, she held up her hand for him to be quiet. 'I'm thinking,' she said, simply. Then: 'Wait a minute.' She sprang to her feet. 'Frank!' she said, decisively. 'We'll take your car.'

Frank took a moment to process the words. '*Val?!*' he said, as though she'd suggested that they take a magic carpet.

'Frank, you know how to get there! There's a car sitting outside doing nothing. *He* can stay here in case Red turns up.' She gestured towards the policeman. 'Red's dad is on the way, too. I can't do anything here . . . We'll take your car.'

'I can't,' Frank said.

'I think Frank's right, you can't just go charging off,' Lowden agreed. 'You're much better off leaving it to us, the experts.'

'Shut it, Tour de France. Your lot don't know where he's gone. Frank does.'

Lowden pulled at the Lycra of his crotch self-consciously.

'I just can't.' Frank felt the familiar panic at the very suggestion of going beyond the gate.

'Frank, Red's *lost.*'

Frank tried to stop his head from spinning. He concentrated on the middle of the living room carpet until the world began to steady. And then he seized on the obvious problem with the plan, as though it was a passing life raft.

'Even if I wanted to. Even if I could. There is no way that car will move. Absolutely no way. Val's not moved in the best part of two years. She's rusted to crap. The battery'll be as dead as a—'

Sarah's ears had apparently stopped working. 'Well, let's try it, at least.'

'It. Won't. Start.'

Marcie was standing by the window, peering out at the old Volvo.

'No,' Frank said, with finality. He was talking to Marcie this time, but Sarah and Lowden assumed he was reaffirming his point.

'He's right, Mrs Evans,' Lowden agreed.

'Frank,' Sarah said dully. 'You can at least try.'

Frank breathed in through his nose and out through his mouth. He looked around, searching for escape, and found none. He caught sight of Red's drawing, and suddenly found himself imagining the boy alone on a bus or a tube, walking through the streets or crossing a London road. In that brief moment, he wanted nothing more than for the old Volvo to make one last journey, as his fear for the boy fought against his fear of *beyond the gate*.

But fear will only get you so far. And it didn't change the facts.

'Jesus, the world's gone mad. It won't start,' Frank insisted.

Sarah just looked at him.

'Fine.' He walked into the hallway and came back with the spare key. 'I'll bloody show you.'

RED

Five minutes passed before the police appeared through one of the passageways that led to the platform they were sitting on.

They were a man and a woman. The man had one of those proper police helmets on that look like upside-down buckets. And they both had bright yellow vests, and lots of things hanging from their belts, like handcuffs and shark repellent.

A couple of trains had been and gone in the time that Red and Carmel had been sitting there, chatting and chewing. One had just departed, so the platform was empty when the two police officers approached the odd pair sitting on the bench.

The lady policeman said something into the radio attached to her shoulder before speaking. 'Hello.' She waved at Red, even though she was only a few steps away from him, and you normally only wave when you're a long way away from someone. 'How are we doing?' she said.

Red didn't say anything.

After a moment, Carmel spoke for him. 'Hi there.' She put a hand on Red's shoulder. 'This is my friend, and he's got . . . well, you've got a little bit lost, haven't you?'

Red looked up at the policewoman and nodded shyly.

'OK, well.' She was interrupted by the sound of another train approaching, so she crouched down, one hand on the metal bench. 'It's a little bit noisy down here to have a chat. How about we head up to our office upstairs? We'll get everything straightened out. How's that sound?'

Red looked at the handcuffs of the tall, quiet policeman standing behind her and suddenly got nervous.

'Am I going to prison?'

'No, of course not. You're not in any trouble at all, I promise.'

'It's just that Noah's brother said that prison is bad, because you only get three channels. But it's not that bad, because you will prolly get bunkbeds, so—' He was rambling.

'Well' – the policewoman stood up – 'prisons are just for baddies, really, and you don't look too dangerous to me.'

Red looked at his cast and hoped they wouldn't ask about that. She might think differently if she knew he'd punched a fish.

Carmel stood up too, and then turned to speak to him. 'Listen, Red, it was an absolute pleasure to meet you. But I need to go and try and get myself unlost, too. You'll be safe with these officers ,and they'll be able to get you where you need to go – okay?'

Red nodded. 'Uh huh.'

She took a card and a pen from her magic bag, jotting down her number. She handed it to one of the police officers. 'You'll let me know he's alright?' she said, before gathering her things.

'Well.' Carmel took one last look at him. 'I'll see you around, Red.'

She seemed to be thinking twice about leaving him, but then stepped away and hopped on to the train that had just pulled in behind them. She waved to him through the glass. And then she was gone.

*

'You hungry? Do you want a drink or anything?' the policewoman asked.

Red shrugged.

She turned to the policeman, who was propping open the office door with a fire extinguisher. 'Just grab him a Coke and Kit Kat from the machine, will you Dave?'

They were sitting at a long table in a room with glass walls. The policewoman was on one side of the table, and Red was on the other. Through the glass, he could see the busy office they had just walked through, with its wall of TV screens and desks, and people busily chatting into headsets. And now he could see the policeman – Dave – making his way through that busyness to a vending machine in the distant corner.

The policewoman took off her hat and put it on one of the unoccupied chairs at the table. Then she removed her heavy vest and draped that over the back of the same chair. She then opened a black folder, looked at her watch and was writing something on the pad inside when Dave returned with two hot drinks and a can of Coke. He set them all down together, then slid the Coke over to Red.

'You okay, big man?' he said, as he produced a Twix from his top pocket and set that down at the side.

Red nodded.

'So, we're just going to ask you a few questions.' The police-woman smiled kindly. 'Nothing hard, I promise. No maths or anything. Let's start with a *really* easy one: what's your name?'

He didn't answer.

'Okay, so my name is Gemma, and you know that this big dope is Dave. So, what do they call you?'

Red thought for a moment. 'Red,' he said.

'Okay, Red. And what's your surname – what's your second name?'

'. . . Gavin,' he said, reluctantly.

'So . . . Your name is Red Gavin?' Dave asked.

'No'. Red looked at Dave as though he was daft. 'My name is Red *Evans.*'

'Evans. Okay,' Gemma said, writing it down. 'That's great, you're doing brilliantly. And where do you live, Red Evans? Where's home?'

Red had been thinking about this question on the ride up the escalators, down the secret corridors and through the metal door you needed to have a code for. He had thought about it carefully. He *could* tell them where he lived, but he wasn't stupid. If they knew that, they would probably take him straight home. Half of him thought this was exactly what he wanted to happen. But there was another half of him that thought this: he had come too far to fail now.

He fell silent again.

'Okay, well, we'll come back to that.'

Officer Dave took a sip of his tea and set it back down on the desk. 'What did you do to your arm, Red?'

Dammit, he thought he had got away with them not asking about that. He would have to be honest, though. This was the police.

'Oh, I punched a fish tank.'

'Okay. And is that why you ran away from home? Because you were in trouble?'

'Oh no, I did it at school.'

'Why?' Dave asked.

'Why what?'

'Well, why did you punch a fish tank?'

'Cos I'm a mountain.'

'Riiight.' Dave took another sip of his drink and sat back with a confused look on his face.

Officer Gemma leaned forward gently. 'Where's home, Red?'

Red looked at his hands.

'Look Red, I'm sure your mummy and daddy are worried sick, and unless we know where you live, we can't let them know that you're okay, and we can't get you home.'

'My mummy and daddy don't live together. Not anymore.' He didn't look up.

'Okay then, different question: where were you going? You told the lady on the train that you were trying to get somewhere. Where was that?'

Red thought about shrugging again, but instead he picked up the backpack at his feet and pulled it on to his lap. He unclipped the top, reached deep inside and pulled out the invitation.

He slid it over the table.

Gemma picked it up and examined it carefully. 'Okay, so this address here, Castlegate Road, South Wimbledon – is this where your mummy or daddy lives? Does somebody you know live here?'

Red shook his head. 'Not really.'

Officer Dave took the invitation and looked at it too. 'So, you don't know the person who lives here? Is it someone famous or something? Is it a footballer?'

'Mmh. I just need to get there.'

Gemma sat back now. She ran a hand through her short hair and exhaled loudly, then looked at Dave. It was his turn to shrug. She took the invitation, put it on top of the pad and closed the folder. 'Okay, Red. Just sit tight for a minute; we're going to see if we can get to the bottom of this.'

*

'Okay, Red. We checked this address on our computers. And we know that the owners of this house are a couple called Michael and Ellie Hayes. But here's the thing. We've just spoken to them on the phone, and they've never heard of anyone called Red Evans . . . and they don't have the faintest idea how you got this.' She tapped a finger on the invite. 'They're as clueless as we are.'

'They've no idea who you are,' Dave added, pointlessly.

'I know,' said Red.

Dave's forehead creased. 'So why were you heading there, then?'

Red shrugged and looked at his hands again.

'Sarge.' Suddenly, Gemma and Dave stood up as they greeted the tall man who had just entered the room. He was tucking his white shirt in to the back of his trousers.

'Hi, young man,' he said to Red.

'This is my boss, Red,' Gemma explained. 'His name is Sergeant Chaney.'

Sergeant Chaney had the black folder in his hands, and he opened it as he sat across from Red, the two police officers standing behind him. Reading the pad in front of him and examining the invitation, he stroked his chin. 'Well, this is all a bit of a mystery, eh? So, you're not going to tell us where you live. Or your mum and dad's names. Or why you're riding on the underground on your own.' He held up the invitation with Mikey's address on it. 'Or what on earth this is all about.' He leaned back in his chair, blew out his cheeks and scratched his head.

'I just need to go there,' Red said, quietly. 'I made a promise.'

Chaney flicked the piece of card in his hand a couple of times. He was thinking. 'Right, okay,' he said, leaning forward. 'So, how's this? I will do you a deal, Red Evans. If these officers take you to this address' – he flicked the card one more time – 'do you promise to tell us what all this is about?'

Red's eyes lit up.

Chaney continued. 'Your mum and dad's names, your address . . . everything?'

Red smiled broadly.

'Deal?' Sergeant Chaney smiled in return. He passed the invitation back to Red, then put his hand out.

Red looked at his hand, then shook it. 'Deal, baby seal. Cross my heart and no backsies,' he said, seriously.

FRANK

He turned the key again. Nothing.

'I told you it wouldn't start,' he said to Sarah.

Lowden was leaning on the car roof and talking to Frank through the open driver-side window. 'You're going nowhere.'

'I did say.'

It had been a long few metres from the gate to the car, but now he was sitting in the driver's seat, Frank felt surprisingly calm, especially given the circumstances. It was partly because he knew that there was no way that Val was going to start, and this was as far as he would have to go. But it was also because, as it turned out, inside the old car felt a little like an extension of the house, familiar and non-threatening.

He pressed on the clutch and turned the key again, pointlessly. Nothing.

Sarah got out of the passenger side, slamming the door behind her, cursing. Frank was about to step out himself when he turned to find Marcie sitting beside him.

'Alright?' she said cheerfully.

'Uh huh.'

She looked around at the inside of the car and ran her fingers over the dashboard.

'Remember taking Val to Northumberland? ' she said. 'Just the two of us. We tried to cross that causeway at Lindisfarne, and the tides came in. We only just made it back to the mainland before she conked out.'

Frank remembered only too well. 'You had to have your feet up on the seat for the last half a mile. That footwell was full of water.'

'Yeah.' Marcie chuckled. 'We stayed at that little B and B, then went back to fetch her the following day.'.

Frank smiled at the memory. 'She started first time.'

He looked out of the windscreen at Sarah and Jimmy Lowden. They were talking animatedly.

Something that had been nagging seemed to settle in his mind.

'I didn't know you taught him,' he said.

'Who?'

He nodded towards Lowden. 'I didn't even know that his first name was Jimmy.'

'I know.'

He turned to face her. 'No, I mean I *didn't know*.'

'Frank . . . I know.'

They sat there for a long time. Or outside of time – Frank wasn't entirely sure.

But after a while, Marcie placed her hand over his.

For a moment, or maybe just the tiniest sliver of a moment, Frank could almost feel it.

She let out a long sigh and then looked at him. 'Maybe give it one last go, Frankie.'

Frank nodded slowly and pressed down on the clutch. He was about to turn the key again when he stopped. 'You're not going to be here when I get back. Are you?' He swallowed.

'I'll be here.' She smiled, as though this should've been obvious.

He nodded again.

'Who are you talking to?' Sarah asked through the open passenger-side window.

'Never mind,' he said, as he turned the key.

Her question was lost and forgotten in the sound of Val's engine firing into life.

'Oh my God,' Sarah said, pulling open the door. She dropped into the passenger seat again and began to quickly pull the old seatbelt across her chest.

'Holy shit!' Lowden shouted through the other window, as he backed away from the car.

Frank revved the engine a couple of times. It sounded like a brick in a washing machine.

Overcoming his shock, Lowden returned, leaning through the open window. 'Frank,' he shouted over the sound of the sickly car. 'I'm sorry, but there is *no* way I can let you drive off in that thing. I doubt it even has an MOT; it's definitely not roadworthy! It's not legal!' He took a step back and, trying to look commanding, held up one palm. 'I'm going to have to ask you to exit the vehicle.'

Frank revved the engine again.

'Please, Frank.' Lowden sounded less certain, a young man again.

Frank started to wind up the window. 'You're a good boy, Jimmy, but piss off,' he said, putting Val in gear.

In the rear-view mirror, Frank could just make out Marcie sitting on their front step. She was smiling, her face turned towards the sun.

He pulled out of the space.

And into a blast of a horn from a passing silver Audi.

'Use your facking indicator, you old twat!'

RED

Red had never been in a police car before. He didn't know whether they all smelled like air freshener in a toilet, but this one did. Like there was a bad smell being covered up badly. To be honest, he'd thought it would be more exciting. They weren't going very fast – in fact, they had been crawling along in traffic most of the way, and there was no blue light flashing or siren telling everyone to get out of the way. That was obviously only used in an emergency or when the police had a murderer in the back – and Red wasn't a murderer, he realised, a little disappointedly.

'You okay, Red?' Officer Gemma turned around in the passenger seat.

'Yuh huh.' He nodded.

'Fancy telling us what this is all about yet?'

Red frowned apologetically and shook his head.

'Okay. Well, we're about twenty minutes away, alright?'

Red nodded again.

Realising he was thirsty, Red leaned over to his backpack and took out his Fruit Shoot. Taking a squeezy drink, he noticed Bonzer smiling up from the bottom of his bag, and he took him out too, whispering into the cuddly kangaroo's ear that he shouldn't worry, things were back on track.

It was a while, though, before Red realised that he was looking at the same shop he had been staring at for ages. A lot of streets in London did have the same shops repeated over and over again, but this was definitely exactly the same shop, because it was called *Jacamo* and had some massive trousers in the window.

They hadn't moved at all in five minutes.

'This is daft,' Officer Dave said. 'We're gonna be sat here all day.'

'It's marathon traffic,' Gemma replied. 'Always the same.'

The radio squawked some numbers. Dave yawned exaggeratedly, and then tapped out a beat with his fingers on the steering wheel.

'You thinking what I'm thinking, Gem?'

'Dave,' Gemma said, disapprovingly.

'Just to get us to the junction.' He nodded through the windscreen in front of them and put his hand on a switch above the gearstick. 'Come on, Gem. Just to get past this little bit.' He turned around to ask Red. 'What do you say – shall I put the blue lights on for a sec?'

'*Cool.*' Red nodded his approval.

'See Gem? It's cool.'

*

'One-three-six, one-three-eight, one-forty, one-four-two . . .'

The police car was crawling along the side of the road as Officer Dave looked for the correct number. The radio continued to beep and squawk and say random things about 'code twenty-three's and 'dispatch'.

'I think it's the one on the corner, Dave, with the open gates.' Gemma turned around in her seat. 'Right, I think we're here, kiddo.'

Red wasn't sure that she was right; he had been watching the world go by much more carefully as they got closer. For the last ten minutes, they had snaked through road after road of similar-looking houses, and he had yet to see anything that looked even a bit like a castle.

'Are you sure?' he said.

'One-four-eight . . . yep.'

'But there's no castle. There should be a castle.'

'Maybe five hundred years ago,' Dave said, as he slowed down. 'I think there's a pub round the corner called The Castle. Does that count?'

The noise of the tyres on the road turned crunchy as the car pulled into a driveway.

Red looked out of the window to see a semi-detached white house, divided from next door by a tidy square hedge. There was a four-by-four-type car parked under a tree to one side, but the driveway was comfortably wide enough for two or three more. It looked a lot like Red's old house, where he had lived with his mummy and daddy, but this one had a small glass building stuck to the front. Red looked through the open door of this porch as they slowly passed; it was cluttered with coats and shoes. A folded pram leaned to one side.

The car came to a stop. 'Right, well, we're here.'

Red nodded. He reached to open the door, but remembered that there was no handle on the inside. It hadn't broken off or anything; it was like that on purpose, so that murderers couldn't open the door and run off. The two officers opened their own doors and, as Red waited to be freed, he suddenly felt hot. Nervous. Probably more nervous than he had ever felt in his entire life.

And for good reason. In that moment, he realised that he had planned how to get to the house at Castlegate Road in great detail. And yes, it had not gone exactly as he had planned, what with the whole barriers thing, and the wrong train thing, on the wrong line and in the wrong direction thing, and then the whole police thing. But Red now realised that there was a big bit of his plan that had been missing all along.

He had no idea what he was going to say.

If this *was* Mikey's house, how was he going to explain why he had travelled all the way across London to see him? And what if Frank was right? What if Mikey wasn't interested? What if he was mad? What if he just shouted at Red to go away?

Officer Dave swung the door open.

'Come on then, sunshine. This is it.'

Red stepped out of the car.

Officer Dave was right. This *was* it.

FRANK

Frank couldn't remember driving being this bloody stressful. He hadn't driven in a long time, but since when had the roads become so filled with crazy bastards? Admittedly, he was stressed to find himself so far out of his comfort zone. (In fact, his comfort zone – specifically his reclining armchair – was currently light years away, on a distant planet.)

But this madness was not helping.

Cyclists weaving between cars, their arses almost touching the wing mirrors. People changing lanes without pause, indicator, or common sense. It was as though in the time he had not been driving, he had missed a meeting at which everyone had agreed that the roads were now owned by dickheads.

To begin with, he had kangaroo-hopped the old Volvo to the end of Merton Road, reminding his feet what to do with the pedals and his hands what to do with Val's stiff gears. It seemed his eyesight hadn't improved since the last time he had driven, either; he squinted at road signs and winced as he pulled out of junctions, waiting for the inevitable blare of a horn or the crunch of a collision with a car or cyclist.

Slowly, though, as they made their way south towards the river,

Frank found himself gaining in confidence, as he barked at the lunatics with whom he was forced to share the highways, and increased his speed to a break-neck twenty miles per hour.

Right now, though, they weren't moving at all.

They were stuck in traffic on a street that led directly into the diverted roads for the marathon. Just sitting there in what was, to all intents and purposes, a car park.

'This is crazy,' he muttered to himself for the fourth time.

Sarah was agitatedly talking into her phone. 'I don't know, we're somewhere near—'

The infuriating thing was that they could see the turning they needed to take; it was 200 metres further up the road on the right, and once they were there it looked like the traffic would clear. But they hadn't edged an inch closer to it in the past twenty minutes. They could be here all day.

Frank angled his head, trying to see if there was any movement at all in the traffic in front, just in time to see a blue light flash ten or so cars ahead, as a police car manoeuvred through. He cursed as the busy traffic stitched itself back together behind it.

Sarah hung up the phone. She looked as though she had aged another five years during this latest conversation. 'Jamie's at the house, and the police have finally got there as well. They've put out an alert, or whatever they do, and they're gonna . . . Oh, Christ, Red.' She interrupted herself. 'Where the hell are you?!' She checked the time again on the screen of her phone, and then looked out of the window, biting her fingernails.

'He's gonna be okay, y'know.' Frank was still craning to see the traffic in front of them. 'The kid's batshit, but he's smart. Really smart.' As the words left his mouth, Frank realised that he was trying to convince himself as much as Sarah. He was certain that Red was headed to Mikey's, absolutely sure of it. But nobody knew better than him just how great a distance between two places could be.

His hands wrung on the steering wheel.

'You don't know that! You don't know he's gonna be okay. He could be anywhere. Red thinks he can do anything.' Sarah returned to the destruction of her fingernails. 'I blame myself. This is my fault. I mean, actually, it's mainly your fault. But I blame myself; I've been so worried about everything and distracted, with me, and his dad and work . . . If anything happens to him, I'll just—' She seemed to notice the traffic for the first time. 'How much further is it? Can we not go any faster?'

The concern they were both feeling seemed to settle on the same wavelength, filling the car like a hum.

Frank looked in all directions. The traffic was inescapable. There was still nowhere to go. The cars remained as static, as though they were queuing to board a ferry. Frank hit his horn once, and then, in frustration, pressed it again, this time for a long thirty seconds. When he stopped, a manicured middle finger was extended casually from the driver-side window of the car in front.

'Ah, sod this,' Frank said, decisively. 'Hold on.'

He put Val in reverse and backed away from the car in front by a few millimetres. Then he spun the steering wheel left, and then right. The BMW in front rocked as Frank nudged it with his bumper.

'What are you doing Frank?' Sarah said, surprisingly calmly.

Somehow, though, he had partially edged them out of their place in the traffic. The woman in front had just enough time to pull her middle finger back inside her window, as Frank then hit the accelerator and Val scraped down the side of her car with a long, high-pitched squeal. Frank enjoyed a moment of satisfaction as they gained speed and Val matched her wing mirror with the BMW's. It was no contest; the elegant old tank sending the other's mirror sliding across its own bonnet.

As they mounted the pavement with two wheels, Frank forced the accelerator all the way to the floor.

'What are you *doing*?' Sarah repeated more urgently, as they lurched forwards. She gripped the handle above the door and drew up her knees, as though bracing for impact.

'It's fine!' he shouted unconvincingly.

'I'm not sure that—'

The last of Sarah's 'calm' disappeared, as they began to career down the pavement.

A moment later, a set of wheelie bins glanced off the bonnet.

'Jesus!'

It was too late now, though, Frank thought, as he swerved to avoid a red postbox, and a recycling crate full of cardboard and plastic bottles exploded in their wake. They were clearly going to die.

All he could hear were the horns that seemed to be blaring from all sides, and the racket of the old car's engine and suspension as they barrelled along, half on and half off, the path.

It only took twenty seconds. And then they finally reached their exit: the elusive right turn. Frank skidded around it and into the narrow road that interconnected the tight streets.

With one final wrench of the steering wheel, they screeched to a halt.

'There we go,' Frank said serenely, his heart about to explode through his arse.

They both released the breath they had been holding for the last minute.

'Bloody hell, Frank,' Sarah muttered, as though she too was entirely surprised that they'd survived.

Frank's hands were still white on the steering wheel, and he looked at them each in turn, as if they had been recently possessed.

After a moment, he pressed the right pedal gently and they slowly drove to the end of the narrow alley. They were both silent as he indicated to turn left, moving on to the vaguely familiar and clear road, in what he hoped was the direction of his son's home.

RED

Red stood on the driveway of 148 Castlegate Road between the two officers. He clutched Bonzer, twisting the kangaroo nervously in his hands. Then he realised that this made it look a bit like he was strangling him, and he thought that might make a bad first impression. So he let the cuddly toy dangle by his side.

It was the second time that Officer Gemma had knocked on the open porch door, and there was still no answer. Officer Dave approached one of the windows. He was holding his hand between the glass and his forehead to peer inside, when a woman's voice chirped from the side of the house.

'Hello?'

They all turned in her direction as she emerged around the corner. Dave looked a bit embarrassed to have been caught peering into the living room.

The woman looked at the police officers, confused. She was pretty and blonde, like his mum, and she had black leggings on, and a long, scruffy white T-shirt that came to her knees.

Must be the wrong house, thought Red.

'Hi. Sorry to bother you,' Gemma said. 'Our sarge phoned earlier?

Sergeant Chaney? We tried to call again, just to let you know we were going to pop by, but we got no answer.'

'Yeah, we're in the garden and you can't hear the . . . I'm sorry, what's this about?'

'Actually, we were hoping *you* could tell *us*.'

Red had been shrinking behind Officer Gemma's legs, but now he stepped out and into view. 'Does Michael live here?' he asked the lady.

She looked even more confused, but smiled kindly at Red. 'Mikey? Yeah.' She looked at the officers in turn, and then back at Red. 'He's in the back garden, with the baby.'

'Look, Mrs . . .?' Gemma began.

'Hayes. Ellie Hayes.'

'Honestly, Mrs Hayes, we're as in the dark as you are. We picked up this young fella, Red, at Vauxhall station. He was on the tube on his own. He won't tell us where he lives. And all we know so far is that he was trying to make his way here.' She gestured towards the house. 'To this address, to speak to someone called Michael.'

'Mikey?'

'So . . . a Michael *does* live here, then?'

Not for the first time, Red thought that Dave was a bit slower than everyone else.

'Yeah, Michael's my husband. As I said, he's just in the back garden. I still don't understand what this is about.'

'Well, if we could just speak to your husband. maybe we can start to get to the bottom of things? I'll be honest,' Gemma said, 'this is a new one for us, too.'

Ellie took off her gardening gloves and put them in her back pocket. 'Okay, I guess you'd better come through.'

They followed her around the side of the house.

'I like your hair,' Red said.

'Oh . . . er, thank you.'

'It's got a stick in it.'

She tugged the branch free of her curls and chuckled, tossing it to the side of the path. 'Sorry, the state of me, I'm just doing a bit of gardening. Red, is it? That's a very cool name. I used to have a dog called Blue when I was about your age.'

'I love dogs,' Red said, matter-of-factly.

'Me too,' the woman agreed.

They reached the end of the path, where there was a tall gate. The pretty woman put her arm over the top and there was a clacking as she popped a latch on the other side and the gate swung inwards.

The garden was bigger than Red's, and it was surrounded by flowers and shaded by a big apple tree in one corner. No trampoline.

A conservatory dominated the back of the house, and by its open doors stood a wide patio with a table and chairs. In one of the chairs was a man in shorts and a long jumper. He was oblivious to the visitors, and was leaning over a baby bouncer, gurgling and goobling at the tiny human bouncing inside.

'Who was that?' he said, without looking up, going straight back to the goobling.

It was Officer Gemma who responded. 'Mr Hayes? Michael?'

Mikey looked up. 'Oh, shit. I mean, hello. Yeah, that's me.' He stood up straight. He was tall, taller than Frank. But Red could instantly see the family resemblance. He was a young man with Frank's eyes.

'We're really sorry to bother you, We were just explaining to your wife: we're really hoping you can solve our little mystery.'

'Mystery? I don't understand.' There was something in that voice, and even in the way he stood, that Red found familiar.

'Do you recognise this fella?'

Mikey looked at Red, who had taken cover behind Gemma's legs again. He looked back at the police, at his wife, and then back at Red. 'No.' He frowned, confused. 'Why?'

'Well, because he seems to know you.'

Mikey shrugged. 'Sorry. Never seen him before in my life. No offence, kid,' he added. 'I don't know what to tell you.'

'Okay, Red.' Gemma nudged him out from behind her legs. 'We got you this far. Remember our deal? This is when you do your bit and tell us what this is all about.'

Red couldn't speak. He was surrounded by four adults, all of them looking at him for an explanation – and all of a sudden, he wasn't sure if he had one.

He peered over at the baby. 'Is that Mirabelle?'

Mikey shook his head, as if shaking off confusion. It was a mannerism borrowed straight from his dad. 'Yeah, this is Bella.' He scooped up the baby, kissed her on the forehead, and held her against his shoulder. 'How do you know—?'

Red wrestled free of his backpack, and dropped it at his feet. He delved into the bottom of his bag and grimaced as his fingers squished against the discarded Lunchables packet; there was still a bit of cheese in it. Finally, he found the invitation, still just about held together with Sellotape. He stepped forward and handed it to Mikey.

Mikey's forehead creased. He handed a gurgling Mirabelle over to Ellie, then took the invitation, turning it over in his hand. 'Eh? This is an invitation to Bella's christening. Where did you get this?'

Red shrugged, 'From Frank.'

'Frank who?' Mikey asked, bewildered. 'Like Frank, as in, my *dad* Frank?'

'Uh huh.'

Gemma smiled at Red kindly. 'Red, why don't you try starting from the beginning?'

Red looked at the confused faces around him. Starting from the beginning sounded like a pretty good idea.

'Okay. So, well, I got this trampoline . . .'

And so Red told them about moving into the house next door to Frank, about the invitation going to the wrong house, about the joke about the man who invented trampolines, about the drawing in the bin, about Jake, about punching a fish tank, and about being suspended from school, and about beating Frank at *Connect 4*, and about the broken fence . . .

He was only part way into his story, but he stopped uncertainly.

They were all looking at him as though he was crazy.

'Red, is it?' Mikey asked, gently.

Red nodded.

'I'm not sure what all this has got to do with anything?'

Red knew he should have planned this better. He was rambling; he knew he was rambling. By now, even Baby Mirabelle was looking at him in confusion. It felt like he was squandering his opportunity to explain, and that he wouldn't get another one.

Ellie put her hand on Mikey's arm. 'Mikey, let him finish.'

Michael raised his eyebrows as though she had gone mad, too.

Red started talking again. He tried to explain in a different way. 'I saw the photographs on your daddy's mantelpiece,' he said, hesitantly. 'Do you remember the one with you at the seaside? Do you remember when you went to catch some crabs and you were upset because you weren't catching any? Did you know that Frank bought one from a shop and then threw it in the water so that you'd think you'd caught it?'

Mikey didn't look any less confused, but he did smile. 'I actually *didn't* know that.'

At this point, Red wasn't sure what he was talking about himself; he was still rambling. He tried to get back on track. 'I know that you stopped being friends. And I know it's got something to do with when your mummy died. And I know that must have made you both really sad and scared, because I don't know what I would ever do if *my* mummy died.'

Red felt tears sting his eyes, at the very idea ghosting across his mind. 'Well anyway, I found that invitation in his drawer in the hallway.' Red gestured to the card still in Mikey's hand. 'And I said to him that he should go to the party, and that he could just say sorry, and then you could just say sorry, and you'd be friends again.' Red took a breath. 'But he got mad and said to mind my own business, and that's when he ripped it.'

Mikey was looking at the invitation in his hand with a sadness that made him look *even* more like his father.

Red saw his face and kept going, more urgently now. 'But he *did* want to go to the christening. And he *does* want to make friends. Because otherwise, he wouldn't have put it in his drawer, he would've just thrown it out straight away, wouldn't he? And even when he did get mad and rip it up, he didn't throw it away properly, not in the proper bin.'

'Red.' Mikey sounded weary. He seemed to be the only one following Red's story.

The tears in Red's eyes finally brimmed over as he continued. 'And I think he just says he doesn't want to go to the christening because he's scared. You don't know that, but he is. He's scared to go outside. He doesn't really even go to the very end of the garden, that's how scared he is. And it's not just of going outside. He's scared that he's too sad, and that he'll make you sad and Mirabelle sad, and you'll think he's not a good person anymore. But he *is* a good person, and he's my friend.'

Mikey sat down. He looked at the invitation again and then at the sky, before sighing loudly.

Red was wiping his face.

'Look, Red. It's nice that you're my dad's friend. I didn't think he had any friends anymore.' Mikey smiled bitterly. 'And you're obviously a good one. Especially to come all this way. I don't really understand everything you just said, but you seem like a good kid, and it's nice that you want to help me and my dad. But it's—'

Red interrupted. 'You're going to say it's complicated! Because that's what he says, because that's what everybody says about things like this. But it's not. Not really.' He had that sinking feeling kids get when adults decide that what you have to say is no longer worth listening to. It felt like something big was slipping away, through his fingers and into the ground.

Mikey just looked at Ellie with a shrug.

Red scrabbled to find the correct combination of words to make him understand. And then he remembered. Somehow, he had forgotten about the letter in his backpack.

'Wait. There's something else. Something that proves I'm right.' Red wiped his face with his palm again, and delved back into his backpack, frantically searching for the letter.

Just then, he heard his mum's voice.

'Red!'

FRANK

The side gate was still open, which was fortunate. Had it been closed, Frank was sure Sarah would have taken it off its hinges or barrelled straight through it, leaving a mother-shaped hole in the splintered wood.

There were two police cars on the driveway by the time they arrived, and as Frank pulled Val into the remaining space, Sarah had all but fallen out of the passenger-side door before he could bring the car to a stop. She was running down the side of the house before his hand had touched the handbrake.

Instinctively, Frank was out of the car too, and before he could feel the usual weight of being outside – the enormity of being so far beyond the gate – he was following Sarah down the narrow passageway.

But she was already through the opening, barging a policeman twice her size out of the way.

'Red!' Frank heard her shout, before he rounded the corner in time to see her lift up her son and hug him so hard that the boy could barely breathe. Frank's relief came in a single outward breath; it felt like the first time he had exhaled since that morning.

'Oh, thank *God!*' Sarah shouted, spinning around once with Red in her arms. She stopped and held him away from her body so she could see him properly. 'Are you okay, are you hurt?' She set him down on his feet, now examining every limb for damage.

'I'm okay, Mummy,' Red muffled as he was pulled again into her chest.

'You scared me to death, Reddy. What the hell were you thinking??'

'Mrs Evans?' A couple of the policemen were already passing Frank, nodding at him as they left. Of the two police officers remaining, it was the woman who spoke. 'Red's mum?'

'Yeah,' Sarah replied, not looking up.

'We've had quite the adventure,' the policewoman continued. 'Haven't we, Red?'

'Y'know, when kids his age run away,' the male officer added, 'they don't normally get past the end of the street. The fact that he made it all the way here safely . . . He's been very lucky.'

Sarah didn't seem to notice the judgement in his tone; she was crouching down, holding Red's face in her hands, smushing his cheeks and showing no sign of letting her son go, not until he was in his teens at least.

'I could actually *kill* you. I am *so* cross. You're grounded for ever,' she said, swiping an eye with one finger. 'I mean it.'

Finally, she seemed to notice the couple: the woman and the man holding a baby, standing there, patiently observing this reunion with awkward smiles.

'I'm so sorry,' Sarah said, standing up. 'God knows what you must think. I just don't know what got into him.' She pulled Red into her arms again.

'Don't worry, It's fine . . . We're just glad he's okay,' Ellie said uncertainly.

'He's a really good boy,' Sarah said. 'He just sometimes gets something in his head and he's like a force of nature.' She looked at Red. 'He won't bother you again. I promise.'

Mikey said nothing; he seemed dazed.

He was looking over everyone's shoulders, at his dad standing at the gate.

Frank took a step forwards, into the back garden.

'Frank?' It was Ellie who spoke first.

'Sorry. I just – just wanted to check that the kid was okay,' he said awkwardly.

The two police officers barely acknowledged his presence, and returned to speaking to Sarah. 'So, we have some questions, but . . .'

Frank heard all this only distantly. He was looking at his own son (when did Mikey start growing a beard?) who stood with a cloth over one shoulder, a baby in his arms, her tiny fingers exploring his face.

There was an unreality to this sight; it felt like he was peering through a window.

'. . . But, in the meantime, I think we'll get out of these people's hair and let them get back to enjoying their garden,' the officer was continuing.

Suddenly, Frank felt unsteady, as though the bones had been removed from his legs. Putting one hand on the gate post, he glanced at the floor, unwilling to look any one of them in the eye.

'Dad?' Mikey said, quietly.

Frank tried to think of something to say in reply, but his mouth was too dry.

'Well, sorry again,' he said finally, gathering himself, still not looking at anyone. 'As I said, I really just wanted to check that the kid was alright.'

As he backed out of the gate he caught the shake of Mikey's head.

Out of sight, Frank leaned against the side of the house and breathed deeply. The adrenaline that had got him this far, across the whole of London, was turning to stone in his limbs.

It felt as though the house wall was leaning towards him, like his hands didn't belong to him, like the sky was lower than it should be, and the ground too wrong. He reached for something to steady himself, and realised that everything that did steady him, everything that was familiar, was now thirty miles away.

Swallowing air, he scolded himself under his breath and put one foot in front of the other in an attempt to make his way back down the passageway to Val.

Reaching the car, he pulled open the driver-side door and fell into the seat. Sensing some relief, he put his head against the steering wheel, waiting for the worst to pass, while feeling certain that it never would.

Because, even as his breathing steadied and his pulse slowed, he found he was feeling something much worse. Frank felt ashamed.

This wasn't new. He had long felt ashamed of his weakness. Ashamed of his fear of the outside and the ordinary. But now, more than anything, he felt ashamed of his long, comfortable anger. An anger that, as he had looked at his son's perfect and tiny family, seemed so terribly pathetic.

Of course his son wanted nothing to do with him. How could he, when all Frank wanted to do himself was go home, close the curtains, and never, ever leave 34 Merton Road again.

RED

'I'm so sorry, again,' Red's mum said, as she turned him away from Michael and Ellie.

She was holding his hand tightly as they followed Officer Gemma back through the gate. Officer Dave waited behind to speak to the still-confused couple. Red could hear him.

'So, I don't think we need any statements or anything,' he was saying, as he scratched the back of his neck. 'This is a weird one, but we'll have a chat with the boy and his mum, make sure he doesn't do anything like this again. I don't think he will. I think he was pretty shook up when we found him at the station and . . . well, we'll leave you to it.'

Since his mum had appeared through the back gate, everything had happened so fast. *Too* fast. Suddenly, nobody was listening to Red anymore. Anything else he had to say was lost in the commotion that had followed. He hadn't had a chance to finish. To do what he came to do. To deliver the letter. To complete the mission.

He began to resist, pulling at her arm. 'Mummy, wait,' he said.

But she either ignored or didn't hear him.

He tried to stop, tried to plant his feet before they went any further, as though the gate itself represented a point of no return.

'Mummy,' he said again, louder. 'Wait a minute.'

'Red. What are you doing?' she said as she continued to tow him along, through the opening and down the path.

'We need to go back!'

'What? No. That's enough! We need to go home, that's what we need to do.'

He pulled one more time. And when she shouted his name again, he gave up on trying to persuade her.

'Mummy, let me go!' he said, trying to slip free of her hand. 'Let me go!' And with one final twist, he somehow wrestled out of her grasp.

'Red!' she shouted. But he was already running. Back down the path, through the gate and back into the garden, where Ellie and Mikey looked on as he snatched his backpack from Officer Dave's hands.

'Hey!' Officer Dave complained.

But Red didn't have time to ask politely. He quickly unzipped all the pockets and emptied the whole bag out on to the patio before anyone had the time to react. He was on his knees, searching the contents, when his mum landed at his side.

'Red, what on earth are you doing? Seriously, that's enough!' She started putting his things back into the bag.

'Time to go, sunshine,' Officer Dave agreed, as he took Red by the arm and hauled him to his feet.

Red was being led away once more, when, looking over his shoulder, he saw it: the letter, stuck to the bottom of his empty Lunchables packet. His mum was stuffing it back into his bag, but it flapped free. It was caught by a light breeze, and landed on the ground where the patio met the lawn.

Red pulled one last time, trying to lurch away from Officer Dave's grasp, but the policeman was too strong.

The last thing he saw, as they turned the corner, was his mum apologising one final time, and the sheet of paper as it flipped once, twice, across the grass and up into the air.

'No!' Red shouted.

But it was gone.

FRANK

Frank looked in the rear-view mirror at the two police officers stood on the driveway beside the remaining police car. The woman was writing in a pad as she spoke to Sarah, who now had Red in her arms. The other was talking into a radio. Frank couldn't make out what they were saying, but he could get the idea.

He still wanted nothing more than to be home, but he was glad of this time. He was slowly returning to his body, but needed to gather himself a little more before even thinking about driving anywhere.

He had never felt so old.

Sarah put Red down, and the woman police officer said something to him with a smile. He nodded, before Red's mum pointed to Val. A moment later, the kid climbed into the back seat behind him.

'Hey, Red.'

'Hey, Frank.'

There was a pause.

'What the hell, kid?'

'I like your car.'

Frank let out the longest sigh. 'What did you think you were doing?'

'I dunno,' Red said, chewing the inside of his mouth. His disappointment was like an aura. 'I just wanted to help. I thought that you and Mikey should be friends again. Maybe then you wouldn't be so sad all the time.'

'Red.'

'And besides, *you* helped me.'

Frank frowned as he looked at Red's face in the rear-view mirror 'What are you talking about, help you? How did I help you?'

'With Jake.'

'Red.' Frank turned in his seat. 'You've got a broken arm and you got kicked out of school. How the hell did that help?'

Red shrugged.

Frank turned back around, and they sat in silence for a while longer.

'Hey, you're outside,' Red said, as though he had only just noticed. 'I thought you didn't go past the gate?'

'I don't. You know, you scared the living crap out of your mum.'

'Mmm.'

'And me,' Frank added quietly.

'I know.' Red looked back at the house and sighed. 'And it didn't even work,' he said, sadly.

'Well, it's like I said,' Frank sighed, with a sadness that made his head feel heavy, 'sometimes adult stuff is not that straightforward.' He paused before continuing. 'But you must never do anything like this, ever again. It was a really stupid thing to do. Y'know?'

'I know.'

'But I know what you were trying to do . . . and, well . . . you're a good kid.'

Sarah swung open the driver-side door. She had Red's backpack over one shoulder.

'Right, I've smoothed it over with the cops; looks like none of us are going to jail. I think they think that we're all mental, and they're going to check on us in a couple of days, but we can go home, at least.' She gestured to Frank to get out. 'Out you get, Frank; I'm driving.'

Frank thought about protesting, but wasn't sure he had the energy.

'I'm serious, you're in no state to drive. You look terrible, and I know a panic attack when I see one. And this must be the furthest you've been from that house in what? Months?'

Years, Frank thought. He got out without protest and walked around to the passenger's side, just in time to see the remaining police car back out of the driveway. As he climbed in, Sarah was pulling on her belt.

'I am still angry with both of you . . . But thanks, Frank. I do know it isn't easy for you, being, y'know, outside. And I know it took a hell of a lot to get us here.'

Frank nodded.

'Let's go home,' she said. She turned the key in the ignition. There was a grinding noise, and then nothing. She turned it again; this time, there was just a repetitive clicking.

'What now?' She tried again. More clicking.

Unbelievable, Frank thought. *Now the thing won't start again.* It was only a matter of time before Mikey came out on to the driveway and found them still sitting there. Frank couldn't face his son, not now; he couldn't stand a confrontation.

'You need to put the clutch down and—'

'I know how to drive, Frank!'

Another few seconds ticked by, and then she turned the key again. This time, the click was followed by a cough. Then a sound like a cannon firing escaped Val's exhaust, along with a ball of black smoke – but the engine fired into life, then settled into a calm idle. Frank grimaced as Sarah ground the gearstick into reverse, slowly backed into the space left by the police car, and then *crawwk'd* into first gear to go forward, out of the driveway and into the road.

The car had only edged a metre forward before she braked suddenly.

Frank looked up. Standing in their path, blocking the exit, was Mikey.

Red leaned over Frank's shoulder to look through the front windscreen. Nobody else moved or made a sound.

'Wait,' Mikey mouthed. He put one hand on the bonnet, as though he could stop Val from moving. Satisfied that the car wasn't going to edge any further forward, he made his way round to the passenger-side window – to Frank.

Frank kept staring forward. He swallowed once as Mikey appeared at the window beside him.

In his son's hand was a piece of paper. He unfolded it against his chest before pressing the page against the glass. Frank looked up and recognised his own writing immediately.

After a moment, Mikey took it down, folded it and stuffed it back into his pocket.

He motioned for Frank to wind the window down. An old gesture from a time before windows were automatic, but one that still applied to Val.

Finding the handle, Frank lowered the window slowly, and waited for whatever Mikey had to say. He looked into the footwell. Whatever it was, he would take it. He deserved it.

But when he looked up, Mikey was turning away.

Taking the baby from his wife, who was now standing behind him.

When he turned back around, his son's lip was trembling, his eyes were ringed with red, and there was a hitch in his voice as he spoke.

'Dad,' he said, crouching at the side of the car. '. . . This is Bella.'

TWO MONTHS LATER . . .

RED

Red ran through the rainbow-coloured streamers of the curtain Frank had put up over his back door to keep the flies out.

'You've got to see this, Frank!'

'You know, if you keep charging through the back door like that, you're gonna pull that blind down. It's only been up five minutes.' Frank was distractedly adding some pieces to a jigsaw of the depressed-looking owl. 'And stop coming under that bloody fence,' he continued, before muttering to himself, 'I need to get round to blocking that gap up.'

Red ignored him and got himself a drink from the sink. Frank was always threatening to block the gap under the fence, but he never did. In fact, the only day Red had had a problem shimmying underneath the panel was because a thistley weed had started to grow on Frank's side. The following day, the thistle had been gone.

'But you've got to see this, Frank!'

'What is it?'

'I can't tell you. You've just *got* to see it!'

'Is it another amazing trampoline "stunt"?' Frank asked, dully.

'Yeah! How did you know? You're like, sidekick or something.' Red sat down across from him while he drank his water.

Frank continued adding some pieces to the jigsaw. 'I thought you were getting that thing off today?' He peered over his glasses and nodded at the cast on Red's arm. It was no longer white; the plaster was covered in scrawls and doodles and words.

'Yeah, this afternoon.' Red gulped some more of his drink. 'And then I'll be able to do some really super-wicked stunts.'

'Uh huh.'

'My dad's taking me to the hospital to have it taken off,' Red offered casually.

Frank nodded. 'Seeing quite a bit of your old fella lately, eh?'

'Yeah, we went to the football again on Saturday, with Noah and his dad. I think he's not as busy because him and Heather fell out.' Red sniffed. 'I asked him if that meant him and Mummy might get back married, and he said, "You never know." But I asked my mummy the same thing this morning, and she said "over her dead body", and she'd rather chew her own foot off.'

'Sensible lady, your mam. So, you got to see Noah?'

'Yep, and Noah's brother came as well.' Red paused. 'Y'know, Noah's brother says that he went to the zoo with school, and he saw this gorilla on a tyre swing, and it was pooing into its own hand, and then it threw the poo at the wall and it spelled out the word "hello".'

'You know Noah's brother is full of it, don't you?'

'Full of what?'

'Never mind. How is school, anyway?'

'Okay,' Red replied.

*

When he'd first returned to St Agnes, Red felt as if he hadn't been there for a very long time, even though it had only been one week. The night before, he hadn't slept too well. But on the morning that he returned to class, he was surprised to find that he didn't feel scared at all.

Red and his mum had arrived early to have a 'return to school' meeting with Mrs Mills. He had sat in the too-big chair, and his mummy sat in the spinny one next to him. And Mrs Mills said some stuff about God and St Agnes, and something about turning another cheek. (Which was stupid, and basically meant that if someone hit you in the face, you should let them hit you in the face again.) His mum said to Mrs Mills that Red understood. And then, through a fixed smile, she told Red to tell Mrs Mills what they had rehearsed over breakfast that morning. Which was that Red had thought a lot about what had happened, and that it wouldn't happen again, and that he was very, very, very sorry about trying to hit Jake in his face.

Which wasn't completely true.

The truth was that Red wasn't sure if he was 'three verys' sorry. Maybe just one 'very'. Maybe not even that.

Because he *had* thought about that moment a lot: the moment when he had stood up to Jake and screamed that he wasn't a mouse, and he had realised something.

In that moment, he may have lost his temper, he may have broken his arm and he may have killed a goldfish called Bubble, but something else had happened too: he had stopped being afraid. And the likes of Jake didn't seem anywhere near as big as they did before.

And besides, everything that had followed – helping Frank, the mission and everything – would never have happened if he hadn't punched the fish tank. So how could he be sorry about all that?

And so, it was with this lack of fear that Red returned to school.

But nothing could have prepared him for his return to the Caterpillar classroom.

Red's plan had been to give invisibility one more go, but as he shuffled to his peg to offload his coat and bag, he heard his name.

'Hi, Red.' A kid whose name he didn't even know was smiling at him.

'Mornin' Red!' Another shout came from across the room. He lifted his head to see Liam waving a hand as he turned in his seat.

Red realised that almost everybody in the room was looking at him. It was just like on his first day, but this time they weren't looking at him as if they wanted to eat him; this time they were looking at him with something like awe.

'Hey, Reddy!' It was Amelie. She was hanging up her own coat as Red reached the pegs. Seeing the confused look on his face, she chuckled. 'Everybody's been talking about you *all* week. Zoe Senior said she'd heard that you had been sent to *prison*. And the police were after you. And Max said that his brother had seen you in Primark and that you'd had to have your arm chopped off and now you had, like, a *hook*.' She held up a hooked finger.

Red remembered his cast, and held it up. 'No. Just got this on. For, like, a billion years or something.'

'Wicked.'

'Hi, Red,' another boy said as he pegged up his coat and then walked away.

Red blushed awkwardly.

'Oh! And I've got you something.' Amelie turned around and fished in her bag. She frowned when she couldn't find what she was looking for, and started to dig through her coat pocket instead. 'It's *this*!' She held up the Mewtwo card, the one that had been ripped. The card had been carefully stuck back together with tape, and it reflected the light from the window. It was encased in plastic. 'Miss Payton let me laminate it.'

'Whoa, it's as good as new!' Actually, it wasn't. Red thought it was *better*.

'See ya at breaktime!' Amelie said, as she skipped away to her table.

Red was still admiring the card as he turned to go to his own seat. Most of the class were still gawping at him, but he'd stopped noticing that.

Because blocking the path back to his desk was Jake.

Red looked at him curiously, waiting for him to stick his leg out or say something mean about his arm. But then Red realised that his nemesis looked . . . nervous.

'Does it hurt?' The bigger boy was looking from side to side.

It took a moment for Red to realise he was talking about his arm. 'Not really. It itches sometimes, but I've got a big needle.'

Jake nodded. And then stood there awkwardly, nibbling at his lip.

Red moved to walk past him.

'Can I write my name on it?'

Red was confused for a second, before realising that Jake was talking about the cast on his arm. There were already some doodles and names on there. A few people had already signed what Frank called his 'pot'. And Red had drawn on it a few times himself, so that it looked like you could see his bones, and there were flames where his knuckles were. Even Fat Ken had drawn something on it. After Red had told him the story of how he had hurt his arm, he had drawn this. Which was kind of funny, but not really.

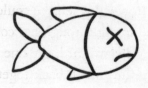

(But kind of.)

'Yeah, okay.'

Jake's face lit up and he took a blue felt-tip pen out of his pocket. 'Cool,' he said, enthusiastically.

Red held out his arm as Jake began to write his name and draw. Soon, Red was surrounded by every child in the class, each armed with a pen, waiting to add their signature or drawing to his arm.

As Miss Payton brought the class to attention and welcomed Red back to school, everybody returned to their seats. He sat, too, admiring the scribbles that now filled the plaster cast on his arm. Rockets and stars and rainbows; a stick-figure dog. Even Miss Payton had drawn a smiling caterpillar that curled around his wrist.

It suddenly occurred to Red that Jake might have written something mean, something that would be made to embarrass him. He turned his arm over, looking for the blue.

He found it near his wrist.

Jake X

'So, is Jake giving you any grief anymore?' Frank asked, slotting in another piece of the owl.

'Nah.'

'So, you're proper friends with this kid now then, eh?'

'Kind of. He's still a bit of a dickhead.'

'Jesus, Red. You've been spending way too much time over here. Enough with the language; your mum'll bloody kill me.'

'Well, we're friends, but we're not, like, best friends or anything. He still likes playing football and games like Shark Attack and things like that. And I prefer playing with Amelie and Warren and all them. But we sometimes play Shark Attack all together, and he's not mean to me anymore. He's not really super mean to anyone anymore.'

'Well, that's good.'

'Yeah, Mummy says that's because he was being a bully, and it's right to stand up to bullies.'

'Oh, she did, did she?' Frank looked over his glasses again, seeming amused.

'Yeah. But she did also say that your advice was bad and rubbish. And to not listen to you ever again.'

'Like I said, sensible lady, your mam.'

Red finished his drink.

'Frank, are you looking forward to tomorrow?'

The christening.

FRANK

On Sunday the 2nd of July, the family and friends of Mikey and Ellie Hayes gathered outside St Wilfrid's church, Wimbledon, to celebrate the christening of their daughter, Mirabelle Marcie Hayes.

Frank wasn't among them.

He had ventured beyond the gate a handful of times since his odyssey across London.

He had been to the park with Red (well, halfway there, anyway, before he remembered he had something to do back home). He'd had two afternoon drinks with Ken in The Flea (just shandies, though, as Frank had been driving). He had even taken Val for her MOT, which she passed – after getting new tyres, new brakes, a new radiator, and a new fan belt, carburettor and gearbox (the mechanics utterly bemused as to why Frank insisted on sitting in the car while it was lifted two metres into the air, and they carried out the work).

Frank had even recently taken to putting his bin out without the aid of a broom handle.

But the idea of making his way across London again, to sit in a crowded church with a vaulted ceiling? He wasn't ready for that. He wasn't sure he ever would be, but that was okay. Because Mikey understood.

412

In fact, it had been his son's idea to invite a few of those friends and family back to 34 Merton Road after the main christening was over.

Frank looked out of the kitchen window at the scene in his back garden. It seemed strange now that this space had *ever* been so quiet. A matter of weeks ago, it had been a cemetery. Now, by comparison, it was a circus.

Ellie was sitting on a step at the top of the garden, chatting to Sarah, who was bouncing baby Mirabelle on her knee. Mark, one of the fellas from next door, was sitting on the grass, chatting with Jonny. Joe was doing the same with Sal, showing her photographs on his phone. Red and his friends – Amelie and Noah – were firing water pistols at Mikey. Beer in hand, his son kept turning around, pretending to be some sort of monster, and the kids would scatter. After the third or fourth time, he shouted, 'Right then!', grabbed the garden hose and turned it on them, sending them shrieking with delight.

The front door opened, and from the hallway, Jimmy Lowden appeared with a bottle of wine in one hand. 'Alright, Frank?' he said, as he walked through the kitchen.

'Why does everyone think they can suddenly just wander through my bloody house?!'

'Sorry Frank,' Lowden said, sheepishly. 'Door was open, and Fat Ken said it'd be alright.'

'Franko!' Ken appeared behind Jimmy. 'Got a disposable barbecue from Home Bargains.' He held up a carrier bag. 'And I got some of those dodgy sausages off of Trigger Pete last night. I'll fire it up.' He followed Lowden straight through the house and into the garden.

'Unbelievable,' Frank said to himself, incredulously.

He was still shaking his head when Mikey walked into the kitchen and opened the fridge. He looked surprised to find his dad sitting there.

'Oh, hey. Just grabbing another beer. You want?'

'Yeah. I'll have one.'

Mikey popped the tops on two bottles and handed one to Frank. 'Thanks for doing this, Dad. We really appreciate it. You know, having the afters in a pub or whatever just wouldn't have been the same. Expensive, too. This is great.'

'Aah, it's no bother,' he said, as he lifted his bottle a little in Mikey's direction.

As much as he and Mikey were similar, he was reminded in this moment that Mikey was his mother's son. God knows, Mikey could afford a few sandwiches in a pub, and having a christening party so far from their own home was no doubt ridiculously inconvenient. But Mikey had learned in the past few weeks that his dad's relationship with the outside world was . . . complicated. And so, without ever asking about it, he had absorbed it as though it was weather, and come up with this way to include his father in the day. Frank loved his son all the more for that.

'You coming back out?' Mikey asked.

'Yeah, just give us a minute.'

Mikey smiled and nodded, then walked back outside – into a face full of hose spray, thanks to Ken. The kids' laughter became hysterical.

'Hey,' Frank said to Marcie, who was leaning against the kitchen counter across from him.

Marcie had been telling the truth that day, in the car, when she had said that she'd be there when he got home. He had thought that perhaps she'd meant that she would be 'there' in his heart, or in spirit, or all around, or some other greeting-card bollocks, but she hadn't. He should have known. Marcie never really did go in for all that spiritual stuff, even after she was dead.

But over the last few weeks, she had been around less and less.

And he had missed her, but not like before, not in a way that was painful, like a missing limb; just in the way that you miss a friend whose company you enjoy.

'I'm not going to see you around here again, am I?' he said.

'Frank.'

He stopped her. 'It's okay. It is. I'm getting a bit old for imaginary friends, anyway.' He smiled and rotated the beer bottle in his hand.

'What you thinking about, Frankie?' she said, sitting down.

'Honestly? I've been thinking about our first cat.'

'Okay. Weird,' she said.

'I was remembering what you said the day we had to have her – y'know.' He made a *cricck*ing noise and dragged his thumb across his throat.

She looked at him with an expression that made it clear that this was a deeply inappropriate way to talk about the death of Mittens.

'God, we were in bits coming back from the vets. And I remember something you said. You said we were lucky to have had her for so long.'

'Riiight, so . . . am I bloody Mittens in this, whatever it is, analogy?'

'Maybe.'

'Great,' she said, rolling her eyes.

'I just mean, I think I was so sad, or angry, or whatever, that maybe I forgot how lucky I was to have had you for so long.'

'Well, maybe that's true.' She nodded. 'Plus, I didn't get hit by a Renault Alpine, and land in next door's pond like Mittens. So, y'know, every cloud and all that.' She smiled thoughtfully. 'You know what I think?' she said. 'I think you saw that I was in pain, and you were mad that you couldn't take it away, so you created some of your own.'

'Whoa, that's pretty deep.'

'And you know what else I think? I think you forgot that the best of us never went anywhere.'

As if he had been introduced, Mikey poked his head back through the rainbow flyscreen. 'Red says you've got to come outside. It's "important".'

'Alright, I'll be right there.'

Michael disappeared back through the curtain.

And when he'd gone, the sound of the garden was gone too.

Marcie looked across at him for a long time, and for a long time he looked back. At the eighteen-year-old girl he'd first met, the twenty-year-old woman he'd married, the thirty-year-old woman who'd carried their son, the forty-year-old mother, and the sixty-year-old woman who'd had no choice but to leave him behind.

She stood up, walked around the table and then behind him. Frank felt her arms as she put them around his shoulders. And her lips as she kissed the top of his head.

And then she was gone.

Really gone.

'You alright?' Red said, sticking his head through the door.

'Yeah, I'm fine.'

'Right, well . . . you really *do* need to come, Frank.'

Frank recognised the tone in Red's voice. 'Why, what have you done now?'

'Well . . . don't go mad, but we were playing with the hose, and I tried to get away and under the . . . and, well . . . the fence has fallen down.'

'Unbelievable. I bloody knew it,' Frank said, as he galumphed through the back door.

EPILOGUE

It had taken a while to find his old word processor. He couldn't remember putting it in the loft. Couldn't remember the moment when he had been so sure he would never write again that he had pulled down those ladders and hidden the machine away.

For his birthday, Mikey had bought him a computer, a laptop. He liked it; it was great for internetting and emailing and face-timing Bella to hear her latest words. All that sort of stuff. But everything he had ever written had been on this thing. It had a familiarity about it. An honesty.

He was surprised when he plugged it in and turned it on that it still worked. It had come to life with a comforting and familiar whir.

The cursor flashed.

—

—

—

'Chapter: 1_,'

—

—

'_This is a ghost story.

—

Not a scary ghost story. Not a haunting. But the story of a woman who loved a man so much that she came back.
To catch a newspaper on the wind. To befuddle a postman, to topple a fence and to start a car. To introduce him to the world again.

—

_And to a boy called Red.'

THE END . . .

TEACHER: MRS M HAYES. Claire Beal, Helen Dee, Martha Bell, Clara Warns, Sue Tull, Bobby Chaney, Ian Wood, Danny Lohia

Tim Pierce, Amit Patel, Mark Savage, Ben Tukow, Jimmy Lowden, Dean Bennett, Tom Cooper, Billy Revitt

Angela Hops, Bridget Foden, Carmel N'sungu, Sarah Mitt, Ellie Brook, Helen Mills, Sadie Franks, Emma Ray, Mary Ireson

ACKNOWLEDGEMENTS

Writing a book is a weird thing. For months you sit at a desk and bash words into a computer. Words that you hope, one day in the future, someone will enjoy reading.

You are on your own most of the time. You don't get on a bus or a train or go anywhere like a normal human. You basically just sit around in your pants, unshaven, rarely escaping your dressing-gown all day, and call it work.

Thankfully, during those months there are people who stop you from going entirely insane. Individuals who stop you from going full Jack Nicholson in The Shining, typing 'all work and no play' – over and over again – and then chasing folk through the snow with an axe.

These are my individuals.

Firstly, my agent at A. M. Heath and top friend, Euan Thorney-croft. Euan, thank you for being such a great champion for my writing. And for patiently continuing to explain, for the thousandth time, how basic publishing works . . . I am listening, honest.

Thank you too to the family Wildfire. My mighty editor and mentor Alex Clarke, who took Frank and Red on when it was just a few thousand words and a vague idea. Without his usual faith and belief, it would have remained exactly that. My brilliant copy editor Tara O'Sullivan, who disentangled the whole thing and made it make sense.

And to the incomparable Areen Ali, who deserves special mention. It has been an absolute pleasure to work with Areen on this book. Incredibly smart and talented, she reminds me of myself as a young man, had I been in any way smart or talented.

To Jess Tackie in marketing and publicist-from-the-Gods, Ollie Martin. Let's be honest, I don't understand any of the things you do. Marketing and publicity is a strange alchemy. But I know that if you didn't do these things so brilliantly, and with such passion and care, this book would struggle to find its way. I thank you for your wizardry.

As always, thank you thank you thank you *dear reader*. Especially those amongst you who have followed my nonsense for years through Man vs Baby. My gratitude for your support is limitless. Without you I would be just another unfulfilled, middle-aged man shouting at the sky . . . and there's enough of them.

My constant appreciation to my family and friends. My sister Jo, her husband Paulyface, The Mad Dog Lady of Lincolnshire (my mum), and to the best friend an idiot could ever have: Andy 'Dr Rectangle' Carrick. These are people who believe in me when I'm not so sure. I can never thank them enough for that.

You may have noticed a dedication in the front of this book to a lady called Lorraine. She was many things, but to us – to me, Lyndsay and Charlie – she was the very centre of our family. Momma, we miss you. We always will.

Which brings me to the loves of my life.

Lyns, *Frank and Red* is for you. You are the kindest most giving person I know. For that alone your mum would be so proud.

And to Charlie. Next year will be my fiftieth-year hurtling around the sun on this rather busy ball of dirt. It took for you to turn up for me to realise what the point was.

I love you to the bones of my skellington.

And no, you can't have a trampoline.

x

Matt Coyne lives in South Yorkshire with his partner Lyndsay, their son Charlie, and a Jack Russell - with 'issues' - called Popcorn. *Frank and Red* is Matt's first novel, but he is the author of two Sunday Times bestselling non-fiction books inspired by his popular parenting blog and social media profile: 'Man vs Baby' (*Dummy* and *Man vs Toddler*). He also writes children's books about monsters and stuff.

When he is not writing, Matt enjoys the pub, obscure Japanese films and falling for clickbait headlines, like: '13 potatoes that look like Channing Tatum'.

You can follow Matt on Facebook and Instagram (@manversusbaby).